Canadian Joseph Boyden is the author of *Born with a Tooth*, a collection of stories. He divides his time between Northern Ontario and New Orleans, where he teaches Creative Writing and Literature at the University of New Orleans. He was born in 1966, and traces his roots to Ireland, Scotland and the Native American Ojibwe and Nipmuk nations.

'An extraordinary novel . . . written with great skill and passion . . . presents a wholly new view of the Great War . . . I was deeply impressed by it and would urge anyone who thinks they have read enough about 1914–1918 to think again . . . they won't find anything better than this'   Susan Hill

'*Three Day Road* is a devastatingly truthful work of fiction, and a masterful account of hell and healing. This is a grave, grand and passionate book'   Louise Erdrich

'You will never forget these two young Cree snipers plunged in the horror of the First World War, where the enemy was so close that one could smell him. A beautifully written and haunting story of survival and innocence shattered, of friendship, death, redemption and love of the land. The three protagonists, Xavier, Elijah and Niska, will be in my heart for ever. Please, please don't miss it'
                                 Isabel Allende

'Boyden tells his story with the starkness and simplicity that does justice to the raw worlds of bush and trench . . . An absorbing read . . . as the reader is drawn into the Cree network of spirits, voices and stories'   Adam Piette, *Scotland on Sunday*

'Every now and then a book comes along that rescues from the mire and carnage a genuinely new perspective on the awful events of 1914–18. Focusing on the rarely told stories of indigenous people enlisted into the Canadian army, Joseph Boyden's first novel, *Three Day Road*, is one such book'
                                 Laurence Wareing, *Glasgow Herald*

'There have been so many novels inspired by the First World War that to read one that is not just harrowing, but fresh, comes as a pleasant surprise . . . a real page-turner . . . poignant and convincing'   *Sunday Telegraph*

'This novel of a Native American family in the slough of its fortunes alternately amazes and moves . . . perhaps the most startling success of this book is the way it combines a tale of racial and cultural displacement with a mystic saga'   *Independent*

'A powerful tale of two young men numbed by the horrors and brutality of trench warfare. Boyden vividly portrays the chaos, fear, cowardice and courage of infantrymen . . . friendship is riven with resentment and war is stripped of glory in this remarkable, wrenching novel, the work of a gifted storyteller'

Publishers Weekly (starred review)

'It's gripping, wrenching, eye-opening, illuminating, stirring, moral (not moralistic) fiction, rooted in closely observed fact . . . Boyden, like Homer in the *Iliad*, is precise and unflinching in his descriptions of the ways in which soldiers fall in battle . . . This novel is a remarkable achievement, and a breathtaking debut'

Globe and Mail (Canada)

'*Three Day Road*, his first novel, will stand beside Timothy Findley's classic *The Wars* as a moving account of the Great War from a Canadian perspective, but Boyden has delivered something new . . . The cinematic battle scenes blaze with intensity and the riveting climax of the boys' friendship feels brutal and inevitable. It satisfies even as it shocks . . . the writing is glorious and shines with real immediacy . . . Boyden is a remarkable storyteller. *Three Day Road* is an unforgettable and valuable depiction of the aboriginal Canadian experience in the First World War and at home'

National Post (Canada)

'Full to the brim with life . . . quite satisfying and believable'

Quill & Quire (Canada)

'Boyden provides a unique prism into the contribution that native Canadians lent to the war effort in the 20th century, refreshingly devoid of the usual clichés of designated victimhood. A first rate read'   Jerry Todd-Jenkins, *Canadian Post*

Three Day Road

JOSEPH BOYDEN

PHOENIX

A PHOENIX PAPERBACK

First published in Great Britain in 2005
by Weidenfeld & Nicolson
Simultaneously published by Penguin Group (Canada)
and Penguin Group (USA).
This paperback edition published in 2006
by Phoenix,
an imprint of Orion Books Ltd,
Orion House, 5 Upper St Martin's Lane,
London WC2H 9EA

1 3 5 7 9 10 8 6 4 2

A CIP catalogue record for this book
is available from the British Library.

ISBN-13: 978-0-7538-2081-0
ISBN-10: 0-7538-2081-1

Printed in Great Britain by Clays Ltd, St Ives plc

The Orion Publishing Group's policy is to use papers that
are natural, renewable and recyclable products and made
from wood grown in sustainable forests. The logging and
manufacturing processes are expected to conform to the
environmental regulations of the country of origin.

www.orionbooks.co.uk

JACOB
kina ntehi

AMANDA
kina ninikamowin

THREE DAY ROAD

We walk through the snow, follow our trail out to the traplines by the willows. I lead, sleepy. Bitter air. Sharp in the lungs. Elijah walks in my tracks. The sun is coming.

I break through the crust with each step. Too cold last night. Elijah tries to be quiet, but his feet sound heavy.

Elijah and me, we are the same age. We have lived twelve winters. The trees moan and crack. The sound is like dying.

'Do you think we have snared anything?' Elijah asks.

I stop, look back at him. 'Stay quiet.'

Tracks everywhere around us here. Footprints in the snow. Shallow prints. Scoops of shadow in the white.

Up ahead, the dark line of it hangs in the air. My heart beats faster.

'Have we caught something, Xavier?'

A marten has sprung our willow trap. It dangles above the snow as if floating. Up close I see the rawhide noose around its neck. Its fur is thick. Auntie will be proud.

Elijah pushes past me, reaches for the marten, grasps the long body in his mittens. He turns to me and smiles. The marten begins to twist and snarl. Elijah lets go, shocked. We did not realize it is still alive.

We stand back and stare as the marten struggles in the air. The black eyes focus on me. It does not want to die.

'What do we do, Xavier?'

'You must club it.'

Elijah finds a stick and approaches the animal. He looks back at me.

'Do it.'

He hesitates, then swings the stick. The animal screams out. The sound frightens me.

'Harder!'

Elijah swings again, and again the marten squeals. My stomach feels sick. I pick up a heavier piece of wood, step up, and give it a sharp blow to its head. The hide noose snaps and the marten drops to the ground. It doesn't move. I club its head once more.

Elijah stares at me.

'We had to do it,' I say.

'We had to,' he repeats. 'Our first night out alone and we have already taken an animal. Your Auntie will be impressed.'

I nod and smile.

I untie the noose from the marten's neck, take out my knife and begin to skin it. I make sure to be careful, to not damage the fur, to keep the body intact. I want Auntie to see that I do not waste.

Elijah watches. His eyes miss nothing. He takes off one mitten and bends down to touch the marten's naked body. 'We are great hunters, aren't we, Xavier?'

'Yes, Elijah,' I say.

'We are great hunters and best friends, yes?'

'Yes,' I say.

EKIIWANIWAHK
Returning

FOR MANY DAYS I've hidden in the bush by the town, coming out when I hear the call, watching carefully for him. This is an ugly town, far bigger than Moose Factory, even. This is a town I have not been to before, a place to which I will never return. More *wemistikoshiw* than I want to see walk the dusty streets in their funny clothes, dressed as if for colder weather, though the sun above us is high and full of summer heat.

I hide well during the day, but when the sound of it reaches my ears I have no choice but to come out and walk among them. They stare and point and talk about me as if they've not seen one of me before. I must look a thin and wild old woman to them, an Indian animal straight out of the bush. Soon I will have only enough food left to get us home, and so I've taken to setting snares around my camp. The rabbits, though, seem as afraid of this place as I am.

Where it comes to rest is just a wooden platform with a small shelter to hide in when the weather turns. The road that leads up to it is covered in dust. Automobiles, just like the one Old Man Ferguson back in Moose Factory drives, rush there at the same time every other day. I have watched them pour what smells like lantern oil onto the road, but still the dust floats up so that it coats the inside of my nose and bothers my eyes. At least I can hide a little in the dust, and not so many of them can see me.

3

The place where I go is covered in soot so that I feel the need to bathe each day that I return from there without him. I have stopped sleeping at night, worried that the words were wrong, that he will never come, that I will die here waiting.

Again today I hear the call. Again today I wait for the others to get there before me, before I step among them.

The old ones call it the iron toboggan. As I watch this thing approach, whistle blowing and smoke pouring from the chimney in the summer heat, I see nothing of the toboggan in it. More frightening than the crowd of people around me is the one bright eye shining in the sunlight and the iron nose that sniffs the track.

Too many people. I've never been around so many *wemistikoshiw* at one time. They walk and jostle and talk and shout to one another. I look out at the spruce across the tracks. Blackened by soot, they bend in defeat.

I stand back in the shadow of the shelter and watch as the people in front of me tense, then move closer to the track as it approaches, not further away as I would have expected. The women in the crowd look nothing like me, wear long dresses made of too much material and big hats. They hold bowed cloth shields above their heads. The men are dressed in black and brown and grey suits, and the shoes upon their feet are shiny, so shiny that I wonder what kind of animal the leather has come from. All of the men wear hats, too. All these people wearing hats in summer. I do not understand much of the *wemistikoshiw*.

It whistles like a giant eagle screaming, so close now that I must cover my ears.

I have paddled by myself against the big river's current for many days to get here. No mind. My one living relation died in a faraway place, and I am here to greet his friend Elijah. Elijah Whiskeyjack is as close to a relation as I still have, and I will paddle him home.

Joseph Netmaker brought the letter out to me. Winter had just started to settle itself into the country. Joseph walked on snowshoes from the town. 'This is for you, Niska,' he said. 'It is from the Canadian boss, their *hookimaw*.'

As soon as I saw the brown letter, the English words written upon it, I knew what it contained. I sat down beside the fire and stirred at it with a stick while Joseph read, first out loud and in his stumbling English, then for me in our language.

"Serial No. 6711. Deeply regret to inform you, Private First Class Xavier Bird, infantry, officially reported died of wounds in the field, November 3, 1918. Director of Records."

I waited for more, but that was all. When Joseph left, I was alone.

Many moons later, when the winter ice was leaving and travel was difficult, Joseph came back with another letter. He explained that it was in reference to Elijah, and that Old Man Ferguson had given it to him to give to me since I was the closest thing to a relation that Elijah had.

The letter said that Elijah had been wounded, that he had only one leg now, that he had tried to rescue another soldier, was given a medal for bravery. It said that although weak, he had healed enough to travel and was expected to arrive in the same town from which he and Xavier had left so long ago.

I had Joseph explain to me how the *wemistikoshiw* calendar worked, what month I was to be there, and I made careful preparations to journey by canoe to that town where Elijah would arrive. I left early in the summer and paddled up the river. It was difficult. I am older now, but I travelled light. Joseph had asked to come along, but I told him no.

I went alone.

I watch the beast pull up and give one last great sigh, as if it is very tired from the long journey, smoke pouring from its sides. People wave from the windows and people on the ground wave back, just as I have watched them do for days. Then men and women and children who have arrived start stepping down into the arms of others. I see a few soldiers and search among them for Elijah's face with his sly grin. The crowd begins to thin, and once again I do not see an Indian soldier with one leg.

I am turning to leave when I see through one of the windows the silhouette of a man inside. He walks slowly along the aisle, on crutches, in a uniform, a small bag slung over his shoulder. I step away from the shadow of the wall.

He wears a hat, just like the *wemistikoshiw* do, but this one is of their army and I cannot see his face for his looking down as he slowly makes his way down the steps on his crutches. He is an old man, I think. So skinny. This cannot be the Elijah I know. One leg of his pants is pinned up and hangs down a little way, empty.

When he is off the steps I begin to back away, thinking it is not him. He looks up and I see his face, thin and pale, high cheekbones, and ears sticking out from beneath his hat. I stumble a little, the blood rushing away from my head. The ghost of my nephew Xavier looks at me.

He sees me at the same moment, and I watch as his eyes take a long time to register what they see, but when they do he begins to rock back and forth on his crutches. He falls to the ground. I rush up to him, kneel beside him, grab his warm hands. He is no ghost. I hold him to me. His heart beats weakly. I am struck suddenly that he is very ill.

'Nephew,' I whisper. 'You are home. You are home.'

I hug him, and when he opens his eyes, I look into them. They are glassy. Even in the shadows of the station his pupils are pinpricks.

'I was told you were dead, Auntie,' he whispers.

'And I was told you were, too,' I say.

We sit on the ground for a while, both of us too weak for the moment to get up. We are crying, looking at one another. A small group of *wemistikoshiw* gathers and stares at us. I help Nephew up so that we can get away, get to the river where he can drink water and I can better protect him.

We do not stay in the town long. It makes me too nervous. Automobiles, they are everywhere. We must cross the dusty road that they travel upon before we can get to the river where I keep my canoe. Nephew walks slowly on his crutches, his eyes cast down. People stare at us, at him. There was a time before he left that he would have stared back, he and Elijah both, not intimidated by them.

What of Elijah? If they made a mistake about Nephew's death, maybe they made one about Elijah. I want to ask, but will wait until he is ready to speak.

We try to cross the road but an automobile honks like a goose and swerves around. I watch carefully and must wait a long time until I can judge that we can cross safely.

I lead Nephew down to the riverbank. I have left the canoe a good walk down the rocky shore. I tell him that it is best for him to wait while I go ahead and get it. He doesn't respond, just sits heavily on the bank. Quickly as I can, I make my way. I am silly to worry about leaving him alone for a few minutes. In the last years he has experienced more danger than anyone should experience in a hundred lives. But I worry anyway.

As I approach him in my canoe, I can see that he has his jacket off and is holding his thin arm in one hand. I get closer and see that he has stuck something into his arm, something he pulls out just as he looks up and sees me. His body has gone relaxed and his eyes look guilty for a moment, but as I get to where he is they are like the dark river in the sun.

I feel better once he is in the canoe and we are paddling away from the town. It smells the same as Moose Factory, the scent of burning wood not quite masking another decaying smell below it. He paddles for a while, but he is listless.

I tell Xavier to lie back on his pack and rest, that we are heading north and I have the current with me for once and it is easy going. He does not seem to hear me. I touch my paddle tip to his shoulder. He turns. I say it again and he watches my mouth intently. He lies back without speaking, and I paddle us back into the bush, looking every once in a while at his thin face in the sunlight, this face that has grown old too quickly. He sleeps, but his sleep is not restful. He twitches and his hands shake. He calls out and this wakes him up. He sits and dips his hand in the river, runs it across his face. His shirt is soaked through with sweat. He is very sick. Some fever is burning him up from the inside. I push down the river in silence.

I take my time, find it pleasant not to have to work constantly, not to fight the current. Only a couple of days ago I battled with every stroke until my arms were dead things and my lower back felt broken. Now paddling home I have the luxury of the current that runs north with me to the Great Salt Bay, to the place the ones who took my nephew call Hudson Bay. It cost me a week of hard work to make my way up the river, but with the wind and weather in my favour, the river is a three-day paddle home. I have many questions for Xavier, and I am like a child inside, waiting to ask them. But I am patient. I am good at waiting.

We do not get far before the sun lets me know that it is time to prepare a camp. I want to go easy with him anyway. No rush. It is summer.

The insects are heaviest just before and during dusk, and so I look for an island in the river that will afford us some relief from them. Ahead, a good one appears with a sandy beach and dead wood scattered about for a fire.

We beach the canoe and I busy myself collecting wood. Nephew tries to help but his crutches sink into the soft sand and he grows frustrated. I want to cry, watching him from the corner of my eye as he bends and tries to pick up wood and then finally sits and pulls rocks to him slowly, making a fire circle.

I cut long saplings with my axe and drag them to him, tie them together at one end and construct the frame for a small teepee. I pull a length of canvas from the canoe and tie it to the frame. The sky right now looks like it will give a starry night, but the wind tells me something different. We are not so far away from the bay that a storm can't rush up on us. Once I have dragged our few belongings into the teepee, I pull food from a pack and lay it out. Nephew has gotten a nice fire started.

On one rock I place salted fish, on another some moose-meat and on a third, blueberries picked fresh from the bush.

I take a stick and sharpen its end. Nephew stares at the river. I lace a length of meat onto the stick and heat it by the flame. He turns his head in recognition when it begins to warm and its scent comes up.

'I have not smelled that in a long time,' he says, smiling shyly. These are the first words he has said since the town.

I give him some food, but he doesn't eat. His skin is the colour of cedar ash in the setting sun.

That night I crawl into the teepee, tell him to sleep when he is ready. He stares at the fire.

Hours later, I awake to a light rain tapping on the canvas. I open my eyes and listen to it. The fire smoke in the rain is a pleasant scent. I realize I lie here alone. Even with the weather, Nephew has not come in. I peer outside. The fire sizzles and pops, and my fear returns when I see he doesn't sit beside it.

There is no sleep the remainder of the night. I toss in my blanket. My body hums with Nephew's pain and with the realization that he has come home only to die.

TAKOSHININAANIWAN
Arrival

RAIN PATTERS ON THE SAND all around me tonight, slowly soaks through the wool of this uniform I still wear, the animal scent of it pulling me back to the battlefields. I do not ever want to go there again. Auntie rests in her little teepee, but me, I can't. When I do, the dead friends I don't want to see come to visit. They accuse me of acts I did not perform. Of some that I did. We all acted over there in ways it is best not to speak of. Especially Elijah. He is the truly skilled one. But at one time I was the better marksman. No one remembers that. Elijah, he is the blessed one.

Where is he? We spent the whole war together only to lose each other in the last days. A shell landed too close to me. It threw me into the air so that suddenly I was a bird. When I came down I no longer had my left leg. I've always known men aren't meant to fly.

They gave me medicine for the pain, and I learned how to fly in a new way. The cost this time is that I can no longer live without the medicine, and in a few days there will be none left. Their morphine eats men. It has fed on me for the last months, and when it is all gone I will be the one to starve to death. I will not be able to live without it.

This is all too much to figure out. Elijah is missing. Auntie is not dead after all. I received a letter in France one year ago saying that she was gone. Nothing in the world makes any sense any more. I lie back on the sand and let the rain tickle my face. The campfire hisses. I should sit closer by it, but the light hurts my eyes.

I watch my body shiver in the cold rain. The morphine is very good, though, a warm blanket that wraps about me like a moose robe. I will lie here and listen to the hollow breathing in my chest, wait for dawn to come, and I will fight the sleep that pulls at me. I do not want to sleep and be taken back.

I stare up at the rain that falls down, flickers of lightning cutting through it every few minutes. My body floats above itself. Oh, this medicine is good. I hear my breathing, how the air floods in slowly then recedes from me like waves on a beach. I listen to myself breathe, and I close my eyes. After a time I can hear others breathing heavy all around me. I want to tell them to go quiet. Lightning, another flare, pops up out of the darkness and throws a white light on us and on the ditch we lie in, our uniforms soaking up the cold water. Elijah is not near. So long has Elijah been around that he is like a part of my own body.

Where is he?

The big guns echo. They shake me.

I crawl with the others up to broken buildings on the edge of the town. Me, I'm so tired I'd rather sleep here on my belly away from the buildings that attract all their shells. The darkness makes me feel safe.

Tomorrow we will go into the trenches. But tonight we're told to go to that town. We have no choice. The *crack crack crack* of rifles keeps us in the ditch and the flares go up and nobody knows who's firing into the night. The rifle fire sounds maybe fifty yards away, to the left and front.

12

'Are those our fucking signal flares?' Sergeant McCaan hisses. 'Can somebody tell me? Are they?'

The one called Fat whimpers like a dog. The others around me breathe too loud. A good hunter will hear us. Another *crack* of rifle fire. Puffs of dirt spray on my head.

'Ross rifles,' I whisper over to McCaan, and he looks at me, swearing more, the words louder and angrier. It's our own rifles firing at us.

Suddenly McCaan crouches and begins screaming at the top of his lungs, 'Quit firing on your own, you bastards!' and I reach up and pull him down as rounds buzz by his head.

We hear a voice in the distance shouting back, and the rifles stop their noise and the voice becomes clear, shouting out to stop all firing.

We make our way up, ready to jump back down, holding our arms in the air and climbing out of the ditch. McCaan's face glows red in the Very lights falling near us. I'm glad I'm not the one who will face his anger. Elijah walks beside me. He's laughing at all this. I don't find it funny.

It is another Canadian company holding the edge of this town, just over from England, too, and as they hand out cigarettes they explain that at this place there seems to be no clear front and that Fritz is all around. McCaan has marched up to their officer and I can tell that he wants to beat the man, but he's a lieutenant and so McCaan must hold all his frustration in. We're given directions to a place we can sleep, and as I march away with the others into the night I wonder what kind of sign this is that the first time I am under fire it comes from my own side.

We are sent to an old farmhouse billet, and upstairs through the glass-less window is a good view of the horizon where the drumbeat of artillery keeps constant and the horizon glows like a wood stove with the door open. The beds in here are long gone and most of the walls are torn down. We lie on straw, so many of us squeezed in shoulder-to-shoulder that I worry the floor can't hold our weight and we'll be sent crashing down to the ground below. The lice crawl over me so that I can't fall asleep for the itching. Sitting up, I search for them in the seams of my uniform, picking them out and cracking them with nails that have grown long for the purpose.

I'd much rather be outside on the cool grass, me, but the officers won't allow it. We've been over here in this place that some call Flanders and others call Belgium for three weeks now. I felt stupid and small when Elijah had to explain that Belgium is a country, like Canada, and Flanders is just one small part of it, like Mushkegowuk. I'm still uncomfortable with the language of the *wemistikoshiw*. It is spoken through the nose and hurts my mouth to try and mimic the silly sound of it. I opt to stay quiet most of the time, listening carefully to decipher the words, always listening for the joke or insult made against me. These others think that I'm something less than them, but just give me the chance to show them what I'm made of when it is time to kill.

This is the closest we've come to the front. It's close enough that I can smell the burn of the cordite, and the guns are louder than I thought anything could be, even thunder or waterfalls. The urge to admit that I want to be home and not in this ugly place hovers close, but I must push the thought away.

For a time this was almost what I pictured it to be from all the stories the others told. Green fields and pretty girls waving to us from windows and doors in the towns we marched through. Then we were shipped further north on old trains and walked through towns smashed to pieces as if by giant children. I saw my first dead body in one of these places, not the body of a soldier but of a small boy, naked and bloated in the sun, a great chunk of his head gone. The child confused me. What did he have to do with any of this? Where was his mother?

I'm confused by many things, by all of this movement, by the loss of my sense of direction here. The rain began soon after I saw the boy, is continuous now so that it has become a part of my world.

Every day we practise drills in it. Bayonet drill, grenade drill, shooting drill, marching drill. My skin is always wet so that I feel like a frog or a fish. All this rain makes keeping my rifle clean and working difficult.

Rain. We lie in the farmhouse, scratching, and I listen to rain and to Sean Patrick and Grey Eyes talking quietly to one another.

'My girl back home wanted to marry me,' Sean Patrick says. He is the youngest of our section and is from a place in Ontario not so far away from where I live. I wonder how they let him into this army. He looks like a gangly moose yearling not yet weaned from his mother. All knees, bigger ears than mine.

Sean Patrick keeps talking. He loves to talk. 'That's the only way I was going to get to see her naked. But I told her that I didn't want my wife being a war bride. "You're too good for that," I says. "I'd just as soon wait till I get back to marry you."' He scratches at the collar of his unbuttoned tunic. 'We all know this war isn't going to last long anyway.' I see Sean

15

Patrick turn to Grey Eyes when he says this. Sean Patrick needs others to tell him he's right. 'Truth is, I didn't agree to it because I was mad at her that she wouldn't do it with me. I'm only just turned seventeen, and that's too young to marry.'

Grey Eyes laughs quietly in the dark.

'You really an American?' Sean Patrick asks.

'From Detroit,' Grey Eyes answers. 'I got me a girl back home, too. Her name's Maggie, and she's a real looker.'

'Oh yeah?' Sean Patrick says.

'Red hair, a figure like Aphrodite. I promised her I'd marry her, too, once I get home.'

I was there when Grey Eyes told Elijah his girl's name was Janice and that she had hair as golden as a wheat field. I'm not sure about this one, the one who's befriended Elijah.

I fall asleep to their voices and to the sound of the guns pounding back and forth in the distance, thinking about Sean Patrick, who's not seventeen winters but fifteen. And that one, Grey Eyes. Him, he's a liar.

The next day, we stand in front of the farmhouse at attention all morning. I don't know why they make us do this. Late April clouds gather in the distance. Elijah stands next to me, moving his feet about so that Sergeant McCaan shouts at him to be still. I can see that McCaan doesn't want to shout at him, doesn't want us standing here at all. The one who tells McCaan what to do is named Lieutenant Breech. The enlisted men call him Bastard Breech. He stands in the shade and watches us all morning. He carries an ash stick with a bullet tip and whips it against his leg when he wants McCaan's attention.

The clouds continue to gather and still we are told to stand there as the rain comes from the sky and soaks all of us until we shiver. The men begin to talk when the downpour is thick enough that Breech heads inside.

'We are to go into the front lines today,' one near me says.

''Bout time,' Sean Patrick answers.

McCaan tells him to hush.

Elijah leans toward me. 'Now we get to hunt,' he says.

I don't respond, am too worried that Breech might be watching.

The rain falls harder and soon I can't tell the guns from the thunder. The men shift and moan. Our packs weigh more than half our weight. The men around me are like the horses I've seen here, skittish. I hear someone behind me talk about officers taking our own soldiers behind the lines and shooting them for the slightest disobedience. Another says that the Canadians just took a beating at a place called Saint-Eloi and now our battalion's to go in as reinforcement. The rumours continue until they become the truth. We will go into the front lines today.

And then the rain stops. The sun comes out, and so does Breech. We sag under our packs. The one called Fat whines. They call him Fat because he really is. Fat as a beluga. I stand and suffer and watch the steam rise up from us as if we are all on fire, smouldering slowly under the weight of Breech's stare.

I am hungry but we are forced to stand here. The time to eat our day meal passes. It is only after that Breech gives McCaan the order. We are to begin marching. A great cheer comes up from the men, and it all suddenly makes sense to me. The ones who order us are as crafty as wolves. To have men cheer as they march off to the front is not an easy accomplishment. This army orders itself very carefully, I see.

I think about this as we march along a crooked road filled by mud and puddles, the sounds of the guns getting closer with each step.

As the others break into a song, the sun settles down behind us so that we walk upon our own shadows. They sing a song I don't know and even McCaan sings out in his thick and raspy voice. From what I can tell it's about a girl and her smell and not a lot of it makes sense. Me, I won't sing their songs. I have my own songs.

I try to remember one of my own but the English words all around stop it from coming, so I hum instead and soon I notice that someone else is humming, too, but it is out of tune and grows louder and louder until the hum is a scream and, with no other warning, thunder and a wave of heat coughs me up from the earth, the river and the exploding trees flashing through my head. And then I'm landing hard on the ground shoulder first and it's raining rock and softer globs of red dirt that it takes me a moment to realize are the flesh and guts of men. In the muffled sound that can get through to my ears that feel full of cotton I hear horses screaming and men shouting and another shell lands, this time in front of me, and men are crawling and scratching at the mud trying to get to the side of the road and past it, anywhere that might offer shelter from the splinters of flying metal. I want to crawl too but can't move, and I feel the tug of hands at my shoulders and I'm being dragged through the mud and pushed under an overturned wagon, and Elijah's face looks down at me, asking in Cree, 'Are you all right?' I nod and Elijah's eyes are full of sunlight like he's smiling. He crawls back out and returns a little while later with Grey Eyes and Sean Patrick and we all huddle under the wagon and listen as the shells creep a little farther away with each boom and shudder, like they are live beasts sniffing and pounding the dirt in search of men's flesh to rip apart.

Once the shelling has gone quiet, we make our way out and survey the damage. I'm surprised to see that very little looks different than it did before. There is the same mud and puddles and torn-up wagons and piles of bricks. The only real difference is the bitter smell of cordite and the sweeter smell of blood that is as rich in the air as if we'd just butchered a large moose. We do what we can to help the wounded, and it is not long before stretcher-bearers appear to cart off the dead, and the living who can no longer walk.

After dark an officer appears and tells McCaan to move the platoon farther to the west along a narrow winding dirt track. I can tell McCaan doesn't like the order. Lieutenant Breech is off to a briefing and has left McCaan in charge with the order to get the platoon to someplace in the darkness. Breech and some others will be there waiting. McCaan's too smart to complain to the officer but his stiff body says how he feels as he listens to the little man with the moustache wave his thin cane toward where the last light fell, squeaking in a high voice what sound like complicated directions. 'Tonight then, sir?' is all I hear McCaan say, and Elijah and me, we give each other knowing looks. A long march still ahead. This Belgium is far more confusing than I ever imagined. Nobody seems to know where to find this Saint-Eloi.

'How many miles from the front line do you think we are?' Elijah asks in Cree.

'Maybe three or four still,' I say. 'Hard to tell. I don't understand yet the sound of the big guns.'

One time when we were little more than boys, we were

out following moose tracks in the deep snow and got lost from one another. When dark was close and I was beginning to worry that I'd be out alone in the cold all night, I aimed my rifle at a tree two hundred yards in the distance toward where I could best figure Elijah had headed. I fired it and listened carefully for a couple of minutes until the thin pop of a rifle answering far away came back. In this way we located one another and at the same time learned the sound of the rifle and how to track it through distance and time. To simply aim a rifle in the air when lost in the bush will not help. The sound travels up and around and seems to come from everywhere. Focus on the sound. I listen carefully now for the sounds of the big and little guns. I try to learn them.

McCaan grumbles to himself and then, after the little officer has disappeared, shouts out for us to shoulder our packs. 'Tiny fucker wants us to march into dangerous land after dark knowing full well we have no goddamn idea where we are. Like fucking virgins into the mouth of a lion!' I like it when McCaan swears. His voice almost sounds like it is singing.

Night swallows us. The flash of big guns comes from what seems to be all sides. We are lost. The road we've been sent on has become smaller and smaller until now it is nothing more than a dirt path cutting through little ponds of stinking water. We follow the man in front and try not to lose him. To lose the one in front means to be lost in this swamp that we walk through, water and the sound of night animals feeding on all sides, thick mud sucking at boots, threatening to pull them from the soldiers' feet with each step. I wonder if my moccasins in my pack would be a better choice right now. This mud is not all that different from the mud of the Moose River.

Tonight's the kind of night to just sit under and wait for it to end. But we can't do that with enemy patrols that might be anywhere near. For all I know the platoon has slipped behind the enemy and is in his country. When I think this I feel a little ball of panic in my stomach, and the sound of wings of large birds in the swamp rustling and pecking and feeding is suddenly the sound of the green-skinned Hun sliding through the mud on their bellies, slipping closer, scratching their way, the points of their helmets ready to impale me in the back.

'We're lost,' I whisper in Cree to Elijah.

Elijah doesn't answer. Black wings suddenly beat up all around us, the tips touching my head, and Fat screams out, 'I fell. Help me!' Men scramble and they follow his voice and with a tremendous tug he is freed from the sucking water beside the little track that we perch on. In Fat's hand he holds a human arm, I can see in the faint light, and when Fat realizes what he has pulled from the mud below him he begins to scream, until McCaan walks over and the sound of a loud slap rings out in the thick fog and stink of the night.

McCaan whispers out to all of us to regain our wits, that this is our first true test as soldiers and that for all we know we may be in enemy territory and that from this moment on our lives hang in the balance. 'You are acting like rabbits,' he says. 'It is time to act like wolves,' and these are the perfect words. I can almost hear the backs of the men around me stiffen and the hairs on their necks bristle and it is exactly this, to be the hunter and not the hunted, that will keep me alive. This law is the same law as in the bush. Turn fear and panic into the sharp blade of survival.

We tread along more slowly now, listening to the noise

around us, watching for the flash of big guns in the distance, trying to judge who and how far away they are. My eyes have adjusted to what little light there is. The horizon glows like there will soon be a sun but as best I can tell, the glow is in the north. Fat's breathing is the only sound that echoes when we stop and listen. Like a horse's breathing, I think, lungs as big as a horse's, but a horse with a cold. He coughs and sputters and whines till McCaan tells him to shut his bloody trap.

When we are very still, the sound of clinking metal and maybe voices travels through the thickness of the fog that has crawled to chest level all around. The fog is so thick that when we drop down we disappear completely as if into water. McCaan whispers something and the whisper travels from man to man until it reaches us. He wants Elijah and me to come to him. We crawl over and he says, 'Leave your packs here, boys. I want you to advance slow and silent like I know you can and figure out for me whether that is friend or foe over that little ridge.'

We nod and slip our packs from our shoulders and I see Elijah slips his coat off too, so I do as well. I pick up my rifle and check the action and snap off the safety with my thumb. Elijah slips into the fog and I follow quick so as not to lose him. I listen for Elijah's quiet step and dip blindly into the fog, surfacing every little while by standing straight up to get my bearings before slipping back down again. I count off two hundred paces and I've lost Elijah, but know that he will be cutting to the left and will expect me to go a little to the right, just like we do when tracking moose. The ridge is a hump in the distance, only maybe one hundred and fifty paces ahead. Suddenly I hear the low warbling whistle of Elijah and answer it with my own. We both advance slow. I wish now I was wearing my moccasins and not these heavy boots.

Near the base of the ridge I pause and listen again. It is not a ridge at all but the lip of a large shell crater. Laughter is clear now and so is the clinking of metal cups. I see the dim flicker of a small fire. Whoever it is thinks he cannot be seen or heard in the fog and in the hole, but he is very wrong.

A voice rises up. The voice isn't English. I lie closer to the ground and strain my ears. If they have a sentry, he might be coming this way or might have his rifle pointed at me right now. I roll into the thicker fog and head left toward where I know Elijah will be. 'It is not English they are speaking,' I whisper in Cree when we are side by side and have retreated a safe distance into the fog.

Elijah nods. 'I think it is the Belgian tongue,' he answers. 'What colour are the Belgian uniforms?'

'I saw one yesterday on a dead soldier that was lighter than the French's,' I answer.

'We'll have to go up the ridge and see.'

We crawl back into the mist and when we reach the lip I signal for Elijah to go first while I cover. Elijah crawls up and peers over the edge, then signals for me to follow. I crawl to Elijah and peer down to where four men sit around a small fire with cups in their hands, as if they are a thousand miles from battle. Two have long moustaches that droop over their mouths. One is old and another looks no older than twelve winters. They wear a dark grey uniform, and round helmets with a ridge along the top sit by their feet.

Elijah suddenly stands up and walks down to them, rifle at his side but still ready to fire if need be.

'Hello!' he says loudly when he is in their midst. The men jump and two of them fall off their seats. 'I am Canadian! Hello!' The men, once they've gotten over the shock, relax a little. Strange guttural words pour out of the mouth of one. Elijah just nods and smiles and repeats, 'Yes! Yes! I do not understand! I am Cree Canadian!'

I stand up and click the safety back on my rifle and join Elijah. Once again the men in the crater look startled and I just nod and smile and take an offered cup. The cup's half full with wine and it tastes bitter in my mouth but I like the warmth and listen as Elijah asks them, 'Where are the Canadians?' Two of the soldiers point and respond in English worse than mine that they are to the west of here, very close.

Elijah tells me as we make our way back to the company in the fog that best he could figure, the Canadians are only half a mile away.

Elijah reports to McCaan, who looks very relieved, orders the troops to pick up their packs and tells Elijah and me to lead them in the right direction. Thinking back on my first test I'm very proud of myself as we move silent and straight through the muck and find our battalion.

Just a short walk from there and we are encamped in the cover of woods, and I'm surprised by the size of the battalion and how well it conceals itself. It was not until we were right upon them that we realized we'd found the group. Sentries called out and McCaan answered and we were taken in among the others. No fires are allowed so close to the front, and in the darkness I begin to make out forms of tents and men lying on the ground in blankets or sitting in small groups talking quietly to one another. They ignore us like we are ghosts float-ing by, and in the darkness with the shadows thrown across their faces and the long stare of eyes in cigarette glow I realize that these are the veterans of the last year's horrible fighting, that it's these men who are the walking ghosts. My first small trial is suddenly nothing in their eyes or in my own.

McCaan asks where the canteen is and we are directed to a large kitchen wagon. Inside, the smell of cooked food makes me realize I've not eaten in a long time. We pull out our bowls and fill them with stew that is burnt but tastes as good as fresh game right now. I clean my bowl with a chunk of stale bread that moistens a little with the dipping, and as soon as I finish my last bite the exhaustion falls across me and all I want is to find a place to stretch out and roll up in my blanket.

Our platoon keeps its distance from the others, the ones who have just been relieved from days on the front lines. My group is not a part of them, I realize, as I lie on my back on the hard ground of the woods. I stare up into the night sky and just as I drift off to sleep I can see exactly where I am clearly etched on the blackness broken by skeleton trees above me. This is where my life has led me. It's as clear as if I've been walking a well-marked trail that leads from the rivers of my north home across the country they call Canada, the ocean parting before me like that old Bible story nuns forced upon me as a child, ending right here in this strange place where all the world's trouble explodes.

I'm up the next morning before first light and reveille. A few men sit in a loose circle, blankets over their shoulders, talking quietly, smoking cigarettes and drinking coffee. After a while one waves me over. I sit with them but they do not talk to me directly or ask my name. I can follow most of what they are saying. They talk of lost friends, of a winter battle where many died, of successful trench raids on the Germans. Bad fighting at Saint-Eloi through March and April, but now all's quiet there. None of them talk of home or what was left behind.

Finally, one of them asks me where I come from.

'Near Moose Factory,' I answer, and the man knows where that is.

'So you're an Indian, then?' he asks. I nod. 'You're pretty short for an Indian, ain't ya?' The others laugh. 'All the Indians around from where I come from are taller than you. But I guess that's the way the prairies grow 'em.'

'Your battalion's just arrived, hasn't it?' the second one asks. I nod. 'They'll be sending you up to the front lines today then, I reckon.'

'We lost a lot of men last month,' the first one says. 'Fritz's getting more accurate with the big guns. With that kind of aim they don't need no offensive. They'll just blow us to kingdom come and that'll be the end of it.'

The second man speaks up again, says, 'A fella like you had better learn quick to keep his head down. Hun snipers are deadly accurate. There's one about, whose signature is shooting a man through the neck. How many has he got now, Smithy?'

The one named Smithy hasn't said a word till now. 'At least a few dozen,' he answers. 'That I know of, anyways.'

'Smithy here's a sniper himself—ain't ya, Smithy,' the first one says.

Smithy doesn't answer, doesn't look like he even heard the comment. I look at his rifle lying down beside him, at the notches cut into the stock of it.

'Smithy's gotten thirty-three confirmed kills, and many more unconfirmed,' the second one adds quickly. 'Most in our regiment. Most of any Canadian. Or Brit for that matter.'

Smithy shakes his head and looks away. He is small and skinny. He's going bald. He looks like a Hudson's Bay Company man I know back in Moose Factory who teaches Sunday school to the children who live on the reserve and not in the bush, the homeguard children. 'That ain't true at all,' Smithy mumbles. 'There's another Indian feller goes by the name Peggy. Ojibwe, I think.' He looks over at me. 'He's got close to a hundred kills but no officer wants to give him credit since he likes working alone.' Smithy suddenly stops talking and looks embarrassed that he's said so much. 'Peggy's salt of the earth,' he adds as an afterthought. 'Every Canadian enlisted man knows he ain't no liar.'

There's a long lull in the conversation. I guess they're thinking about what Smithy just said. I'd like to meet this Peggy.

'You sure don't say much,' the first one says to me after a while. 'You're a lot like Smithy here. Man of few words, eh?'

The second one laughs.

I smile. 'I don't know much English, me,' I say.

'You don't need to know much,' Smithy says angrily, 'for the job you been sent here to do.'

I nod but know enough not to smile again.

After a time I go back to my sleeping place and lie on my back, stare up at the tree branches standing out black against the lightening sky. I close my eyes, and when I open them again it is Niska's face above me. She shakes me lightly in the new morning.

'You are shivering,' she says, and asks me to sit by the fire.

MONAHIKEWINA
Trenches

I LIE STILL BY THE FIRE and even the scent of warm bannock does not make me hungry. My guts are cramped like ropes bind them. My eyes ache in the sun that rises across the river, and the mist hanging over the water reminds me of the mist in early morning France. It's a heavy mist this morning, almost as thick as fog. The day will be warm.

Niska nudges me, her eyes questioning. She looks older than when I left, her hair mostly grey now. She's thinner, too, but wiry strong still. 'I said that we will take our time on the river today,' she says.

I watch her mouth to understand. All I am hearing this morning is a dull roar like rapids in the distance.

'Do your ears trouble you?'

I nod to her. My hearing leaves me more than it is with me any more.

The relief of taking a syringe from my kit and readying my arm washes over me almost as sweetly as the medicine itself. With Niska loading the canoe, facing away from me, I slip the point in the vein at the crook of my bruised elbow and lay my head back with a sigh. The struggle to keep memory away is no longer worth it, and minutes later as Niska helps me into the canoe and I settle against my pack, I let my mind go where it wants. She steers us into the current.

The mist still hasn't lifted much. McCaan tells us what a

good thing that is. Sean Patrick and Fat are in front of me, and we crouch and move along a communication trench that leads us to the front trench. The whistle of shells keeps our heads down and when someone up the line slows down or stops, the ones behind bump into him. It is hard going. The bottom of the trench is covered in duckboards that keep our feet out of the mud and water that collects at the bottom. Normally, McCaan told us earlier, we'd come in at night, but the fog allows for us to move during the day. We were taught in training that everything happens at night. Digging and repairing, raids on enemy trenches, scouting and laying out of wire. 'Darkness is your best friend,' McCaan says over and over. 'Not to learn that lesson will kill you, boys.'

When stretcher-bearers come by, we squeeze to the side of the trench. I try not to look at the men being carried away, but occasionally I glance down at a face that is either contorted in pain or marked with a yellow *M* that means he has been given the medicine and is dreaming of the other place. It makes me think of Grey Eyes, and in thinking of that one I think of Elijah, too, who has become withdrawn and focused and serious since we came here. I see how Elijah's eyes glow, how he is feeding off the fear and madness of this place. He makes a good soldier. McCaan is very happy with him, I think.

Finally we reach the front trench. At least this is what those in front whisper. This trench looks the same as the others we've been working our way through for hours. But the soldiers here sit in twos and threes in holes in the walls, their faces thin and dirty so that their eyes look too white and big. Other men hold tall metal boxes against the wall and peer into them, watching what the other side is doing. These are the periscopes we were shown how to use not long ago.

McCaan stops us and goes out in search of an officer.

The one named Gilberto lights a smoke. His thick arms are covered in black hair as shiny as a bear's. He'd scare me if his eyes didn't crinkle kindly at the sides when he smiles.

Graves, the oldest of us, hisses at him, 'Stomp that out, man. Fritz will see your smoke and lob a few right on top of us. Worse yet, an officer will come along and do far worse.'

Gilberto is big and wide-shouldered and grows fruit back home. I like him because his English is as poor as mine. He drops the cigarette immediately and two soldiers sitting in a dugout beside us laugh at us as they light up their own.

'The action left Saint-Eloi a while back,' one of them says, fitting the butt of his cigarette neatly into the place where his front tooth should be. 'The dance is on the Somme now.'

McCaan returns with an officer who is tall and hunch-shouldered and looks like he wants to cry. He speaks so quietly that I notice McCaan must lean toward him to hear, and they look for a moment like two old grandmothers telling secrets. The officer holds a long club with a heavy end and bangs it on the toe of his boot. McCaan motions to us and we begin to walk, heads bent, through men sitting and sleeping or talking in low voices to one another. Once in a while we pass a few snipers who have their Ross rifles ready behind squares of iron. A little door in the iron slides open and the sniper fires his gun before closing the square again, and then I hear the *ding* of German bullets hitting the plate. It is like a game, I think, but one that you don't want to lose.

We find the stretch of dirt and mud that is our new home and immediately start working to make it into something livable. Little shallow caves are dug into the sides as places to stretch out and sleep. We each claim what we can, and Fat begins complaining because there's not one big enough for him to fit in, so I grab his shovel and help him to dig out something larger. When I'm done I find Elijah, and we agree silently to share a space.

The rest of the day is busy and the men are nervous. We listen for the different types of shells, and McCaan introduces us to a corporal named Thompson. He's not much bigger than a big child, but his face is old. It's impossible for me to tell what age he is.

Thompson does a lot of explaining, but me, I can tell he doesn't like strangers much. 'You hear the *thunk* of a mortar land close to you, know you can run away from it if you're quick. It's the only bomb you can do that with. The big shells you can hear coming from a long way off and just pray that they aren't heading for you. Now listen careful, boys, it's the smaller shells, the whiz-bangs, that are the most damaging, the ones that sound like a mosquito whining in the distance. You hear that coming and you dive flat into the earth and bury your nose deep as you can into the mud.'

We listen wide-eyed and careful, and as if to emphasize Thompson's point, shells whine and roar and explode not so very far away. When one sings over us that is exceptionally clear, Thompson says, 'Now that's Fritz's version of our eighteen-pounder. Blow a hole the size of a ditch into the earth.'

Another shell flies overhead, this one whistling like a teapot come to a boil, and then it's gone. 'That's the whine you've got to learn to be fearful of. Shell's only a four-incher but deadly accurate and efficient.'

He stops talking and puts his hands in his pockets. Then he turns from us and walks away whistling.

We look at each other. 'Now that's an odd one,' Fat says.

I know, though, to listen carefully to what Thompson teaches me.

In the late afternoon when we've reinforced our section of trench, Elijah and I lie on our backs and watch the aeroplanes above us soar and dive and fight one another. They are close enough that we soon learn to tell the shape of our own grey-and-black aeroplanes from those of the Germans. They swoop like ospreys and puff out little bits of black smoke. Once in a while a plane will falter, then spin down to earth and disappear over the hump of the trench.

'I wish I could fly like that,' Elijah says to me in Cree. 'I wish I could fly like that, like a bird,' he repeats, staring up like a little boy. 'Maybe a pilot will take me up sometime.'

'Me, I'm happy to stay on the ground on my belly in the dirt,' I answer. 'Thinking about falling from up there makes me sick.'

Every night near sunset we are all ordered to stand-to, rifles at the ready, our heads just below the crest of the trench. We stand on what McCaan calls fire-steps, crouched, waiting for a German attack. This is ritual at dawn and at sunset, when both sides like to attack each other best.

This evening, McCaan squats beside me and smells of sweat and tobacco. He stares into a periscope over at the German lines and swears a lot because he has only the weak light the setting sun throws from behind us and can't see much of anything. He's jiggling around his periscope so much that he attracts a swarm of Hun bullets. I want to shout to McCaan to drop his head but the English words don't come in time, just a stream of Cree, but it's too late.

McCaan flies back onto the duckboards. The periscope is smashed beside him. I think that he has been shot in the head, because he doesn't move, but then he gets up groggily as if he's just woken up from a deep nap. One eye is so puffed that it is already shut closed, blackening by the second. He picks up the periscope and stares at it, muttering to himself. A bullet hole is punched neatly through the front, and the metal in back is ripped open. A medic rushes up, but McCaan pushes him away. A confusion flashes in his eyes that I've not seen before.

WE SPEND OUR FIRST MONTHS in and near Saint-Eloi. I like the nights best there. When evening falls the flares go up. Red and green, they illuminate the sky around us in the strangest hues of colour. These are the signal flares both sides use. It is as if I'm dreaming, staring up at this painted sky, shells whizzing above my head and once in a while crashing around me.

Corporal Thompson, the one who knows all the sounds, has taken over most of our training. He's been in the trenches since almost the first day. Tonight he will take five of the new soldiers out to get them accustomed to working in no man's land in the dark. As Elijah and Sean Patrick and Gilberto and McCaan and me sit waiting and smoking, Thompson appears as if from the wall of the trench, and I realize that it is the hole where he sleeps.

'Corporal Thompson,' McCaan says.

Thompson nods to him sharply, a cigarette dangling from the side of his mouth. He is short enough that he doesn't need to hunch over in this trench. 'Yes, Sergeant,' he answers.

'How do you feel about taking us up above to give us a little taste of no man's land?'

'Very good, Sergeant,' Thompson answers, and disappears into his hole.

33

Thompson reappears with a small bag strapped by his side. I see that he doesn't carry a rifle.

As if Thompson knows what I think, he says, 'Not much good a rifle will do you up above when you're working. It will only get in your way.' The others of us in the party unshoulder ours and lean them against the trench walls. 'I want two of you to hold onto them, act as sentry while the rest of us work.'

McCaan and Gilberto are the first to pick theirs back up.

'This way, gentlemen,' Thompson says, and moves along the duckboards with almost silent steps. He leads us to a ladder, then climbs it, peering over the top before disappearing onto the earth above. First Elijah goes, and I follow. The others are close behind. I wait for the zing of bullets to come any second, but see that Thompson has led us to a place of mounds and craters where we seem to be covered from direct fire.

A white flare goes up nearby and Thompson, on his belly, goes very still so that I have a hard time seeing him just yards away. I follow his lead, looking at the scarred landscape all around without moving my eyes. Under the bright glow of the flare it is strangely peaceful, rock-strewn and muddy and silent so that it isn't difficult to forget I'm in the middle of a terrible place. In the dimming light I make out a grinning face next to me. It belongs to a soldier long dead, but I cannot tell from which side. His face is frozen in a perpetual smile, as if he is chuckling at what he knows.

When the light has died, my eyes have a hard time re-adjusting to the darkness. Thompson crawls up to me. I hear him rather than see him in the black that's descended.

'Blind as a bat right now, ain't ya?' he says close to my ear. 'Next time keep one eye closed when a flare's up. It'll help your eyes adjust back faster.'

I hear him scuttle away. My night eyes are back in time to see him stop in an especially large crater. He motions for the rest of us to come close.

'They say a shell never falls twice in the same hole, but don't believe them,' he whispers. 'I've seen it happen. But in a pinch and there's no other choice you are safest in a freshly blown crater.' He pauses, listening. I listen too, and a sound like scratching comes to my ears. I listen as carefully as I can and to me it sounds like mice chewing through something. Elijah listens as well, and we look to Thompson to explain.

'That's our engineers below us digging,' he says. 'They're digging tunnels toward the Hun lines. They'll fill those tunnels with explosives underneath Fritz. When the time comes—boom!' He spreads his fingers, lifts his hands.

Elijah and I look at each other in disbelief. Thompson seems to be a serious one, so I have no choice but to believe him. 'From this point forward,' he says, 'keep a close eye for Fritz. He's been busy here again. Look at our barbed wire. Make sure that it hasn't been cut. Note places that look like they've been mucked with. That's where Fritz crawls through.'

We slip out of the crater one by one and make our way parallel with our own line, stopping often to listen. It is a quiet night. Even the constant shelling seems to have moved away from us. We make it to the stretch of barbed wire in front of our own position and Thompson examines it carefully. He motions and points to a place that has been cut through. We have no rolls of wire with us. Someone will have to come out later and fix it.

We turn and go back the way we've come. In another crater Thompson explains to us in a hushed whisper that he doesn't want to go farther down the line tonight. Our group is close to the point where the new companies are dug in, and the sentries will be nervous and inexperienced enough to mistake us for Germans and shoot at us.

When we are within yards of where we first emerged, I feel relieved. The others slip back down into the safety of the trench and I am standing, about to follow Elijah down the ladder, when a flare pops up and hovers right over me. I'm frozen there in full view and turn my head and get my first look at the German line. It is much closer than I had assumed and I realize how exposed I am now that the flare is dropping right above me, illuminating the ground like it is morning.

But still I do not move. I stare at the enemy for the first time. No faces, just a line of mounds behind barbed wire. I hear the bullet whip past my temple before I even hear the *crack* of a rifle, and all around me the ground sends up splats of mud and dirt and I feel an impact on my hand and it goes numb as other bullets whiz by very close. I dive like an otter toward the trench and before I know it I'm sailing down the wall and land hard on my side on the duckboards at the others' feet, the wind knocked out of me.

'You'd better lose that habit quick, Private,' Thompson says, staring down at me, then walking away casually as I struggle to find a breath.

McCaan bends down and sits me up. My chest relaxes a little and I gulp some air. I clutch my hand to my chest. McCaan takes my numb hand into his own and looks at it for a moment. 'No Blighty for you on your first night out,' he says. 'You're just hit by a clump of mud knocked up from a bullet. It'll be sore for a while is all. Teach you a good lesson.'

Back in our section of trench I lie in my little cave. My mind races with what's just happened, the sneaking about in such a dangerous place, being shot at for the first time. It is real. All of this is suddenly very real. The other side wants to kill me, and I've never even seen their faces.

I won't see it. It will just appear. The bullet so close to me tonight could have been a little more to one side. It is thrilling and horrifying at the same time. My hand begins to ache. I listen to Elijah carry on in English and laugh with Sean Patrick and Gilberto and Grey Eyes and Graves. Already Elijah is telling of his exploits. I hear him making this story bigger, more dangerous, though he wasn't even the one shot at.

I watch the flashes of an artillery barrage far down the line. The night sky is on fire.

NOOHTAAWIY
My Father

XAVIER TWITCHES AND MOANS in his sleep. I arranged it so that he lies back in the canoe, his head on his pack. I found him this morning on the beach, shivering and half conscious. What happened over there has wrecked him. He thinks I don't see him putting those needles in his arm. They are a part of what's killing him. But something far worse is consuming Xavier from the inside. It's this that I must figure out how to remove. I wish it were simply a matter of finding the right root in the bush. This is a sickness I've not had to face before. I must figure out the right cure or I will lose him, and he's the last of my family.

The river water is black this early in the morning before the sun has a chance to warm it and the light to turn it the colour of tea. My father used to tease my mother and younger sister and me, telling us that we were the colour of the river water in high summer but that in winter we turned as pale as the Hudson Bay traders and he was afraid he'd one day lose us in the snow. My sister—your mother, Xavier—we called her Rabbit. We'd look at my mother's brown face as her eyes narrowed in laughter and then look to my father smiling back. He was the last great talker in our clan. He told stories softly so that you had to lean close to him to hear, so close you could smell the smoke in the hide ribbon my mother weaved into his hair, the scent of his neck like the wind coming off the Great

Salt Bay. I used to imagine that he weaved his stories all summer, his words forming invisible nets that he cast over us on the long winter nights, capturing us and pulling us in closer together so that we collected each other's warmth. And sometimes his stories were all that we had to keep us alive.

I steer the canoe into the faster current and let us drift with it, using my paddle only as a rudder. The mist is disappearing now and I can see a long way down the bank, can keep an eye sharp for the movement of animals along the shore. Nephew cries out but then goes silent again. The sound of it, the animal fear at the very bottom of that cry, makes me think something I haven't thought about in a long time. It is the story of my childhood. Now I tell it to you, Xavier, to keep you alive.

The snows were settled in so deeply that winter had become a part of us. This was long before you, Xavier, when I was still a child. Thirty Anishnabe lived on the traplines that season, half of us children. All the past winters we'd survived in much smaller numbers. This time we had no choice. Three families' hunters had been taken away the autumn before, two by the North-West Mounted Police, one by Hudson's Bay Company rum.

I was a young girl with waking dreams of all the trouble that was to come into my life, sharp pains like ice arrows through my temples that dropped me to my back and caused me to convulse. Except for Rabbit, the other children avoided me. Damaged is what I was to them, but they wouldn't say this to my face. I was lean and bony with knotted black hair that I refused to let my mother comb. If they thought I was crazy, I let them. Laughed at them.

Autumn had been promising, many geese and ducks shot, four beaver families snared, and many grouse and sturgeon.

But no moose, and the old women among us immediately began their chatter that no moose early in winter meant starvation later. Me, I think it was their idle complaints, their greedy talk as they chewed their hides and drank their tea, that put a curse on us. And in the harsh North Country near what the *wemistikoshiw* call Hudson Bay, shaking a curse once it settles upon you is like trying to shake a fat bloodsucker from your hand.

Early winter, the time of the blowing moon, sat upon us. Our hunters came back wide-eyed and frozen, reporting to my father the absence of animals, even of tracks. They worried by my family's fire. I know all this because I watched them from the corner of our *askihkan,* hidden under my father's moose robe, quiet and observant like a hungry lynx.

By the end of that month, all of us scrounged for food. The women peeled tamarack bark for tea, dug through the deep snow in hopes of finding a few dried fiddleheads. The men continued to go out on the traplines and to hunt, returning silent, their blank stares scaring us children.

I was nearing the time of my strawberry ceremony, when the women closest to me would keep me in our *askihkan* all day, talking to me, praying, telling me stories, preparing me for my first blood of womanhood. Until the spring came, I was allowed to wander. But I wanted nothing of that. I wanted to stay close to my father, to watch over him.

When talk began that soon we would be forced to boil our moccasins, a group of hunters returned with a small black bear slung on a pole between them. Some of the old ones among us were bear clan and muttered bitterly. Who would dare disturb a brother's winter sleep? They brought the bear directly to my father. I hid in my usual place and watched as he spoke with them about where they'd come across the den, how they had recognized it in the deep snow.

Marius, the oldest hunter, spoke first. 'We followed its tracks.' My father looked puzzled, but he remained silent. Marius continued. 'At first I thought I was mistaken, but there they were for all of us to see. We followed them.' My father and the four hunters sat silent for a long time, staring at the crackling fire. 'The tracks ended near a cliff by the river,' Marius said after a while.

My father waited.

'They just stopped,' one of the younger hunters blurted. 'We walked with them, and in the middle of an open field they just stopped.' The others stared at him.

'We'd been led to a den,' Marius went on, as if the young one hadn't spoken at all. 'We could see its indent on the side of the cliff. But the tracks stopped short of it at least the length of a tall man. Clearly the den had not been disturbed since autumn. We dug and we roused the bear and took it quickly. We wouldn't have disturbed it, but we were hungry.' My father nodded and again they all stared at the fire.

I looked over at the bear hanging from the pole, tied by its hind paws so that its nose pointed to the ground and its tongue lolled out. Normally they would have skinned and quartered the animal where they took it, but this time was different. The bear was thawing now near the fire. I smelled the musky smell of piss. I could see from where I lay that it was only a little taller than me.

The young hunter spoke again. 'All of this is not good!' His name was Micah. He had a pretty wife who'd had her first child the summer before. I thought he was handsome, and I blushed whenever he was around.

'Do we continue to starve or do we eat the animal that has been delivered to us?' my father asked. 'If no other game is found in the next day, the choice will be apparent.'

I listened to this as the wind threw itself against our *askihkan*. An early storm wind, young and strong. Even I knew that. There would be no hunting for the next day at least.

The following afternoon my mother and father prepared the bear for us. Normally we did our butchering outside, but the bear was our brother, and so he was invited in. Nothing was rushed. Nothing was to be wasted for fear of angering him. The knife used couldn't touch anything else. Any of the hair that the bear shed was carefully collected from the floor and clothing, and burned in the fire, whispered prayers drifting up with the stinking smoke. My parents carefully laid the animal on his back on freshly cut spruce boughs, talking to him, whispering prayers for what seemed like hours. They rocked back and forth on their haunches, my father sprinkling bits of powder into the flames that brought into the room a sweet smell I recognized as cedar. I was alarmed when at one point my father began to cry. I'd never seen this before and was frightened, but I remained beneath his heavy moose robe.

When the prayers were finally done, the bear was pulled up on the pole by his hind paws once again and a large cooking pot placed below him. My father took his knife and ran it along the bear's stomach. With a ripping sound the *askihkan* filled with the powerful smell of insides. The guts filled the pot. Then he and my mother cut along the inside of the bear's legs and gently peeled the fur from his body, cutting carefully where they had to separate flesh from fur, until the animal hung there naked. He looked like a small, thin man dangling from his feet, blood dripping from his head. For the first time I realized why we were told the bear was our brother.

For many nights after, I was jolted from sleep by dreams of this bear-man waking from his death slumber, bending up to untie his feet and then jumping onto the floor, eyes bulging from his fleshy skull, pacing on two legs between the bodies of my sleeping family, sinew of white muscle glistening in the moonlight as he searched for his fur.

With the skinning and cleaning done, the hunters who'd killed him were invited in to prepare the meat for roasting. He was a winter bear, grown thin in his sleep, and although young, was tough already. But we were hungry, and all thirty of us crowded in and ate until every part of the animal was gone— his meat, brain, heart, kidneys, liver; his bones cracked open for their marrow and carefully collected to be boiled down later. We ate until our stomachs grew taut as drums, until beads of sweat dotted our foreheads and our cheeks flushed red. My father warned all of us that not a scrap should be wasted. Even the smallest piece of gristle that no one wanted was collected in a bowl and added to the bones or burned in the fire over prayers. We were always careful not to waste for fear of insulting an animal, but this time stood out to me. I did not understand my father's concern, his eyes following everything, anxious. Later I would come to understand.

The young hunter Micah took his new baby girl from his wife's lap, then chose a bit of flesh and put it in the baby's mouth. 'Your first taste of meat,' he said to the child, who hesitantly, then hungrily began to chew. We all smiled at the expression on her face, but then she turned red and began to gasp. Micah shook her upside down to try and dislodge the meat. Like lightning my mother grabbed the child, sticking a

43

finger in her throat so that she gagged and threw the meat up. I saw the meat drop to the floor. I glanced at Rabbit, but she did not pick it up and place it in her bowl. No one else seemed to have noticed.

We didn't taste fresh game again for a very long time. It got so that I would remember the tough bits of gristle that I had not wanted at the feast and my stomach would grumble moodily.

The real cold settled in with the moon of the exploding trees. This was the time of the year that we depended on the hare to help us live. Its hides were sewn together and worn fur-side-in from our feet to our heads. Its meat was tender. We ate the stomachs that were filled with bitter greens to stave off the coughing disease and the yellow disease. But like everything else this particular winter, even the hares began to abandon us. The hunters continued to return with very little or nothing at all. Marten partially eaten by wolves, the odd grouse, a skinny and starved beaver. Some of the men began to complain about what we already knew, that there were too many of us for this part of the bush to sustain. They were going to head off with their families in hopes of surviving. In the end only the headstrong young Micah and his wife and baby walked into the bush alone.

The next day broke bright and cold as any I'd ever felt. The children who had energy played a game where they let spit drool from their mouths and measured how fast it froze once it hit the air. Micah pulled a toboggan with their few possessions, his wife with her child slung in her *tikonoggan* walking behind in the track that he cut. Although his wife did not speak a goodbye or look back to us, we all knew that she did not want to go, that it was Micah alone who had made the decision.

From what we were to find out later, they travelled the day

through deep snow, Micah stopping along the way and wandering off to find animal tracks. When dusk threatened they'd only made it a few miles and had set up camp by a creek where he hoped to find tracks in the morning. He didn't. They pushed on.

Micah and his wife and their child made their way west. They moved inland and away from the Great Salt Bay only a few miles at a time, Micah searching for tracks. On the fourth day he made a difficult shot at a snowshoe hare bounding toward a tree line, and later watched proudly as his wife cooked it. A good enough sign for him. As they ate the hare he declared that this place marked where they would build their winter shelter.

For a while, anyway, we thought Micah's decision to head out on his own must have been right. That or he was dead. We did not see them for many weeks. From what his wife was later able to explain between her fits and in words that we understood, many tracks crisscrossed the area, fox, marten, wolf, lynx, hare. It was as if Micah had discovered that place in the forest where all the animals had come to winter. But for all the tracks he followed, Micah did not see a single animal.

At night, the *Wawahtew,* the North Lights, flickered so brightly they awoke the baby from her sleep. Strange sounds echoed from the forest, groaning and shrieking. Micah said the trees were popping in the cold, or wolves were snatching rabbits. His wife claimed to us that they'd found tracks near their lodge early in the morning after those long nights, tracks that resembled a man's but much larger, holes in the snow gouged where claws instead of toes had dug in. Tracks of the *windigo.* By the time she told these stories, though, Micah's wife had become unreliable, had become something else. At that point she was only trying to save herself.

Out in the bush, their situation became more desperate. Micah blamed himself for his inability to find an animal despite so many tracks. The baby's hunger cries suddenly stopped. Instead now she stared reserved from her *tikonoggan,* her eyes like the eyes of an old person. Micah grew desperate enough to dig through the snow, chop through the ice and try to catch fish. He spent long hours with a line of sinew and a bone hook, constantly stirring the water of the small hole with a stick so that it would not freeze up. The cold was the brutal kind, bullying. His wife begged Micah to give up his fishing but he refused. 'I will not return to our lodge until I can feed you' is all he would say. He caught nothing. He began to stay by the hole through the night, too, a small fire to warm him.

At first light one morning, the wife bundled up her child and herself and went to check on Micah. She found him sitting in the snow, his fire long burned out, a grimace carved on his face. The wife sat and mourned her dead husband, her tears freezing on her cheeks. The baby stared listlessly.

The two of them somehow survived the cold of that day. As dusk settled she made the promise, whispered just loud enough for the forest to hear, that if she and her baby survived the dark, she would feed the child well the next morning. Later, when we tried to get this from her, all she could do was growl and whimper at us. But that morning the sun did rise, and with the last of her strength she collected wood and started her cook fire. She drew her knife from her shawl and leaned toward her husband. He was keeping his promise to feed her and the child.

None of us knew any of this at the time. We continued on best we could. Even the smallest and sickliest game was a welcome change from the roots and bits of dried fish we still had left. The hunters came to my father and asked him to divine. He prepared his fire. When all was ready, he had the hunters bring him the shoulder blade of the last moose that had been killed, a young bull. I watched as the men huddled around the fire and my father prompted them to discuss in detail the day they'd taken the animal.

'What was the weather like?' he asked, holding the shoulder blade in his scarred hands. 'Was the moose feeding on red willow? Tell me exactly where you found the tracks. Tell me everything. Leave nothing out.' The men described the day, the tracks, the location. My father placed the shoulder blade in the fire and urged them to talk on, to say everything.

After a time, he took a small cup of water and dipped his fingers into it. He leaned over the fire and dripped water onto the shoulder blade. He studied it carefully, then dripped more. 'Keep speaking,' he urged the hunters. 'Describe the river, the animal's movements, everything.'

The men continued to talk and my father continued to drip water onto the heated sheath of bone, the water sizzling, then disappearing. Soon cracks began to appear in the bone. The men talked on, reminiscing about the day, the place, how they felt as they tracked the wounded moose silently so as not to panic it, deep into the bush. They did this until the fire died down.

My father removed it from the fire, still hot so that I didn't know how it was that his hands weren't burned badly. The others gathered around him as he explained the map of cracks and splits. 'This is the Albany River,' he said, pointing to a long, thick split. 'This is where the Wakina Creek pours into it.' They nodded and listened carefully. 'You will find a moose here, close to that creek. Leave early tomorrow morning.' They smiled and rose to leave.

In the days that the hunters were gone Micah's wife and her baby returned. She appeared with the sunlight behind her, walking steadily, powerfully on her snowshoes so at first we mistook her for a man. Her face was flushed and healthy-looking. Her eyes sparkled.

All of us children gathered around to talk to her, asking questions. Had Micah found game, was he still on his lines, had she any food in the large pack slung across her back? At first she didn't answer, just stared at us quizzically, as if she didn't know who we were or what we were saying. When we began to wonder what was wrong, she finally spoke. 'Micah is back in the bush,' she said, smiling. 'He has supplied me with more meat than I can eat.'

We children jumped around at word of this, energized for the first time in weeks. 'Give us some! Give us some!' we shouted.

'I will cook some for you,' she said. As she walked away I swore she'd grown taller.

My mother and father knew something was wrong. My mother's father was Ojibwe, and my mother had seen this once before. So had my father. He told some of the young men to keep an eye on Micah's wife and to take away her pack. Later, I heard her screams from where I lay hiding under my father's moose robe, dreaming of roasted meat. The men entered her *askihkan,* and it took four to hold her down.

Even then they barely managed. My father ordered her bound and guarded day and night. He then sent out a search party to see what had become of Micah. My parents already knew, though. They'd seen the contents of her pack. My father strung it high in a tree for the *manitous* to watch over.

The next days we listened to her fall into madness. She

begged and pleaded in a child's voice, first for Micah to help her, then for her child to be brought to her. At nighttime her voice went hoarse so that she sounded like some monster growling in a language we did not understand. None of us slept. We became tense and restless. Some days she turned back into her old self and talked normally. This is when she confessed everything, explained to us what had happened. She said that on the night before she cut into Micah's flesh, a strange man-beast came out of the bush. He threatened to take and eat her child if the wife did not feed it the next day.

'It was not my fault. Don't you see?' she pleaded. 'I was only trying to protect my baby.' And then she'd cry again, her sobs turning into angry growls as she began to quake and squirm so fiercely that we thought she'd break her ropes and attack us.

The baby cried constantly. One of the other women who was breast-feeding agreed to nurse it. We couldn't trust Micah's wife any more. The child sucked hungrily on the other woman, who became worried the child would drain her of all her milk. When the woman tried to remove it, the baby bit hard and the woman screamed in shock. My father had to pry the child's mouth from her bloody tit.

Micah's wife and the baby were turning *windigo*. The children in camp stopped sleeping, cried in fear, no longer felt their hunger. We'd grown up on stories of the *windigo* that our parents fed us over winter fires, of people who eat other people's flesh and grow into wild beasts twenty feet tall whose hunger can be satisfied only by more human flesh and then the hunger turns worse. I listened to the adults of the camp talk nervously among themselves, their voices interrupted by the wife's growls and mad language. They talked of my father's reputation as a *windigo* killer, of how as a young man he became our *hookimaw* after killing a family of them who roamed near where we trapped, a family who had once been part of the caribou clan but had turned one hard winter and begun preying on the camps of unsuspecting Cree. 'He must kill *windigos* once again,' the adults whispered to one another. 'We are too weak already and Micah's woman's madness can surely spread in these bad times.' My father knew this too, and made preparations to act as his own father had taught him.

Micah's wife must have sensed what was coming. She pleaded and begged, screamed and howled, whispered to the children to untie her ropes. On the day that my parents called for her, it took five men to carry her to them. Once again I hid under my father's moose robe. My stomach ached with what I thought was hunger but the ache turned to a dull throb when my father sprinkled crushed cedar into the fire and muttered prayers. Micah's wife watched him with eyes sparkling, her body shaking, her mouth gagged now. The baby lay sleeping beside her.

He didn't take long to do it. His eyes looked sad. He leaned down and whispered something I could not hear into her ear. She immediately went slack and her eyes reflected fear and then expectation as he straddled her chest. My father covered her face with a blanket and placed his hands on her neck. He looked up above him and the muscles of his body tensed. Her feet quivered, then went still. At the moment when the quiet came like a shadow into the room, I felt warmth between my legs. My father turned to the baby. Again he wasted no time. He covered the sleeping child's head with a corner of the blanket, placed a hand about its small neck and, looking up once again, squeezed until the life left it.

He sat silent for a long time after, staring into the fire, his back to me. 'I allowed you to watch, Little One,' he said when he finally spoke, 'because one day I will be gone and you might have to do the same.' The ache in my stomach was gone. When he went outside I placed my hand between my legs and then brought it to my face, stared at the little smear of blood on my fingers, hoping to see some sign of what awaited me.

Within days, our hunters returned with as much moose-meat as each of them could carry. They'd found a large bull where my father had told them to look. Something unwanted had left us. A thaw settled in the very morning we prepared the feast. Winter's back had been broken. Colour came into the children's faces. The adults once again walked with purpose.

More than ever I kept to myself now, too old to play with the children, too young to be accepted by the adults. From that time on, I realized long after, the rumours about me began, talk fuelled by full stomachs, whispers of half-truths that grow wings as they leave the speaker's mouth and flit around like sparrows, landing where they please. I had been witness to brutal deeds that no child should see, I'd been struck mute by shock, my womanhood had come to me like a tainted thing, a sick animal, at the moment it should not have. I heard all of this and it pushed me deeper into my shy silence. My fourteenth year had come, that time when the wisdom of the world begins to show itself but cannot be expressed in childish words. So I chose not to speak, always watching. What the gossips did not realize was that I wasn't afraid of my father's actions, his gifts. I desperately wanted to possess them for myself.

*

W HEN THE SNOWS RECEDED, the clans came together at the mouth of the Albany River not far from where the *wemistikoshiw*, the pale ones of the Hudson's Bay Company, had built a post. It had been a poor winter for furs, the bad side of the seven-year cycle, which did not make the company men very happy. Those Cree who did have furs were treated well, given flour and sugar for their bellies, rum that loosened their tongues. Some began to talk.

All the clans that had gathered already seemed to know the others' winter hardships and triumphs. Unspoken law said Cree business remained Cree business and was not to be discussed with the *wemistikoshiw*. But rum is a sly and powerful weapon. I've watched it drown our people all of my life. In the month of the frog moon when the fishing is at its best, the rum drinker George Netmaker, father of Joseph, brought an important message to my father. What my father had done over the winter seemed to have angered the Hudson's Bay Company men, and they demanded he come to them to discuss his actions so that they might decide whether or not he should be considered a murderer. We laughed at this. Wasn't it the *wemistikoshiw* who were on our land? Was it not they who relied on us? My father ignored the news.

For the most part, our lives continued as they always had. Hunting, fishing, trapping, socializing late into nights that stayed bright, storing up on food and laughter, preparing as best we could through the brief summer for winter's return. This was my summer of bitter happiness, moods sweeping over me like summer thunderstorms. I hated the changes, the monthly blood, the sprouting of breasts. I was appalled and mesmerized by what I was becoming.

As we prepared that autumn for the path of the geese to

cross ours, the *wemistikoshiw* came with many rifles. They were North-West Mounted Police, and their uniform buttons shone brightly in the sun. Their leather boots squeaked with each step, and their strange words broke harshly from thin, tight lips. George Netmaker translated. They had come for my father. He was to sit in their circle to discuss if what he'd done last winter violated their laws. He was to go with them now and wait in one of their jails because we were a people who would not sit still, and who knew if we might run away and never return?

My father was led away with his big hands bound behind him as our women wailed for the future. To take the *hookimaw* who was to lead us into the bush for the long winter was unimaginable. Ignorance. Malice. I cursed them with everything I had as they receded with my father into their own world.

Most of us survived the winter and returned in spring to the Albany River where news awaited that my father was dead. But I had already known this. The convulsions had come back to me in our winter camp, convulsions that I thought had left with my childhood. I saw it all. The tiny room with no windows that they locked him in, no natural light or fresh air or game. I saw how within a week he'd stopped talking, how within a month he'd stopped eating. I saw how they kept his body from us, how they buried it underground, a place where he'd surely be unhappy.

My mother carried on with my education, teaching which roots and leaves could heal and which could kill. Rabbit never seemed interested. What my mother could not teach me was something that I already had. The vision to see little parts of the near and far future, have moments to come wash over me, left me drained and shaken so that I could not stand. Once I considered this a gift. I no longer feel so sure.

I had the power and watched it slowly recede. I am the second to last in a long line of *windigo* killers. There is still one more.

At the time of my birth the *wemistikoshiw* were still dependent on us. Like little children they came for handouts. When the winters grew too cold we gave them fur to wear against their skin and dried moosemeat for their empty stomachs. When the blackflies of spring threatened to drive them mad we taught them to use the green boughs of the black spruce on their fires. We showed them where in the rivers the fish hid when summer grew warm and how to trap the plentiful beaver without driving them away forever. The Cree are a generous people. Like forest ticks the *wemistikoshiw* grabbed onto us, growing fatter by the season, until the day came when suddenly it was we who answered to them.

Long past my father's death I remember how they laughed at me, a woman living alone in the bush and trapping animals after all my relations had gone to the reserves. Their laughing came less often as season after season my furs continued to be the thickest, the most plentiful.

The world is a different place in this new century, Nephew. And we are a different people. My visions still come but no one listens any longer to what they tell us, what they warn us. I knew even as a young woman that destruction bred on the horizon. In my early visions, numbers of men, higher than any of us could count, were cut down. They lived in the mud like rats and lived only to think of new ways to kill one another. No one is safe in such times, not even the Cree of Mushkegowuk. War touches everyone, and *windigos* spring from the earth.

PASITEW
Fire

I AWAKE TO THE RHYTHMIC SCRATCH of Auntie's paddle on the gunwale. The pain in my body is a long moan. Something tells me to sit up, so I force myself. This is the place. 'Here,' I say to Auntie. My voice is hollow in my head. Auntie stops paddling.

On the bank, taller trees give way to the green shoots of new growth. This strange dividing line stretches off as far as we can see. A fire line. This is the place where the great fire tired out and stopped, the line of its death so sharp I can imagine the fire simply dropping into the earth. 'Elijah and I found a dead moose not far from here,' I tell Auntie. She leans closer to hear me. 'It had roasted in the fire. We were hungry and ate a part of it.' It's strange to hear my own voice. 'When we reached this place I thought we'd crossed into their world.'

I sit up for a time and look at how the bush has grown again. Baby black spruce no higher than my chest stretch out before me, and wildflowers sprinkle themselves across the damp ground. Fire is sometimes good for the bush, makes it come back more fully. But back there, back at Ypres and the Somme, I think the earth is so wrecked with shells and poison gas that nothing good will ever grow again.

I lie down, exhausted from the small effort of sitting. For a moment I think I feel the acrid scent of charred wood tickle my nose. The moment I close my eyes I am on the river again, but it is the one of years ago, before the war, when Elijah and I paddled it together.

I follow a lynx's tracks early in the morning. They are near the river. A short trot into the bush, the tracks suddenly double back toward the water, heading south to the shore. Near the ashes of last night's campfire, we can see that the lynx made its way to the bank and casually headed south. Here on the riverbank its movements are easy to follow, the broad pads of its footprints perfect. Elijah and me, we follow them out onto a wide plain of river mud where the water has dropped over the last weeks. In the centre of the plain, the tracks end. Both of us look around to see if the lynx bounded, but in all directions the mud is unspoiled.

Elijah, he tries to make light of it, but I see in his eyes that even he is nervous. 'Water came up last night and washed them away,' he says in English as we load the canoe and push off. He doesn't say this in Cree. Their tongue is better for lies.

We stick close to the shore of the river, heading south against the strong north-flowing current, making good time. The August days are warm, the night's coolness chased away by a campfire. I've never been this far south of Mushkegowuk before. When we come to rapids, I pole and Elijah pulls with a rope from shore. Both of us have lost the laziness and weight of the summer's feasting.

This new country, it isn't so bad. Not so different from home. I like the thought that each paddle stroke takes me farther into a new land. This is good, I say in my head as my paddle dips. I'm in new country.

Days after the lynx, with the river calm and the paddling easier, great grey clouds rise on the horizon. Flecks of ash dot the water. Soon the smell of smoke surrounds us.

Elijah is the first to put words to it. 'The world is burning.' We both stare. This part of the river is a long, straight stretch. To the south, grey columns billow, heavy like they're full of rain. 'Let's paddle closer,' he says.

I feel the warm breeze blowing to the west. I say the obvious. 'The wind is in our favour.'

We push toward the smoke in the distance until it perches on our heads, in our clothes and hair. Elijah guesses out loud that the fire travels away from us.

I want to tell Elijah that even so, trying to get any closer seems foolish. But is there any point? Elijah, him, he lives for what the day will bring.

We canoe upriver for many more hours, and my hands grow sore from fighting the current. I'm happy when Elijah suggests it's time to make camp. The smoke swallows the sun far to the west and a pall falls over the river. I think I can hear the fire, growling in the distance. A living thing.

'Which direction do you think it's travelling now?' I ask. The wind has died and the night sky to the south is orange.

'I don't know,' Elijah finally admits. 'Your Auntie's the conjurer. What would she do?' He laughs and slaps my arm. 'Maybe you should sleep with your eyes open.'

The danger of the fire so close seems to do something to Elijah that I am not sure I like.

We sit on our blankets and watch the sky. To the north the black of night lies, a sleeping bear. But here, it's as if the North Lights have gone south and soured, their cool blues and greens sickened to an orange that dances just loud enough to keep me awake. We talk. Elijah bounces his legs like a child having to pee.

'You say you don't believe in signs,' I tell him.

'Hmm,' Elijah says, looking toward the south. 'And just what is this fire trying to tell us?'

I don't answer.

I must sleep soundly for some time. Distorted dreams come. Deep grey mud along the riverbank tries to pull me under. I hear whispering and mumblings in a strange tongue. A fog all around me rises, and when it is a man's height off the ground it begins to shower down like a burning rain onto my face. I hear a booming in the distance like an elder's drum. My body shakes with the noise.

Elijah shouts and kicks me. 'Get up,' he says, as hot ash and cinders swirl around us.

I stand, confused, shading my eyes in the bright light of trees burning. My throat constricts in a gag.

Elijah scrambles with his blanket wrapped about him, grabbing our few belongings and our rifles. 'We've got to get to the canoe,' Elijah shouts. '*Ashtum!* Come!'

I feel a burn like wasps stinging my scalp, and when I reach up to brush the annoyance away, the cinders that smoulder on my head burn my fingers as well. I run in the direction of the river just in time to remember that our food, the flour and lard and moosemeat, is tied in a tree away from animals. Too late to get it now.

Not able to breathe, I bend closer to the ground and continue on, listening for Elijah's voice. We'd camped only ten yards from the river, but I can't see the water. The smoke suffocates me, and a stand of trees to my left bursts into flame with a whoosh and crackle, hurting my ears deep inside. I drop to my knees and crawl, shouting out to Elijah. I cannot hear him answer.

The mud between the stones tells me that I'm close to the

river. A few feet more and my hands find it. A line of trees close to the bank lights up, illuminating the surface of the water for a few seconds, burning my back. I dive, sure that I am on fire, but when I emerge I find that I'm all right. I lie there with just my nose and mouth and eyes above the surface. The sudden image of Elijah being burned alive forces me to move. I rise out of the water as much as I can, shouting out, 'Elijah!' but my voice sounds tiny and weak in the smoke. The fire's a continuous thunder in my ears.

The smooth pull of the river helps to orient me. Every time I can muster a deep enough breath, I call out for him. Panic slips itself inside my body. I am trying to brace myself for the frantic charge up the bank in search of Elijah when the weight of the canoe bumps into me. I grab for the gunwale and feel my way along it until the shock of a warm hand makes me jump.

Elijah bursts up from the water. He too has taken shelter in it. I shout, 'It's me. We've got to go.'

'Look at this!' Elijah hollers. 'Incredible!' His eyes sparkle in the firelight. 'Why didn't you follow me?'

'I lost you.' I do not know if he hears me. I cannot hear myself.

'Drape your wet blanket over the canoe,' he yells at me. 'The cinders are going to burn holes in the canvas.' He points to his own blanket stretched across the canoe. I follow his direction.

'It didn't look like you were too concerned about me,' I shout, but Elijah doesn't seem to hear. A large tree cracks and crashes close by and a moment later a red rain of embers falls on us. 'We've got to go with the current.' I point. 'It will be easier. Just hold on and float out.'

'No! The fire's running north faster than we could.' We look around at the exploding world, the flames lighting up the night. 'If we head back north, all we'll do is keep pace with the worst of it. It will eat us up.'

I am not sure. I ask, 'How far south will we have to travel to get out of this?'

'It burned along the river already, burned up all the bush,' he says, and I think I see Elijah grin, his teeth glinting. Why? 'I'm sure that a couple miles upriver it will be clear. Smoky, but clear.'

Around us, there is fire on all sides, bright walls of it. I hear a building roar and the hiss of embers falling into water. I breathe in and cough. 'Let's go then,' I shout. 'For a little while. If there's no let-up, we try floating out.' I look. Yes, Elijah, he is smiling.

I hold onto the stern and push while Elijah pulls on the bow. When our hands are on the gunwales, the falling embers burn them, so we both place our hands closer to the water's surface. I feel the embers hit and sizzle on my wet head. We wade forward clumsily in the dark, feel our way over the rocks and sinking mud. Elijah tries to keep us chest deep, but often he loses his footing completely in the depths and is forced to float, holding onto the canoe. I can feel the both of us, at these times, drifting backwards.

'Let's work our way shallower,' I shout up to Elijah, but when we're waist deep we soon learn that the smoke's too thick to breathe and the heat burns through our wet shirts. Sometimes, though, we find the right depth on a flat stretch where just our noses and half-closed eyes remain above water.

A long time passes and the burning world around us doesn't let up. On a smooth stretch I bang on the canoe's side to signal Elijah. We meet in the middle. 'It's not easing up,' I say.

'It will,' Elijah answers.

'Let's rest here awhile.'

Elijah doesn't answer.

We wait, not speaking, leaning into the current's pull with lolling heads. Just as I motion to Elijah that we should move forward, Elijah points above, then ducks underwater. I look up as an arc of yellow fire shoots across the river. Carried on the wind's back, it swoops over the wide stretch of water, a bridge of flame. Just as quickly as it appears, it's gone.

Time moves slowly. We push the canoe against the current in the fire rain, stopping often to splash the blankets and our hair. A film of grey covers the water's surface. 'Maybe it's coming time where we should go back the way we came,' I shout out finally, but if Elijah hears me, he doesn't respond.

Many fires onshore flare up at once, and I notice that the wet blankets on the canoe are smoking. Soon after, the stink of burning wool fills my nostrils. I pound on the canoe again and shout, 'I think the blankets are on fire. The canoe might be too.'

We pull the canoe in as close to the shore as the heat will allow and fill it with water so that it sinks. We load it with all the rocks we can find. Keeping our legs and bodies in the canoe, we sit again with our noses and eyes above water and wait.

'We're only a few days' paddle away once we get through this,' Elijah says. 'Just keep focused on that.'

My eyes are closed later when Elijah's foot pushes at me. 'It's getting lighter out,' he says.

I peer through the thick haze. To my left I see some light,

greater than the fire's. This little change boosts me. 'Maybe the smoke is thinning out too,' I say.

We wait. My nose keeps going underwater, and the shock of breathing it in causes me to jolt awake, coughing. I can tell that Elijah's tired too. I slip into half dreams, go back to my short time in the residential school, old Sister Magdalene and her stinking breath like burnt wool. I see her mouth moving as we boys sit frightened at our desks, her words pouring out like the river. 'The old Cree are heathen and anger God,' she says. 'The Cree are a backwards people and God's displeasure is shown in that He makes your rivers run backwards, to the north instead of to the south like in the civilized world.' She smacks my desk with her ruler and sparks fly from it, a thin tree on fire. 'When you accept Him He will perform a great miracle. He will cause the rivers in this barren place to run in the right direction.' I gasp awake when my head sinks into ashy water.

I see a hint of morning through the smoke. We are able to climb back in the canoe and, with heads bowed low, begin to paddle through the morning. On a long curve of river, we see a sand bar splitting the water. There is enough room for the two of us to curl up. The sand is warm from the fires that still burn up and down the river. We can get a little good air close to the ground.

'One of us should stay awake and keep watch,' I say to Elijah, but he's already dozing lightly. Before I can fight it, I too am taken by sleep.

We lose all track of time in this soot-coloured place. All that's left to us is to keep paddling, one stroke after the other. Find our way out.

Fires continue to rumble, but a little farther off now. The

smoke lies so still and heavy above us that no sun is visible, and I no longer know what part of day it is.

A darker shade, possibly night, has approached when Elijah spots the hulk of it on the shoreline. We'd have missed it if not for the unmistakable scent of burnt hide and underneath that the smell of cooked meat that makes our hungry stomachs groan. We beach the canoe and see that it's a bull moose, a big one, charred and blackened. Smoke rises from what is left of it. 'That doesn't smell so bad to me,' Elijah says, looking to me for my reaction.

I take my knife from its sheath and cut into the animal's haunch. The rest of the meat will be poisoned by its fear. I cut past the blackened muscle to a large strip of warm, tender meat that's undercooked but not too bad. I taste it. 'Good,' I say, cutting off more. Elijah takes his knife out as well. We work our way up and down the animal's leg, choosing the best-cooked parts.

When I've had my fill, I skim ash away from a spot on the river's surface and take a long drink of water. Elijah drinks too, and we sit together looking out at the haze of darkness approaching.

'Do you think we'd be safe to sleep here a few hours?' Elijah asks. We look around at the blackened stretch of stumps and smoking ground.

'There's nothing left to burn,' I answer.

Elijah shivers. I realize how cold I am too. At least the ground's warm. 'Mind getting a little fire going?' he says.

I laugh.

The next couple of days remain the same. It is as if the river has taken the two of us down underground. The smoke refuses to lift and the lack of wind makes us feel as if we're being suffocated. No birds sing. There are no trees for any wind to rustle through. The sounds of the river travel differently now, and it's impossible to estimate distances, which only worsens the feeling of suffocation. Still, it's the complete lack of animal sounds that makes me begin to feel more sad than I've ever been.

We both find it better not to talk at all if we don't have to. The scrape of paddles on gunwales as they dip into the ashy water is the only sound. The earth, in all directions, is burnt black and continues to smoke angrily.

Elijah finally breaks the silence. 'How far do you think the fire burned?'

I've been wondering. 'Miles and miles,' I answer. 'Hundreds of them at least.'

'I hope it doesn't reach our home,' he says.

It strikes me suddenly that I might not hear any news from home until I return, if I return at all. Something very much like regret begins to rise in me.

I remind myself that I made the decision to do this. I will protect him. It is what I do, what I have always tried to do.

By afternoon there's less smoke. The world unfolds a little of itself around us. As far as we can see, the ground is scorched black. What must have been bush too thick to walk through is now a great dead plain. Charcoal stumps stick up from the ground.

'I know this place,' I whisper to myself.

TO KEEP MY HEAD CLEAR, I ask Elijah to teach me more English.

'Good day, sir,' Elijah says. 'Do you know the time?'

I repeat, my tongue feeling thick and stupid.

'You are the best shot in all of the world,' Elijah continues.

'You are the best shot in all of the world,' I repeat, looking for birds, for anything with colour, only half paying attention.

'Thank you,' Elijah answers. 'You're not a bad shot yourself. If you had a father, he would be a heathen like your Auntie.' We keep paddling. After a while he says, 'The sky looks like rain.'

'Rain will kill the fire,' I answer in English.

'Good,' Elijah laughs. 'Very good. You didn't even sound much like a Frenchman. Now say, "I am a Cree Indian from Moose Factory, and I have come to kill Germans." They will like that.'

'Will they really ask questions like that?' I ask in our own tongue.

'Maybe,' Elijah answers. 'Better to let them know you're an angry warrior than some fucking bush Indian.'

I think about this for a while.

I rely on Elijah to help me in their world. Since we were boys Elijah has always had a gift for *wemistikoshiw* language. Once the nuns taught him to speak English, they couldn't stop him and soon learned to regret that they ever had. In school, it got so that Elijah learned to talk his way out of anything, gave great long speeches so that his words snaked themselves like vines around the nuns until they could no longer move, just shake their heads hopelessly at the pretty little boy who could speak their tongue like one of their bishops.

'What if they mistake us for Plains Cree and give us horses to ride?' I ask.

'They'd better not.' After a pause, Elijah continues, 'Maybe we'd learn and be good at it.'

'I can just see us climbing onto horses and falling off as

soon as they start running. All the *wemistikoshiw* would stare. They would wonder just what kind of Indians we are.' We both laugh. After a long time of silence, I speak again. 'Are they going to teach us to fight their way or will they just send us over there?'

'I don't know,' Elijah says.

A SHRILL SCREAM close by jolts me from sleep. The night is at its deepest black and I feel blind reaching for my rifle.

'Another lynx,' Elijah whispers as we lie on our stomachs with our guns ready. 'Very close, too. Take a shot if you get the chance.' Maybe the pelt will bring us some money in town.

It screams again, but from a different place. Something in its tone tells me it's the same animal. It sounds hurt. Maybe a mother who's lost her children.

The sound doesn't come again. Eventually we relax once more, but I sleep restlessly, not sure any more what's dream and what isn't.

Before leaving the next morning, we scout out the lynx tracks in the black soot, following them once again on their circuitous route around the camp before they lead down to the water. Their size and shape are identical to those of the others. Once again they stop in a flat open plain of mud. 'It's the same lynx,' I say.

'Impossible,' Elijah answers. 'And besides, there's no mystery where its tracks went this time.' He points to the water. 'A lynx could jump that distance.'

I do not believe him.

By mid-morning the blackened ground gives way to thick green bush. The change is not gradual but sudden. One can walk the jagged fire line of damage stretching west, the lush of high summer to the left, the black of fire on the right. I take a deep breath of the returned season.

We keep a close eye out for game all that day, and as dusk approaches put out our lines. No fish bite. I smell the scent of smoke in the early evening air, but it is the smell of town smoke, of people.

'It will be night soon,' I say. 'I don't wish to enter that place in the dark.'

Elijah nods. 'We'll camp and go into there in the morning.'

We find a good spot on a small island and soon have a fire going. The sun is sinking and we haven't eaten since the morning. 'My mother,' Elijah says, 'she told me stories of her mother having to boil their moccasins in deep winter to make soup.'

I look at Elijah talking, his face blackened. His eyes stand out against his skin. He lost his mother at a young age and rarely talks of her. Both of us are filthy. 'We can't go there looking like this,' I say. I walk to the river and wade in, remove my clothes and wring them out. The water isn't as cold as I'd imagined. I scrub my scalp with sand. Elijah walks in too, does the same. I dive under the water, let the current carry me in its darkness like I am flying in my dream world.

After, we sit naked on a rock and braid each other's hair, tying it tightly with strips of moosehide. The two of us still wear it in the old style. We are hunters, not homeguard Indians.

'Will they make us cut our hair short?' I ask, staring at the sun going down behind a stretch of spruce.

'I don't know,' Elijah says. 'Me, I think it would look good on me. But you, your ears would really stick out then. And your bald head would be so big it would make a nice target for the enemy.'

We roll our blankets about us, going to bed hungry once more. I try to find sleep, listen to the sounds of the town crossing to me in the night, men shouting and laughing, the tinkle of glass breaking on hard ground. Sleep is far away. Tomorrow I'll go into a place from which there is no turning back.

'Do you think the Canadians will separate us, Elijah?' I ask. I try to sound relaxed, a little bored.

It takes Elijah a long time to answer, so long that I think he has fallen asleep.

He finally speaks in the darkness. 'They'd better not.'

NTAWI NIPAHIWEWAK
Raiding Party

I JOLT FROM A LIGHT SLEEP. Feet pounding by on duckboards. Who is running around at such an hour? The night's very dark, that time just before dawn. I peer out from my hole and see another form pass by. I can tell by his breathing that Elijah is awake beside me. A shout down the trench and the boom of a rifle firing, followed by the *pop pop* of a pistol. Elijah rolls out of our cave and crouches, me following. With our rifles we bend and run toward the noise. Sergeant McCaan appears with his red hair sticking up and follows as well.

More shouts and the boom of a grenade going off close by, just ahead at the traverse where the trench cuts at an angle to the right. A shower of earth falls on our heads. We stop and wait. Elijah signals for McCaan to give covering fire, then peers around the corner, waving for me to come ahead. Half a soldier lies on the ground. His eyes are open and looking around in a panic. From the waist down there is nothing left of him, just ropes of red gut and intestine where his hips should be. McCaan shouts for a medic and other soldiers appear, looking about dazed and uncomprehending. I figure it out quick enough, though. It seems to dawn on Elijah at the same time.

'Trench raid,' Elijah says. 'Those were Hun running by us.'

I nod in understanding. 'They might still be around,' I answer in Cree. 'We should look.'

McCaan barks out and details are formed. A search goes on until dawn. The Germans are long gone, appearing then disappearing like phantoms. One soldier complains after stand-to that his helmet and rifle are missing. Another claims all his rations are gone. The soldier blown in half is carried away by the medics and his guts and blood covered by a few shovelfuls of dirt.

There are rumours about that Gerald, a young one in our company, was found sleeping at his sentry position last night. Some say that he has been taken a few hundred yards behind the lines and shot already. I don't know if this is true. All I know is that no one has seen him in the last few hours. After breakfast we clean our rifles and uniforms as best we can and speculate out loud. When McCaan appears he is ashen faced. No one dares ask him anything.

Over the next days a quiet falls on the lines, although it seems that no one is sleeping well at night. Talk starts of retaliatory raids and the talk builds until it is a given that one of these nights, tonight maybe, the Canadians will raid the German side.

Elijah pals around with Corporal Thompson as much as he can. Thompson tells Elijah many helpful things, one of which is how to kill rats. It is simple but effective. Tie a little cheese or bread to the barrel of a rifle and the braver rats appear within minutes for their treat. Then, just a matter of squeezing the trigger. The *crack crack* of rifle fire is common during the day and the victim more often than not is a rat rather than a German. They are as bold as pet dogs but will run over your face while you sleep to get at your rations, even bite your nose or other exposed flesh if they are hungry enough. Elijah and I have taken to sleeping with our heads under our blankets.

We find that the rumours about young Gerald are true. He was court-martialled a week after the raid and taken behind the lines. Six soldiers were ordered to go with him, a dummy round put in only one rifle so nobody is quite sure if he is the one who did the actual killing. Rumour is that they were all poor shots and Gerald did not die immediately. The officer had to stumble through the mud and take out his revolver and shoot him in the head as if Gerald were no more than a mule. According to someone who talked to someone in the firing squad, Gerald cried and begged the whole walk to the place where he was to be executed. He tried to run and screamed so much that they had to gag him and tie him up. He was shot in the rain, crying like a child.

When our time in the front trench is done, we are sent back to the support trench. I soon learn that the biggest worry here is not enemy rifle fire but shells that occasionally scream in and explode close by. Harassing fire, Thompson calls it. Our days are spent filling sandbags and repairing sections of trench, working up and down the communication trenches that lead to the front line, fortifying them. The work would be monotonous if not for the constant worry of a German shell taking us by surprise.

Rumours are more rampant than truth, I discover. Now that the spring fighting along and around Saint-Eloi has died down, the men talk of being shipped to another place where a great summer battle is building. The other talk is of the Hun's newest weapon, shells filled with poison gas that fall like a plague from the heavens. There must be some truth in it. We are all issued strange-looking hoods with goggles for eyeholes and a tube that sticks out for breathing.

We are told that if the scream of 'Gas!' ever reaches our

ears, we are to place these hoods immediately over our heads and tuck them into our tunics. McCaan makes us practise this, Lieutenant Breech nearby and watching with a smirk on his face. The hoods are hot, and difficult to breathe in. I feel like I might smother in mine, but Breech demands that we keep them over our heads for hours, that we go about our work wearing the hoods so that we may become used to them. The chemical that coats them and neutralizes the gas gives me bad headaches. They are ill-fitting as well, slipping about so that I can't see through the eyeholes. I can hear my own breath echo in my ears, and feel like I am suffocating. It's easy to hate Bastard Breech even more on these days.

Finally we are sent back to reserve where we can rest without too much worry or work. My first round in the line seems to have faded to a distant memory already. Corporal Thompson says that the last few weeks since he's met me and the others are the quietest that he can remember in a year. Only seven casualties in the company, four to shrapnel wounds and three killed, including the private blown up by the trench raider's potato masher. I wonder if young Gerald is counted among the casualties, but I keep the question to myself.

Back of the lines we fill up on hot food and clean ourselves as best we can. We keep occupied by playing soccer in a fallow field near the farmhouse where we've been billeted. I don't like the game. It's pointless and tiring. Instead I spend my time watching. Grey Eyes, the one who is a liar, he is a prisoner of the medicine they call morphine. I've seen him take it with a needle, and the way he goes slack and calm after. The idea of it scares me. So much easier, too, to find medicine here than I ever imagined. The medics carry plenty and are not always careful keeping an eye on their kits. Many men even carry it in their packs in case they are wounded and there is no help close by.

Elijah is fascinated by Grey Eyes' use of it. He even goes so far as to watch Grey Eyes when he is in that other place. I tell Elijah to let Grey Eyes get caught by an officer and taken away. He's a bad one and his actions will lead us all into trouble. But Elijah says no. This is all like a game to him. Elijah can out-talk even the officers with his nun's English and his quick thinking. The others in our section are drawn to him and his endless stories. I am forced by my poor English to sit back and watch it all happen, to see how he wins them over, while I become more invisible. A brown ghost.

When it is time to go back to the front trenches, the men are sombre once more. Instead of heading back to where we first were, we march a couple of miles south, and those in the know mutter that we are marching directly to Saint-Eloi craters, the ugliest place on the earth. Corporal Thompson explains to us that seven huge craters and countless smaller ones dot this area. On any given night they might be in different hands. We come up to the craters through what once was the town of Saint-Eloi, now just laneways of rubble and burnt timbers. We file along the communication trenches when night falls, going still when flares go up as we near the front lines. Only a few shells whistle by on their way to somewhere else.

Elijah and I are given sentry duty that first night, and are amazed at the condition of these trenches. They aren't really trenches at all but shallow ditches where even Thompson must keep bent at the waist. All attempts at drainage have failed, and water up to our knees soaks through our boots, making them too heavy. It would be better and more comfortable to wear the moccasins that I made for Elijah and myself, but I don't want to ruin them. As we pass by the troops we listen to the low mutters of discomfort. There is nowhere dry to sit and sleep, never mind lie down.

When dawn finally comes, little more than a greying of the black, I get my first glimpse of the craters. It's like the tundra I'd once travelled to, but devastated and pocked, so empty of any vegetation that it's impossible to imagine anything once grew here. The area in front of me is pitted with craters of different sizes, some too small for a man to take cover in, others so large they might be small valleys. This is the place where each side took turns tunnelling underneath the other and placing huge amounts of explosives, then setting their fuses just before offensives.

One night, late, Thompson appears in front of Elijah and me and says, 'Let's go.'

He leads us to where Sean Patrick sleeps and wakes him up. 'Let's go,' he repeats. I watch Sean Patrick climb tired like a tall, thin child from his blanket.

We make our way to Thompson's house, as he calls it, and there he tells us to take off anything that might make unnecessary noise. McCaan and Graves have joined us there too. I wonder why Graves is coming along. He is old, probably too old for this war. He has been in a war already in a place called Africa. Maybe that is why Thompson and McCaan have included him.

Thompson pulls out a chunk of charcoal and blacks his face and arms and hands and any other exposed skin. He doesn't say anything, just expects us to watch and to learn, and I think to myself that Thompson is very much an Indian this way. He hands the charcoal to me and I do the same, then hand it to Sean Patrick. When his face is blacked, the whites of Sean Patrick's eyes glint in the night and it makes me think he is afraid. Sean Patrick's hand shakes a little when he passes the charcoal to Elijah. Thompson hands each of us a black woollen cap and shows us where he straps his knife to his chest for quick grasping. Like all of us, he has ground off the wicked and sharp teeth along the blade's spine that are meant to do maximum damage in the thrust and removal. The Germans would kill the Canadians on the spot if they were to capture us and find those teeth on our knives. The Canadians do not blame them. We would do the same.

It is only then that I notice how closely McCaan watches us. I nod to him and he smiles, his swollen eye that was hurt from the periscope still evident even in the darkness.

We have all heard about the party that was sent out last night that did not return.

Thompson and McCaan have revolvers strapped around their waists. Graves is in charge of a Lewis gun, and Elijah and I are told to carry the extra drums of ammunition for him. Elijah, Sean Patrick and I carry our Ross rifles and as many extra rounds as we can. McCaan hands everyone a small sack of Mills bombs, the ones that remind me of heavy pinecones. 'Useful in close quarters,' he says.

'We'll travel in teams of two,' McCaan goes on. 'Keep in mind where the others are. Observation balloons spotted Fritz in some of the big craters the last few days.' He rubs at the charcoal on his forehead. 'Frankly, we don't know which ones are ours and which are theirs at this point. Our job tonight is to get some idea of what's going on.'

Elijah nudges me and says in Cree, 'We're going over the top. We're going Fritz-hunting in the craters.'

'Take care of any business now,' McCaan says. 'We go over the top in five minutes.'

Above the trenches the world feels opened up again. Elijah and I are teamed, following Thompson and Graves. McCaan and Sean Patrick take the rear. Although activity in the area has been quiet, Fritz continues to keep this part of the line reinforced. They battled too hard to lose any ground. Tonight our group is responsible for scouting out one of the bigger craters.

They call what we do crater hopping, moving from crater to crater, peering over the sides first before slithering into them like snakes. The bottoms of each are filled with water. Some of the holes are almost full.

Thompson makes the sign that the next one is the object-ive. Elijah and I spread out to his left, McCaan and Sean Patrick to the right. At the same time we all peer over the side to see what's below. This crater is the biggest I've seen, twenty or thirty feet of deep wall before the water starts. Something down below moves along the water's edge. As a flare goes up, I see three figures. There is enough eerie green light that I make out the cut of their Canadian uniforms. Elijah slides in before the others and is down beside the three men before they even know he's there. I make it down to him. Two soldiers lie still and one is awake but weak-headed. Elijah takes a canteen lying beside him to give the soldier some water, but it's empty.

McCaan slides in beside us. 'Next time, you wait for my direction, Private Whiskeyjack.' He pulls his canteen from his belt, unscrews it and pours a little water into the soldier's mouth. 'We've got to get this one back,' he says.

The others join us at the crater bottom. I can tell that Elijah

76

is about to ask what we should do about the two unconscious soldiers, when we see at the same time that their faces are hardened with death.

'Whiskeyjack, Bird, Graves, crawl to the lip and keep watch,' McCaan says. 'I'm going to help the private here in carrying this one back to our line.' He points to Sean Patrick. 'We're still close enough that it won't take long. When I come back we'll get an idea of who's in what crater.'

We have no choice but to nod.

'Let's go,' McCaan says.

All of us pick up the wounded soldier and help to carry him to the lip, where McCaan and Sean Patrick take him under the arms and begin dragging him into the darkness. Elijah, Graves and I lie with our weapons pointing at the black, and I am wondering what I should do next when the familiar whistle comes to my ears, faster than I can react to. An explosion close and to my right lights up no man's land for a moment, and when the brightness from it dies, flashes of light remain behind my eyelids.

I slip down for protection as another shell crashes in. From its sound I know that it is not big, not something terrible like a seventy-seven. I realize with a bit of satisfaction that I'm beginning to recognize enemy artillery.

But Fritz has spotted us out here. The bombing intensifies until we are forced down to the bottom of the crater. I lie curled in a ball, my face buried in mud and arms covering my head, my legs in the water, wondering if a mortar is going to land in the bottom of this hole and kill us all in one shot.

'They've got us just about pinned,' Thompson says in a brief moment of quiet. 'Got to get out of here.' He scrambles up the side and we follow. It is not until we are at the top that

I realize I've left the machine-gun ammunition down below. Too late for that now.

We dash for another smaller crater and roll into it, wait a moment, and then make a dash for another one that we hope will be deeper. The whiz-bangs come in then, going off with pops, their splinters chasing me like great angry insects. This crater is deeper, but the bottom too is filled with water. The stench is horrible. Another explosion lights the darkness. Arms stick up from the pool of water, some with fingers curled like they are grasping something I cannot see. A few bare feet stick straight out of the water as well. I wonder what has become of the boots.

The sky flickers as if full of lightning, and when I look I see that the water is more a stew. Besides the limbs, rotted faces peek over at us. I see the eye sockets are empty and their lips have pulled back from their open mouths so that they look like they're screaming.

'Xavier, see those faces there,' Elijah says to me in Cree, pointing with his rifle barrel. 'They look alive.'

He is right. When shellfire flickers, the water shivers with explosions and the faces come alive. I feel like I'm going to be sick. The stink is worse than animal rot. I look away at the others. Graves, too, seems like he is about to become ill, but Thompson's face remains passive as he listens carefully for the bombardment to recede. It doesn't.

I slip into a strange half-sleep lying there below the earth's surface with the dead. I know that I'm safe here, know that my time to join them is not going to be today. When I open my eyes again, the sky is noticeably lighter, and I realize just before Thompson mutters it that we won't be getting back to our side until after another nightfall.

'The good news, as you can tell, gentlemen,' he says, 'is that the bombardment is done, but there will be enough light behind Fritz in the next short while that we'll stand out like silhouettes if we try to get back to our side.' He points his rifle at the terrible mess below us. 'I vote that we find more agreeable accommodations before it's too late, and hole up for the day.'

One by one, we slip out. I'm surprised that Thompson leads us closer to the Germans rather than toward our own side. I trust Thompson, though. He must have his reasons. We crater hop, but none of the holes offer enough shelter.

In one hole the four of us lie still beside one another. I can feel the morning chill up my back. I realize I've been clenching my teeth so that they ache. I have lost my sense of direction, but then realize that the lightening sky to the east is obviously where Fritz is. I'm exhausted.

What appears to be a tall parapet is clearly visible ahead of us. I'm not sure if it is Fritz's front line or one of the great craters that Thompson talked about. The landscape is stranger than anything I've ever seen. Pocked and pitted, little valleys of mud filled with water and corpses. Thompson goes first toward the parapet, Graves follows with his machine gun, then goes Elijah, with me pulling up the rear. This had better be the place that we will stay today. With the sun on the verge of rising, we will be spotted and killed.

We make our way up the ten feet of mud that is the side of this pit and carefully peer down. It seems deserted. Some water fills the bottom, but plenty of places look very good for hiding. We crawl down into it, rifles ready in the event that we surprise any Hun. Scouting around the perimeter, we can see it is abandoned for now. Lengths of tin roofing and chicken wire lie scattered about. Thompson says it must have served as a listening post for Fritz at one point. Apparently, Canadian artillery found its mark.

He points to a trench that runs east from the crater. 'That one there goes straight to Germany,' he says. 'We'll have to post a man fifty or sixty feet in to keep an eye out for any visiting Fritz.'

We group around a stretch of old canvas and count out our arms and ammunition. Ten Mills bombs, two rifles and plenty of rounds, Thompson's revolver, and Graves's machine gun with only a couple of drums of bullets. I wish now that I'd turned back last night and retrieved what I'd left behind. 'Two rest, two keep watch,' Thompson says. 'Fritz doesn't know we're here, but the bad news is that neither does our side, so try to find a place that gives a little cover from shellfire.'

We decide that Graves and I will rest first while Thompson goes down the trench as a sentry and Elijah keeps watch in the crater. I pull some chicken wire over a cut in the crater that will make for a comfortable nest. I cover the chicken wire with a few boards and a layer of mud. Slipping into it with my rifle, the exhaustion washes over me. I know I'm invisible here and the tension slowly recedes from my jaw. Sleep comes fast and deep.

My eyes open to sunlight cut by diamonds of shadow. For a moment I'm not sure where or who I am. I just am.

The brightness of late morning shines through the chicken wire and across my face. I wiggle myself a little so that my head is free of my nest and I stare up at the blue sky. Not a cloud, only the blue of morning. Small birds dart across the crater chasing one another. One swoops in and lands close to my head. It doesn't know I'm there and begins to primp itself, just a few feet away from me, its feathers shining in the sunlight. It is a type I've not seen before. The eyes are black as night. I blow on it and, startled, it hops, then flits away. For a while nothing moves. Pure silence. It's not something I'm accustomed to any more.

I inch out of my nest in such a way that my movement won't be noticed. I peer about, rifle at my side and ready. Graves is curled up close by, sleeping lightly. Elijah sits at the other end of the crater, rifle across his lap. Every few seconds he scans the parapet above him. I wave to him. He smiles and waves back. I make my way to him.

I feel good but a little groggy. Sitting side by side, we pass a canteen of water. 'Get some sleep,' I say. 'You look tired. Crawl into the place where I slept. It's comfortable.' Elijah doesn't put up a struggle, just gets up and walks to the nest and goes in.

I find a cut in the crater that gives some cover and sit there with my rifle on my lap, listening. Big guns have started up in the distance but they are miles away. It's as if the war has moved to another place. It has sucked the life from Saint-Eloi and left it like this, has moved on in search of more bodies to try and fill its impossible hunger.

I figure it's safe enough to light a cigarette. No one will notice it in the sunlight. I started smoking to fit in. Now I like it. Sometimes I send up prayers on the smoke.

I take a cigarette out of my kit. The flare of the match makes me want something more, but I don't know what it is. Maybe I'm reminded of the danger of the night, see the shell-fire in the match's light. I don't know. All I know is that I've got a little time alone. I pull the smoke down into me. It tastes like bitter spring greens on my tongue. Reaching into the inner pocket of my tunic, I undo the moosehide bag in which I keep the tobacco that protects me. It is the bag Auntie gave me before I left. I put the bag back in. It feels warm against my skin, like it is filled with blood.

I hear the scuffle of feet and train my rifle on the trench that runs out of the crater. Thompson appears, looking tired. He sits beside me and lights up a smoke too.

'It's as if Fritz has headed back to the Rhine,' he says. 'I went down that trench a good hundred feet but no sign of anything. I came back half that way and sat all morning long. You wouldn't think there's a war going on.'

I must listen carefully to understand him.

An aeroplane drones above us, silhouetted by the sun and hard for me to identify. 'Looks to be one of ours,' Thompson says. 'You can see by the outline of the wings. Observation plane. Stay still. If it spots us it might take us for one of them and call a bombardment in on us.'

I listen, basking in the warmth.

'Did you send Elijah off for some rest?' Thompson asks. I nod. 'You're a quiet one,' Thompson says. 'I'd have said that's an Indian trait, till I met Elijah.'

We laugh.

'Why's his English so good?' he asks after a time.

'Him, he stayed in residential school a long time,' I say. 'Him, he had no parents, so the nuns kept him.'

Thompson leans back and stares up at the sky. 'Your English is getting better,' he says. I smile. 'I watch the way you two walk about,' Thompson says. 'I figure I know true hunters when I meet them.'

Another plane drones somewhere we can't see.

'A cup of coffee and something to eat sure would be nice

82

right now,' Thompson says. 'I'm going to rest awhile and dream about it. You take the trench, but don't let your curiosity get you and go down too far. Fifty or sixty feet is plenty. If Fritz does decide to come along, you can get back here and warn us.'

We both get up and Thompson rouses Graves. I head down the trench. Nothing's in it but the mud walls. I find a place to sit where I can get a view down the laneway but can't be seen. I don't mind sitting here, waiting for the darkness that is still many hours away. My head floats up above this cut in the earth and into the blue swatch of sky above me. I listen to the rhythm of bombing in the distance.

The afternoon is waning when I make my way back to the crater. The sun has begun its slide down behind the Canadian lines. Graves sits by the side of the crater, his machine gun pointed at the trench I emerge from. Graves nods to me as I walk out. We wake Elijah and Thompson.

When it is dark enough, Thompson gathers us and we make our way out of the crater. As I crawl out, I see an old German helmet. It is the rarer kind, made of leather and cloth with a spike on top. Elijah grabs it. He straps the helmet to his pack.

Instead of leading us back to our own trenches, Thompson has us wait by the lip of the crater. He hands each of us two Mills bombs. 'I've got a feeling they'll be coming this way soon enough to look around,' he says. 'If you hear them scrounging about below, pull the pins and throw these in. Then we'll make our way back quick.'

When twenty or thirty minutes pass and I begin to think that Thompson is mad, I make out the sound of men sneaking about below. I can hear them whispering, can hear the step of boots all around where I'd slept this morning. Thompson gives the nod and we set and throw the bombs in at the same time. They explode in a series of concussions. Men scream. Thompson takes Graves's machine gun and crouches at the lip, sprays into the crater until all of the rounds are spent. I'm amazed at the little man's actions. He kills with such ease.

'Let's go, boys,' Thompson says.

We move from crater to crater, the ground a little more familiar now, and finally drop into the safety of our own lines.

I replay it over and over in my head so that I don't sleep all night, pulling the pin on my Mills bomb, throwing it and watching it arc until it disappears into the crater, the concussion and screams. I have killed someone now.

The next morning after stand-to, Thompson approaches Elijah and me. He talks to both of us, but his words are for Elijah. 'What do you think of the last days, Whiskeyjack?' he asks, lighting a cigarette, exhaling and looking at the sky.

I can see that Elijah knows exactly what Thompson's asking. Thompson is asking if Elijah likes killing. Elijah considers it for a moment. 'It's in my blood,' he finally says.

Thompson smiles, then walks off. He didn't ask me the same question. Does he sense something? How am I different? A strange sensation, one I do not recognize, surges up my spine.

KISKINOHANAASOWIN
Learning

A COUGHING FIT makes me open my eyes. This stretch of river is still new growth. I'm amazed that Elijah and I survived the fire only to end up in the trenches. All along the bank the bush struggles back to what it once was. I wish I were so resilient. The cough doesn't leave me, and each one feels like another rib breaking. I lean over the gunwale for a handful of water and the pain of my rotting guts causes me to gasp out.

'Are you all right, Nephew?' Auntie asks. 'Should we stop and let you rest?'

Her words make me angry. I don't know why. *'Mona,'* I spit into the water. 'Leave me alone.' Immediately I feel remorse. I look at my empty pant leg, the material of it pinned up, and think once again, for a moment, that I can feel the foot and calf that aren't there any more. The medicine is loosening its hold on me. I want more, but so little is left.

'Do you want to know something, Auntie,' I say, cupping my hand and taking a small sip from the river. 'So many dead men lay buried over there that if the bush grows back the trees will hold skulls in their branches.' I laugh, and it makes me feel worse. 'I saw it already. We once left a place covered in our dead. When we came back a few months later flowers redder than blood grew everywhere. They covered the ground. They even grew out of rotting corpses.' Knives of pain stab me low in the gut. My arm screams out high in the place where a bullet entered it. My head throbs with the cut of sunlight. She doesn't respond, but I know she listens. 'Those flowers grew back, but that was all.' I hurt so bad. 'Useless things.'

'Sleep, Xavier,' she says. I want to tell her I'm sorry for this anger, but I close my eyes instead.

Thompson and Graves and Elijah and I have returned from the big crater. I can't sleep for wondering if I've killed someone now. We all threw Mills bombs into that pit and heard the screams. We are all equally guilty.

The rain begins the night of our return. It falls for five days and makes me wonder if *manitous* are unhappy with me. The Germans shell this section of line more heavily than normal and the Canadians, we are miserable, cold and wet and muddy and scared we are going to die soon. Some say Fritz is doing it to avenge the crater raid.

Soon we will be sent back for a few days, and this is the only thing that keeps me going.

Elijah is happy, though. He marches around the trench, up and down in the rain, wearing that helmet he took from the crater. The rotted thing looks silly sitting on his head, and this must be partly why he does it.

To make it all worse, Elijah's taken to talking in an English accent in the last days. This makes the other soldiers laugh, but I wonder why he really does it. It's like he wants to become something that he's not. He tells jokes and makes the others laugh and brags that he has now killed men, all of them close enough that he could hear them die. But is it the truth? I do not think so. I was there and know Elijah was scared too, and know that when we all threw the bombs into the crater there was no telling how many men died down there. But what is

86

the truth in a place such as this? It might as well be Elijah's version. After all, he makes the others happy, he keeps their spirits up, and that is worth nearly as much as good food and a warm, dry bed.

He is already a hero to them. I can see that. Me, I can feel the eyes of the section on me. They try to figure out what makes me different from them, different from Elijah. I know I am a better shot than Elijah, that it was me who taught him the ways of the bush. But they are drawn to Elijah and his easy smile. Me, I won't give in to this army's ways so easy. I learn their English but pretend I don't. When an officer speaks to me I look at him and answer in Cree.

Lieutenant Breech—Bastard Breech—he doesn't like me speaking my language at all. He has disliked me from the moment he saw me. Elijah is partly to blame. I remember the morning not long after we'd joined up. Elijah and I had travelled for days together on a train from the north. We had been sent to a huge place of stone and glass called Toronto, were kept in an area called the Exhibition Grounds by the big lake. Every day, I was up before the others, before the bugle call, taking care of the horses. I couldn't get used to sleeping in a cot surrounded by all these strange men in the great echoing stall. I wanted to sleep outside and asked Elijah to ask Lieutenant Breech. My English was no good. But Elijah taught me the words instead, told me I had to begin fending for myself in their tongue. We had finished lunch and men were sitting around smoking. Breech sat laughing with some others. He seemed in a good mood.

Breech broke into a big grin when he finally understood what I was asking. His smile made me feel good. 'So the Indian wants to sleep under the stars,' Breech said, loud enough that everyone around stopped what they were doing to listen. 'If you don't mind,' Breech said to me, 'would you please repeat the question so that the others may hear?' His smile wasn't so nice any more.

'May I be so bold as to request different sleeping quarters?' I stuttered. 'Perhaps outside away from the atrocious snoring of my fellow soldiers?' It had taken me all day the day before to learn it. Even though I had practised, it did not come out like I'd wanted it to.

'Is there any other way we might accommodate you?' Breech asked. 'A separate and private mess hall? A maid perhaps?' I wasn't sure what Breech was saying at the time, and had to ask Elijah later.

Breech's smile disappeared and his face turned red. 'This is not a day camp!' he screamed. 'There will be no special treatment! Where I prepare you to go there is only misery, fear and death.' I looked over to Elijah then. He was covering up a laugh with his hand. 'I have a mind to put you up on charges, Private,' he yelled into my face. 'I can't even think of what those charges might be other than buffoonery. Get out of my sight.' Breech then sent me to clean the horse stalls, not knowing I enjoyed it, did it every day already. My relationship with Breech never really improved after that.

Corporal Thompson says that the Hun are reinforcing their lines somewhere else and that their manpower is low around here right now. He tells McCaan that he wants to go over with Elijah and me again. He admires our calm in the face of battle. 'Nothing against Graves, Sergeant,' he says. 'He acted as a soldier should. But your two Indians are blessed. They've got the charm about them. And I'd like a little of that charm myself right now.'

I like Thompson but don't know if I deserve all this that he wants to give me.

At nighttime when I am not on sentry duty I lie in my little hole in the side of the earth and fondle the medicine bundle around my neck. It still has the faint scent of the fire's smoke when I put it to my nose. Sometimes I'm tempted to open it, but have decided not to any more, for fear of losing something important, something of you, Niska.

I dream of home. The sleeping's no good here, but I've taught myself to dream with my eyes open. Where I live the river is as wide as a lake and now at this time of year, spring, is when the fishing is best. It is also the time when we all come together from our winter camps to socialize and to live easy a short while. We build goose blinds on the bay and set our decoys. We pluck and smoke birds over a fire late into the night and fill our stomachs as often as we please. It would be interesting to take Gilberto and Grey Eyes and Sean Patrick and Graves there. I wonder what they would think of such a place. All the bush and water and not very many people like all of these other places I've been now. The children would be amazed by Gilberto's hairy body and strange accent. The girls would surely think Sean Patrick was handsome. Graves would impress the elders with his stories of fighting wars for most of his life. Grey Eyes would probably steal things.

Grey Eyes tried to talk Elijah into going to the medicine world with him last night. They'd come from up top where they were in charge of repairing a stretch of wire and there were still many hours until dawn and stand-to. They squeezed into my hole and Grey Eyes asked me to keep an eye out for officers, then he went through his ritual with the needle. He turned to Elijah while he slipped the point into his arm and asked Elijah to try it as well. He smiled at Elijah like a lover. Elijah turned away from him with disgust, but I could see something in the flash of light as Grey Eyes lit a cigarette and lay back. Elijah's eyes told me all I needed to know.

When Grey Eyes takes a lot of it, he lies still like he is dead until I worry he has joined them. Then he groans a little and breathes deeply like he is sleeping, and I guess that is actually what he is doing, sleeping with the dead for a short while. I wonder what Grey Eyes would do if the trench was overrun.

He doesn't always take enough that he goes unconscious. I have seen him glassy-eyed and calm, breathing deep and staring like he is concentrating. He speaks carefully then, worried, I think, that his words will be slurred. Me, I don't think he can hide this forever, though. If McCaan and the others know what Grey Eyes is doing, no one says anything. But I don't think anyone but Elijah and me know. We're the keeper of the secret for now.

Not many days pass before the pattern of the trenches is a part of me. Dawn and dusk all soldiers must stand-to, up on the duckboards, rifles loaded and cocked, prepared for a Hun offensive. After stand-to, we gather in our small groups, open our tins of bully beef, smoke cigarettes and clean our equipment. We try to stay dry in the rain by erecting pieces of canvas over us like little tents, but it's near impossible. We repair trenches blown apart in bombardments the night before and collect the dead for the stretcher-bearers to pick up when they can. Those who aren't collected we bury the best we're able in the trench sides when they begin to swell and stink. I make sure to thank them for helping to strengthen the trench line, tell them that even in death they are still helping.

In the afternoon, our section is allowed a sort of rifle practice. The snipers stand aside for us while we wait by the steel plate. Each of us takes his turn lining his rifle up and listens to what the spotter beside him says as he peers through the periscope. When a possible target is sighted we are told approximately where it is, and as soon as the shooter gives the call, the steel plate drops and he is given a very short, panicked second to fire his rifle before the plate swings up again. More often than not, there is not much of a target to try and hit in such a short time, but twice now for both Elijah and me the spotter has called out, 'Good shot, you hit their plate.' More often than not, too, a German hits the Canadian plate the moment it closes, and the loud *whomp* of the bullet crushing itself on the metal barrier rings in our ears. We constantly move our firing position so that the Hun don't get too used to where the firing comes from. We also try to keep many sniper spots operating randomly at the same time. Too much of a pattern and someone is dead.

Sean Patrick is proving himself a very good and natural shot. Sometimes the Hun like to play a game where they place an old helmet or a tin can on a stick and see if the Canadians can hit it. Right now, Sean Patrick has hit these targets more than anyone else. The fact makes Elijah irritable. Sean Patrick keeps both eyes open when he shoots and this allows him to find and aim at his target quickly. I was shown the same way of shooting as a boy. I talk to Sean Patrick about where he grew up, a place called Ahmic Harbour, and I tell him that *ahmic* means beaver in both Cree and Ojibwe. Even though he is a *wemistikoshiw,* he grew up with many Ojibwe who taught him how to hunt and shoot.

Gilberto doesn't like to do anything that takes chances.

Every day he says how he wants to get sent back where he can become a cook where it is safer and there is always enough to eat. He writes one letter every day, no matter how busy we are or how much it rains. He makes sure to give them to soldiers heading back for rest or to stretcher-bearers who will make sure they get posted. Elijah asks him who he writes to and Gilberto replies it is to his wife and young family left behind on his few acres in Southern Ontario. He writes in Italian and he has let me look at his letters and has even read a couple of them to me. His handwriting is large and childlike, like mine, although he knows how to put down far more words than I ever will. Gilberto keeps his hair very short but his moustache long and bushy.

After ten days on the line we are finally relieved. I feel good packing up my few possessions and stuffing them into my sack. We head out down the communication trench as shelling goes on nearby.

'They're sending us off in good fashion, eh?' McCaan says to no one in particular.

'You couldn't wish for a better stretch to lose your virginity, fellas,' Thompson says to our section as we squat and allow a fresh company to pass us on their way up, shells whistling by overhead. I'm not sure what he means. 'I've never seen a stretch with so few casualties,' he continues. I think of all the shells that have missed us so far and of all the sleepless nights and try to imagine how it can be worse than that. 'Oh, it will get far worse than we've seen, boys,' Thompson says as if to answer me. 'This is the calm before the storm.' A shell explodes fifty yards away and wet clumps of dirt rain down.

We make our way out of the last communication trench and for the first time in a very long time I can walk erect up on top of the earth again. It is a strange, good feeling. The moon threatens to come out from behind the cloud cover and we fall into step, dreaming of sleeping through a whole night on beds of straw and of eating hot food and of lying on our backs in the sunshine for a few days with nothing else to do but watch the aeroplanes twist and dive and fight. We head down the road pitted with shell-holes and weave around the craters like a line of ants, rifles slung over our shoulders, packs heavy with muddy clothing and mess kits, our skulls and uniforms crawling with lice that have become a part of us now.

We stop for a ten-minute rest along the side of the road. Up ahead a column of soldiers comes toward our own, uniforms clean and boots shining in the moonlight, their stride long and timed right, their faces open, eyes wide. They stare at our platoon from the corners of their eyes as they pass. We pretend not to notice them, our column leaning against rifles or sitting in the mud, cigarettes dangling from mouths and eyes squinted. We pretend that these new ones are not even there. But we know. They were our platoon weeks ago, years ago, lifetimes ago. I look at a few of the faces as they pass and wonder which ones won't come back this way again. Elijah sits beside me, whistling a song that he's heard the others whistling a lot lately too.

I look over to him and say in Cree, 'It will be good for a few days.'

He smiles. 'I'll miss the excitement. But yes, it will be good to relax.'

We stand and begin to walk again with feet dragging, back to somewhere behind Sanctuary Wood.

We're billeted in a barn once again, the roof full of holes

from some earlier fighting, but the rain has stopped for now, so nobody really cares.

Outside, their backs shining in the sun, a line of soldiers stands naked. They hold their clothes in their arms, and when they reach the front of the line they hand them to a man who throws them into a long steaming machine that is supposed to kill all the lice. The men stand around and chat and smoke cigarettes and scratch themselves, naked as the day they came into the world. Elijah and I laugh at the sight, something worth taking home with us and telling a story about when the elders ask us what we saw. I can see myself telling the story of being surrounded by naked *wemistikoshiw* with hairy bums standing around in the sunshine talking, their clothing in a machine that cleans it for them.

I will tell the elders the many strange things I've seen, the aeroplanes that fly high up in the sky and fire machine guns at one another, the bodies of the dead everywhere so that one gets used to the sight of them swelling in the rain, the spoken threat of little bombs that release poisonous gas that burns a man's throat and lungs so that he chokes to a painful death, the sneaking about like a fox at night, repairing wire and raiding the enemy craters, the shells that whistle from out of nowhere on a quiet morning and blow the arms and head and legs from the man you talked to the day before. But especially I will tell the elders how after a shell attack life returns to normal so fast, how one's mind does not allow him to dwell on the horror of violent death, for it will drive him mad if he lets it. That is why they can stand around naked talking to one another without a care as the Belgian farm girls giggle at them from a distance, how they can light up a cigarette with fingers still bloody from the soldier they have just finished burying, how they can cheer as a man in his aeroplane hurtles to his death after being riddled by machine-gun bullets. How they can accept without blinking the execution of one of their own for sleeping on watch. I keep my head attached to my body by doing the simple things that it knows to do.

The day is sunny and warm and the only reminder that we are in a war is the rumble of shells on the horizon like thunder threatening to bring rain. I watch the others play a game of soccer, and when they ask me to join I do, running after the ball, not understanding the rules but running like a child anyway, until my lungs burn and the sweat stings my eyes. We line up at the food wagon and fill our plates with runny stew. We soak the stale bread in it so that it can be swallowed. I want to taste goose right now. I know the people who have this farm keep some. I saw them.

Our days of rest pass too quickly. Elijah and I discuss capturing and plucking a goose for dinner but decide against it. It would be obvious that the Indians were the guilty ones.

It rains again the day we are ordered back in line to march the ten miles to the front.

Spring warms into early summer, and we put our time in on the front line by Saint-Eloi. We spend this time digging in and avoiding German shells as best we can, waiting to be relieved again so that we can get back to a safe place. Most nighttime activity has dropped off, and through May there is none. But something is in the air, and I cannot forget Thompson's words that far worse days are just over the horizon.

THOMPSON GETS PERMISSION to begin taking Elijah and me to learn the art of the sniper. A long natural slope rises up a hundred yards behind our own line that offers a view of the German-held craters. That is where we set up our position. Thompson calls this place the Ypres Salient. Here we stumble upon old dugouts in the waist-high grass. Good places in which to hide, I think, but they seem too far away now for a good shot until Thompson mounts a looking-glass on Elijah's rifle that you squint through with one eye. It brings the target up close. What was once just a bump on a field seven hundred yards away suddenly appears as a tree stump. Even better, they have somehow put a cross of thin hair on the glass so that you can put the point where the two lines meet right in the centre of your target. These *wemistikoshiw* amaze me sometimes.

We practise with the rifle and scope for hours every day, and Thompson teaches us how to sight it in by twisting the two knobs on the side. We practise at different distances, taking turns with Elijah's Ross until we are comfortable and accurate. Thompson explains that at this distance we must take into account all kinds of things, mostly wind speed and trajectory, which is how high to aim above a target at very far distances to hit it. He is an excellent teacher, patient and calm.

He teaches us the importance of blending into our surroundings, to lie still and only take a shot when it is a good one. He shows us that one man needs to spot with another scope that he holds in his hand while the other shoots, that at times of the day when the sun is high our guns and especially the glass of our scopes will glint, which will give away our position. We begin wrapping our rifles in rags. He points out that the puff of smoke from firing is enough to give us away when it is sunny, that the only way to avoid being detected on those types of days is to fire once and then immediately move on and build a new place to hide somewhere else. It is just like hunting, I think. It is hunting.

Thompson calls the little mounds of earth and cover that we construct in the middle of the night nests. He finds it very funny to be able to say, 'Bird, go to your nest.'

I am made for this, I think to myself.

Elijah and I spend long hours at nighttime building our nest, paying attention to every little detail, the colour of the earth, the surrounding stumps and pieces of twisted, rusted metal, routes to take if we are discovered that offer a little bit of cover. This is just like building goose blinds at home. If they are not well constructed, the geese will avoid the hunter. We lie for hours during the day, me spotting, Elijah with rifle ready, not flinching a muscle, breathing long and deep and very slow so that a rhythm comes to the both of us. A spell descends on us and makes us a part of the earth.

May turns into early June and a little heat comes. Talk of the Canadians joining up with the British south of here still rumbles about, but nothing comes of it. Elijah and I have made a nest that is covered so well it is not even visible from our own line of craters fifty yards in front of us. I went down and tried to spot it myself but could not, even though I'd built it. The nest is in a smashed pile of trees splintered and crushed by a shelling earlier in the winter. We've propped our rifle steady on a thick stump with a wide view of the Hun. I peer through my scope while Elijah rests his eyes. We both learned that it is easy to strain them after hours of staring and scanning.

We have been lying here for many hours now, unable to see much of anything in the grey early afternoon. We lie very still so that I wonder if my body can remember to move. I tell my foot to wiggle and it does. All is good. Even the lice have gone to sleep, I think. Sometimes, with them crawling from the seams of my clothes and onto my skin, it is near impossible to stay still for the itch.

During the night we became tired of being wet and so put a bit of canvas above us and covered it with wood in such a way that we didn't change the look of our nest too much. Fritz has spotters over there who pay very careful attention to any change in the surroundings. Such changes let them know that those like Elijah and me operate in the area.

Even with the canvas over us the drizzle manages to sink into everything and soak it. I must keep one hand cupped over my scope to keep the drops of rain off it and steady it with my other hand. The Hun line is staggered mounds of earth in the gloom, joined by trenches, a little more than four hundred yards away from us. The Germans are smart in the way they set up their lines at odd angles. They even drape their parapets with bright pieces of cloth so that there seems to be no order or reason. This makes the hump of their trenches look almost pretty, but also makes it difficult for us to spot irregularities that will give away soldiers' positions and the places of other sharpshooters in the line. The Canadian lines are kept exact and orderly like the British do it, and I imagine it must be easier for the Hun to notice when something is where it shouldn't be. I know this is why their snipers have such high numbers of kills, and I imagine if I know this then the officers above me must know this too, so why don't they change it?

My stomach grumbles with hunger and I want a cigarette and I need a break from staring and am about to nudge Elijah from his rest when I spot movement right behind a distant mound, just a flicker of something in my scope. I train my eye on it and wait with breath held. It might only be a large rat scurrying for all I know. And then I see him. The top of a soldier's head bobs above the cover of their secondary trench for a moment before disappearing again. I watch as shovelfuls of dirt appear over the side. He is working hard on fixing his section of trench and doesn't realize he's visible to anyone. I nudge Elijah and he opens his eyes calmly.

'There,' I say in Cree.

Elijah looks through his scope, his rifle aimed in the direction of where I point. I peer back through my scope and we both can tell that the soldier is standing on duckboard. He's taken a break and his head is a target now as he wipes sweat from his forehead with a handkerchief. He has no idea that he can be seen, and as I look at his face, young and pimply and scowling from the work, I begin to whisper to Elijah that he's got a good shot if he wants it, when the sudden concussion of his rifle makes my body jump involuntarily and the familiar whine in my left ear so close to his rifle begins immediately. The young soldier's face is a red smearing explosion that exits the back of his head in a spray before he crumples from sight.

Elijah smoothly ejects the old shell casing that flies out with a clink of metal on metal, then he loads in a new round. The image of the soldier's head exploding makes my stomach churn. I retch a little and spit up bile from my empty stomach, my throat burning and the acrid smell of my own insides making me retch a bit more. I look over to Elijah.

Elijah stares through his scope still, smiling to himself. 'I got him, didn't I?' he whispers.

'You did,' I answer.

KIPWAHAKAN
Captive

I KNOW THAT Xavier wants to talk to me. He goes so far as to let words come out of his mouth when he sleeps. He says very little when he's awake. I'm not able to make out more than the odd sentence when he is sleeping, though, and sometimes when he dreams he speaks aloud in English. I can't help but smile a bit when he does. As a child he was so proud that more than once he claimed he would never speak the *wemistikoshiw* tongue. And now he does even in his sleep. He cannot speak to me yet, and so I decide, here on the river, that I will speak to him. In this way maybe his tongue will loosen some. Maybe some of the poison that courses through him might be released in this way. Words are all I have left now. I've lived alone so long that I realize I'm starved to talk. And so, as I paddle him gently with the river, I talk to him, tell him about my life.

After the death of my father, your grandfather, Xavier, our people were directionless. Flakes of snow in swirling wind. Some went back to Moose Factory and never really left it again, became homeguard Indians where they learned to stomach the *wemistikoshiw* food and ways. You could tell you were approaching Moose Factory on the river by the stink of sewage and refuse piled up onshore. And they all wondered where the diseases came from.

A number of us chose to risk starvation and to go into the bush instead, roving bands who went back to the old ways as little families, retreating into the muskeg a century, hunting with bows and vine snares when there were no more bullets to be had. My mother showed me the magic deep in the bush that is as real, as alive as the flashing glow of the *Wawahtew,* the North Lights. She spent the next years teaching me some of it.

Their killing my father was a hard and bitter seed lodged in the pit of my stomach that bloomed over the years into a dark flower of anger. My mother recognized what grew in me. In her own way she tried to teach me not to use it in negative ways, for to do that was to enter a spiral near impossible to escape. I listened to her, but on those nights when I was shaking with the cold and my stomach ached dully with hunger, the black flames of that heat were comforting. I pictured pursuing those police with my skinning knife, tracking down each one and gutting him like I would gut a skunk, spitting my hate into his gaping belly.

The Hudson's Bay Company had instilled in the Cree a greed for furs that nearly wiped out the animals, and because of this the time finally came when even the most experienced of the bush men and women were faced with the decision to move to the reserve or die of hunger.

I remember the first day walking into Moose Factory, the bowel-loosening fear and confusion of a prisoner being led into the prison for the first time. There were eight of us. My mother and Rabbit and me, and an old man and his family who were friends to my parents. The old man had broken his leg a number of years before and had never had it set properly so that he dragged it behind him uselessly. His wife helped him, along with their three grandchildren, the children younger than my fifteen winters. It was mid-winter and cold, the sky an aching blue. Our dogs pulled

101

our sled and our few possessions and even they were twitching and afraid surrounded by all the strange smells. We were a ragtag and defeated enemy, and the fat proctor was smug in announcing our surrender.

'So ye all come for handouts now, do ye?' He spoke to all of those gathered in the Company store, white and Indian. 'Do ye bring furs to trade me, or are ye like the rest of them devils that expect to live on credit?' My uncle sent his grandson to retrieve the few marten and beaver pelts we'd managed to snare that winter. The proctor shook his head when he saw their condition. He gave us a little food and we scattered around the reserve to different relatives who had room for us.

I watched as the other children around me went off to the residential school across the river. One day Rabbit asked our mother that she be allowed to go and join her friends. My mother gave in to Rabbit's wish. Your mother, Xavier, only wanted a better life than the one we could offer her.

The nuns gave the children funny haircuts, the girls' bobbed to above their shoulders so that their faces looked round like apples, the boys' cut very close to their heads so that their ears stuck out. Even though the walk was not far, the parents were not allowed to visit the children. My mother told me this was so that the nuns could work their spells without interruption. When the children came back, they were different, speaking in the *wemistikoshiw* tongue, talking back to their parents, fighting and hitting one another, crying in the middle of the night for reasons they could not explain. I wondered what happened to them over in that place and was thankful that I was not sent there.

Then one day I was. Word had filtered through to the Company men that there was an Indian girl wandering Moose

Factory who was not yet old enough to marry but who was as uncivilized as an animal. A priest arrived at our cabin on a day when the first signs of spring were showing. A greasiness was in the snow, the breeze did not hold warmth but hinted at it. He came with a soldier from the fort in the case that the odd-sounding Cree that came from his bearded mouth was not good enough. My mother stumbled a little when he told her I was to come with him to learn about God. 'She is all I have,' my mother said to the priest in English. It surprised me to hear that she could speak it at all.

'It is for the greater good of God that she come with me,' the priest answered. 'She will be clothed and fed and kept warm.' Nothing my mother could say would change what was about to happen, and she knew it as well as I did. And so I did the only thing I could do. I ran. But the soldier surprised me with his quickness, catching up to me not a hundred yards from our cabin, throwing me to the ground roughly, trying to hold my arms. I fought like a lynx then, scratching at his eyes with my fingernails, biting him through his thick coat so that he screamed in shock and pain. I punched and kicked until I had nothing left, until the soldier dragged me away from my mother.

The building was large and white, bigger than the Company store, bigger than any structure I'd seen. They had us sleep in long rooms, on rows of cots, and because I was older and knew very little of their language, the nuns paid very close attention to me. They kept me away from my sister. They didn't want me changing what they had taught Rabbit, who they now called Anne.

The nuns would wake me in the middle of the night and drag me to a brightly lit room where I was made to repeat words over and over until I pronounced them correctly. When I was caught speaking my tongue, they'd force lye soap into my mouth and not give me anything else to eat for days. I watched as the younger children were beaten with switches and forced to eat food from the floor like dogs, but something in my eyes must have warned the nuns not to do the same to me. Every waking moment I planned my escape, sneaking bits of food into my scratchy dress pocket when no one was looking, noting the places where the warmer clothing and tools were kept that would serve me in the bush.

The one in charge, Sister Agnes, took an immediate dislike to me in those first few weeks. She personally cut my hair, making it shorter than the rest of the girls'. It took all that I had not to strike out at her to prevent her from doing it, but I knew to choose my battles carefully. They were going to remove the black hair that reached to my waist as a symbol of *wemistikoshiw* authority, of our defeat. She sat me in a chair, other nuns hovering in expectation of a fight, but I sat and smiled serenely as she tugged at my hair, pulling it hard to get a reaction from me that wouldn't come. When she was done and my scalp ached, I refused to look in the mirror that they shoved in front of me. I did not want to give them the reaction of shock and sadness that they so wanted. I'd already planned my answer to their actions.

Deep that night when even the most vigilant nuns were sleeping, I crept down to the basement to the room where they sheared us like sheep and found the clippers used for the boys. I cut the rest of my hair from my head so that all that was left was a stubbly field.

I lay awake in my bed all the rest of that night, rubbing my hand over my scalp in anticipation of the approaching dawn. In the morning the nuns walked up and down our rows, pulling our covers from us and shouting at us to get up. When that moment finally came and I was left exposed, the room went silent, and child and adult alike stared at me. One of the nuns whispered *devil,* and knowing better but not being able to help it, I smiled at this word.

They dragged me from my bed then and pulled me down to the basement, locking me in a room with one window high above me. That was when I thought of my father and his last days. I wouldn't let the same cloud cover me.

After a week of talking to no one and of being given a single bowl of porridge to eat each day, I began to have strange visions. Sister Agnes had told me that I would not come out again until my hair grew back. My hunger, combined with the thought of being in this little room with the single high window, caused the shaking to come to me, something that hadn't happened since my father died. It felt like a warm current running up my back and filling my head until I grew dizzy. Then my jaw tightened and the tremors ran through my legs and lower torso, building in intensity until my whole body quaked and I fell to the ground. My vision turned red and that was the last of my consciousness. There was no more room around me for this world then, only glimpses of the other place and of what it took me a long time to realize was the future.

I saw the bush once more, summertime or maybe autumn, with the sun high. A beaver dam that had not been abandoned, a new lodge of freshly woven branches. I sat in a canoe with a young man paddling ahead of me. I did not recognize him. His hair had been short like mine but was already growing out. On a bend in the river, a large moose, a bull, stood on the shore. The same excitement that always comes with spotting one, especially one so large, swelled in me. But we did not take it. We drifted silently by with the current.

Sitting alone in the room, I realized that I was not going to be able to escape it. The window was too high, and the door that locked me in was solid. My hair had grown to a soft down, and still I did not regret my actions. I waited and dreamed and plotted.

One night I awoke to a soft scratching at the window. I looked up and saw a shadow hovering by it. Before the panic even had a chance to grip me, the window crackled with a tinkling of glass. I crouched behind the bed and watched as the rest of the window was smashed out. With a flourish of long hair, my mother stuck her head in, and in the language I had not heard in weeks she told me to throw her my bedsheet. I stood and did as she told me, all the sleep quickly gone. She twisted the sheet and threw one end down and told me to grab it. She then hoisted me up and pulled me through the window, where I smelled the first fresh air in a long time. Spring had come while I sat in that room.

'Ashtum,' she said. 'They have probably heard us. We must go now.'

I wondered where we were going, but that soon became apparent when she led me to our two dogs, both tied to travois with all of our possessions bundled on top. 'Did you see Rabbit?' my mother asked. 'Will she come with us?'

'She is called Anne now,' I said, and watched the under-standing cross my mother's face.

We led the dogs out of Moose Factory at that part of night when it was darkest, and I did not look again upon that place for another two years. My mother and I walked out of there and back into the time of our ancestors, living on what the land would give and slowly becoming wild like the animals around us.

KAKWAPASKINAATOWIN
Competition

LATE IN JUNE our battalion is moved near a place called White Horse Cellars where the remnants of the town run between the two lines. The mud is less of a problem as we have been stationed almost on top of the Ypres Road that leads into here. No man's land is strewn with rubble and the carcasses of rotting farm animals. It is ground rich for hunting Fritz, Elijah says.

I like the name of this place. When I sleep a little, the dreams are good, of the big white horses running free across open green fields, of cool dry cellars filled with food.

More and more Elijah and I are given permission to go out on our own, me spotting and Elijah shooting, because we come back with kills. There is plenty to hide in around here, old brick piles, blasted wagons, the fallen walls of houses. This part of the line is confusing and temporary. In some stretches, the Hun line is only one hundred yards away. The area has claimed many lives on both sides.

Thompson has been out and watches us work. He says he is amazed by how long we can lie still despite the lice and without falling asleep, how we can spot movement that he is not able to see. Elijah explains to him that it is hunting, and hunting is what we have done all our lives. I do not correct Elijah. There is no point in telling Thompson that I am the only one of the two of us really from the bush, the only one who

107

has truly hunted for a lifetime. I have no reason to say it.

Over the early summer that Thompson calls the quiet season and the calm before the killing, Elijah's numbers grow. Three, five, ten. I have become very good at spotting movement, at seeing the men in the jumble of brick and mud. My job is to find the unfortunate ones who for just a moment forget the danger. But it is Elijah's job to dispatch them.

I am learning to come to terms with what he does. And that I am his accomplice.

Now when Elijah and I come back in to the trenches after a day or two out, the others look at us differently. We are becoming the talk of the battalion, Thompson says. We're also beginning to draw attention from the German big guns. When we hunt in one area for more than a couple of days, the shells begin to pour in. This in turn makes us unwanted by our own, and so we spend longer and longer periods of time out of the trenches and sniping from our different nests. The really good nests we keep as long as we can, moving between them as randomly as possible. I like it better out here away from the trenches anyway. There's no boredom, no officers to answer to, no stand-to.

One night when Elijah and I slip back into our line for a hot meal and a little rest, I overhear Sean Patrick and Grey Eyes talking about us. I hear my nickname mentioned, then Elijah's, and realize that they don't know I'm right beside them. I'm becoming a ghost.

'What do they do out there?' Sean Patrick asks.

'They sneak around and kill Fritz,' Grey Eyes answers.

'Don't they see?' Sean Patrick says. 'The more they shoot, the more shelling we get in our sector? I'd rather they do their dirty work somewhere else.' The two of them are silent for a time.

'It's Elijah that's the killer,' Grey Eyes says suddenly. 'X just spots for him. Elijah told me how X threw up the first time he saw Elijah get a kill.'

'How many do they have now?'

'Elijah's got dozens, I imagine, if you include the crater raid they did a couple of months ago.'

I leave without a sound so that they do not know I have been there, my ears hot.

A HORRIBLE OFFENSIVE BURNS like a giant fire south of us. The continuous rumble of the big sixty-pounders hammering the Germans doesn't let off, beats for days like the biggest drums, the earth below me shivering, shuddering even though the bombing is many miles away.

Elijah and I lie in our nest at night or volunteer to sit in listening posts in no man's land. 'Those are our guns,' Elijah whispers to me tonight. His eyes reflect the little light and he has the smile of the mysterious on his lips. Lately, I notice he sleeps less and talks all the time about hunting. He says he can see things over the horizon. Glimpses. We sit in a listening post, a small crater twenty yards out from our own line. We spend this night listening for what Fritz is up to, but all we hear is a German soldier moaning and mumbling, wounded badly but still alive and in the middle of no man's land.

'Sergeant McCaan says a big attack's coming,' I whisper, 'and that the British are preparing a big offensive.' The night's at its quietest, with the sun only an hour away but still buried somewhere deep below. The wounded soldier continues to moan and mumble. He is talking some sort of secret language now, I think, speaking with the spirit who will take him on the three-day road.

'Fritz is dug in too well in France,' Elijah says. 'Tommy will fail.' The wounded soldier suddenly laughs, as if to agree with what Elijah says. Maybe they see the same thing.

Elijah has killed more men already than I can count on both hands. It doesn't seem to bother him. Me, I've killed no one that I could see yet, but I've helped Elijah. I don't think it bothers me, but I won't let myself think of it, just push it away whenever it appears.

Elijah smiles and stares out into the black. The guns in the south cause the sky there to glow and pulse. They are the North Lights, in the wrong place, reminding me of home. The line across from us is still. The only noise over the booming in the distance is the muttering and cries of the wounded soldier.

'I'll be back,' Elijah whispers to me and crawls out of our listening post quick and silent. I know it's useless to try and stop him. I also see that Elijah has left his rifle behind.

Staying still, I listen and try to fight off the anger that comes to me when Elijah does these stupid things. It isn't fair. I'm left here like a worried wife, wondering if Elijah's going to make it back this time or if he will be spotted and shot. I hear the wounded soldier suddenly cry out what sounds like 'Nine, nine, nine ...' and then in a lower voice, he begins to speak as if carrying on a conversation with someone. Finally, he stops talking. I sit and listen for a long time, the emptiness of the night striking me now that the wounded voice is silent.

When the sun begins to threaten and I am sick with the worry that Elijah will not get back in time or at all and I will be forced to squat in this hole all day until night comes again and I can make it back to the line, Elijah slithers into the crater and leans back on it, breathing shallow and a little hard.

'Where were you?' I ask in Cree, trying not to sound upset, the tone slipping out anyway.

'I helped that soldier find his way to the spirit world,' Elijah whispers.

'We must get back before the sun comes up,' I say.

'I was good to him,' Elijah continues, staring up into the sky. 'He'd suffered enough and I didn't want him to leave violently, so I covered his mouth and nose with my own hand and whispered good things to him till he went.'

'Enough,' I say sharper than I want to, and crawl out of the crater and toward our line.

THE OTHERS IN THE BATTALION have begun to treat Elijah like he is something more than them. I walk beside him or behind him along the trenches between stretches out hunting, and very few seem to notice me at all. When we are given our daily rum ration, Elijah likes nothing better than to sit and talk about his latest exploits to anyone who will listen. And there are many. How soon they seem to forget who is the better shot. None of them know that I am the one who taught Elijah what he knows about hunting. My English isn't good enough to correct what I see happening, but even if it was I would only sound like a bitter old woman to them. After all, I have not pulled the trigger on a man yet. That is Elijah's job.

When I am able, I find a place away from their talking and slip into a light sleep that creeps across me like smoke. I drift back to the training place we were sent to after our time in Toronto, in the cool of autumn, back to where we first learned exhaustion. This memory, this pretty little stone, I examine it with my eyes closed tight. Turn it over in my fingers.

Our days of training in these farm fields in Ontario are all the same, the company sleeping lightly and in shifts, working at digging trenches and then filling them back in again, learning about sap lines, fire-steps, parapets, parados, stand-to morning and evening, learning a little of what we will do once we get to France.

Some officers have arrived from over the sea to train the men. The men around me whisper that these officers have seen a lot of action. They have a certain look about them, a certain hollow stare. One of them is older, British. The other two are Canadians. One of the Canadians is missing his left arm to the shoulder. The British one always looks like he's crying. The other Canadian, him, he looks like he's fine to me. Those three sit long hours at night by a fire and talk with Lieutenant Breech and sometimes Sergeant McCaan.

Nighttime is when we learn how to string barbed wire without tearing our hands, how to lie still when flares pop up over us so that we melt into the ground. Nighttime is when we learn to patrol quietly and sneak up on one another. This is what Elijah and I like best, and what we are best at.

McCaan has taken notice of how good we are at this and it makes me feel a little important. During these games at night the men are sent out into the darkness of forest or meadow and told to find the other group that has been sent out or are simply told to make it back to the camp first. The others can't keep up with Elijah and me, though. In the darkness I feel that Elijah and I are owls or wolves. We have done many night hunts over the years. McCaan reports our talent to Lieutenant Breech. Elijah tells me Breech says that it is our Indian blood, that our blood is closer to that of an animal than that of a man.

While the men are out on night training I know that the visiting officers sit by the fire and talk with Breech. They talk about France, about places with strange names. Popperinghe. Flanders. Festubert. Loos. They talk of the Hun using a gas that when breathed turns the lungs to fiery liquid so that a man drowns in the flames of his own insides. The crying officer was at the place where this gas was first used on the Canadians. He saved himself by pissing into a handkerchief and breathing through that with his face buried in the mud. But the gas got his eyes a little bit anyways.

One or two places over in France will decide the war next summer, these officers say as they sit by the fire. And it's the soldiers here around them that will help decide it. I find out all of this through Elijah. Elijah comes back late at night to the tent where we sleep, shaking me awake and whispering to me in Cree all the things that he has overheard them say as he lay in the dark spying on them. Elijah sneaks up and stays silent in the shadows for hours while they talk, mimics their voices, their postures, their stares. He cannot wait to get over there. He tells me he's afraid the war will end before we arrive.

Elijah, he has a talent, him. He has become as good as me at sneaking, and maybe has more patience. Elijah's like a shadow when he wants to be, lying flat and breathing silent so that he becomes the ground. I know that I am a good hider, a good worker, a good shot. We will both be very good over there. But Elijah, all he wants is that place. This war will make him into something.

One night Elijah and I lie in our tent and talk. The quiet evening with nothing to do is rare. Autumn has come to stay. The air is sharper. The trees glow in the sunlight as part of them dies.

Talk's started up of the battalion moving again, maybe this

time to the ships that will take us overseas to the war. Elijah tells me this in our language as we sit in the tent near the warmth of the wood stove.

'Just a matter of time before this came,' Elijah says. I sit up to hear better. 'Before they separated us.'

'What is this?' I ask. 'Who says?'

'It is the talk.'

'That's shit,' I say, then ask, 'Will they separate the two of us?'

Elijah stays silent for a while. 'Most probably. You must prepare yourself for that, for being on your own, Xavier. Your English is getting better, and that is good, but the army cares nothing for friendships.'

For the first time since arriving in this place the panic begins to come back to me. 'Surely they'll keep the two of us together if we ask,' I say.

'They don't give a damn about us, Xavier.' We sit without talking for a while. 'It might be better that they separate us,' Elijah says in the dark. 'It will teach you a little about in-dependence. It will give you a chance to make a name for yourself, to grow a little.'

The words anger me. I wonder why Elijah says all of this.

The next day, two full battalions stand at attention in the great field where the men shoot their rifles. The 48th Highlanders stand across from us, the Southern Ontario Rifles. We all stand tall as we can, the Rifles especially, taller now than we were a few months ago. I can see slight looks of disgust on the faces of the Highlanders facing me. Not one of those men across from me thinks in the slightest that the 48th will lose. They are professionals who have seen many battles. Our battalion is a bunch of farmers and labourers with a couple of bush Indians thrown in. Me, I want to change those looks on their faces.

The British officer sent here to train us, the one with the weeping eyes, marches out into the middle of the field and another officer shouts for the men to come to attention. There is a flurry of movement as they do, and then the British officer clears his throat, preparing to speak. I have to listen carefully to understand as the officer holds his rifle out in front of him and begins shouting.

'The soldier's Ross is the soldier's best friend,' he says. 'If you care for her working parts what you will hear is the bolt pushed smartly and the clickety-click and one up the spout and there you 'ave 'er, one dead Boche!'

He pauses and stares out at the men on either side of him. His face is red from the effort of shouting and his eyes cry salt water. I wonder if he is mad. I hear a snort beside me and carefully look over to Elijah, who has begun to giggle and seems to have trouble controlling it. The officer begins shouting again.

'You men must really cultivate the 'abit of treating this weapon with the very greatest care, and there should be a healthy rivalry among you growing!' He shakes with the effort of his shouting. It is a strange sight to see the tears rolling down his cheeks and wetting his collar. He pauses and his eyes wander up and down the lines of troops until I am not sure if he is finished his little speech or not. Just when I think the officer must be done, he begins to shout again. 'It should be a matter of very proper pride. Marry it, man! Marry it! Cherish your rifle for she's your very own!' He looks a little confused now, like he has forgotten what else to say, and that is when Elijah erupts into laughter, great gasping laughter so that

115

everyone around him turns at the same time and stares in horror wondering what Sergeant McCaan and Lieutenant Breech will do.

I look to McCaan ahead of me and he has turned toward Elijah now, a look of pure red anger on his face just as a cheer goes up from the 48th across from us. The Rifles join in the cheer. It's the first time the 48th save Elijah, and I don't think it will be the last.

When the cheering dies, the best shooters from each company are asked to step forward. McCaan could not choose between Elijah and me so he tells both of us to step up, and this makes me unsure. I can feel a heaviness in my stomach as so many eyes fall on me and the others in the group of marksmen. We stand at attention with rifles at our sides, facing down the field to where green balloons bob on strings fifty yards away. They look small from where I stand, easy to miss as they shift and bounce in the cool wind.

The crying officer shouts out the rules. We are to shoot in groups of ten, and will be eliminated immediately on the first miss. I see that Elijah has been placed in the first group. I have been placed in the last. The wind picks up as the first group takes their position. The balloons jump around like they have a life of their own and know what's to come. The shooters hold rifles loosely at the ready. When the officer shouts, they raise them and sight in, then fire. After the noise, only Elijah's and one other's balloons have disappeared. A cheer goes up from the 48th. The other is their man, small with sand-coloured hair.

The second, third and fourth groups do better. Most make their shot as the wind dies down. As I line up with my group the wind kicks up again. We are ordered to the ready, then to fire, and I raise my rifle, imagining the balloon is a goose float-ing on wind currents. The wind whips the balloon and I hesi-tate so as to sight in better. I squeeze the trigger and my balloon disappears. When I lower my rifle I see that mine is the only one gone. My company cheers. The officer warns me not to hesitate again or I will be disqualified.

Less than half of the original group is left and once again we are divided, this time into four. Elijah and I are put in the same group. We smile to one another. It's like the old days when we'd shoot against each other till we ran out of bullets. The British officer orders us all back many yards so that the balloons look the size of coins from where we stand except for their moving in the wind. The first group falls into line, and when the order is given they try and draw a bead on the balloons. With the roar of the guns, only one disappears. The little marksman from the 48th smiles broadly as his battalion hurrahs.

My group is second and my luck is good. The wind slows just enough as we are commanded to fire, and Elijah and I hit our balloons. Our ones, the Rifles, answer the cheer. I smile and settle back on my haunches to watch the rest of the shoot-ers. Two men from each of the two groups are able to hit their balloons in the calmer wind. Only seven are left after two rounds.

I watch carefully as soldiers prepare the next competition. Seven bully beef tins are set along a ridge of earth 150 yards downfield. The seven of us soldiers circle around the officer and pull straws from his closed fist. Once again the little sandy-haired soldier from the 48th goes first. The officer barks out for him to start and pushes the button on a stop-watch. The soldier drops down from attention, unslinging his

117

rifle from his back smoothly, and as he lands on his stomach the breech is already open and a round slammed in by the time he is lining his sights up on the first tin. He is fast and smooth. The rifle fires, followed by the distant metal rip of the bullet tearing apart the tin, followed by the slide and click of his bolt opening. I watch his hand reach for another round, followed by another slide and click as he pushes the bolt closed and *crack,* another tin is torn apart. When he is done he has hit all seven in a very short time, and not just his own battalion but everyone cheers.

The next four shooters are not nearly as good as the first, two of them hitting four tins, two of them five. But when my name is called, I talk to myself, tell myself to go to that place. I stand at attention and go through my movements in my head. When the officer barks out to begin, I fall to the ground, my knee striking a stone sharply. Wincing, I open the action of my rifle and grab a round from the ground beside me, slipping it in and slamming the bolt shut, both eyes open and staring down the field, searching out the first bully beef tin. Breathe in, breathe out, breathe in, half out, and the sights line on the first tin, the sharp *bang* and kick of the rifle and the tin ripping apart. I work steady, sliding open the breech and letting the spent cartridge fly out before I replace it with the cool casing of a second shell. I do the same thing over and over, in my own quiet place now, ears ringing with the noise of the rifle. By the fifth tin I know my time is good, but I fumble and drop a round because I have let myself think instead of just doing. I force myself to slow down. Seven hits will guarantee my advance. I drop the last three tins and stand to the cheers of the battalions, muffled by the ringing in my ears.

Elijah is the last to shoot, and he is very good. There's no pressure for him, I see. I think Elijah is like a wind across a field he is so smooth and sure. When all seven of the shiny little tins are punched through, Elijah stands and waves to the cheering crowd. He has always been the one who is not afraid of others. But there was a time when he knew nothing of the bush or of hunting. I was the one to teach him.

The officer huddles with some of the others. I hear talk of more balloons, of more bully beef tins, of paper targets. Carefully so that it won't be noticed, I take a sidelong glance at the little Highlander. He is short and thin with bright eyes that don't miss much. He leans with one hand on the barrel of his rifle, the butt of it firmly on the ground. With his free hand he plays with a piece of string, tying it into sure knots with his fingers. I see the power in his confidence and look away. I look toward my battalion and make out Sean Patrick and Gilberto and Fat in the crowd. Sean Patrick gives me a wave. I smile at them all.

The sound of Elijah clearing his voice causes me to turn to him. Elijah has approached the officers and begins speaking. There's trouble in that. Everyone knows.

'Sirs,' he begins. 'Place matches in the ground twenty paces from us and the man who can light the match with a bullet wins.'

Breech turns to him angrily but is prevented from acting by the British officer's voice. 'What's this?' he asks.

'It's simple,' Elijah says. 'You place matches in the ground and each man takes a turn. Whoever can light the match by touching the tip with a bullet wins.'

It is a game Elijah and I played when we were young. A game impossible to win. The officer rubs his chin and nods, smiling. I watch word ripple through the troops who are sitting or standing at ease. Immediately men begin to talk and reach in pockets for money. I look over to Elijah and he smiles at me. It is the same trickster grin he's flashed since he was a boy. I am the only one who knows, though, that Elijah has not always gotten by in the world so easily. As the officers continue to debate and the soldiers near us continue to exchange money, I think back to the winter shortly after Elijah left the residential school and came to live with me in the bush.

We snared rabbits and used their fur and ate their meat and their stomachs full of greens. I showed Elijah how to find their runs, taught him that rabbits, like people, are creatures of habit. One morning as we checked our snares we noticed that a fox followed our lines. The fox had eaten a rabbit that had been snared. Its tracks were fresh, and so we followed them. I could tell by the impression that it was a large one.

I walked along its trail, Elijah following noisily, snapping twigs and breathing heavily. 'That school taught you nothing useful,' I whispered back to him. Elijah didn't like that, but I knew the fox was close. We climbed a rise, and through some thick tamarack I caught a flash of red. The fox sensed us too, and stopped. I removed my mitten and raised my rifle, levelled my sight on its centre. An easy shot.

'What do you see?' Elijah asked, and as soon as his voice left his mouth, the fox darted away.

I didn't speak to Elijah the rest of that day. When we returned to our winter camp he went out in the bush, dragging back dried spruce branches. I thought he was trying to make up for his mistake by collecting enough wood to guarantee us a night of warmth. As he spread dry branches around our *askihkan,* I wanted to ask him why, but I was still too angry to talk to him. The fox's fur would have looked nice, felt even better, as a collar for my parka.

Late that night the cold woke me, and as I built back the fire I noticed that Elijah wasn't in the *askihkan*. I was still not happy with him and so fell back asleep. Near dawn the sharp snap of a twig outside woke me. I crawled from my blanket and peered outside. As my eyes focused in the early light, I saw the tracks going round and round our sleeping place. They were unmistakable. Elijah's prints. He rounded the *askihkan* carefully, stepping one foot at a time, watching intently where his foot would go, trying not to disturb the twigs he'd sprinkled. He noticed me and smiled, looking exhausted. 'I have been walking around you all night and didn't wake you until now,' he said. 'I will try not to make any more mistakes, Xavier.'

When matches are placed in the ground, Elijah and the Highlander and I line up beside one another. Twenty paces away the matches stick up from the ground. The tips are tiny, almost impossible to see clearly. Elijah shoots first, and his match disappears. Men whoop but then go quiet when they realize that he hasn't done it. I shoot second, but can feel the eyes of so many on me. I can't find that place, jerking the trigger so that my bullet thuds uselessly into the earth a half-foot in front of the match. The Highlander takes his time, and when he fires he too makes his match disappear completely.

On Elijah's second turn, his bullet goes just over the top of the match tip. I can see that it was very close by where the bullet pierces the ground behind it. I lift my rifle and take my turn. I am steadier this time and actually hit the match so that it too disappears. I'm beginning to think that, even as adults, we will find this impossible. The Highlander fires and he misses, grumbling.

The officer announces that the third shot will be the final one. There will be no winner today if the match remains unlit. Elijah takes a long time sighting, makes a show of it for the spectators, gently squeezes the trigger, and misses. The Rifles groan loudly. I breathe in, breathe out, breathe in and lift my rifle to my shoulder. If I can do this I will no longer be so much the outsider. I will gain respect. I let half my breath out and place the very tip of the sight on what must be the tip of the match. The world has grown silent. My body feels as steady as it ever has. I squeeze the trigger and as if by some magic the match flares and then lights, the flame wavering in the wind. The men roar. I feel a little dizzy and lower the rifle.

My head is light and today has turned into a good day for me. The Highlander raises his rifle and aims a long time. I hold my breath. The rifle fires and the match quivers, then falls over. Men shout once again and rush on the field. I am surrounded by arms reaching out to me and men talking into my face. The ones in my section, Gilberto and Graves and Grey Eyes and Sean Patrick and Elijah, grab me and lift me above their heads. I look down at the sea of men around me and notice the officers pointing to me and talking.

McCaan approaches, beaming, and shouts up to me. 'From now on you will no longer be called Xavier. You have a new name now. Your new name is simply X, and when men ask you why, you tell them, X marks the spot on any target you wish to hit!' The others laugh and cheer, shout out to me, 'X marks his spot!'

It strikes me then. None of these who are here today can call me a useless bush Indian ever again. They might not say it out loud, but they know now that I have something special.

ONAHAASHIWEW
Sniper

THE SHORELINE THAT WE PASS is still new growth, green and wild, nothing grown taller than a man. I watch it for some time after I awake, listening to the gentle dip of Niska's paddle. In places blackened tree stumps jut up like burnt fingers. They look like the dead trees of Ypres, make me wonder if the battlefields have begun to grow over yet with red flowers.

'Maybe Elijah is still over there, Auntie. Maybe the army has kept him there longer,' I say out loud, not meaning to. I turn to her and she smiles down at me, passes me a cup of water that she's dipped into the river to cool my scratched throat.

'Maybe,' she answers. I watch her lips. 'When is the last time you saw him, Xavier?' she asks. She is not used to asking questions. I can tell she is afraid to voice this one.

I look at the shore. 'Near here is the place where the fire caught up to us,' I tell her, pointing to the bank. 'We had made camp and fallen asleep with the wind blowing the fire away from us. But sometime in the night the wind shifted and the fire snuck up.' I lay my head back on my pack, too tired to speak more. I want to be able to tell Niska this story but cannot find the energy inside me that I need to do it.

Sean Patrick's at his sniping post, Grey Eyes working the steel plate, swinging it up when Sean Patrick calls for it, shutting it as soon as the shot is fired. I noticed them earlier in the day and am surprised to see them still shooting in the afternoon. I want to warn them not to use the same position too long or they'll give it away, but figure they know as much. I don't want to offend them. I also see that Grey Eyes has the glassy look of the medicine in his veins and he is not paying close enough attention, but McCaan has given me a shovel and told me to fill sandbags.

'Don't want you snipers thinking you're above all this,' he says.

I notice Elijah isn't given a shovel.

An aeroplane drones overhead and I look up from my work to see if it is one of ours, or Fritz come to strafe us. I bend back down to fill sandbags when I hear Gilberto shouting for help. When I look over, I see ten yards from me Sean Patrick on the ground writhing like a snake and grabbing his neck, blood spurting out in impossible amounts, his eyes wide with terror of what is coming. I run to him. We all run to him, McCaan and Elijah, Graves and Fat who've become closer and closer over the last months like a skinny father and his heavy son. We stand over Sean Patrick dumbly, none of us really knowing what to do, in shock at the sight of bright red blood pumping from between his fingers clenched so hard that he appears to be choking himself, McCaan kneeling and fumbling to help.

'Shot through the neck,' Graves mumbles as if to no one.

Immediately I think of the snipers rumoured to be around here, of one especially, the one they say stalks our lines and has impossible numbers. Elijah claims that the man doesn't really exist.

McCaan pulls gauze from a pack near him and tries to

move Sean Patrick's hands. 'Help me,' he shouts, and the tone in his voice sets us all into action.

Elijah and I pry Sean Patrick's hands away and hold them above his head while Graves and a stunned-looking Grey Eyes clamp onto his long skinny legs. McCaan applies the gauze to his neck, but we all know it is futile. I stare into Sean Patrick's eyes near to my own. He stares back at me in pure fear. I smile to try and reassure him that soon he will be on the long road and he won't be scared or in pain or cold or wet any more. I can see the fear die a little at the same time that the bright light drains from his eyes. They turn glassy as those of Grey Eyes. McCaan quits working. I let go of Sean Patrick's arms and watch the muscles relax into the slow release of the dead.

Grey Eyes stands back from us. 'I told him to take a break,' he mumbles to no one. 'I told him that he's too tall to be sniping here.'

Sean Patrick's height has nothing to do with what has happened.

That evening McCaan gives me and Elijah and a couple of others permission to carry Sean Patrick back behind the lines near one of our nests for burial. We dig silent and steady, the body beside us wrapped tightly in his blanket. When the hole is deep enough, we put him into it. I prefer the old way of placing the body high in a tree so that the soul can leave it without hindrance, but no trees stand for miles around here. I say my own prayers to *Gitchi Manitou,* and Graves and Fat touch their fingers to forehead and chest and shoulders. It surprises me that Elijah whispers his own prayers in Cree as well. We burn a little sprig of sweetgrass that I've carried with the leftover moosehide in my pack from Canada and whisper more prayers to drift up with it. We cover Sean Patrick's body with shovelfuls of dirt and then sit, watching the flash of the big guns and feeling the rumble beneath as the real darkness begins to settle in.

'Hun sniper,' Elijah says. I nod to him. 'He's a good shot,' Elijah continues. 'To be able to hit a man through the neck with such a short window of opportunity.'

I want to tell Elijah that Grey Eyes is at least partially to blame for operating the slot so slowly, but then I realize that I am to blame too for not saying anything to them when I noticed the mistakes they were making.

Sean Patrick is not the only one to be killed by their snipers. All up and down the line the Germans are taking a toll. Although the shells kill far more, the snipers eat away at morale like a fast disease. Thompson says that Fritz are using this area as a training ground. McCaan orders Thompson, Elijah and me to do whatever we can to impede them, to get a little revenge for Sean Patrick.

For the next days we stay out of the trenches as much as possible, finding places to hide and scout for snipers. I am glad not to be in the trenches. McCaan is angry that Sean Patrick died so needlessly, and keeps a closer eye on Grey Eyes. He is not as good as he thinks he is at hiding what he puts into himself. I must remember what he has done to Sean Patrick next time Grey Eyes asks for something.

ELIJAH GOES INTO ANOTHER PLACE when he is hunting. He forgets his British accent and his bragging, is patient. And he becomes more watchful. He moves with no wasted movement, like a wolf on some smaller animal's trail.

Sometimes late at night when we are in a listening post or in one of our nests, Elijah will comment on what Fritz is doing in his own line, on what his actions will be in the next few days. It is as if Elijah is lifted from his body and carried to the other side where he can float around at will. His eyes stare as if he can see very far. Some elders talk of this experience, but more often a man takes the form of an animal when he leaves his body—a bird or a fox or even a bear. Sometimes I wonder if Elijah is taking Grey Eyes' medicine, but I know that he isn't. He wouldn't be able to hide it from me. This *wemistikoshiw* medicine, sometimes I am tempted to try it, late at night, lying out here and listening. Plenty of it around. Many of the soldiers carry it in tablet form in their packs. They put it under their tongue if they are wounded. Some even carry a needle full with them at all times, the same type of needle that the medics carry. Most are deathly afraid of pain, of prolonged suffering, even more than they are scared of death.

I begin to adopt Elijah's ways. I try to think like the Hun, particularly the very good one who killed Sean Patrick. The sniper has been operating in this area for a while now. Many shots through the neck. His numbers continue to grow. Proof that it is the same man is that he uses a rare type of round in his rifle, one that does not flatten and expand on impact like most of the cheap rounds but is hard and copper and cuts through nearly anything like a tiny, deadly knife.

We spend more and more days out in our different positions, watching for hints of the others who are no doubt in turn looking for us. Elijah and Thompson and I go into our own line only once in a while for small supplies of food and water. Lieutenant Breech lets us come and go as we need to, on the promise that we deliver results. The summer remains quiet on this part of the line, hot like I have rarely known heat.

I am always thirsty. We hear the constant rumble of the big battle going on down the line. It is not going well for Tommy. Graves keeps us informed when we come in. There's a new urgency to find the snipers operating across from us. Word is out that very soon the Second Division, my company included, will be sent down to take part in that fight.

'We bombed 'em straight for days on end,' Graves says. 'Literally tons of shells we dropped on 'em thinking we were going to soften 'em to mush before the assault.' Graves talks more now that he has a listener in Fat. 'We figured it would be a Sunday stroll across no man's land after the bruising we gave 'em. But little did we know they've got some very deep trenches to hide in. Soon as we stopped the bombing and the whistle blows for us to go over the top, here comes Fritz crawling from their deep holes and setting up their machine guns. From what I heard, a man couldn't advance for all the dead Tommies lying like cordwood on the field in front of him.'

McCaan tells Graves to pipe down and stop stirring trouble.

'If we'd had those same machine guns in the Boer War,' Graves continues, muttering now, 'I tell you it'd have been a different outcome.'

Here where the Ypres Road bisects the front line, where the piles of brick and wood and debris add to the chaos, nothing stands out and everything stands out, it seems. I peer through my riflescope for hours at a time. I've taken to spotting through my rifle now in the chance that I, too, might get a shot. I want to see if I can do what Elijah does. But all I am able to spot are rare glimpses of a helmet or shovel. Easier for me to picture soldiers with antlers on their heads, I tell Elijah.

It will make it all the easier when the time comes to shoot one. Elijah laughs at this. Even though I make light, I spend my hours wondering what I will do when it is my turn to pull a trigger on a man.

'Antlers,' Elijah says. 'Do you remember the time you had antlers?'

I wonder for a moment what he is talking about, force myself back to Mushkegowuk, a place I try not to think about for fear it will make me homesick. 'When we were caribou hunting?' I ask. He nods. I smile. 'We were young then, weren't we,' I say.

We were only sixteen winters, had wandered as far from Auntie as we ever had before, far up the coast, near where the *Ayashkimew,* the raw flesh eaters, lived. I'd promised Auntie we'd return with enough caribou meat to feed a village. Now it was deep winter and we'd still found none. But tracks were everywhere, and so we pushed on.

On a bright morning that was so cold we were forced to keep moving, we crossed onto a plain surrounded by black spruce. At the far edge of the plain, we spotted a herd. We were downwind of them, but I knew if they sensed us and ran, we could never catch them. Elijah wanted to shoot at them, but I knew the distance was still too far.

'I have a better idea,' I said, remembering what you'd once told me, Auntie. 'Conceal yourself here,' I told Elijah.

We sat and watched the herd from a place that was a natural funnel if I could force them this way. I dug through the snow until I reached dry, yellow grass and collected as much as I could. Using my knife, I struck my flint above the grass I'd collected until part of it glowed red embers and sent a thin trail of smoke into the frozen air. I picked up the smoking grass, breathing on it every little while to keep it alive.

'They will soon come,' I whispered. 'Wait until they are close before you begin shooting.'

I crept along the way we'd just been, the smoking grass in my hand, and cut into the tree line. Careful as I could, I made my way along the edge of it back toward the herd. Wherever the trees opened up onto the plain, I stopped and placed some of the grass into the crook of a tree, blowing onto it until it smoked. I continued in this way for a long time until I made my way behind the herd. You'd told me, Auntie, that caribou were afraid of the smell of smoke and would move away from it.

When I'd reached the far side of the herd, I found a thicker branch and picked it up. Holding it above my head, I bent at the waist and walked out of the tree line, crouched and swaying, directly toward the nervous herd, bending the branch in a curve so that it looked like antlers. The animals swung their heads and looked at me, not sure what they saw. I continued walking toward them, cutting off their escape route to the north and east. The animals let me get so close that their musk tickled my nose.

And then they ran. I straightened and ran after them, watched as they approached the places I'd left the burning grass before they veered away and toward the spot where Elijah waited. I began to shout when I saw that they could not escape, my voice leaving my mouth in great puffs of air, the cold stinging my lungs. I whooped and ran, and didn't stop even when Elijah's gun began to bark out and the animals fell as they tried to pass him.

'We ran out of bullets that day,' I whisper to Elijah as we stare out at the Ypres Road. 'How many did we kill? A dozen?'

'Yes,' Elijah says. 'It was a good day. And the day of butchering that followed.'

FRITZ HAS A SIMILAR SNIPING SYSTEM to ours. He hides in his nest and moves frequently, uses the steel-plate method in his line too. Elijah and I now know the location of four plates. The one on the far left of their territory appears to be the most used. We doubt that the talented sniper is using any of those, though. The true snipers like to work alone or in pairs. They don't like to work in the trenches, but outside of them. They're more exposed then, but they are exposed to more targets too.

It's an obsession now for Elijah to take out a sniper behind one of the plates, a message to Sean Patrick's killer. While I scan for possible positions behind their lines, methodically Elijah searches for some pattern in how they are working the plates. So far the killer has been very careful, very random. He does not take any shots unless they will be sure. He doesn't give away his position. But Elijah and I also feel the pressure increase every day that we don't make a kill. Lieutenant Breech will call us back into the line with all the others where we will be forced to live like rats once again. Breech has already done this to Thompson, ordered him back in to train new virgins.

One afternoon when I think that Elijah is sleeping, he suddenly says calmly that he has figured out a pattern. I lie and listen, resting my eyes. 'I see it at sunrise,' Elijah says, as if talking to more people than just me. 'I hear a succession of shots on the mornings when there is no cloud and the sun rises over their line. Their chances are good of hitting a soldier's head at stand-to. They use the light to spot us and know that all we can see of them is covered in shadow.'

I think about this for a while. 'How will we be able to see their position to shoot at them, then?' I ask.

'We'll make sure to train our rifles on two plates in a little while, then leave it be till morning.'

'But how will we know the precise time to fire?' I ask.

'The last two days they have fired exactly when the sun comes up behind them. We will lie facing them, and soon as you see the first light that shines bright enough to blind you, we will both fire.' Elijah breathes in deep, then releases his breath. 'They have grown comfortable thinking that they cannot be seen at this time of morning. They know that we are at stand-to on our line and there are plenty of targets for them. They've taken to leaving the plates up long enough to take two shots. You will hear their first one, and then we will immediately answer it.'

We carefully train our rifles on two plates, the rifles anchored by sandbags so that they won't move accidentally. Elijah goes back into his head then, and for the next hours I lie and listen to the evening sounds.

The night is relatively calm and the air is clear. Stars litter the sky above me. I fall into a light and troubled sleep, then jerk awake when I dream I've accidentally nudged my rifle out of position.

When dawn approaches, we lie facing it, and I breathe my deep breaths in preparation. The sky above us is the black-blue of early morning, and clear. The sun lets me know it's coming by the slow brightening of the sky to purple. When the first ray shoots out and over me, I whisper, 'Be ready,' in Cree to Elijah. My hands loosely grip the rifle so as not to move it even a fraction.

Sighting through the scope is useless. It reveals nothing. Seconds later the sun breaks over the other line. The thin crack of a Hun rifle rings out and Elijah answers it before its echo has died in my ears. The sudden concussion makes me jump a little, even though I am ready for it, the familiar whine rising inside my head. I fire as well, but am worried I waited too long. 'Do you think you got yours?' I whisper to Elijah. He nods, and in the silence that falls back over us I know as surely as I know anything that Elijah has done it.

I wonder about myself, though.

NAATAMAASOWIN
Revenge

THE FREQUENCY OF GERMAN FIRE from behind their steel plates drops off almost completely in the next days, and this is proof enough to McCaan and Lieutenant Breech that Elijah and I are accomplishing what we need to. We come in for a little food and rest and the others ask if it is Sean Patrick's killer we have gotten. We shake our heads and explain that he does not work from the trenches but is somewhere behind, where he has a better view of the Canadians. Elijah warns everyone to keep their heads down.

'Remember, chaps,' he says, 'Xavier is sniping behind your line too now and might mistake one of you for bloody Fritz!' Everyone laughs and Elijah laughs and talks with them.

I do not laugh as loud.

Elijah's reputation is growing, I know, and Elijah's vanity being fed makes him content and happy. But the real job still lies ahead of us, and if Elijah can get the Hun whose reputation grows like a legend in this place, bigger than Elijah's even, then Elijah's reputation will be secured, and mine will be too, and we will be given a higher rank, and we will make more money and have more freedom. Thompson tells us all of this. While I lie still at night, though, I begin to wonder about this Hun sniper.

When it comes time for us to go back for a few days of rest behind the lines, I'm surprised that I don't want to go.

A short while earlier, the promise of rest in a safe place was the only thing left to keep me going, but now I've become as obsessed as Elijah. I'm tempted to ask permission to stay in the line and continue hunting the sniper, and tell Elijah as much.

'It will be good for us to take a few days' rest,' Elijah says. 'We will gain a new perspective on things. We'll come back with steadier nerves and fresh eyes.'

We march the five miles on the Ypres Road with the others. Socializing now isn't as easy. Sean Patrick, I realize, was a kind of bridge between me and Graves and Fat and the others. He was always the first to say hello or invite me to sit with them for a meal or to offer a cigarette. It isn't my imagination that now when Elijah and I walk by a group of soldiers, the soldiers stare at us and wait until we are out of earshot before they begin talking again.

Still, I see that Elijah and Grey Eyes fall back into their old ways when they are once again together. They sit together and eat together and disappear for long stretches together when they know no officers will be about. I realize one night as I sit alone along a creek that runs by the farm, listening to the talk of the others by their campfires, that I am angry with Elijah. Elijah isn't really even friends with this man who is directly responsible for Sean Patrick's death. I know that Elijah spends time with Grey Eyes because he likes the pull of the medicine. He likes to test himself, to see how well he can fight trying it. Is there not enough stress for him here in this place? I am tempted to go and find McCaan and tell him what I know about Grey Eyes.

Me, I try to ignore all of the bad feelings that well up inside of me. Enough bad feelings around here for a thousand

135

lifetimes. I enjoy this little bit of time off, and sleep and eat well and stay mostly to myself and don't think about my work on the lines at all and maybe that is why I'm jolted out of the deepest sleep I've had in months with a knowledge as sure as anything I know. It's so clear to me suddenly that I think nothing of immediately getting up from my blanket in a corner of the barn with a little bit of straw for a bed to search out Elijah.

Elijah and Grey Eyes have taken to staying in a little well-hidden tent that Elijah constructed out near the creek. It reminds me of the old tents that the elders build back in Moose Factory and into which they bring heated stones and pray and sweat and wait for visions or for knowledge. Elijah has built this one in the old way, with sturdy saplings that form the round structure that he covers with canvas, a small flap for a door. When inside the tent, the dark's like what a womb must feel like, the air close and hot and the universe feeling endless even when you stretch up your hand and touch the roof.

I make my way to the creek and squat outside the tent, listening to hear if Elijah's awake. I hear nothing and crawl inside, where the black is so complete that my eyes won't adjust. I feel around, hoping Elijah's the one I find first and not Grey Eyes. I know my friend well enough to be sure that he constructed this tent not so much to seek visions as to protect himself from the prying eyes of officers. It would be easy for him to claim that he is conducting mysterious Indian cere-monies in his tent. This would be enough to keep most of them away.

'Elijah, wake up,' I say, shaking the form in front of me. He sleeps hard tonight. 'Wake up. It is important.' Elijah takes a long time to find consciousness.

'What is it?' he asks in Cree. 'An officer?' His voice is disjointed in this darkness, hollow and childlike.

'No. I've made an important realization.'

'Can it not wait until tomorrow?' he says.

'It is about the German sniper,' I say.

Elijah's blanket rustles. The little light from the moon outside is a welcome thing as we crawl out.

Elijah lies on the ground and stares up at the stars. His eyes glitter wetly in the moon's light. 'Tell me,' he says.

'Think of the bullet that killed Sean Patrick,' I say. He nods. 'Its angle was not right.' Elijah looks puzzled. 'Sean Patrick was not shot by someone level with him or even from above him like we assumed. The bullet entered his neck from below him.'

'Then why did you not say anything at the time?' he asks.

'It's not a great angle,' I answer. 'At the time, I just believed it had ricocheted on his spine and that was why the exit was higher than the entry. You saw it too.'

'There was too much blood to see anything.'

'There was a lot of blood,' I answer. 'But it was obvious where the bullet opened up his neck. Just below his Adam's apple. And then when we turned him over after he was dead it was obvious as well that the bullet had passed clean through, but near the base of his skull.'

'How do we know it wasn't just a ricochet?'

'You know as well as I do that the Hun sniper uses copper bullets. The chances of one ricocheting on something softer than it is slight.'

We sit silent for a while. The air is almost chilly at this time of night out on the wet grass.

'That can only mean one thing, then,' Elijah says after a

137

while. 'He's hiding somewhere where he is looking up at our trenches, not down at them like we assumed.'

'And the only place that he can do that from is no man's land,' I answer for him.

We look at each other. Elijah no longer seems sleepy.

WE LET MCCAAN KNOW that we are on the verge of something important, and he gives us permission to go back out to where we keep our nests hidden. Three days pass and we continue to wait, searching no man's land for any sign. I peer through the scope of my rifle at the magnified images, the craters whose bottoms are filled with water, the splinters of black trees, a blasted wagon, a bloated horse, the belly expanding with gas each day so that it has become grotesque in its size as it bakes in the sun. Old rifles are scattered about, old Hun helmets, the wool coats of soldiers disintegrating into the mud just as their bodies do below the coats. Newer corpses lie out there too. A number of times I'm startled to see a man sprawled out and grimacing at me with big teeth, his lips and gums pulling back, and for a second I think the man is alive and is aiming his rifle at me. But they are dead, all of them. Everything out there is dead.

When we are bored, we whisper back and forth to one another. We are well hidden. We never talk of home. It is too far away.

Today in one of our nests, I comment on the dead horse whose belly has grown impossibly bigger. It reminds me of other horses. In the big ship on the way across the ocean I watched over horses in the ship's hold. I haven't thought about those horses, haven't thought about anything from the past in a long time. To focus only on what is around me now is enough—if the shell that screams overhead will fall close to me, if I have chosen a careful enough concealment, if any of the metal of my rifle glints in the sunlight, if I can find the sniper.

It is the long part of the afternoon. Elijah laughs. 'Do you remember the bull moose that came back to life?' he asks.

I nod slightly, smiling. 'You thought it was dead,' I whisper. 'And as you straddled it to pull its head up by its antlers it stood up with you on its back.'

'My first and only horse ride,' Elijah answers.

We stare out at no man's land. Elijah breaks our silence with his whisper. 'Why did you care so much for those horses on the ship?' No answer comes to me.

After a time, he speaks when he sees that I won't. 'Did you know that I tried the medicine, the morphine, on that ship to England?' he asks.

I stare at him in disbelief.

'Grey Eyes is to blame for that,' he says, and I know he will tell me the story. Elijah, he can't keep anything from me. He never has been able to. It is easy, hearing his voice, for me to be in Elijah's stories so that I live them myself, and this is why, even before I hear the story of Grey Eyes and the medicine, I dislike the man more.

It was when we had set sail from Canada on the falling tide, and as soon as we cleared the breakwater, the sky dulled and hung low and the waves built up so that the rocking of the ship felt comfortable at first like a mother. But not an hour on the rolling swells of the ocean and Elijah said he was cold to the touch and when he felt his forehead he was sweating as well. His stomach churned and its contents rose so that he stumbled best he could to the railing and expelled them into the black sea below. He retched until nothing was left and continued retching until his stomach hurt like it had been punched hard. He lay on his side on the metal deck and slipped into broken dreams of horses on fire on the river we'd travelled.

He remembers a hand shaking him. He turns and sees that the sky is dark now. The ship pitches horribly. The hand belongs to Henry Grey Eyes.

'You're sick,' Grey Eyes says. 'And you're freezing out here.' Elijah stares up at him. 'You need medicine.' Grey Eyes smiles. 'Smoke one of my cigarettes with me. It will calm your stomach.'

The thought of the thick sweet smoke makes Elijah's stomach churn. 'I have other medicine,' Grey Eyes says. 'I'll help you below.'

They make their way along the heaving deck and inside. Elijah only realizes how cold he is now that the heat and stink of all the crowded men rolls over him. He and Grey Eyes make their way along the aisles defined by swinging hammocks, voices grumbling and moaning in the shadows. They descend further into the ship, down below to where there are no longer any men, just the thick smell of horses.

The animals are nervous as the dull thud of waves hitting the ship echoes somewhere above them. Elijah reaches his hand out to one but it pulls back.

In a corner near the stable, Grey Eyes falls to his knees and digs behind an old crate, pulls something from the burlap. Elijah shivers violently. A good thing that Grey Eyes found Elijah, Elijah thinks. He might have frozen to death up there. His fingers are numb so that he can't feel them or the tiny bottle Grey Eyes passes to him. It glitters in the little light. Grey Eyes' brows arch when he sees how Elijah stares.

Grey Eyes sits beside Elijah on the soft burlap and fondles another one. 'I have all this medicine, but no way to take it,' he says, laughing. 'Cut my arm,' he says.

Elijah looks at him.

'Cut me,' he says again. 'Deep.' Elijah pulls out his skinning knife. His head's dizzy. He runs the thin blade hard across the bone of Grey Eyes' forearm. Elijah watches in fascination at the skin separating, red blossoming out against the silver of his blade.

Grey Eyes takes a handkerchief from his pocket and wraps the wound. 'I'll be back shortly,' he says, as Elijah wipes the blade on his pants. Grey Eyes disappears into the shadows of the ship.

Lying there with a sick stomach, Elijah listens to the *thump thump* of the ship's engines, the pound of waves, the nervous shuffle and stamp of horses' hooves.

Maybe a couple of hours pass. He tries to find the energy to stand up and get back to his nest under the lifeboat on deck. It's better on the deck in the open air, he realizes, than in this place below the water in the groaning ship. Elijah hears Grey Eyes before he sees him. He has a way of walking heavy on his heels. He'd be no good as a hunter. White-faced out of the shadows, the dark under his eyes making him look sick, he smiles. He sits beside Elijah and pulls up his sleeve, exposing a bandage. He pulls the bandage back, and Elijah sees a neat row of black stitches puckering Grey Eyes' skin where Elijah had run the knife.

With his other hand Grey Eyes pulls a small sharp object from his pocket. 'Take off your jacket and roll up your shirt sleeve,' he says. 'Give me one of those ampoules.' Taking the bloody handkerchief from his pocket, Grey Eyes loops it around Elijah's biceps and pulls tight so that his arm and hand throb dully.

Grey Eyes snaps off the top of the glass ampoule and inserts the needle of the syringe into it. 'I nicked it up in the infirmary,' he says, focused on the needle. He then carefully draws back on the plunger, and Elijah watches a little golden liquid flood the glass tube. It's the same colour as the ring on each side of the syringe where Grey Eyes places his fingers for grip. 'I don't know how strong this is,' he says, taking Elijah's arm in his lap, 'so I won't give you much.' Grey Eyes flicks his thumbnail against the tube and pushes the plunger so that a bead of golden liquid appears at the needle's tip. 'Hold still,' he says, placing the sharp needle along the vein of Elijah's arm and pushing it in slow so that Elijah feels a tug and burn under the skin. Carefully, Grey Eyes presses the plunger down, and Elijah feels like his arm's being filled with warm air.

Grey Eyes takes the needle from Elijah's vein and unties the handkerchief. Elijah looks down at his arm, wondering if this is all, when suddenly his breath hitches in his throat and light floods all around. His head floats from the pain of his body, hovers there, watches Grey Eyes remove his jacket, roll up his sleeve, tie the handkerchief around his arm, dip the needle into the ampoule, tap it with his thumb, and slide it into the bump of his vein. Grey Eyes lies down on the burlap away from Elijah and shivers. Elijah stares up into the dark, smells the horses, floats just above the ground on warm golden water, listens to it hit the ship, the beckon of snuffling and snorting animals like whispers from thirty paces.

He tries hard to keep his floating head tethered. It hovers above him, tugging gently, wanting to float, to drift and see what there is to see. When he thinks of releasing it, just letting it go to explore, a panic swells up, so big it forces air from his lungs so that a low groan escapes his mouth.

'Don't fight, Whiskeyjack,' Grey Eyes whispers. 'Just let it go.'

'No,' Elijah whispers, 'it won't come back, my head won't come back.'

Grey Eyes laughs softly. Elijah fights the fear by himself, and then just decides to let his head float away.

Elijah remembers seeing the horses' stalls from above, and in one of them he sees me with a horse, feeding it by hand. Elijah floats further, peering into dark corners, reading the names on wooden cargo boxes. AMMUNITION. FOOD. CLOTHING. Everything we will need over there. He floats to the next level. Waterline. Men in hammocks sleeping. Some tossing. Others sick. Rows and rows of meat, they look like meat wrapped in wool blankets. A couple of men talk, talk about girlfriends left at home. Children that they might not see again. Elijah lets himself float up the stairs and up out onto the lowest deck. Black night. No stars. The water below blacker, deeper than the sky. Cold. Two night watchmen stroll, cigarette tips glowing. Will they check the cargo hold? Watch. Don't panic. Breathe. The upper deck and officers' quarters. More sleeping men. Two are not sleeping. They touch tender fingers to mouths. Taste one another. Bite.

The whisper and laughter of many voices up the final stairs. Elijah can hear them coming from the little glow of the wheel-house. A party? The voices are excited. Not a party. Something. Crackle. Static. Anger. Women's voices speaking Cree. Elijah is pulled back to his body. He disappears into himself on his burlap sacks that itch his back.

'That was the one and only time I experienced the morphine,' Elijah says to me, the pounding of artillery rumbling low in the distance. 'It allowed me to leave my body and see what was around me. I see how it might be a very powerful tool for me in such a place as this.'

'You will not take it any more,' I tell him.

He nods and smiles.

We lie on our stomachs and scan the ground hundreds of yards in front, the sun reaching its peak and then beginning its descent toward the earth behind us. Its warmth causes me to grow sleepy, and I find myself nodding onto my rifle, head sinking. A bird behind me sings a shrill song, and I realize that I've not heard this in many days.

Elijah's voice startles me awake. 'I'm going to check the accuracy of my rifle.'

My eyes dart open. The sun has moved some since I fell asleep.

'Is that wise?' I ask. 'What if the smoke gives away our position?'

'We've got the sun pretty much behind us now,' he says. 'No sniper can stare into it and see anything but sunspots.' He preps his gun. 'I'm beginning to think that their sniper is a phantom.'

'What are you going to shoot at?' I whisper.

'The bloated belly of that horse,' he says.

I focus into my scope and fill it with the body of the horse. 'That will be a very bad mess you cause.'

'It should explode in an interesting way,' he says. 'Watch carefully.'

I watch, tense for the explosion in my ear. As soon as it comes, the horse's belly disintegrates in a red and brown cloud of spray, the animal's head jerking as if it is still alive. I continue staring through the scope, scanning the ground all around, tracing the ribbons of intestine and brown hide littering the mud around the animal.

That is when he captures my eye. Not fifteen feet away a corpse moves slightly and a puff of smoke comes out from it. Almost simultaneously wood splinters and dirt clods explode between Elijah's head and my own and Elijah yelps in pain, the sound of his trying desperately to reload his Ross setting me into action.

'That body just shot at us,' I blurt as I train my sights on it and can suddenly see the barrel of a rifle pointing out at us from under the corpse.

'I can't see,' Elijah says. 'My eyes.'

I know that the sniper is reloading and it is a matter of seconds before he will fire at us again. My rifle is steady on a place just above the rifle poking out from under the corpse and without any more thinking I pull the trigger. There is the explosion and the kick. As the smoke clears, I see that the rifle I aimed above is now lying on the ground at an angle. The knowledge slowly sinks in. As I peer through my scope for movement, I know that there won't be any.

'Fire one more time,' Elijah says. 'Put one more round in the same place.' His voice is tense. He is in pain.

I reload smoothly, draw a bead once again at the space just below the corpse, then fire.

We drop down into the cover of the nest. 'Give me a canteen,' Elijah says.

I reach between us and pass it to him. He lies on his back now and pours water into his eyes.

'Can you see?' I ask.

'Yes, but things are fuzzy,' he says. 'You got him, didn't you?' he asks.

I don't answer.

'That was their phantom sniper,' Elijah says with awe. 'The one who killed Sean Patrick. He was hunting us too.' I see that Elijah can't speak with his British accent when he speaks in Cree. 'Can you imagine?' Elijah asks, beginning to laugh. 'The intensity of such a man? He could lie there for hours among the dead and the rotting. He lay there in that stink of death like death itself. But we got him.'

I ponder this for a while.

'We will go out there tonight and learn his tricks,' Elijah says. 'We will get you a souvenir of your first great kill.'

SHAKOCIHEW
Seducing

IN THE EVENING I find a good spot for camp. This first day has been a strange one for me. Twice I came around a bend in the river, expecting to recognize land I'd passed not so long ago as I travelled up this burnt stretch to the town. Twice I was surprised to feel lost, like I'd somehow never been on this river before. I'm feeling unsettled, like Nephew and I are on a very different journey from the one we began.

I try to feed Xavier, but still he doesn't eat. He is disappearing in front of my eyes, sitting across the fire with a blanket over his shoulders, the smoke causing him to shimmer. I feed him with my story instead. He's listening, I think, his eyes staring at the water.

We weren't always alone out in the bush, Xavier. Although my mother never let another man very close to her after my father, she sometimes liked their company, their quiet talk and easy ways. Like us, there were roving bands of hunters who lived in the old way as much as possible, sending in hunters to trade furs for bullets and flour once in a while when that was possible. The Indian name for us was *awawatuk,* and we had the unfair reputation of being thieves and murderers, all because we rejected the *wemistikoshiw*. Rarely did the *awawatuk* travel in groups bigger than five or six, but in the summer, just as in the old days, we came together in bigger numbers when the land would support us.

147

In the years I grew into a young woman, my mother taught me all that she could about the shaking tent and the *matatosowin,* the sweat lodge. She taught me about the healing and killing power of roots and herbs that grew around us, what parts of the skunk would cure snowblindness and what parts of the owl gave night vision. She saw my occasional fits the same way I did, as an unwanted gift, but one to be nurtured regardless.

The *awawatuk* accepted that I was the natural extension of my father, the new limb through which my family's power travelled. By the time I was living my seventeenth winter, men would come to me not for what men usually seek women out for, but to ask questions and advice. Most often, they wanted to know where to find game, and so I divined for them, placing the shoulder blade of the animal on coals and dripping water onto it as I had watched my father do. The rare hunter came to me wanting to understand the symbol of a dream and sometimes to learn his future. If I had not experienced a fit in some time, I constructed a shaking tent and crawled into it, summoned the spirits of the forest animals to come inside and join me, so many of them sometimes that the walls of my tent puffed out and drew in with their breath, becoming a living thing all its own. Most often, though, it was the spirit of the lynx that came to me first and stayed through the night, showing through its sharp eyes the secrets of the forest.

When I was left free with my time, I travelled through the bush, hunting and stalking. My hair grew long and tangled and wild. I stayed out for more and more days on my own, worrying my mother who was growing older now. But I was restless. The void inside me was aching, needing to be filled.

That is when I came across him.

He began to run a trapline farther out than the other *wemistikoshiw* and was apparently not afraid of the bush and its dangers. I knew he was a *wemistikoshiw* trapper by the way he systematically placed his traps and by the way he baited them. At first his insolence angered me, and I would follow his line and spring all of the metal jaws before they could take any animals. But still he persisted. So I played tricks on him, taking the leg of a fox or a marten, placing it in one of his traps, and leaving him to wonder whether the animal had escaped by chewing off its own leg. I covered my own tracks by sweeping the snow with a spruce bough, or else I'd strap carefully whittled branches to my mukluks so that they resembled great clawed feet and leave prints where I knew he'd see them and be left frightened and wondering. That's when the idea came to me.

At first it was less an idea than an image that came late at night while I sat alone by my fire in my little *askihkan,* the thought of me catching him and keeping him like a pet. This kept me warm, and even for brief moments stilled the ache in me as I imagined stroking him, feeding him berries with stained fingers, licking the juice from his lips. When the winter was at its deepest and the hunger had set itself in the pit of my stomach so that the world was more a dream than a real thing, I acted in desperation, frustration.

Openly, I followed his trapline in my snowshoes, knowing he would follow. I led him to a copse of cedar where I'd placed a rope high in a tree from which I could swing clear of my own tracks, leave him wondering how I'd disappeared. From a hiding spot I'd built, I sat and waited for him to take my bait. It did not take him long to come.

He might have been an Indian in his fur and hide, his beaver hat tied down and covering most of his face. But when he came to the place where my prints disappeared, he pulled off his hat and scratched his pretty head. One hand went to a lean, bearded jaw as he studied the scene carefully, so carefully that I worried for a moment that I'd not been wily enough in playing my trick. Then he looked around him, his copper eyes flashing. My heart beat so wildly I thought he might hear it, but if there's one thing in which I excelled, it was becoming invisible. He moved on after a while, and I was tempted to follow, but I knew he'd be back. He was as intrigued as me.

I continued my game through the rest of the winter until I was sure he'd grow bored of it, but still he'd follow my tracks out. And every time he appeared, I felt that same aching pull in the pit of my stomach so that I thought I might go mad.

With the spring thaw coming, I knew he'd be prevented by the sucking muskeg from travelling out this far into the bush and it was because of this that I decided to snare him. For weeks I'd schemed and figured, but still nothing came to me. I could dig a pit and have him fall into it and in this way capture him. But he might injure himself in the fall and be very angry. I could snare him with a vine about the neck, but surely that would kill him. And then it struck me. The simplicity of it was perfect. I was the bait, and my *askihkan* was the snare. I saw no point in denying it any more. Soon the water would be flowing, the sap trickling, the bear waking.

I prepared my *askihkan,* paying attention to what I'd need. The herb that would make him sleep deeply, the length of rope to tie him, dried berries and moosemeat to feed him, my knife carefully tucked by my sleeping robe if all did not work as planned. The thought of my removing his clothing as he slept, of exploring his pale body, made me want to rush.

On the day that I did not hide my tracks but instead walked carefully about his lines and then straight to my *askihkan* a wind blew that was as warm as any wind I'd felt in months. I crouched and waited inside, worrying that the weather was all wrong and he would not come. That is when I heard him walking toward me, whistling a song that I'd heard the children sing at the residential school. I looked up to my door as he threw it open, the light silhouetting him so that he was featureless. He said nothing, and neither did I.

He came in and closed the flap behind him. As my eyes adjusted to the dark I watched him remove his coat, and then his boots and rabbit fur pants. He wore cotton pants beneath them. I couldn't move. That's when it dawned on me that maybe I was not the hunter any more.

I look over at Xavier lying by the fire. His eyes are closed, but I'm not sure if he sleeps or not. The rest of this story belongs only to me, and so I let my voice rest for the night, float back to that time when I was young. I remember how the trapper came into my lodge that first time, how he began to speak in French, words that I did not understand. He spoke in a quiet voice, staring at me boldly with his golden eyes. Although I did not understand the words, I understood the tone. He was asking me, gently telling me. I stood up in front of him, stood there for a long time. He wore a slight smile on his lips. I could feel that my face was flushed.

As if in a trance, I stared into his eyes and then removed my shirt. I slowly unstrung my own hunter's pants and removed them too. I was naked now, stood there in front of him, the smell of my own musk touching my nose.

He stood as well, removed the rest of his clothing until he also was naked, close enough to touch. There was a light fur

151

on his chest so that immediately I thought of a wolf, long and sinewy. Hungry. His cock stood out straight in front of him and it bobbed slightly as if it had a life of its own. It seemed very big for a man whose frame was so slight. I'd seen many men's cocks. We Cree are not a shy people. But I'd never seen one in its hardness, in its desire for me. He pulled me to him and he brushed his lips against mine, then over my cheeks and neck. The lightness made me shiver. He brushed the hair back from my face and stared boldly into my eyes, smiling slightly. I looked up at him then, and took his cock in my hands. It made him jolt. He moaned out, and so I rubbed him slightly up and down until he moaned louder. I knelt before him and licked him gently.

He picked me up and held me to him, leaning me back so that my weight rested in his arms. He bent forward and began to lick and nibble me so that a small bolt of lightning ran from my breasts to between my legs. He continued to kiss me lower so that I found myself upside down, supporting my weight with my arms, the blood rushing to my head. I wrapped my legs around his neck and he kissed me there, slipping his tongue into me as he did it so that I cried out. His slight beard rubbed against me. Behind my eyelids the world was blue, red, orange. I felt fire in water. I was flame in water. Something inside me ignited, then melted, and a great shudder racked me so that my arms went numb and we collapsed together on my soft sleeping robe. I slipped into dreams then.

I awoke with my back to him, his arms wrapped around me. He'd nudged my legs apart and was gently pushing his hardness against me. He whispered in my ear and I let myself relax so that suddenly I was full of him. I gasped. So much. He cupped my breasts in his hands and went deeper so that I thought I might scream. He whispered again, and although I did not know his tongue, I understood. I arched my back and pushed against him so that he filled me again. I clamped myself to him and rocked slightly so that he wouldn't leave. His breathing shortened and quickened. He called out, and I felt him flood me, the pleasure mixing with the sudden fear, the immensity of what I'd just let happen. Again I fell asleep.

When I awoke a short time later he was gone.

MOOSASINIWI PASKISIKAN
Rifle

AUNTIE CRAWLS INTO HER TEEPEE. I open my eyes and stare at the fire a while longer, and in its flame I remember Sergeant McCaan. I remember how McCaan liked to boss Elijah because he'd seen how Elijah didn't like being told what to do. He wasn't a bastard about it, not like Lieutenant Breech who bossed us with a sneer. McCaan ordered Elijah with a slight smile on his lips, enjoying that he could madden Elijah easier than lice could.

I remember the evening of the day I killed the sniper. Everyone around us speaks about it excitedly.

McCaan tells Elijah that he must take Corporal Thompson out into no man's land with us tonight to frisk the dead man.

This bit of news angers Elijah, but he doesn't let it show. 'Yes, Sergeant,' he says. 'Yes, Sergeant.'

I can see that he'd rather go out alone. He'd rather leave Thompson in the trench, and me too, for that matter. Elijah likes to go out of the trench at night and do his own patrols. Just him and the mud. He'd get court-martialled if Breech knew. But he must take me out with him tonight. The kill was mine after all, wasn't it? My first as a sniper. Elijah can't believe he didn't get the shot. He told me himself he was more surprised than anyone.

'The lads down on the line are happy about this new bit of

news, though,' Elijah says. 'Bloody fine shot, that sniper used to be. No longer!'

Elijah complains that his sight's a little blurry from the dirt spray of the bullet so close to his head, but it's dark out anyway, and he likes to rely on the other senses at night. Elijah claims that he can smell Fritz from a long way off, swears that Fritz smells differently than an Englishman or a Frenchman or a Canadian. Elijah says he picks up a vinegar smell when one's close. He always knows.

Thompson comes by our little dugout near two a.m. and whispers through our blanket door that it's time to go. Elijah picks up the wooden war club from beside our door. He made it himself. Thompson has one and he showed Elijah how to make it. Heavy hardwood driven through with hobnails. He's dying to try it out on a Boche skull. Bash a Boche.

'Bloody good,' Elijah says, exiting our blanket door and pulling his black wool cap low over his eyes. His good-luck sniping cap. McCaan gave one to me and one to Elijah when we first started our specialty work. 'Can't very well be wearing those shiny tin pots,' Elijah says. The army issued us helmets a few months earlier. They are terrible, uncomfortable things. 'A soldier might as well wear a beacon on his head!'

Thompson, Elijah and I sit together, away from the others, and charcoal our faces. It's our ritual. It's what I call a *wemistikoshiw* smudging ceremony. Elijah laughs at me. No Indian religion for him. The only Indian Elijah wants to be is the Indian that knows to hide and hunt.

'Jolly good night for a little snooping, eh, Thompson?' Elijah says.

Thompson shakes his head at the words, and his teeth are

white almost to a glow. 'You do a better British accent than a Brit,' he says.

'Right-o,' Elijah answers. He began talking this way to get the others to laugh, but he likes it now. Makes him feel respectable. He told me there's a magic in it that protects him. Elijah told me the accent came to him while deep in a slumber. 'Woke up speaking like a lord,' he said.

I've got my animal *manitous*. Elijah's got his voices. He says he couldn't speak in his old voice even if he wanted to now. It's gone somewhere far away.

Word moves down the line that a patrol's going out. We don't need our own firing upon us. We go over the top at the designated place where a rise in the field keeps us hidden from the other line. Thompson signals for me to take the lead. It was my kill. I know best where to find it. I know that this must sting Elijah a little.

According to the others, he is the resident expert, although I am a fine shot too. As fine as Elijah. But I don't have the killing instinct for men. I believe that Elijah sensed my hesitancy to shoot the sniper, even when our lives were threatened.

We keep our rifles loose in our hands and run, bent at the waist. A good shell crater looms twenty yards out. The big guns of the Somme pound in the distance. The sound that has been with me so long now that I rarely notice it any more. It has become, for me, the sound of Belgium and France.

Flares go up from Fritz's side, and we hit the mud, lie flat as bright light hovers overhead. It's too early to tell if Fritz knows we're out here or if it's coincidence. Elijah knows as well as I do that the three of us work well together. We press ourselves to the ground at the same time and rise at the same time and know which direction the lead man is going to head before he does it. When the white flare light dies away, I rise and in a crouch run to the next crater. The bottom of this one is filled with stinking water, and so we lie along the side of it. The smell suggests bodies rotting in the bottom, a smell I cannot grow accustomed to. We move out when it is safe and make our way like this—leapfrogging, Thompson calls it— until Elijah and I can make out the hump of the horse he shot earlier. Elijah signals to us. The smell of vinegar must have risen to his nose. He tugs at our tunics to let us know we should stay put in this crater for a little while. We trust Elijah.

Sure enough, three shadows catch my eye. This is just on the Fritz side of no man's land here. I've never known a sniper to work so far out from his line. That explains this one's excellent record. And Elijah tells me later that this sniper's boldness gives him some ideas.

The three shadows crawl into a crater and are obviously scanning the area best they can. Fritz must have really cared for their dead sniper to send a party out to investigate his bad luck. The urge to shoot them all and be done with it is hard to wrestle down. We'd be giving up our position then, though, and all that would do is get us blown to bits and pieces. The Germans crawl out and head in the wrong direction. Thompson lets them pass. They have no idea where their dead man lies.

We can smell the horse from here. The rotten meat smell of it is different than the smell of dead human, much gamier. Elijah whispers, says to me again that the unlucky Fritz was a special one, that he must have been a lover of the dead. He could lie with them for long periods. Stay as still as them.

While Thompson and Elijah offer cover, I go out to where the dead man lies. I know my slight form is swallowed up by the darkness.

Elijah told me later that when I was gone, he closed his eyes to rest their soreness, his nostrils flaring for any warning scent. He said I was gone for too long and that he wanted to go out and look for me and to see the dead sniper up close. He hoped that I would get a good souvenir from him.

And I do. When I find the sniper, I see in the darkness that his face is a black smear. I had hit him dead on the nose. I go through his pockets. Except for cigarettes and a nice brass lighter, they are empty. I cut his stripes from his uniform and take his rifle and bayonet.

I slip back into our crater, smiling. Elijah says later that he sees why. I am cradling the Mauser. Elijah can see even in this darkness that the gun is a very good one with a scope. Wrapped in cloth like we keep ours when we are working. He can smell the gun oil on the cloth, and just below it the stink of dead animals. The rifle is one Elijah's wanted for a long time. He's angry with himself that he didn't grab one back in the big crater. All he took back was the old helmet. I can see that he begins to think of things he might trade for it.

Thompson tenses and pats my side, points toward the Hun line. He sees or hears something. He has noticed even before Elijah. Under the sound of the big 5.9s in the distance we pick it up. The sound of shovelling, dull yet steady. How did Elijah miss it? Me, my ears have troubled me more and more in this place of noise, but I know Elijah will be hard on himself for relaxing. Obviously a Fritz work party. Thompson makes the gesture for Elijah to investigate while he and I offer cover.

He lays his rifle down and picks up his war club. McCaan was especially impressed with its wicked design. He calls it a knobkerrie. Elijah checks his Mills bombs in their sack attached to his belt and listens for the direction of the sound. While two or three of them work they will no doubt have the keenest eye on sentry duty. Elijah will approach them dead-on and get an idea of what they are up to.

Slithering out of the trench, he makes his way toward the sound of the shovelling. I watch him stop and lie still every few yards. I imagine I can see what he sees.

He is close to their barbed wire, stops and re-gauges his direction and progress. It is unerring. He feels invincible, makes a note to keep track of how far he's gone. Perfect. Steady breath. Focus of an osprey. They have no idea how close he is. They are just on the other side of their wire. Elijah closes his eyes and lets himself drift to them. He sees three workers and one sentry. The sentry looks out into the darkness but cannot see a thing. He whispers back to the others. Elijah doesn't understand what he says. They are digging a machine-gun placement. It will be a good one once finished, will cut the Canadians down like thin bulrushes, brown-haired heads toppling heavily to the earth. Elijah must swallow a giggle that rises up from his throat. The temptation to sneak in on them comes to him, to club them like one would club martens caught in snares. Elijah memorizes where the weakest point of their wire is and turns around. Not much night is left.

We make our way back carefully to our own line, no longer focused like we should be. We are coming down from the rush of adrenaline, and the fatigue crawls in.

In the officers' dugout, I show off the sniper rifle and the shoulder patch of the dead sergeant. We smoke his German cigarettes and Elijah reports his findings to Lieutenant Breech. My head pounds now with the approaching day. There will be stand-to far too soon and I must sleep before that.

Breech dismisses us finally after giving us double rum rations for a job well done.

Elijah and I walk to our dugout. It has begun to rain. A warm, steady drizzle. We will sleep well to the sound of it puddling in the trench.

Later as I fall asleep wrapped in my damp wool blanket, the lice make their way from the seams of my uniform and crawl over my warming skin. My filthy clothing must be why I dream what I do, of that day we first arrived in the *wemistikoshiw* town after making our way through the fire. Elijah had sold our canoe to a trapper for enough for train tickets with plenty left over. It was his idea to take us for new clothes.

I remember the store owner watching us carefully. 'Hurry,' he says. 'I need to close shop.' I wonder if he is afraid of the fire moving this way.

Elijah smiles when I come out of the little room wearing a red long-sleeved shirt and black pants. I look good, my shiny hair dark against the shirt. The dirty moccasins on my feet are the only problem with my outfit, Elijah says. But I won't part with those.

When Elijah strolls out, I laugh. He has chosen a black suit and stiff, high white collar. In the mirror he looks like a preacher. This appeals to Elijah.

'That is what you will wear to join the army?' I ask.

Elijah ignores me, pulls out the money and hands it to the store owner. The owner looks surprised. Elijah counts the money when it is handed back. We have ten dollars left, but Elijah doesn't tell me that we are short a dollar for the train passage. *Wemistikoshiw* money is a funny thing. There's always more of it somewhere.

The two of us walk down the street, staring into the store windows. Most of the shops are deserted. When a car passes on the dusty road, we stop and stare at it, argue over how it moves itself. 'The driver does something with his feet,' I say. 'He must be pedalling it.'

'No,' Elijah answers. 'They pour lamp oil into the engine and then light it on fire. You've poured lamp oil on a fire.' Elijah spreads his arms in a whoosh. 'Little explosions inside make them go. Old Man Ferguson explained it to me.' I only stare as the car passes, coating everything in dust. 'Let's go to that tavern we saw beside the hotel,' he says. 'My throat is dry.' Mine is too. 'There might be women there.'

'What about the train?' I ask. 'It must be leaving soon.'

'The train doesn't leave till tomorrow,' Elijah says.

'And what of the fire?' I say. 'What if it does come this way and burns down the town while we sit and drink?'

'Can you imagine anything more glorious?' Elijah says.

LIEUTENANT BREECH SELECTS SIX OF US for a raiding party tonight. Far too many. There will be Thompson leading, Elijah and me, Grey Eyes, Gilberto and some other new one that I do not know. None of this is good. He might as well have invited Fat out with us. At least then if we came under fire the whole raiding party could take cover behind him.

Lieutenant Breech orders Thompson to lead us behind the lines and practise our raid all day. Cold and wet and miserable, my heart isn't in it. I can tell Elijah's isn't either. Gilberto is clumsy and nervous. Grey Eyes is glassy-eyed and far away. Thompson marks out our line and Fritz's machine-gun nest with white strings. We crawl through the mud in the drizzle for hours, leapfrogging one another and figuring out who will be where in the darkness of tonight, while Breech watches from a distance with an odd smile on his face. Thompson and Elijah and I would much rather just the three of us go out again tonight, but Breech has gotten reports of increased activity by Fritz and wants to claim a little glory for himself. He wants to show his superiors that he is a warrior of the highest order. Elijah says that Breech should be coming out with us tonight. That way he can guarantee that Breech won't be coming back.

We're restless as night crawls across the front. The rain hasn't stopped and is the kind that will drizzle steady for a long, long time. I am with Elijah and Grey Eyes in our little dugout. Our door is a blanket strung across the entrance to our cave, and it doesn't allow the stink of the kerosene lamp to exit. Elijah bounces his legs up and down, up and down, until finally Grey Eyes says, 'Quit your shaking. You're making me nervous.' Elijah takes out his trench knife and sharpens it with a stone.

The big guns keep up their drumbeat far south of us on the Somme. We hear word that we will be moved out of this quiet place in Saint-Eloi and marched down there as re-inforcement. Words. The rumours fall like rain here.

When will we go? Many dead down there in the Somme, though. Many, many dead. British coal miners tunnelled their way from under their line to under Fritz's and then filled the tunnels with high explosives. The idea was to collapse the Huns' world from under them, send them to their white man's hell. It didn't work as well as planned, but the blast was so tremendous that miles away the ground shook and trembled under our feet in sickening waves so that I swore I was on board that troopship again. Grey Eyes was shaken badly by it, swore it was the gates of hell opening up below us. He hasn't been the same since and is taking more morphine than is wise. Elijah tells me he will talk with Grey Eyes very soon about it.

I know Elijah can't keep anything from me, has never been able to. To tell me what he thinks and does releases a sort of pressure from inside him. Tonight, though, he thinks I'm not awake before our raid. I lie with my eyes closed, pretending to sleep. We've already begun shelling Fritz in preparation for our raid. We are lobbing mortars at their wire. I hear Elijah say to Grey Eyes that Breech is attempting to weaken Fritz's wire near the machine-gun nest.

'I told him that there is a place weak enough already for us to get through unnoticed,' he says. 'All Breech is doing with this shelling is letting Fritz know that we plan on coming over.'

Even with my eyes closed, I can tell Elijah's mood blackens more.

'Dear Henry,' Elijah says, using their code, 'would you be a kind chap and make me a cup of tea?'

'I'm afraid I'm out of tea, Elijah,' he answers. The tea they talk about is a tobacco they sometimes smoke together when it is available. It calms Elijah and makes him smile.

'But you had plenty only yesterday,' Elijah says.

I can tell he's holding the anger inside him as best he can.

'It really wasn't that much,' Grey Eyes nearly whines. He is a weak man. 'Why don't you find the medic and tell him that you've sprained your ankle. Maybe he will give you an extra rum ration or even a tablet.'

I open my eyes a tiny bit and look over to Elijah. Through my eyelashes he looks blurry. I see that Elijah contemplates what Grey Eyes has suggested. I can also see that Elijah's tempted to take his knife to Grey Eyes' throat. I can almost feel the black anger rising from his gut and filling his head so that his eyesight dims. Me, I don't pretend to sleep any more. I open my eyes. It's as if a silent explosion has gone off in the room and emptied the air from it. Elijah gets up and walks outside into the rain in search of something for his pounding head. I know Elijah so well that it is just a matter of me closing my eyes so that I can follow him.

The rain is cold and relentless as Elijah splashes along the duckboards, peering in dugouts for the medic. No doubt Breech will order a box barrage when we head over, try to cut the machine-gun nest off from the rest of their line so that we can get in and destroy it properly. So noisy! Such a waste, like fishing with Mills bombs! McCaan wouldn't listen when Elijah told him earlier in the day that Thompson, he and I could sneak over and do the job in silence, mine it once we killed the work party so that we might destroy not only the nest but as many of the enemy as possible. The problem is that McCaan would have to suggest a better plan to Breech than Breech's own, and there's never any of that.

Nothing feels right about the raid tonight. A good hunter knows to rely on his feeling. Elijah should just tell them that he is too sick to go out. But surely some of them would take this as cowardice, and he cannot bear to have them think this of him.

Finally he finds the medic huddling in a dugout, trying to keep out of the rain. The water has formed little rivulets that pour in, running down the mud walls, gradually collapsing them. His name is Driscoll, and he is short and chubby with small round-rimmed glasses. He is generous with the medicine, Grey Eyes says. Driscoll's way is to make a little joke and smile as he digs in his kit for an ampoule, his eyes remaining serious as they look for signs of the addict. Driscoll's tried to give it to Grey Eyes in pill form but the effects are not the same, and Grey Eyes says he finds it much harder to achieve the place he desires.

Elijah truly considers trying the morphine again tonight. He tells himself it is because of the bad feeling he's got about this raid. What he cannot yet face is that he wants the morphine to wash away a fear that he feels for the first time in this place.

Elijah crouches by Driscoll and offers a cigarette. 'Bloody awful weather,' Elijah says. 'Not fit for man nor rat.' Driscoll smiles, takes the offered cigarette. Elijah lights Driscoll's, then his own. 'That toe I was telling you about, the one I broke when I dropped the eighteen-pounder on it, it's really acting up in this weather.' Elijah smiles at him. 'Can you spare just the tiniest bit of M? I've got a big job to do tonight and I'm afraid I won't perform too well for the pain.'

'I'm sorry, Private Whiskeyjack,' he says, offering his own smile. 'Supplies are very short. The shipment that was to come in yesterday was destroyed in a barrage half a mile from our lines. I can't do it. Orders.'

'Just a little bit? A push to get me through this difficult evening?'

'If I didn't know better, I'd report to McCaan that you're displaying symptoms,' Driscoll says, smiling. 'But I know better, don't I, Private?'

Elijah smiles as he stands up. 'Yes, Corporal, you do.' He walks back to the dugout, his anger watered down by fear.

165

KIMOCIWINIKEWIN
Raid

THE RAIN HAS NOT LET UP, but Thompson has decided that it will offer good cover. Our attack party slips out of the trench in teams of two. That time in the night has come once again when the world is at its blackest. Elijah tells me his stomach is sick so that he would throw up if it held any food. His head pounds along with the big guns. He's with me in the crater closest to the weak part of the wire now. We are in advance position and the others flank us in their craters on either side. The plan is simple.

Elijah and I will approach as soon as the box barrage begins that will cut off the machine-gun nest. When the barrage ends we will drop Mills bombs into it and kill the work party. Then we're to place cotton charges into the nest, set the fuses, and retreat back to our line.

Thompson sends up a signal flare, and this immediately draws Fritz's fire upon him. The Canadian guns begin to drop shells behind Fritz's wire, but Elijah and I can tell the shells land too far behind to be effective. Fritz has a good idea where the attackers are. Elijah and I have to advance now and complete the job so that we can all get back to our line as soon as possible.

Elijah crawls out of the crater and cuts through strands of barbed wire while I keep a careful eye out for movement in front of him. The nest is behind the wire about twenty yards, just to the left. When he is through the wire, he crawls on his belly to a trough of mud thrown up by a mortar and takes position behind it, tensing as he goes, listening for the crack of the rifle and the bullet that will explode his skull. He checks carefully to see if the nest builders have spotted him, but the rain obscures them. He motions for me to come through the wire and join him. My stomach is knotted and I have to piss so bad that I try to right here, lying in the mud. I try and can't and feel small and ridiculous that I'm unable to do even this.

Fritz has concentrated a lot of fire on Thompson's and Grey Eyes' positions. I'll be amazed if they are still in one piece. So far, no one seems to have noticed Elijah and me. We leapfrog closer and Elijah reaches for a Mills bomb from his belt. He pulls the pin so that it is ready. We edge up closer to the nest. We can see it through the rain now, well hidden in the mud. We notice no movement. Elijah says his head feels ready to explode. He can't take it any longer.

'I'm going,' he whispers to me in Cree, and before I can stop him he is up and running.

I lose sight of him in the rain and dark. This all feels wrong. A shout rises up from the nest and I see the flash of a rifle come from it at the exact moment that I hear its discharge. The sounds of scrambling and of more rifle fire cracking in the rain. And then a strange silence before the bright flash and muffled bang of the Mills bomb. Mud and speckles of flesh rain onto me.

I wait, but Elijah doesn't come back. When it feels too long, and maybe it is minutes, maybe it is only seconds, I run toward where I last saw him. He isn't far, maybe thirty steps. He is on his stomach, not moving. I throw myself on top of him. I can feel Elijah tense for the pierce of a bayonet into his kidney. He doesn't know it's me. I reach into his sack on his belt and prime another Mills bomb, then lob it. One more explosion blasts up from the nest as I bury my head in my arms and try to cover Elijah with the rest of my body.

I roll Elijah over. We are both covered in red mud. He looks like he can't see anything, but he appears conscious. I crouch and dig in my bag for the cotton charge.

I light it and drop it into the nest, then drag Elijah back to where we came from, bullets splattering in the mud around us like hailstones, their mortars popping and exploding. As I pull Elijah into our crater, the cotton charge booms and sucks the air up and away from us for a second before it crashes back down like a wave full of earth. We're kept pinned in the crater as mortars and whiz-bangs continue to pop in the rain. I wonder where the others in the party are, if they are still alive. I want to get up and run with Elijah back to the safety of our line, but realize he can't. He's injured.

Fritz's mortars begin to move away and I shake Elijah, say, '*Ashtum,* we must go now.' I grab Elijah by the collar and drag him back as best I can toward our side, the rain falling hard and the blasts of the shells around us threatening to split our heads wide open with their concussions. I look about for the others in the raiding party and when finally Elijah and I roll back into our trench, we are flanked by McCaan and Driscoll. Driscoll searches Elijah's body for wounds. He smiles down at Elijah when he is done.

'Just a few scrapes, possibly a broken arm,' Driscoll says. 'And what I imagine must be a pounding head.' Elijah moans out in pain, cradles his arm. Driscoll digs into his kit and pulls out a gleaming needle filled with the amber liquid.

I watch him sink it into Elijah's arm and flood it. I see Elijah nod to him, then watch as he goes away to hands grasping him and carrying him to a different, calmer place.

Elijah's wounds are worth nothing more than a few days' rest behind the lines on the outskirts of a small, half-destroyed village. The whole unit joins us back here, having spent our designated days on the front.

'Just a sprained arm,' McCaan scoffs at Elijah as he and I sit together. 'That and a minor concussion ain't enough to send you to Blighty.'

'I'm glad for it,' Elijah says. His arm's in a sling. 'I'd go mad stuck in a hospital so far away from it all.'

'You fared better than Thompson and that new kid,' McCaan says.

Although McCaan tries to hide it, Elijah and I can see that he takes the blame for this raid gone wrong. But it isn't his fault. It's Breech's. Elijah tells me he wants nothing more than to take Breech out into no man's land and show him the young private, here not even a week. The kid was unlucky enough to be hit by a mortar and bits of him lie scattered in front of Fritz's wire. Thompson took a bullet in the leg and shrapnel to most of the rest of his body and is close to death somewhere away from here. His loss to the section is not a good thing. I can see how the men are quiet even though they now have days to themselves without the worry of dying. I watch Elijah wander about and tell jokes and some of the men laugh with him. But the atmosphere is more one of a funeral. 'Thompson will be back,' Elijah tells the others. 'He'll miss this place too much.'

A bullet had cut through Elijah's wool tunic and grazed his other arm, leaving a little burn mark. Elijah shows off the hole in his uniform to the others. Another bullet grazed his cheek so that it still stings, he says. But again he was lucky. I escaped with nothing. There's talk of a medal for Elijah for rushing the nest. Nothing mentioned of me finishing things up for him out there.

We try to stay out of the late summer rain as best we can, holed up in tents by a small copse of trees and a field. A barn and a blasted-out farmhouse is saved for the officers. There's no shortage of the medicine for Elijah if he wants it, but I don't see him take any, can tell he isn't luxuriating in its warm grasp. I believe he wants to save it for when he truly needs it out there.

Elijah has decided to forgive Grey Eyes for his greed, he says. He's not sure why. Grey Eyes and Gilberto made it back all right from the raid. Grey Eyes was back long before Gilberto tumbled into the trench with a bleeding Thompson over his big, hairy shoulders. There's talk of a medal for Gilberto too.

I watch as Elijah helps Gilberto compose a letter to his wife and children, telling them of this latest accomplishment, Elijah using his best nun's English to describe Gilberto's heroics and the saving of the corporal's life. They sit in a tent as rain beats on the canvas, Gilberto writing in his big, awkward cursive, Elijah dictating. 'My sweetest little grape,' Elijah begins. 'A few nights ago I faced death and emerged victorious.'

'But I don't want her to worry for me,' Gilberto says, looking up from the letter. 'I want her to think I am somewhere safe behind the lines cooking food for the hungry soldiers.'

Elijah ignores Gilberto's concerns about worrying his wife. 'With enemy bullets falling like rain,' Elijah continues, writing, speaking for the big Italian, 'I attacked the enemy and made him run. Sadly, my corporal was wounded in the struggle. He was near death, and so I carried him on my broad shoulders back through the dangers of no man's land to safety. They speak of a medal for me. Tell our children so that they may be proud of their father.'

'Oh, too much, too much you say!' Gilberto tells Elijah, smiling. 'My wife, she will think I brag and lie!'

'She will see you as the hero that you are,' Elijah tells him, patting his shoulder. 'She will know that you are over here away from your beloved vineyard for the good of the Empire.' They laugh.

An innocence in Elijah's eyes, that desire to help somebody else with his words, reminds me of the short time as a child that I was in residential school. I barely remember my mother, the one Auntie calls Rabbit. She gave me up when I was just old enough to begin having memories, and the nuns took me in. Elijah was the first boy I met. He became my only friend.

I do remember having to sit in hard chairs with little tables in front of them, and Elijah made sure to sit beside me. He was fascinated by the boy who knew no English. We were taught the letters of their language, and how to string those letters together to form words. None of it made sense to me. Elijah always tried to help, whispering to me, even if this led to the both of us being switched.

One morning I remember him sitting beside me in the schoolroom as Sister Magdalene watched us children struggle to form words in her language. It was one of the rare times she allowed us to speak in whispers to one another. 'You take this letter here,' Elijah said, drawing a *g* on a piece of paper. 'And then you put this letter beside it.' He drew an *o*. 'And then if you place this letter beside it, you have a word.' He drew a *d,* and I stared at the strange marks and asked him what it meant. 'It says "god," stupid!' he laughed.

Sister Magdalene scowled at us in warning.

'And what is "god"?' I asked.

'Gitchi Manitou,' Elijah answered.

I was very impressed by this. *God* is still the only word in their language I know how to write.

'Teach me another,' I said, staring down at the paper in front of me. Elijah drew another word from letters. Again I stared, this time at four letters squiggled on the paper. 'And what does this mean?' I asked.

Elijah's eyes brightened, and a smile stretched across his face. 'It is what comes out of Sister Magdalene's bum,' he giggled.

I looked at him, beginning for the first time to understand the power of these letters and words. Elijah's giggles entered me too, and we tried to keep them in, but this only made us laugh harder. Sister Magdalene stormed up to us and Elijah tried to crumple the piece of paper, but she ripped it out of his hands.

She stared at the paper for a long time, her mouth a tight little line across her face. We stopped laughing. She began shaking, then dragged both of us from the room by our ears. I was sure mine was partially torn from my head. Outside of the schoolroom, in full view of the children in it, she tore a thin branch from a tamarack and pulled down our pants so that we stood exposed. First she forced me to bend over and struck me until I cried out in pain. She continued the switching until I fell over in a ball, tears falling onto the dirt.

Then she did the same to Elijah. I looked up at his face

above me and he winked as she began hitting him, then smiled to me as he cried out in mock pain. When it began to truly hurt him, though, his cries became real, until he too crumpled on the ground beside me. For good measure, Sister Magdalene struck us a number of times while we lay on the ground and covered our heads. 'I will strike the heathen from thee,' she chanted over and over. I was not allowed another pencil or piece of paper again in my short stay in that place.

I look to Elijah and Gilberto laughing together, and even as they do, something tugs at my insides. I can see that Elijah is pulled away from this moment by the strong tide of wanting to try the morphine again. I know now that it is more than medicine. Much more.

OUR SECTION SITS TOGETHER, our socks and boots off, carefully examining our feet for signs of rot. In a couple of days we will be back in the lines, but for now we enjoy the warm weather and the rest in this place by the field. Graves talks under his breath to Fat. I wonder what he speaks about.

We all know Graves has seen far more battles than the rest of us. He is many years older, although how many years we are not sure. He was in Africa fighting the Boers when I was just a baby. I wonder how it is that he never made it to Officer after so many years in the army, until he explains to me that he left the army and came back only when this war began.

'I had nothing at home,' Graves says. 'My wife left me. We never had children. I had a factory job that the army's wages could match. They all said it would be over by Christmas. I remembered my youth and the hills and valleys of Africa, the beautiful black-skinned women, the horses and cannons, our khaki uniforms. I says to myself, it all must sure as hell beat what I have here in Toronto. So just like Sean Patrick I lie about my age and the deal's done. This hell,' he says, looking around us, 'is not what I signed up for.'

Fat, Graves's puppy, nearly Graves's son, asks, 'And you, X. Xavier Bird. How is it that a man comes by a name like yours?'

I've learned my English over this last year but still have trouble sometimes understanding Fat. I've told them all already where I am from, that I am James Bay Cree. What more do they need from me? I tell Fat once more the story of me, of my name.

Next time, I think to myself, if they want talk, I will tell them to talk to Elijah. We've been in the trenches for only five months in their time, but Elijah's killed five men for every month that has passed. He is Whiskeyjack the Indian and Whiskeyjack the killer.

The other soldiers often ask Elijah about his name too. And he is happy to talk. His Cree name is Weesageechak. But that is something he doesn't share with the *wemistikoshiw*. Whiskeyjack is how they say his name, make it their own. He has told me that what they do to his name is what sounds to my ears like a longer word for *bastard,* making his name a name without a family.

Weesageechak is the trickster, the one who takes different forms at will. Hudson's Bay Company traders could never pronounce it with their thick tongues. But they saw the trickster in the whiskeyjack, the grey jay that loves to hear his own voice, is bold enough to steal food from their hands when they were not watching.

But here in this place Elijah is something more than just a bird, something more than the rest. Bigger and yet still more slight. Invisible.

The last few weeks in Saint-Eloi are quiet again. The end of August has arrived already. I know that it won't be too long now until we are sent to the Somme. Oh, how Elijah wishes that we would be moved down now. Me, I can wait. Word travels to our company of heavy trench fighting in places with names like Sugar Trench, Candy Trench, even a place called the Sugar Factory. And we are stuck here, Elijah says, as the newly formed Fourth Division is moved in to take over Saint-Eloi.

Between stretches at the front we are given leave to go into the village behind the lines five miles to a small house that serves as a pub, where we drink French beer and wine and cognac and shout back and forth to one another over the noise of living men. The soldiers call these places estaminets. Sometimes women come here and men line up to be with them in little rooms in back. The owner, he sees what happens but seems to ignore it. I watch it all, absorb it, but I am too shy.

Elijah takes me to the estaminet every chance he can in the weeks we are in this area. I learn to drink like the soldiers around me and get drunk enough once in a while that I talk freely with them. Twice I've seen a girl come in here, but she isn't like the others. She's shy like me and is thin with long hair that she wears on the top of her head. Elijah notices her too, and I feel a sharp sting when he sees me notice her and then boldly approaches her. They talk for a while, but I can't make out what they say over the noise of this place. She smiles at him and I begin to feel very sad.

Elijah returns to our table after a while. 'See that one there?' he asks in Cree, not wanting the men around us to understand what he says. I nod without looking to him. 'She's the daughter of the owner. Nice girl, but not worth the wasted effort when I can just pay one of the others for what I want.'

'True enough,' I answer, my sadness beginning to lift. I look to the girl across the room and think I see her smile at me before she turns away.

'Never mind her,' Elijah says, pushing back from his chair and standing. 'Let's get you a little something special. My treat.'

I shake my head, but he grins and walks toward a backroom to line up with the others.

When we return to the front lines I can't take my mind off the girl. She smiled at me. I'm sure of it. I smoke cigarettes in my section of the trench, send prayers up that we remain in this place just a little while longer.

And we do, despite the rumours that we are to head further south. This time when our section is relieved, I am the one to lead Elijah back to the estaminet. I walk quick along the dark road, and the night's late when we arrive, but still the place is busy. I've been here with Elijah till morning sun has come up, and still the old man behind the bar won't close it.

I look about, but his daughter isn't in here. My heart sinks. I buy a bottle of wine and drink most of it very fast. Elijah watches and drinks along with me. He buys another bottle when the first one is gone. And then another. When I am afraid I won't be able to stand any more, I see the girl walk in the side door of the place, carrying a large box that is obviously heavy. Standing without thinking, I almost fall over and have to grab the table. When I feel balanced again, I walk to her, bolder than I ever imagined I could be.

'I am Xavier Bird,' I tell her when I get to her, reaching

clumsily for the box and almost dropping it. She stares at me, her eyes afraid. 'I am not here to hurt you,' I blurt in English, my words slurring. 'Me, I don't even like hurting Germans.' The words sound stupid, but she smiles and nods like she remembers me.

'You will help me, then?' she asks, and I nod too much. 'I have many boxes still to carry.'

Her accent is not one I have heard much. It is beautiful. She is beautiful.

I place the box on the bar and see that her father ignores me.

'Come with me,' she says.

I follow, trying to walk straight as I can.

She leads me outside, and I keep my eyes on the ground so I do not have to meet any of the soldiers' eyes that I can feel staring at me.

The night is cool and helps me to focus. 'Where are the other boxes?' I ask.

She looks down at her feet. 'There aren't any others. It is too loud in there, and I wanted to talk to you.'

I'm surprised. 'Me?' I ask. She begins to walk away, and I don't know if I am supposed to follow her. I do anyway. We walk along a path that leads away from the lines and don't say anything for what feels like a mile.

'Your friend, he says you like me,' she says. Once more I feel surprise. 'I do not like him, but I like you.' She looks at me and then away.

I don't answer. I don't know what to say.

We walk again and I feel her take my hand. My heart begins beating like I've run a very long distance.

'I have to go back now,' she says. 'My father will be

worried.' I look at her and want to kiss her. 'Will you meet me tomorrow?' she asks.

'Yes,' I answer without even figuring out if I am to be in the line again tomorrow. We walk holding hands, and I remember through the fog of drink and scent of this girl that I still have another day before we are to march back.

When we can hear the noise of the estaminet down the path, she stops and looks up at me. I lean to her and kiss her. She kisses back. We kiss until my lips are sore and I do not know how much time passes. When I kiss her neck she makes little moans.

'Is it tomorrow yet?' I ask, and she laughs, kissing me again. I didn't mean to be funny.

'I have to go,' she says. 'Meet me here tomorrow after supper.'

I don't know when her supper is but don't mind waiting. I will get here in the early afternoon.

'Your name!' I ask as she walks away. She stops and looks at me. 'I don't know your name.'

She giggles. 'Lisette,' she says, turning, going.

With all of the drunken men around here, I worry for her safety, and so I track her back to the estaminet. I watch with a chest that feels full of light as she walks to the door of the little building beside the estaminet and enters it. This must be her home.

For fear of losing any of this memory of her, I don't go back into the estaminet. I walk past it and return to our camp. I see that Elijah has not returned, and I am glad for it. I lie until sleep comes, remembering her eyes, her mouth, her hands on my face. Just below the smell of mud on my tunic I think I catch the smallest trace of her.

I am up early and my head pounds from the wine. At a stream near the camp I strip down, entering the freezing water, bathing myself carefully, trying to remove the lice and mud from my hair. I scrub myself with sand for a long time, and then I take my uniform into the water and scrub it with rocks, holding it under to try and drown the lice. Once I put it back on, still wet, I feel the lice return to my skin for warmth. I remove my tunic and run a candle flame along the seams to kill as many as I can.

It is still not even afternoon when I am done. I avoid the mess area. I'm not hungry and don't want others around me right now. I'm forced to meet with them for roll call, but avoid talking. Elijah's head hurts too, I can tell, and this keeps him from prying. When we are all relieved, I force myself to walk away from camp until I am out of sight. Then I rush to the path behind the estaminet, and I sit at the place where Lisette showed me.

I wait for a long time, long enough that I am worried she won't come. In the bush I find a few little flowers past their bloom and collect them for her. I wish I had something else to give.

Night approaches when I hear her coming. I stand up and make myself visible. Lisette walks toward me. *Lisette*. I've repeated her name over and over today. It comes easy off my tongue.

She smiles when she sees me and takes my hand. I want to pull her to me and kiss her, but instead we walk back the way we went last night. We turn off the path and she leads me to a small pond. Enough light is left that when she stops by it and begins to remove her clothes, I can see how thin she is below them. Now I wish I had brought her the lunch I did not eat today. She lies back in the grass and shivers a little. I take my clothes off too and place my tunic over her, worried about the lice that might crawl onto her.

She smiles and we hold one another, feel each other's heat. I am hard against her belly. She places her hand on me and I can't stop the noise that comes from my throat. I place my hand on her warmth. We kiss deeply and, before I know what is happening, she is on top of me, her head back and mouth open.

She calls out and I worry others might hear. I raise my hand to her mouth and she bites me hard on the soft spot between my thumb and finger. Lisette drops her head down then, and her hair falls between us, tickling my chest. I can't take that for long, and roll over gently and push inside so that we both groan. I want this to last, I want it to go on so that I never have to return to the front, but when Lisette grabs my waist and pulls me into her so hungrily, I feel myself slip over the edge like a canoe over rapids until we are both rushing down, the trees and rocks around us flying by, warm white water reaching up and swallowing us, sucking me down into a beautiful darkness until I can no longer stay under. I burst up for air, and look down to her. We are both wet from our movement. Lisette glistens under the rising moon.

We hold each other for a time and don't say anything. When the night chill finds us, I pull our clothes over us and we kiss again. This time is slower. I stare down at the beautiful girl and she holds my head in her hands. When I sense that she is close I lean and kiss her small breasts, suck on them until she begins to shake and, without knowing that I do it, I move quicker too until we both shiver together once more.

'I must get back now,' Lisette says to me not long after,

pulling her clothes back on in a hurry. 'I have much work to do for my father.'

'I can walk you back?' I ask.

She shakes her head. 'If anyone saw us, I would be in trouble.'

I want to ask to see her again, but she leans down and kisses me. Then she is gone. I lie in the little bit of moonlight and think of the ways I might find her again.

TWO DAYS LATER we are sent away from Saint-Eloi. We march to the trains and are packed on like livestock and begin the crawl to this place of brutal fighting. I am silent and unhappy for the whole ride, and it is obvious why, but Elijah knows enough to let me suffer. 'The only cure is time,' he says to me, but I don't answer.

Behind the lines we are given fresh clothing and new long winter coats and we are deloused once more and are infested again by the next morning. The command sends the Canadians new rifles, British Lee-Enfields.

The Ross proves to jam at the worst of times and is responsible for the deaths of many Canadians in the heat of battle. Once again it is the fault of the commanders, I see. They supplied the Canadian troops with British-made ammunition, and the British ammunition, a tiny bit bigger than ours, jams in our rifles when fired repeatedly. I keep the Mauser taken from the German sniper, and Elijah opts to keep his Ross, far better than the Enfield as a sniper rifle.

The troops pore over their equipment, especially their weapons, and are resupplied with fresh stocks of ammunition. Grey Eyes has sniffed out a medical box packed with morphine syringes. I lovingly disassemble my new Mauser and reassemble it, go out to the makeshift range with Elijah where we sight it in carefully and Elijah re-sights his old Ross. Not many rounds of ammunition for the Mauser can be located, and so I am careful not to waste any, but Elijah promises me that we will go on a raid specifically to acquire some more. The weapon is beautiful and accurate, lighter than Elijah's rifle. Its scope is magnificent. A leaf can be examined fifty yards away. I politely refuse all that Elijah offers in trade for the rifle.

Behind the Somme we make camp at a place called The Brickfields, a miserable landscape of rubble in which, like rats, we dig holes to sleep in. We mingle with many others who along with us await their turn to move up and fill the forward trenches. Brits and Canadians and blue-uniformed Frenchmen with long moustaches and even Australians in bush hats and Scotsmen in kilts queue up. Some approach Elijah and me and talk with us, and only then do I realize that we are building a reputation as a sniping and scouting team. Do these strangers know that Elijah has most of the kills and Elijah is the one who volunteers for most of the raiding parties? It seems obvious that his reputation around here precedes him. Gilberto, Grey Eyes, Fat, Graves, even McCaan puff up a little when complete strangers approach our section with handshakes and offers of cigarettes.

The only sight at The Brickfields that is not depressing is straight up in the air. Despite the wreck of the world below, the birds continue to fly above it as if nothing has changed. Elijah and I lie on our backs when we are afforded time from sentry duty or drill. Flocks of small sparrows swoop and chase each other endlessly.

A little over a year ago Elijah and I were very different from the soldiers we are now. But Elijah is still daring, still talkative. He still wants to fly.

He talks about the time we took a train from that town where we'd bought our clothes. It was our first time on a train. I felt sick to my stomach with the swaying, amazed and frightened at how fast the trees and creeks swept past us. We headed south. A man in a uniform said to us, soon as we got on, 'No Indians in this car.' He pointed down the aisle. 'You belong four cars to the back.'

I remember Elijah turning to explain in Cree to me, but I understand. We pick up our packs and walk through the river of people who ignore us. We push our way through the doors to the next car, then the next, then the next.

Here it is much different. A few other Indians sit here, staring out the windows, not bothering to look up when we walk down the aisle. The seats are wood and uncomfortable. The smell of animals in the next car is strong.

We choose a bench and once again settle in with our packs at our feet. Elijah's mind is not on being forced to leave the good car. He thinks taking this train will be something like flying. But he can see that I'm unhappy.

'Did we not pay the same price for tickets as the *wemistikoshiw*?' I ask angrily. 'Do we not wear clothes just as fine as theirs?' If the situation were different, Elijah would egg me on more than he decides to do.

'Look at your moccasins!' he says, pointing down at them. 'Not only are they falling apart, but the stink of them! That is the real reason we've been sent back here with the bush Indians.'

A few older ones close by laugh at his words.

Soon after, Elijah tells me that he does not think this is at all like flying. The train groans and lurches. It is more like we are on the back of a sick cow than an eagle. Elijah glances over at me. I know I look a little green with the swaying. The other Indians in the car do too. Some stare at their feet with their arms wrapped about their midsections. Others sleep restlessly. Elijah is impressed, though, with what passes by the window, the green smears of trees and the flash of black creeks coming into view, then gone for good. He stands up to see what this movement without moving his feet feels like. That is more like flying. He walks along the length of the car with arms outstretched, staring out the window. I know he imagines himself weightless.

'Xavier!' Elijah shouts. 'Try this!' He swoops past me and caws, turning by the door to take another dive.

'Idiot,' I say. 'You embarrass me, you.'

Elijah flies by me and drops an imaginary turd. He can feel the eyes of the other Indians on him. 'What?' he says. 'Have you never seen an osprey?'

Two young girls and a boy giggle at him. He winks. Their young mother is pretty. Elijah gains altitude with a few sweeps of his arms. The train hits a curve and throws him onto a bench beside an old sleeping man. The man's eyes open.

'Whiskeyjacks should fly better,' he says.

Elijah looks at him. 'How do you know my name?'

'I don't,' the man says. 'I was dreaming. There was a flock of whiskeyjacks.' He looks confused. 'They were pecking at something dead.'

Elijah stands and walks back to me.

'What did the old man say to you?' I ask.

'He knew my name. Claims he was dreaming of whiskeyjacks.'

'It's a sign,' I say.

'Everything's a sign to you.' Elijah looks out the window. 'Hey, *there's* a sign,' he says, pointing outside. 'It says Abitibi River. But you wouldn't know that, considering you're a heathen.'

I look at him, then look away.

A wide river passes a hundred feet below us. Our stomachs rush up as if we are falling. We stare at the river running north back to our home, and for a moment I know that Elijah feels as sad as me.

'Look at that island,' Elijah says, pointing to a spit of sand that forces the river to split, a few trees on it. 'It's like the island we slept on when we finally made it out of the fire.'

He stares at the black water, then at the bank of mud and sand, lighter against it. I know he will miss this place, he realizes at this moment. But he will not dwell on it. Just as quickly as we came upon the river, we are past it.

MAMISHIHIWEWIN
Betrayal

I AWAKE EARLY on the second full day of our paddle to find that once again Nephew has slept outside by the fire. The morning is cool, and so I build the fire bigger. I brew some tamarack tea and sit by him, begin talking even though his eyes are closed and he may not hear. My words will sink in.

Listen carefully, Nephew. My Frenchman came back to visit me often in those first months of our bonding. I moved to my summer place when the season arrived, letting him know where to find me. He visited me there too, and like the frozen rivers that gave way to the warmth, something inside me broke and flooded so that all I wanted was him.

You must realize once more, Nephew, that in this world of hardship we must grasp the moments that are offered to us. My Frenchman and I were voracious, consuming one another so that we were constantly sore in the most pleasant way. We said little, but over the summer we each learned some of the other's tongue. Our language was the physical. We loved against trees, on riverbanks, in the water when it was warm enough. It was a good summer. I'd visit my mother and she saw the difference in me, knew what I was discovering. She made me drink bitter tea that kept me from becoming pregnant. She warned me with her eyes to be careful of this one, that *wemistikoshiw* were not to be trusted, but I ignored it, too full of him, too flushed with him.

The autumn called us away from each other, he to hunt moose for his town for winter, me for a very different reason. That feeling came back to visit me, the one that brought warning of difficulty to come. I went back alone into the bush to decipher it, rebuilt the shaking tent frame that I'd let collapse and grow moss.

For days I tried to summon the souls of animals to come to me in my tent, but it was as if I'd somehow offended them and I sat there for hours at a time, praying and rocking, burning sweetgrass and searching the blackness for something to show itself to me. My first thought was that by losing my childhood I'd also somehow lost my power to see beyond the day. Or maybe it was that I'd chosen a *wemistikoshiw* for a mate. I realized that this is how I thought of him now, as my mate.

It struck me that I could not focus on both. And so I chose him. I was young and the emotions of the young are as strong a pull as the Arctic tides that suck fishermen's canoes out into the bay to be lost forever. I walked out of my shaking tent with no answers to what was coming, and the not-knowing was a strange relief. Not having to be the one divining answers was a weight lifted from me. I could just be normal, suffer the sweet pains that came with my young age. The bad feelings of danger still nudged at me, but I pushed them away with thoughts of him.

Winter came upon us again, and I kept my own dwelling now, having made sure that my mother was safe and living with other *awawatuk*. The Frenchman came to me often, and we kept each other warm through even the coldest nights, but as spring approached once more, a mood came over him. He did not smile as often and visited me less. When he did come to me, he did not love me as frequently as he had. I thought I smelled another on him, but the scent was never the same, and so I pushed those thoughts aside.

At the time when the snow begins to melt during the day and then forms a hard crust at night, an *awawatuk* from the marten clan came to me with a request. I knew when I heard the man approach on his snowshoes that he came to ask me a favour, that it would begin a chain of events that I was powerless to stop.

The Frenchman was with me. We brewed tea inside my shelter. We both went quiet at the sound of snowshoes approaching. A visitor in winter is rare and not always welcome. A winter visit often means that bad fortune has descended. I motioned for my man to sit and wait while I went outside to see who'd come. Outside I recognized his face. He was an old hunter who was known to be one of the last of the great trappers. His look confirmed what I sensed, and I knew then that what I'd been trying to push away had arrived now as surely as a blizzard.

After a formal greeting he told me how he knew and respected my father, how he also knew that I was my father's daughter and had inherited his gift. He explained that his clan was hungry and had bad luck finding meat. He wanted me to divine for him, had brought a moose's shoulder blade along with him from his part of the country.

I had no choice. Turning around, I walked into my lodge and told the Frenchman he had to leave. He didn't put up a fight, but packed his things. Although he could not understand what the old man requested of me, he suddenly understood that I was not simply a young woman living in the bush alone. I lived alone for a reason. I had a gift that others wanted and needed. I was frightened by how sullen this made him, how he stopped speaking to me.

Before he left I whispered to him that it wasn't his fault but that I had to be alone to do what was needed. I asked him to come back soon, but he didn't answer. He left the lodge, leaving only the sting of his anger.

I walked out behind him, saw the surprise on the old trapper's face at the sight of a *wemistikoshiw,* a look that he quickly covered, pretending indifference. When the Frenchman disappeared into the bush, I opened my door to the old *awawatuk* and built up my fire.

With the return of spring and of the blackflies, life grew a little easier again. But my Frenchman did not come to visit me. By early summer I wondered what had happened and spent long nights inventing stories. He'd hurt himself and lay prone in a bed in that town pining for me. Or he was all right but waited stubbornly and patiently for me to come to him and tell him I was sorry for so briskly dealing with him that late winter morning. In my darker moods I imagined him with other women.

I visited my mother and we spent long hours fishing and not saying very much. The silence was comfortable. I knew that she knew I had been visited by an *awawatuk* in a time of crisis and had done what I had to. She could also sense that I was alone again, that I ached for the Frenchman and the ache was not going away. My mother finally broke the silence.

'I would never have married your father if I had not pursued him,' she said. 'I hunted him like you hunt a bear. I found out where he lived and I paid him a visit.'

I smiled at this story, my first smile in months, it seemed. For the first time in a very long time I felt sure now of my next move.

Late that summer I packed a few clothes and a few days'

rations and left my spot by the river. I began to paddle my canoe back to that place I had promised myself I would never return to. For the couple of nights I was alone on the water I built small fires onshore and stared up into a sky that took many hours to turn dark.

Some part inside nagged at me about what I was doing. I counted shooting stars like I was a child again. Every time I predicted the swath of light that cut through the sky just before it happened, I'd dare myself to turn back home before it was too late. But I didn't. When I smelled the rotting garbage smell of that town again, I was immediately brought back to the day years ago when I had come here with my mother and young sister.

I beached my canoe close to town around midday. The sun was setting by the time I built up the courage to walk through that place and look for him. I went through the Indian part of Moose Factory first, looking for faces that I knew. There were many that I recognized from my childhood and from my brief time at the residential school, and immediately it was obvious that an invisible wall, one impossible to breach, lay between me and the homeguard Indians of this white town. My clothing was in the old style, a style that only a few of the elders still knew how to make, most of it from the hides of animals.

But that was just the most obvious difference. The Indians here seemed full, full of food, full of drink, full like I saw the white men look full. I became almost envious walking around, feeling the stares burrowing into my back. For so many years it was as if I'd gone hungry. My body was smaller than the others', having rarely been able to feed itself to full. But I was struck as I listened to families talking and friends laughing and children running and shouting that what I had starved for was the company of others, others like me. When I realized that day that there were no longer others like me, my legs shook so hard in the middle of the dirt street with people all around that I thought I would fall down.

Parents called their children to them when I came close. The old converted Indians blessed themselves and closed their doors when I walked by. Young men pointed to me and stared when they thought I was not looking. The other talent the Cree have to rival their hunting ability is their ability to gossip.

When the sheer weight of the attention became too much for me, I looked for the fastest route out of this part of town. As I reached the edge of it, an old woman, her face as wrinkled and round as a dried apple, beckoned me to her with a long bony finger.

'*Ashtum*,' she whispered. 'Come here.'

I walked to her and she opened her door to me.

'You are the one,' she said, smiling toothless at me when I was safe inside. Her little cabin smelled of tanned hide and good food. She sat me down at her table and brought me a bowl of stew. 'Eat, then we'll talk.'

I ate and she watched me carefully, none of the formal politeness of averted eyes in her at all. 'You must watch yourself around here,' she said. 'Or the same thing that happened to your father will happen to you.' I looked up to her, at her bold words. 'The Indians around here know. You can't stop talk from travelling. Some of them are happy that the old ways are still alive out in the bush. But there are lots of them Christian Indians now who are not.'

I nodded my thanks for her warning. 'Do any *wemistikoshiw* know? Should I leave this place?'

'I don't know,' she answered. 'Probably they don't. You'll know as soon as you see them what they know. They are not very good at concealing their thoughts from their faces.' She laughed at this and I did, too. It felt good.

'Tell me more, *Kokum*,' I said after a while. She brought me tea and I sipped on it and waited.

'There is talk that a certain *wemistikoshiw* trapper was fucking you,' she said, smiling at me. 'But that rumour I am not sure of, since it comes from their side.'

My smile dropped. 'So that is the rumour?' I said.

She looked at me. 'So it is true!' she said. I didn't respond, didn't need to. 'Be careful of that one. They say he has a taste for red meat that he can't satisfy. There are little half-French, half-Indian children running around this place that he refuses to claim.' I nodded thanks for the warning. 'This is not the place for you, Little One. You are a *hookimaw*, from a strong family. Happiness is not yours to have. You are a *windigo* killer.' She said this as if it were a sentence being passed down.

She got up and went to a trunk near her bed, rummaged through it for a while, then came back to me with a handful of clothes. She held them up one by one so that I could see them. They were the clothes of *wemistikoshiw* women, a long cotton skirt, a white cotton shirt, a brightly coloured bandanna to tie about my head.

'Wear these,' she said. I shook my head. 'You must wear them so that you fit in with the others. Those clothes you wear make you a target. You look like a bush animal come too close to this human place.'

I took the clothes from her, thanked her as I made my way to the door.

I could feel her eyes on me as I walked back to my canoe.

I camped that night a little way from that place, my head buzzing with the knowledge that my world was not nearly as secret as I thought it was or wanted it to be. So they knew everything! I grew angrier with each passing hour, so that by dawn a plan had formed in my head. I bathed for a long time in the river, scrubbing my hair until it shone, rubbing my body to pinkness with the soft bottom sand. I changed into the clothes the grandmother had given me and carefully and tightly braided my hair on each side of my head. At high noon, I walked back into the town, a smile on my face so that I appeared a different woman, a shy, young homeguard Indian.

I walked toward the spire of the church, to the place where the residential school sat blank and white as a dumb child's face. I had not meant to go here, but suddenly the idea of seeing Rabbit—your mother, Xavier—swept over me. Staying a distance away, I waited until the nuns released the children for afternoon play. I looked carefully through the group of older girls, for my sister would be fifteen winters now, but I did not see her. I stayed and looked until the nuns herded the children back inside.

Nobody stared as I walked through the *wemistikoshiw* part of Moose Factory. The grandmother had been wise about my clothing. All of these people seemed too busy themselves with talk or movement. Most of them seemed late for something, rushing about with heads down. No one paid me any attention, and this made me more confident. I walked down the dirt road of the big street, staring into the trading post, the livery, the butcher shop, the pub.

It was in this last place that I spied him, eating his dinner with another man at a table near the window. A long day had passed, and I realized how hungry I was suddenly. I stood a ways from the window and waited, willing the other man to leave. Seeing my trapper again brought back the feeling in my stomach, made that place low in my belly ache. To my delight, the man sitting with him picked up his hat, stood and left. I waited as long as I could, then walked in.

At first he looked at me like he did not recognize me. He thought I was another young Cree woman, and in that second I saw that everything the old woman had said about him was true. But when he smiled at me with his white teeth, his whiskers pointed like a wolf's, I didn't care. I would take him back to the bush and keep him there, change him so that he no longer desired this place of humans.

'Niska,' he whispered, smiling at me. He stood, walked to me, hugged me.

I felt all of the eyes of this place on me and I pushed myself from him. A flash of anger sparked in his eyes for only a second, then something else that I could not read.

He made a motion for me to sit with him, called to a man who worked there and spoke to him in French that I did not understand. Then he looked at me, his hands on the table, one crossed over the other. He began to speak slowly in his tongue, staring into my eyes. 'I missed you,' he said, putting one hand closer to mine. I just stared back. 'I miss you here,' he said, 'and here.' He moved his hand to his heart, then to his crotch just below the table's lip. He smiled at this, and I did everything in my power not to smile back. The man he'd spoken to returned and placed two glasses filled with yellow liquid before us, then left.

He held his glass up to me and smiled again, waiting for me to raise my glass too. I knew what it was he offered, but I didn't care. I could no longer bear the weight of the last days, and in that first sip realized that this might be a way to let them sit someplace else for a little while. The drink tasted bitter, like bannock gone bad, and the taste did not leave my mouth quickly enough. I watched him raise his glass to his lips and drink deeply so that the bump in his throat bobbed. He put his mostly empty glass down and ran the back of his hand across his mouth, staring at me. I took it as a challenge and picked my glass up, choked it down fast as I could. I almost gagged, then smiled back at him. He made a motion with his arm to the man who'd bring more.

Outside the window of this place the night came. At first I watched the sky's colours change with a child's awe, but as we drank more, a sadness came to me just as the last of the bright light left and the serving man brought candles to all the tables.

'No more,' I said to him, standing up and walking out suddenly, so suddenly that I surprised even myself. My legs felt like a new calf's, loose and long under me so that I had to grab the door frame as I passed through it. I walked down the dirt road, trying to figure out if I was going in the right direction or not, the night sky beginning to spin above me. I did not know or care if he followed me at this point. The cool air on my face felt good.

I was not sure if it was me or some other force that carried me back to that school and the tall peak of the church, but I found myself standing in the same place I'd been in the morning, looking for Rabbit. I called out her name, softly at first, but when nothing came back but the sounds of the crickets, I cried out louder. Over and over I called out her name, willing her to find me, to comfort me, to bring me back to our mother, to our father. I felt hands on my shoulders and spun around, but it was him instead. He hushed me with a finger to his lips, whispering warnings as he looked around him with wild eyes.

'*Ashtum,*' he said to me in my language. 'Come with me.'

He took my hand and led me toward the church. When I realized he wanted to take me inside, I struggled against him. '*Mo-na,*' I said. 'Don't take me in there.'

'It is safe here,' he said. 'It is a holy place. A place to talk to the Father.'

I followed him as he pushed open the big door, then shut it behind him. The smell was everywhere in here, like cedar, but too strong. He walked straight down the aisle, and I could do nothing but follow, running a hand down one row of benches as I went, letting them steady me. He stopped by the table in front of all the benches. It stood on a small rise of wood.

'This is where a man takes a woman to be his forever,' he said to me, pulling me to him and kissing me.

I began to wonder how well I felt as he kissed me, but pushed the thought aside and let my tongue touch his.

'This is a good place, a holy place,' he whispered, biting at my ear. 'You are a holy Indian, no?' he whispered. 'The other Indians say you are very holy, very strong.'

His lean body pushed against me. I could feel his hardness. I did not answer him but kissed him back instead. 'You want me for you?' I asked as best I could in his tongue. He smiled and nodded. 'Here is the place?' I asked, looking at him. He smiled and nodded again. I kissed him. 'Us?' I asked.

He smiled and picked me up, sat me on the table. He pulled my cotton dress up so that I was exposed to him, then lowered his head and kissed me there with his tongue. I held his hair in my hands, and when I could not take it any longer I pulled his mouth up to mine and kissed him deep. His hands struggled with his belt, and then I felt him thrust in me until I called out. He panted and we rocked and then I felt him tense inside of me too fast, too soon. I wrapped my legs around him so that he would stay inside a little longer. Finally he pulled out of me, and I stretched out on the table, looking up at him, my head spinning.

He laughed. 'I fucked you in a church,' he said, and smiled. I smiled back at him. 'I fucked the heathen Indian out of you in this church,' he said, but this time the smile was not happy. 'I took your *ahcahk,*' he said to me, the smile gone now. 'Do you understand? I fucked your *ahcahk,* your spirit. Do you understand that?'

He stared down at me, his eyes wide with a look that made my stomach feel ill. I pushed him away with my legs and covered myself up.

'It's too late,' he said. 'You are nothing special, just another squaw whore. I took your power away in this place and sent it to burn in hell where it belongs.'

Suddenly I felt my guts churn and only knew that I needed to be out of this place. The too-strong smell of cedar made my head pound so that I needed to throw up. I jumped up and on shaky legs ran toward the door. It felt like forever, but finally I reached it and flung it open, the contents of my stomach rushing up and spewing onto the steps below me. I fell to my knees, but heard his boots approaching from behind. I reached for my knife on my belt but realized that I did not wear it with these white clothes. Pushing myself to my knees, I ran fast as I could toward the river, expecting any moment to hear his footsteps catching up with me, to feel his hands grabbing at me.

I made it down to the river, my head pounding, my mouth dry and sour, the world around me spinning. I looked back to see if he followed, but all I could make out in the darkness was the blunt block of the school on the ridge overlooking the river and the tall arm of the church stretching up into the night sky. I crouched and sobbed, afraid that his magic had killed my family's fire inside of me, and it was only then that I realized he was a spell-caster of some kind and he'd stolen my strength.

The stink of their tobacco and drink and especially of him wafted up from the clothes that I wore so that I thought my head would split. I stood and tore them from me, ripped every stitch from my skin and flung the material into the river and finally I stood naked under the moon, my head back and mouth open, the howling of a hurt animal constricting my throat.

Falling on all fours, I drank deeply from the river to ease the burning in my throat and my pounding head. Then I stood shakily and began to run. I ran along the riverbank, not caring about the sting of bushes on my naked thighs, about the sharp rocks under my feet or the branches of the trees that hung low. I ran until I closed in on my little camp and my canoe. I ran fast enough to try to catch up with what I'd lost back there.

I did not wait till morning but began to paddle my canoe immediately, and I did not stop paddling until I reached my home, keeping up my strength by vowing a thousand times never to return to that place. The fear that he really had taken my power from me chased me all the way down that river.

I slept long and deep as soon as my head touched the floor of my lodge. When I awoke I knew what to do. Choosing the stones carefully from the riverbank, I heated them up in a fire for a full day as I carefully constructed a lodge according to my father's directions. Round after round I opened the flap to that small place and crawled inside, poured water on the rocks so that the steam became a living, burning thing, and prayed to the four directions and to the earth, the sky, the water and the air, pouring more water onto the rocks until I thought that my lungs would catch fire. I prayed harder for purification until the pain became ecstasy, and when I completed the last round I crawled out of the lodge and collapsed on the cool ground, the world around me a fresh and clean place again.

When I heard the Frenchman's voice in my head, my fear and anger came back to me so that I needed to prove to myself that I still had power. I constructed my shaking tent and went inside to pray. It did not take long for the spirits to come to me. My tent filled with a light as if a thousand fireflies had entered it. And then the spirit animals began to arrive, the spirit of the bear, the moose, the fox, the wolf, the sturgeon, rallying around my hurt in that tent like night insects to a fire. It was the lynx that came to me most strongly, his growl puffing out the walls of my tent like a great wind trying to escape. And I asked the lynx a favour that would change me forever. I asked him to go out and find the source of my hurt and extinguish it. As soon as I whispered my request, the tent went silent and the light of the spirit animals left it, so that I lay on my back in the dark of night, alone and shivering.

I tried not to think of that night again. A sense of peace came over me as I prepared for another winter alone in the bush.

It was just shortly after the first hard freeze that my old

mother travelled out to see me. I was surprised at her visit, had thought her days of travel were behind her. But I was happy to see her. I heated up water for tea and warmed moosemeat over a fire and we sat comfortably with one another for a time. We ate and talked of small things, and as the evening grew dark she told me that word had come to her that the Frenchman had gone mad in that town and taken to running up and down the streets trying to escape pursuing demons. She watched me for a reaction, and when I did not give her one, she finished her story by saying that no matter what he did he could not escape them and so he ran to the top storey of the hotel on the main street and flung himself through the window. The same priest who had taken me away to residential school years ago deemed the death of the Frenchman a suicide and refused to give him a Christian burial.

I stared into the fire for a long time after that story, not able to look at her.

MISTATIMWAK
Horses

IF I AM TO TAKE ALL of it at once and in this way end my pain for good, I will have to do it soon. Only a few needlefuls are left, and I do not know what I will do when it is gone. All morning Auntie paddles me further north in even strokes, sometimes humming songs to herself, sometimes speaking directly into my muffled world with stories of her youth. My body cries out for the medicine so loudly that I decide not to even try to hide what I do.

Right there in the canoe, I extract the needle and the rawhide from my pack, prepare my bruised arm and inject some directly into a vein, just enough to take the knife's edge of pain away. I can feel Auntie's eyes on my actions, and I feel like a pathetic criminal under her gaze even though I know she does not judge me. I want to talk to her about all of this and know that soon I must, but for now I allow myself to drift back to the comfort of old friends.

On the day before we are to move up into the trenches once more, Sergeant McCaan comes to Elijah and tells him that it will be at the very least a couple of months before Thompson returns and that he would like Elijah to be acting corporal until then.

Elijah barks out, 'I'd be delighted, Sergeant,' and as he walks back with this news swelling inside him he begins to count the freedoms that come with the rank. But it still doesn't help him to take a shit, he tells me. He's been bunged up from the moment Driscoll gave him the morphine. At least his arm is out of its sling.

Me, I'm clearly invisible to the officers. How is it that Breech refuses to recognize that it isn't only Elijah out there killing Fritz? We are a team. If nobody will recognize this, maybe I will force them to.

Our battalion is sent to a village named Albert, close enough to the front that Hun artillery reaches it easily and constantly. The Allies hold the town, but with a good view of the surrounding countryside I can see it is clearly a prize that Fritz would like. Not much left of the one side of this town except for rubble. But on the morning that we move up to the front of the town, Elijah and I see the most amazing thing since our arrival in France. The Virgin Mary, golden and thirty feet tall, rises up from the ruins of a great church. She leans at such an angle that we wonder how she's not tumbled to the ground. She holds a cherubic baby Jesus in her arms, and his chubby weight seems to threaten to topple her further. Elijah tells me he thinks he sees a look of serene disapproval on her face as she stares down at the fighting below.

It seems that this leaning virgin has become a symbol for the troops that surround her. Talk circulates that she's a miracle come to life, that as long as she stands the Allies will not lose this town. Some go further and say that as long as she stands the Allies will not fall, either. But if she does tumble so will they, at the hands of the Germans. There must be something magical to her, Elijah says. Fritz has played a game for months, sending artillery in her direction, but thus far has not been able to send her to the ground.

'Her crown would make a perfect sniping position,' Elijah

jokes to me, and the joke suddenly becomes an idea he can't shake. If only we were within sniping range of any Hun!

Our company moves out of Albert and up the Albert–Bapaume Road under cover of darkness. Everyone is tense. We are entering the place that has devastated the British all summer, the place of the thundering artillery that echoed in our ears for months. But tonight is eerily calm. Near the place called Courcelette we take cover by the road and await morning anxiously. Courcelette is held by Fritz. The Canadians are to try and take it.

While the others close their eyes and pretend to sleep, I watch Elijah sit and jiggle his knees, wishing for the light to come so that he can see the layout of this place. Breech has ordered that Elijah and I are to move out in an advance position and do what damage we can when the Canadians go over the top and attack Candy Trench, one of the trenches guarding Courcelette. We have been told that a candy factory once stood nearby, but I do not know if this is true.

McCaan has already warned us not to go out directly in front of the Canadian line. The Canadians have thought up a new strategy, something called a creeping barrage. Our own artillery will walk through no man's land, and the infantry will follow. 'You and X don't want to be caught in front of it when it happens,' McCaan says. He shows Elijah on a map the approximate width of the creeping barrage. Elijah has already figured a plan. He and I will head as far to the right of the platoon as we can, which will put us directly south of Courcelette. We can enter no man's land that way, find a place of good cover and snipe as many Fritz as possible when the Canadians go over the top.

Elijah and I sneak about on higher ground behind our own

lines the next day, peering through our scopes for hiding places in the field. There seem to be plenty. Destroyed barns, tumbled houses. Sunken roads and old sap lines crisscross the area. Now we must find a good place from which to shoot at Boche and still not get smashed by our own artillery.

I spot the site first. A slight ridge crests up from a wrecked farmhouse halfway across no man's land, maybe five hundred yards in. This means a five-hundred- or six-hundred-yard shot into the town itself at any Hun support troops and no more than a two-hundred- or three-hundred-yard shot at the front trenches. The distance is perfect, the cover seems like it will be perfect, and there's a natural escape route out behind the ridge if we are spotted. It seems almost too good to be true.

We spend the rest of the daylight hours peering through our scopes at this place, Elijah working out in his head all the possible scenarios. Good cover from artillery and machine-gun fire. A wide view of the German lines, although this might leave Elijah and me open to snipers from the other side. The Hun trenches curve gently around the farmhouse so that they are exposed on a wide angle, which is good for us but also makes us more open to fire. And then there's always the possibility that the farmhouse is being held by Fritz. Neither Elijah nor I have seen any movement around it all day, but that means nothing.

When dusk settles, we lie on our backs beside one another and stare up at the evening sky. Purple-streaked, fading into black, the sky is pinpointed with the light of stars rising in the east.

'What do you think of that place?' I ask in Cree.

'I've a good feeling about it,' Elijah says.

'Me too,' I answer.

'Then that settles it.'

We make our way carefully back to our own line and report to Breech. McCaan has made sure to join us so that he knows where we will be. Elijah and I see how little McCaan trusts Breech. Elijah tells them of the wrecked farmhouse and the ridge, the good line of fire that he and I will have, the escape route if necessary. Breech holds his chin, doesn't answer for a long time. Is he going to say no, I wonder, with us forced to stand here like children awaiting a parent's decision? Apparently Breech is reconsidering sending us out. Elijah tells me later that he had decided already that he would go anyway if Breech ordered us to go over the top with the others tomorrow.

'All right, gentlemen,' he finally says. 'But I want results.'

Elijah and I salute and turn to leave. McCaan follows. We walk along the trench together, McCaan instructing. 'Bring enough food and water to last you at least a couple of days. Bring plenty of ammunition. Don't forget anything. You won't have a chance to make it back safely until tomorrow night at the soonest.'

'He's like a worried father,' I say in Cree.

Elijah smiles.

We take off our boots and pull on our moccasins before we make our way down the trench and slip over the top while no flares brighten the sky. We carry more gear than we normally would out here, Elijah's and my ammunition and rations tied into sacks that we wear strapped tightly to our backs so that they don't slip or let the contents rattle. Elijah cradles his Ross, the scope carefully wrapped in rags. I carry a rifle in each hand—my treasured Mauser and another Ross. We do not have enough rounds for the Mauser alone, and when I run out I will have to resort to the other. I have even sighted it in.

We go slow, taking cover and waiting behind whatever we come across. We plotted our route out carefully earlier in the day, finding the way that offered the most protection. We blackened each other's faces with charcoal. We checked each other's gear. Elijah checked his moosehide bag. I didn't know at the time what it was that he was checking inside.

Now we are only a couple of hundred yards from the collapsed farmhouse. The desire to crouch and run to the ruins is very strong, but I know to ignore it.

We slither closer like snakes until we are a stone's throw away, lie still and listen, watching for a glint of movement. Nothing much is left of the barn's structure but the cellar and beams collapsed across it. We stare at the outline in the low light and see the best place to enter, the place by the ridge. Elijah signals to me that he's going and for me to follow and take a position to cover him.

The cellar is black, and if anyone is in there, he is very good at hiding.

It is easy for me to see him, imagine Elijah closing his eyes and asking the medicine to help him. A low glow behind his eyelids. He can't smell the vinegar stink of the Hun. He slips in, trying not to make noise, but kicks a stone that rattles on the floor. Something on the other side scurries then settles. A rat, maybe. Elijah crouches and removes his pack, lays his rifle beside it, slips his knife from its sheath and his revolver from its holster. He looks up above him, senses more than sees me above, rifle ready, as I lie with most of my body out of the cellar. I will cover Elijah.

Elijah makes his way along the littered floor. Beams and bricks make most of it unmanageable, but a small path weaves through to the other side. He takes a few steps in his moccasins, stops and listens. A few more. Slight moonlight through the beams by the place from which Elijah wants to shoot at the German lines. Something on the floor below it? A body, maybe, wrapped in a blanket. He looks around carefully but he senses nothing else here. He sneaks up to the form on the ground and prepares to stab the knife deep, but the bundle is just a sheet of rolled-up canvas. The blood pumps through Elijah so that he can feel its heat on his skin.

One more long look about the place to quell his nerves, and Elijah gives a low whistle for me. I come up soundlessly with all of the gear. We break it open and prepare ourselves for the coming morning.

A round of howitzers down the line and behind us shakes the broken beams near where I sit. I would sleep if my nerves allowed it. Elijah is fidgety, stands up from beside me once in a while to peer over to the German line. Rifle fire crackles out in bursts, but other than this it is a relatively quiet night.

Elijah sits back down. 'Tell me a story, X,' he says. We still have a number of hours before daybreak.

For a moment I have no words, then ask, 'What do you want me to tell you?'

'If I knew that then I would tell *you* a story,' he says. 'Tell me something that will take my mind away from this night. You never talk much, and it might be good for you.' I see his teeth flash in the darkness.

A long time passes before a memory comes to me from somewhere in the night. It is not a happy memory, or a welcome one, but Elijah asks again for me to speak and so I give in. It's a memory he already knows, but one that I know he likes. And so I tell it to him as we wait for morning.

Elijah remembers the ship we rode on to England. I'd never have believed a ship could be so big if I had not ridden in one myself. And I did not know waves could be so large as those out on that winter ocean.

Early in the voyage and at dawn the seas are twenty and thirty feet high. Men hold onto whatever they can. All of us violently sick. The ship does not give to the waves like a canoe but rams them, fights each one, metal groaning. I've taken the horses as my own responsibility. But down here is far worse, the boom of waves bouncing, horses panicked and kicking stalls. Elijah visits me and sees that I am so sick I can barely stand, but still I stay with the wretched animals, trying to calm them. He knows me. I feel comfort with animals. They make me feel closer to land.

Elijah tells me about up top where he stands in the blasting wind, the salt spray freezing to the deck so that it's impossible to walk on. He tries to stay out of the wind best he can, squeezes against a wall behind a post, staring out at the mountains of water and angry whitecaps all around him, imagining himself slipping as the ship climbs a wave, sliding down and off the icy deck to the freezing water below. This much water frightens him. He is so drained that nothing is left to come out of him. They've not served a meal because it's too rough, but Elijah cannot imagine eating anyways.

Below decks, men talk of German U-boats patrolling like great iron fish all around the North Atlantic. They find a ship like this one and fire torpedoes until the ship is ripped apart, then surface to watch the men struggle in the freezing water before drowning. They take no prisoners. Elijah talks about this with me down below when he has the stomach to do it. The waves have not receded. They've gotten worse. The animals look frightened, but they're gaining their sea legs, bracing themselves at the right moment, learning to relax when they can.

Elijah and I lean against a stall. Being this deep in the ship is confusing to our senses. It is harder to gauge when we are climbing a wave or when we are falling, and the boom of steel smacking water echoes like the deep bellows of a wounded moose. The ship groans down here horribly. The smell of the horses' shit, of their fear, is overwhelming.

'How do you stay down here?' Elijah asks me in Cree. 'Why don't you come up above with me?'

'I like it with the horses,' I say. 'I'm worried I'd be flung off the ship into the sea up there.'

'You know about the U-boats?' Elijah asks.

I look at him, wanting a story.

'They are boats that can travel underwater like fish and fire great bombs at ships and sink them.'

'Boats can't travel underwater.'

'Where we stand,' Elijah says, 'we're underwater now. Their U-boats operate according to the same thinking.'

'They can't do anything to us in this weather,' I say smartly.

'Under the water you don't know if it's stormy above. It's the perfect time to hunt us. Our attention is focused on surviving the storm.'

'I can't worry, me, about what I can't control.'

Making it to the troops' sleeping area is difficult. I only bother to go once. Some men lie in hammocks that swing wildly. Sean Patrick seems to be having fun, his long legs dangling over the side, him calling out like a child when we pass the crest of a bigger wave. Graves and Gilberto sit on the floor lodged against footlockers. They attempt a game of

Crowns, cards slipping around on the crate between them.

Graves looks up at me and says, 'You look like death warmed over, X. I warned you about these winter gales.'

Elijah is beside me. He translates. My English is still quite poor. Elijah looks over to a groaning Fat who lies on the floor like a stranded whale. 'That's no way for a soldier to act,' Elijah says, but not loud enough for Fat to hear. The others chuckle.

Elijah steps toward Fat and bends. He asks if he can help in any way.

'Make the waves stop,' he pleads, and Elijah realizes that he means this. Fat is delirious. 'Can you shoot them with a rifle?' Fat asks. 'Deflate them before they hit us?'

All forms of routine have been stopped by this gale, exactly what the officers don't want to happen. Even their regular lectures have been postponed. For them to pass up a chance to hear themselves speak surely means this is a serious storm.

I go back to the horses, calm one with wild eyes. I see a large bloody spot of skin on the horse's flank where it's been rubbed violently against the stall. I try to apply a salve, but the animal is too frightened. I squeeze myself between the horse and the stall's side and begin rubbing in the ointment. The other animals grunt and whinny. A wave hits, sending them all to one side, pinning me hard between the heavy beast and the wall. I groan and slip out, slick with the salve, my face and clothing smeared.

I have heard Elijah tell this next part of the story to others in our battalion. He tells them how he remembers the shaking and slapping that woke him. His eyes are glued shut, and when he manages to open them, he sees me slapping him, my face ashen. I did not know then that he had tried the morphine only the evening before.

'Two horses. Broken legs,' I say.

Elijah can hear them. They kick the sides of their stalls, give high-pitched whinnies of pain. How did the noise not wake him? I pull on him, and we head back to the stalls. A young soldier stands by them, looking scared. As I climb into the stall where the horrible screams pour out, Elijah peers in. Two horses lie on their sides, awkwardly trying to stand. They are both crying loud, eyes turned back so that the whites show. I stand uselessly between them. They've shit a horrible liquid stench. This whole sight is not good so early in the morning.

'What happened?' Elijah asks. 'Were you with them when this happened?'

I shake my head. 'I was over there resting.' I point to a little place between crates padded by burlap. 'This one was with them.' I thumb to the soldier who stands there. The soldier obviously can't understand what Elijah and I say, but he understands our tone. He looks like a boy about to be switched by a nun. The horses scream louder.

'We've got to get a sergeant, get a gun,' Elijah says. 'Wait here.'

And so I wait. Elijah tells how he runs along the stalls and to the stairs that lead up. He makes his way along the crowded passageway. Most of the men appear asleep. The ship still tosses but not as badly now. The odd, larger wave sends the ship off centre. It must have been one of these that scared the horses.

Up on deck a fine mist blows, not quite snow, not quite ice. The deck is treacherous so that he must pad cautiously and keep a hand on any purchase he can. The waves are long, rolling the ship up their backs and sliding it down. Cross waves hit from a completely different direction at times, jolting the ship in a way that's unnerving.

He gets to the officers' mess and sees four or five of them sitting, trying to drink hot tea from porcelain mugs. They act as if he isn't there.

'Sirs,' Elijah announces. They stare up at him. 'There is an emergency with the horses. Two are down. It appears that their legs are broken.'

'Who's your section officer, Private?' one of them asks. From his insignia, Elijah can see that he's a colonel with the 48th Highlanders.

'Lieutenant Breech, sir,' Elijah says.

'Ah, Ontario Rifles causing this disturbance,' the colonel says, giving the others glances. They smile.

'Aren't you the one,' another speaks up, 'who beat our man in the marksman competition?'

'No,' another one says. 'He was in the finals, but it was the other Indian.'

'Sirs,' Elijah says. 'Yes, I was there. But there are injured animals in the hold.'

'They can wait,' the first officer says.

All of them seem tall and look the same with their carefully groomed hair and moustaches. Elijah recognizes two of them from his medicine vision the night before.

'Where did you learn to shoot?' the officer asks.

'Near Moose Factory, where I am from, sir.'

'You're a hunter, then?'

'Yes, sir. With all due respect, sir, the horses.'

The officer waves his hand, as if shooing insects. 'In that part of the country do you stalk your game?'

'Yes, sir,' Elijah says. 'Sometimes for days.'

'That skill will come in handy,' another one says. 'He'll make a fine scout. We need to recruit more Indians to our regiment.' The others laugh.

'But will he perform so well amidst the roar of cannon?' the first officer asks. 'It's one thing to hit a still target on a range or chase an animal through the forest, an animal who won't shoot back.' He rubs his chin and stares at Elijah.

Elijah looks around him. They all stare at him, appraising him as if he is some interesting new creature they've not seen before.

'You speak nothing like any Indian that I've ever imagined,' he says. He looks at the others. 'You speak better than I do!' They all laugh.

'I was raised by nuns and have a talent for language,' Elijah says, then pauses. 'Sirs,' he says once again. 'Two horses are gravely injured and are panicking the others. We must do something immediately.'

'Go raise Breech,' the lead officer says to one of the others. He gets up and walks past Elijah.

Elijah continues to stand impatiently at attention. The others go back to their tea, talking in low voices. Finally Breech appears, pink-eyed with his uniform jacket undone, McCaan behind him, dishevelled, his heavy coat thrown over his undershirt, his red hair standing up. Elijah sees, though, that he has his revolver strapped on. Elijah explains the situation and they turn to leave.

'I think we'll join you,' the lead officer says. 'The storm seems to be abating and it's been too long since we've been below decks.' The officers stand as a group and all of them head out into the wind.

They are more surefooted than Elijah would have guessed. Breech is the only one to slip, banging his knee hard and cursing. Elijah smiles. He leads them along and into the passageway, then down the stairs to the troops' quarters. Inside, the air is heavy with the stink of many men squeezed into one place, the smells of vomit and sweat and stale cigarette smoke like a fog so that the air is almost unbreathable. Below all of this is the smell of horses.

'Bloody hell,' Breech grunts out.

The looks on the men's faces as they see officers approaching makes Elijah smile once more. All routine has fallen apart. Men are unshaven. Clothes are wrinkled and dirty. Army habits are gone. But now with the officers among them, attitudes suddenly change. The more observant ones crawl out of hammocks, smooth clothes, pat down hair, stand erect with heels together, fight to hold that pose against the ship's rock. Elijah looks back and sees some men getting up and standing straight even after the officers pass them.

As they make their way down the final steep stairs that lead to me and the horses, Elijah realizes that something is different. Another thick smell comes up from the hold. He can't hear the horses screaming. The young soldier who'd been on watch bolts up the stairs toward them, face pale and mouth open. He pushes past them with crazy eyes, not seeing or caring that these are officers he jostles in his rush to get away.

'You!' Breech shouts at him, but he has pushed past and disappeared.

Elijah is the first to get to the long row of stalls. Horses snort nervously through flared nostrils. Elijah recognizes the smell now. It is the smell of a successful hunt. In front of the injured horses' stalls the floors are sticky wet. The lead officer

214

looks down at his shiny boots and lifts one up. His reaction is calculated.

'Open these stall doors,' he says to Elijah.

He does as he's told. All of them stare down at me. I look up, sitting cross-legged with one of the horses sprawled beside me, its head on my lap. I look like I've been painted red. The smell of blood is heavy. It covers the wooden walls, the floor, the straw upon the floor. Elijah sees that one of my hands rests on the floor with my skinning knife in it. The horse's neck gapes open along its big artery.

'My God!' Breech says.

'What in the bloody 'ell?' McCaan spits. The other officers stand there, staring.

I look up at them all. Elijah told me later that the white of my eyes was ghostlike against my red-smeared cheeks and matted black hair.

'The other, it is dead too,' I say in English. 'No choice. Legs broke.'

Elijah is told to open the other stall. It too is sprayed red. A horse lies awkwardly in the little space, neck slit and tongue hanging out as if it is tasting the bloody straw.

'I'll have you up on charges!' Breech shouts to me.

'Now, now.' The colonel speaks up immediately. 'Let's consider this for a moment.' He stares down at the scene, twirling the tip of his moustache between two fingers. 'It was no mean feat to dispatch two powerful animals with only a knife. What choice did the private have?'

'Shall I have him arrested?' one of the officers asks.

'On the contrary,' the colonel says. 'I suggest we commend him for valour.' A couple of the others laugh nervously. 'He exhibits the best traits of an officer. The ability of judgment under duress, the will and strength to carry out unpleasant and dangerous duties, decisiveness.' The others nod at his words, bracing themselves against the ship's rock. 'Lieutenant Breech, dispatch some soldiers down here to help these two Indians clean up this mess.'

'What about the two horses, sir?' Sergeant McCaan asks.

'Throw them overboard.'

The officers leave except for Breech. Elijah watches as Breech leans to me and hisses, 'You will never become an officer.' Breech walks away.

'Did he say what I think he said?' I ask in Cree. Elijah nods. 'Why does he hate me?'

'I'm not sure.'

Within an hour Elijah, myself and a number of others are shovelling out the stalls and wheelbarrowing out the old straw and manure and blood into a pile where it is collected in burlap bags, brought above deck and thrown overboard. Now that the seas are more manageable, Sergeant McCaan has our section cleaning not just the stalls of the dead horses, but all of them. A big task to deal with, the shit of these fifty horses.

Elijah watches as his burlap bed is dismantled. Gilberto and Sean Patrick throw themselves into the work. They are happy to stretch their muscles after days of inactivity. Fat shuffles about uselessly, getting in everyone's way, complaining bitterly of the stench. Graves takes charge of things, directing a group of privates to get the cargo winch and slide rope under the dead horses. They lift them up and out of the stalls that way, position them below the cargo hold opening. They will have to wait until the seas are flat or risk waves pouring in and sinking the ship. Grey Eyes, Elijah and I work side by

216

side, shovelling and lifting until our backs ache to stand and our arms burn.

The skies stay grey and heavy for the next five days. Finally the order is given to open the cargo hatch and winch out the horses, stiff now with death and beginning to smell. Elijah and I watch as the horses drop awkwardly over the ship's side, tumbling and bumping before splashing into the water. They bob black before being sucked down by the wake.

OMAWAHTONIKEW
Collector

As THE MORNING LIGHT GROWS STRONGER, Elijah climbs onto a beam that allows him a view from the cellar. He can make out the landscape more clearly. The German trenches appear to hover in the mist ahead of him and not so very far away. If he didn't know better, he would think they were abandoned. The Canadian lines stretch off to his left. From this position he and I will have a hawk's-eye view of the action if the smoke from the barrage isn't too thick. I sit beside him, my eyes closed. I'm resting but not sleeping. Elijah knows this. He removes a syringe from his hide bag and injects just a little of the medicine into his arm. Since being wounded in our raid, he has given up fighting the morphine. 'I'm just dabbling with it,' he likes to say with his English accent.

'Soon,' he says now in Cree.

I open my eyes and stand and stretch. I take a piss in the corner and climb onto the beam beside Elijah. Our rifles are perched there, waiting for us, resting in a space between the thick wooden supports that offer good cover and a wide view. Elijah peers through his scope at Fritz's line, notes the position of smoke rising from cook fires. He trains his scope on the town behind the lines, the place called Courcelette. The place isn't big but is full of smashed houses. Even if the Canadians can take Candy Trench and Sugar Trench, he can see the town will prove difficult and dangerous.

A whistling sound fills the air and the earth erupts a couple of hundred yards away from us. The beam we stand on vibrates crazily so that we wonder how secure it is. We cover our eyes from the light and wait. It is the creeping barrage that McCaan spoke of. Elijah nudges me, shouts to me over the din, 'Watch our lines. Soon you will see us go over the top.'

Sure enough, a few minutes later we watch as Canadians begin to climb over the side of the trench, move in waves, walking almost calmly, bent at the waist with their rifles pointed ahead. The barrage steps closer to the Germans, and smoke and dust block their lines from view. The Canadians advance unscathed, and I think that this creeping barrage is the answer. The *thud* and *crunch* of shells hitting the mud and exploding washes over us. A hundred yards away the men approach in thick groups, closing in on Fritz's trenches. We can tell from the explosions that the barrage falls directly on the Hun's line now. But then as suddenly as the barrage began, it stops. I wonder why out loud, my voice hollow in the cellar. My ears ring. They have begun to do this more and more in this loud place. I'm worried for my hearing.

'We're afraid of crushing our own,' Elijah says. I read his lips to understand.

An odd silence suddenly descends for a short time, enough that I can hear the clinking of the Canadians' gear over the ringing in my head, the *thump* of their boots on the ground. Elijah is so caught up in this that he forgets everything else. He stares at the advancing men, swears he can see light shining from the ones about to fall. Everything seems to move as if underwater, but then the silence is sucked up by the swift drumming of machine guns. I begin to fire my rifle right beside Elijah, shocking him out of his reverie. I aim at the

Hun lines, firing at the yellow cough of the machine guns through the haze. Waves of Canadians begin to fall with the noise, as if on cue.

Elijah turns, sights into his scope and finds the machine guns through the smoke. We set in just above the flashes and fire mechanically, pumping round after round at each bright spurt until it stops. Then we move to the next. Much rifle fire sounds now, and our targets seem endless. I choose a flash of light through the smoke, aim just above it and fire. I know that my bullets penetrate skulls.

Elijah must stop to reload magazines, the world outside erupting, ending for so many. His fingers work fast as they can. I fire a shot, pull back the bolt and push it forward with the simultaneous *clink* of the spent cartridge ejecting, aim, then fire again. Elijah joins me, firing quickly but steadily just above the rifle and machine-gun flashes. Dozens we must have killed in this last short time. Dozens!

'We should have brought a light machine gun with us!' he shouts as the Canadian troops advance to the point where aiming at the Hun is becoming tricky without hitting one of our own. 'Look, X! Look! We are going to take their trenches!'

The ringing has dissipated, but I pretend not to hear him, just keep shooting when a target presents itself. Elijah turns his attention back to the firing.

An hour later the Canadians have swarmed that part of Candy Trench and they move along its traverses, Fritz falling back to Sugar Trench and beyond. Elijah and I hurry to pack up our gear and leave the cellar, dragging the piece of canvas with us. We have an idea.

Along another rise, a much higher one, we find a spot with a view into Courcelette. The good positions to fire from don't offer any cover, though, so we get to work with our knives and the canvas, slicing holes into it and slipping branches into the holes. In ten minutes we've created a blanket to cover ourselves with. Elijah crawls under and asks me to stand back and look at it from a short distance. When I crawl back inside I tell him that we've become a part of the earth. We poke our rifles from underneath the canvas and scan the ruins of the town for Hun.

From here we have an excellent view of the fighting going on in the trenches and of what's happening in much of Courcelette. I spot a group of Fritz setting up a machine gun on its tripod beside a crumbled wall, but it must be more than seven or eight hundred yards away.

'What do you think?' Elijah asks.

'I've only got a few rounds left for the Mauser,' I say, 'and I am not used to this Ross any more.'

'I'll shoot,' Elijah says. 'You spot. Tell me where you see the round hit and direct me to the soldiers if I miss.'

Elijah peers through his scope and finds the target. The men are a long way off, even through the looking-glass. A little wind blows, and he estimates he must aim just above them to hit them from this far away. He sights in on the one instructing the others, aims above his head on the assumption he will hit him in the chest, and pulls the trigger. His bucking rifle doesn't allow him to see the outcome, but I immediately report, 'He's down. You hit him in the neck.' I know Elijah focuses in and sees the man writhing on the ground. Immediately I think of Sean Patrick. Elijah reloads quickly as the other three bend to the man, aims at the one with his back to him and fires again. The man drops. 'He's down too,' I say. 'Fire again before they take cover.' Elijah reloads and takes aim at the blond-haired one who looks up toward him with a look of wonder on his face. Again, Elijah aims above his head and pulls the trigger. 'You hit that one in the neck as well!' I whisper. Elijah sees through his scope it is the blond one's turn to writhe. Before Elijah can fire at the fourth, the man scrambles behind the wall and out of sight.

The best shooting I've done, Elijah says, looking at me.

I stare at his lips and nod. My hearing has left me once again with Elijah's gun so close to my head.

Are you having trouble hearing? Elijah asks.

I understand from the way his lips form the words. 'Too much loud noise,' I say in English.

Before dusk, the town is overrun by the Canadians. Elijah and I make it back to the trenches of the night before. Exhausted, we find Lieutenant Breech and report to him. Sergeant McCaan is somewhere in the field. Breech listens to the report, Elijah talking, me standing wordless behind him. Breech sounds incredulous when Elijah reports taking down the machine-gunners in Courcelette.

'Was an officer present to verify?' Breech asks, standing and stretching.

'No, sir,' Elijah says.

'Your claim seems a little exaggerated to me.' Breech laughs, as if other officers are in the room to laugh along with his humour.

'I'm a good judge of distance, sir,' Elijah says.

'Yes, I'm sure you are,' Breech answers. 'How many canoe lengths did you say they were from you?' he says, smiling, sitting down and picking up his pen. 'I'll make sure to note it in my report.' He stares at Elijah, his smile daring him to respond.

Elijah smiles back. 'Very good, sir. Very good joke!' He's good at hiding his anger.

'Get some hot food and an hour's rest, then re-equip yourselves. Report is that Courcelette is putting up stiff resistance still.'

Elijah and I salute and leave. The medicine is almost gone now, I can see, and Elijah feels the headaches coming. Although he cannot remember the last time he ate, he's not hungry.

'I need to sleep for a while,' he says to me, finding our dugout and crawling in.

'I'll be here,' I say, crouching by the entrance and leaning on my rifle.

Elijah lies down and feels the lice crawling, closes his eyes to the artillery exploding and rifles cracking not so far away.

For the next two weeks Elijah and I move about, searching out the enemy from a distance. Breech orders us to report back often, noting any enemy movements we see, even the sighting of smoke from cook fires. The Canadians have cleared out Courcelette and now focus on taking the Hun trenches to the north, trenches with names like Hessian and Kenora and Regina. Elijah and I concentrate on harassment fire, finding weaknesses in their trenches and shooting at parties as they try to work.

Eleven days after Courcelette, another big push begins, and we watch for the first time a tank rumble across the field. I'd heard the rumour of them during the attack on Candy Trench, didn't know whether to believe that these great iron monsters were real. But there one is, rolling past our nest on the very edge of Courcelette. To the left of us, troops march behind it, and Elijah and I ready ourselves, searching out machine-gun nests in the smoke and rubble hundreds of yards away. Fritz is not so ready to give up these trenches today, and Elijah and I fire our rifles and watch as hundreds of Canadians fall ahead of us. For a moment I feel like I'm watching something private that I shouldn't be, Canadians on the ground screaming out in pain or lying still as the earth, but then the black anger washes over me and I fire the Ross I'm forced to use until the barrel is too hot to touch and the poorly made rounds begin to jam.

No more ground can be won in this area, and after the Canadians' gains, both sides dig in once more. Our company is sent back to Albert for respite. The men drink hard. We join in even though I'd rather retreat to somewhere private. I'm not enjoying this war like Elijah is.

Elijah, he tells me a story of a night in Albert. He has no choice but to tell me. I am his listener.

One evening he climbs the steps of the basilica, rifle in hand. He's drunk on wine and the morphine courses through his veins in such a way that he floats more than walks. He makes his way up the crumbling bell tower, scaring pigeons out of their roost. Their wings beat into the night and he watches as feathers fall about him, reminding him of fat snowflakes, then of home. It is the wrong time for melancholy, it will ruin his mood, and so he straps his rifle onto his back and makes his way out the window of the tower and onto the ledge. Above him the giant virgin leans straight out, glowing gold in the night, her baby Jesus in her hands as if in offering to the war below. He climbs up to the roof and scrambles onto the foot of the statue. He scuttles up further so that he straddles her. Shimmying, he makes his way out along her back, daring himself to see how far he will go. She seems to be anchored to nothing, and Elijah's weight as he rides her back like she is a great horse threatens to knock her down, smash her into a thousand pieces on the ground below.

He's made his way to mid back and makes the decision that he will reach her golden crown. She shakes with the effort of holding him as he slides out further onto her. Elijah is surprised to find he's become hard with the excitement of this. He has his first erection in months, it seems. He lies flatter on his stomach and continues sliding himself up her back, the ground below beckoning them to it, Elijah shaking now as much as she is, her crown almost in reach. He stretches his arms up to the rim and grimaces, pulls himself the last foot to her head and begins to convulse in waves, the virgin below him vibrating along with him.

He lies there a long time, staring down at the world below. Reaching into his pocket he pulls out a cigarette, lights it and inhales. He unstraps the rifle from his back and peers through the scope into the night. There isn't much light, just the rage of battle on the horizon. He focuses in on that, the dancing colours just like the *Wawahtew* back home. He cannot escape thinking of the place he comes from on this night. He slips off the safety and aims at the dancing colours, squeezes his trigger, firing a single bullet into the light.

In the freezing rain of late November, we march back into the forward trenches, and Elijah tells me his world would be a perfect place if only he were able to rid himself of what he eats. It seems the medicine won't allow him to.

Constant back-and-forth shelling around here and the trenches have been pummelled so often that some of them are more like shallow ditches than trenches. A constant threat of being attacked looms over us. More days of cold, relentless, pelting rain than days of dryness, and even with duckboards, the trenches fill with water. Many men fall to pneumonia, and many others suffer skin irritations from being constantly wet that turn into nasty festers. We've been issued tall rubber boots that reach up to the thighs, but in many places these are not even tall enough and fill with water. A new expression to describe the condition of feet rotting in watery boots has appeared. When the soldiers see that their feet are black and swelling, they call it trenchfoot.

Elijah and I immediately think of home here. In the spring and autumn when we goose hunt along the rivers and the sodden, soft shores of the Great Bay, we live in cold rain for days on end and must learn to navigate the mud. It is a part of Cree existence. Elijah and I don't complain like the others but focus our energy on staying alive and finding the little comforts, wait out the autumn, and avoid the shells that scream in randomly from the grey sky. We wear the tall moccasins I made for us a long time ago back in Canada. They dry quickly and allow our feet to breathe, and in this way we avoid foot trouble. The moccasins are the one break in dress code that McCaan will allow. 'Just don't let Breech see them,' he mutters.

Trench raids against Fritz are impossible right now as they are too well dug in, and even night patrols are rare in this weather. The mud and water hold the Canadians captive. We dig deeper into it and await what winter will bring.

I am sick of the corpses around us, but in his boredom Elijah volunteers for burial detail, taking the dead out of the line and down the dangerous alleys of support trenches that are constantly bombarded, stacking the corpses in rows like cordwood and helping with the digging of graves. 'It isn't all that difficult in this soft muck!' he says. They try to bury the dead out of range of Fritz's guns so that they won't be disturbed again. Elijah goes through the dead men's pockets and takes out coins and combs, pictures of wives and girl-friends and children, Christian medallions to help ward off death, letters from home and letters not yet sent, billfolds, knots of hair, baby teeth, bullets, cigarette cases and lamb-skins, morphine pills and wedding rings and baptismal certificates and prayer cards and maps and wills and poems. Elijah places these things in envelopes and marks the names of the owners of them and brings them in piles to the officer.

Before he leaves a corpse, Elijah tells me he has taken to opening each man's eyes and staring into them, then closing them with his calloused right hand, letting a strange spark of warmth accumulate deep in his gut each time that he does it, noting the colour of the iris, knowing that he, Elijah, is the last thing that each will see before being placed into the cold mud and water here. Before they go to their place.

Elijah, he says the spark fills his belly when it gnaws for food.

PAHKONIKEWIN
Skinning

ON CHRISTMAS, what seems like an uneasy peace settles over the trenches for a few hours. For the first time since I've been here, the pounding sound of the big guns does not serve as background to everything that we do. The quiet is unsettling. Our section is one of the lucky ones sent back in a nice bit of timing to behind the lines where festivities for the troops are planned. In a nearby village a great rowdy affair begins and the rum runs freely and we run from house to house drinking and visiting with soldiers from many different places. Gilberto is as happy as I've ever seen him and has become close with Graves and Fat. The three walk ahead of Elijah and me, arms around each other's shoulders, singing an Italian song that Gilberto knows, a bottle between them.

Grey Eyes catches up to us with his glassy eyes dulled a little by the drink. He has been scouting around and brings with him half a goose stolen from the table of some British officers a few houses back. We all tear off a chunk and I eat mine as I walk, the taste reminding me of that place where I was born that feels so impossibly far away right now. I look to Elijah, his lips smeared with the fat of the goose's skin, and in his eyes I see the sadness of what he too feels.

The sound of an accordion and a fiddle comes from a darkened house along the street and we are all drawn to it at the same time. Inside, Frenchmen with blue uniforms and dark hair and unshaven faces sit around a room lit by candles and sing in accompaniment. The words are soft and pretty and the music swirls around my rum-filled head so that I feel a peace I've not felt in a long time. I look over to Elijah. He feels the same thing, I see. He goes to a corner of the room and lets himself slide down the wall so that he's sitting on his haunches, eyes closed and head swaying with the sound. The music stops but I know it continues to echo in his head as it does in mine. Eventually, he sits and stretches his legs and opens his eyes, seeing that only I remain in this room with the Frenchmen, keeping an eye out for him.

The men act as if Elijah and I are not even here, talking and gesturing and drinking from the many bottles on the table. A few of them hold long knives with thin, wicked blades and brass knuckles for handles and play games with one another, placing their hands out on the table and spreading their fingers, allowing the other to tap the point of his knife as fast as he can between the digits, a blur of glinting metal between fingers. Elijah is mesmerized by the game. He stares with his head tilted and his mouth held loose. One man, tall and thin and wiry strong, stands and gestures wildly with his knife, then acts out a scene of struggle with an imaginary enemy, sneaking up behind him, making the motion of slitting his throat, then grabbing the head of his crumpled enemy on the floor by his hair and slicing the scalp from the skull. He is good with his movements, fluid so that I can tell he has done that very thing many times before. The men all raise glasses and repeat words that I don't know, then drink again. I'm as fascinated as Elijah.

Just when I'm beginning to wonder whether they even remember that we are among them, the tall, wiry one turns to us. He neither smiles nor sneers, but just stares for a while. Elijah is looking away, but I know he sees everything anyway. I meet the man's gaze and hold it till the Frenchman motions for us to join them at the table. We are given a bottle of thick red wine. Elijah takes a deep drink.

'You do not look like the Canadians that I have seen,' the wiry one says. His voice has a heavy accent, but his English seems good.

The other men continue to talk with one another, but I can tell that they are listening.

'I'm an Indian,' Elijah says. 'From the North. This one too, but he doesn't speak much English.'

'Does he speak French?' the man asks.

Elijah shakes his head. 'He is a heathen, speaks his own tongue fluently, nothing else.'

I look to Elijah and I think only then does he realize how much my English has improved these last months that I understand his joke.

'I've heard of one of you Indians, a Canadian too. They say he has killed many, many men, that he is the best hunter of us all.' Elijah smiles and is ready to nod his thanks for the kind words when the Frenchman continues, 'His name is Peggy, and he works alone.'

Elijah has heard of this Peggy just as I have. Neither of us has spoken about him lately since he hasn't been active.

'I hear rumour that he is dead,' Elijah says.

'No, he is not dead,' the thin one answers. All in the room are listening now. 'He just works alone. His C.O. refuses to acknowledge all the kills he makes since he doesn't like to work with a spotter. But he is the best. He has killed many Hun.'

'I would like to meet this Peggy,' Elijah says.

We all drink and Elijah and I listen to them talk their French, and I can see he grows angry thinking about this Peggy. What kind of name is that, anyway? I can hear him say to himself. Getting up, I watch as he makes his way outside and to the back of this house, the voices and music wafting out the open window. He notices the cold as he rolls up his sleeve and searches for skin that is not too bruised. Even in the darkness he can see the black discoloration running up and down his arm. He takes the short needle from the moosehide bag in his chest pocket and slips it in quickly, efficiently, wincing as he hits a tender area. His whole arm is tender. Elijah practises self-control, knowing as he floods his vein that he is using the medicine right now out of anger. Just enough goes into him that he no longer feels the pain of his arm or of the cold. The golden halo settles down around his head, and he's protected once more.

When he turns to go back inside, he's startled by me standing there, watching him.

'I don't like these ones,' I say. I talk in Cree. 'Let's find the others.'

'I would like us to stay for just a while longer.' Elijah wants to find out more about this Peggy.

'I will wait outside, then,' I tell him.

I wait, listening and watching.

Inside, the men continue to drink and some of them are very drunk, fighting with their knives in a type of practised dance that Elijah hasn't seen before. They come very close to cutting one another but always manage to pull back at the last moment, even in their condition. Elijah sits back down with the thin one. He tells Elijah his name is Francis G.

'I know who you are,' Francis says. 'There is talk about you and the silent one.' Elijah nods to him. Everything really is better with morphine. 'You two killed the Boche sniper by Saint-Eloi.'

'We did,' Elijah says. They sit without speaking for a time.

'Avoid what happens to Peggy,' he says. He smiles at Elijah now. 'Do what we do. Collect evidence of your kills. Do what my people taught your people a long time ago. Take the scalp of your enemy as proof. Take a bit of him to feed you.'

Elijah doesn't know how to answer this. He smiles. 'And what will collecting these trophies really do for me?' he asks.

'They will buy you honour among us,' Francis says. 'And we are honourable men.'

WE ARE MOVED NORTH before the new year. This place that we have been sent is called Vimy Ridge, rolling country-side near a smashed town named Arras. I can see that it was once beautiful country, but is now mashed earth. I look around at the ruins and wonder if this place will ever heal. I try to imagine the countryside here in ten years, in fifty years, in a hundred years, but all I can see in my mind are men crawling in and out of the tunnels in these hills like angry and tired ants, thinking of new ways to kill the other.

Elijah and I are back in the front line. Breech acts as though he wants to keep a close eye on us. 'This war would be a fine thing if not for that man,' Elijah says to me.

It seems that every private who is sent in to replace Sean Patrick dies soon after arriving. The men have taken to calling it The Curse. Right now we wait for a replacement to bring our section to strength. Elijah tells me he feels sorry for the one who arrives. Word comes that Thompson is recovering nicely and will be sent back to us sometime soon. Elijah wears the power that he's been given as acting corporal comfortably. But we are kept from going on raids in this new place.

This Vimy Ridge is quiet compared to what we endured at the Somme in the autumn. And I'm glad for it. Fritz's line runs along the high ground to the east. The Canadians sit hunkered below him, our every movement visible. Troops must move at night or be pounded by Fritz with great accuracy. This is the place where the French army was nearly wiped out two years ago, and the British last year. Although the Canadians are not supposed to hear of it, word is that the French lost 150,000 men in the fighting here, and the British 60,000. Those numbers are impossible to keep secret. They are impossible for me to understand. I ask Elijah, 'How many does that mean?'

He smiles. 'A very difficult question to answer,' he says.

I can see that he has the medicine in him. His lips curl at the edges in a slight smile and his eyes shine. When he is taking the morphine he forgets all about his British accent.

'Think of all the trees we passed canoeing to the town. Think of how many trees the fire ate. That many, maybe.'

I sit and contemplate this for a long time.

The cold weather finally comes and the rain turns to snow. The mud of no man's land turns hard, which makes movement easier, but when a shell lands close by, the earth thrown up is as sharp and deadly as needles. With the snow on the ground, Elijah and I find that night patrols are more difficult. We stand out in our dark uniforms against the white of snow, and so McCaan is issued white tunics that we throw over our coats.

The cold is exhilarating. Elijah and I watch through our sniper scopes for puffs of breath on the German line that rise up from the trenches like steam and give away positions. When our artillery knocks out chunks of Fritz's line, we watch and wait for the poor soul who doesn't know any better to appear in the opening just long enough to disappear in the red spray of Elijah's bullet, or mine.

Breech lets us go hunting out of the trenches. Elijah has been on his best behaviour the last weeks as January has deepened. He and I work as a team again, me spotting and Elijah shooting. We move constantly and find new and better places to hide in the ruined earth and crushed brick of this place. At nighttime we come alive, constantly patrolling and planning large and elaborate raids on Fritz's supposedly impenetrable trenches.

It's as if the winter weather has inspired the Canadians dug in here. In this place that is a gigantic cemetery for the French, we raid Fritz at will, making him jittery and afraid. The officers like these big raids, and although Elijah tells me he prefers to work alone or with one or two others, he has no choice but to go out with so many other men to patrol and attack. He breaks off from the group when they are in no man's land, never so far that if spotted by them he will be accidentally shot, but far away enough that he feels invisible.

On a night in late January, word goes out for volunteers to go on a mission to overrun a section of Fritz's trench that has been pinpointed as a sector of accurate sniping. Elijah's excited at the prospect of finding his own Mauser with a scope, and uses the medicine sparingly so that he has all of his faculties sharpened. Our artillery isolates a section of Fritz's line, the booms of the guns sharp in the cold air.

I don't volunteer for this one. I'm not sure why. A slight buzzing like a wasp in a burlap sack tells me not to go, and so

I listen to it. I've talked even less than usual lately. I think of needing to get back behind the lines soon so that Elijah and I can build a *matatosowin,* a sweat lodge, so we can sit together for a while. I realize I miss home.

I sit back instead and watch as faces are blackened. Elijah carries his war club and the revolver that has been issued him as an acting corporal. They have carefully outlined their plan of attack, and the forty volunteers who will charge into the enemy trenches and go berserk upon Fritz before running back to their own lines again are as focused as any soldiers I've ever seen. I don't know most of the others by name but recognize many of the faces, all of them Second Division who came over at the same time.

As I watch them prepare for the raid, I'm reminded of those Frenchmen back at Christmas. They put the chill in me. I think that they are *windigos.*

I watch the raiders slip from the trench and get eaten by the night. Back in my dugout, I listen for the box barrage that is to come. When it does, I light a cigarette and watch the smoke curl up, carrying its message. No sleeping the rest of the night. I wait for Elijah, troubled by our separation.

When maybe two hours pass, I hear a different shell attack, this one coming from the German line and landing a long way from us. Not long after that I hear a rustle outside the dugout. Elijah climbs in, his face blackened and his eyes standing out white. He lights a cigarette with hands covered in blood. He sees that I am awake and waiting for him.

'How did it go?' I ask in Cree.

'It went very well,' Elijah answers. He waits a few moments, sees that I am listening. He begins to tell me the story of his night.

The raiders crawl along their listening-post trench that juts out toward Fritz's line, then slip over the top. It is a starless night, and Elijah can tell that by morning it will snow again. They spread out in a thin line and advance on their bellies across the frozen ground. Leaving by way of their listening post puts them close to Fritz's wire without having to pick their way through their own. When star shells and Very lights pop up and drift down toward them, they lie still, their white tunics becoming a part of the snow-covered ground. This will be a good raid. He can feel it.

At Fritz's wire he finds a place easy to slip through and this puts him ahead of the raiding party by a couple of minutes. He lies still and scans the sandbags of the parapet. The knowledge that yards from him there are sentries with guns pointed out at him and sensing he is close but not able to see him is exhilarating. The Canadian artillery is spot-on tonight. It lands with crunching thuds and blasts of fire and frozen ground one hundred yards on either side. This will cut off reinforcements from entering this section of trench that they plan on demolishing, and also keep the heads of the sentries down so that the raiders can slip in without notice and catch them by surprise. Still, the window to do this is small. The artillery can't keep the fire up for long without giving them away.

As soon as Elijah knows that a good part of the raiding party is close by him, he crouches and moves toward the parapet, the others following. Vaulting over it, he feels as if he is flying, not knowing or caring what is below. But he does not fall long. His boots thud on a sheet of corrugated metal that collapses below him so that he crashes in the midst of three soldiers staring at him with wide eyes. It seems that he landed on the roof of their dugout and caved it in. They begin to scramble for their rifles as he tries to pull his legs from the crumple of metal and dirt. He is stuck in the old fallen roof up to his waist and can only move his torso.

He acts immediately, pointing his revolver into the face of the closest and pulling the trigger. With a flash of light the soldier's forehead explodes. The gunpowder burns Elijah's nose. As the soldier furthest from him grabs a rifle leaning on the wall, the other grabs Elijah's revolver with both hands and begins twisting it away from him. With Elijah's free hand he swings his war club hard and sinks the sharp nails deep into the soldier's skull. The soldier stares in shock as Elijah struggles to pull the club out and hit him again, but it is stuck too deep and he lets the soldier fall with the club embedded in his head.

When Elijah turns, the third soldier stands calmly now with a look of anger on his face. The soldier's rifle is levelled at Elijah's chest. This moment freezes in Elijah's head as men all around scramble and shout and the artillery explodes in the background and the German pulls the trigger and Elijah waits for the impact to throw him back. But the look of confusion on the soldier's face lets him know that something has gone wrong. The soldier stares down at the useless rifle in his hands as Elijah raises his revolver and takes his turn aiming it at the other's chest, pulling the trigger so that the gun jerks in his hand and his enemy falls backwards and lies still.

He feels a little ridiculous struggling to get free from the collapsed roof as the raiding party runs through this section of trench whooping and screaming, throwing bombs into dugouts and clubbing dazed Fritz with their knobkerries. Elijah's worried there will be nothing left for him. Finally he is out and leans toward the first of the three soldiers. The face is gone and he is obviously dead. Elijah places his foot on the head of the second soldier and wrenches his club from it. The soldier mutters and speaks gibberish, his eyes making crazy circles. Elijah points his revolver at the soldier's forehead as if he is a wounded dog and fires.

Elijah finds no thrill in this part. This is simply what this place and these conditions have done to him. He makes his way to the third soldier. He is close to death and his chest makes a sucking sound with each laboured breath. His eyes are open and staring, and so Elijah covers them with one hand and with the other squeezes the soldier's throat hard until he stops breathing. The soldier struggles a little and in the madness of the shouting and bombing, and rifle and revolver fire all around, this is an oddly peaceful moment.

Elijah stops this night's story here. It is not until a long time later that he is able to share the rest with me. He does not think I will understand. He is right.

Elijah looks down at the soldier he has just dispatched and thinks of the earlier look of anger on the man's face. He reminds himself that this just as easily could have been him lying there. He turns the dead man on his stomach and removes his sharpened skinning knife from its sheath and pulls the man's hair back and removes his scalp with careful motions as simply as he would remove the skin from a pike. He places the hair in his kit bag, assuring himself that just as some other Indians consider it a sign of honour in battle, this counting coup and taking scalps, he will too.

The medicine pulsing in his veins slows and he knows it will not be long before it begins to thin and the headaches come and his body tires so that he will not be able to move. He begins to run with the others who continue to scream like wild things, throwing their bombs into the sleeping places of Fritz, the odd dazed soldier with bleeding ears crawling out only to have his hands tied as he is taken prisoner. The Canadians own this section of trench now and Elijah makes sure that no dugout has been left untouched, hurling his bombs into them so that his load for the trip back will be lightened. A look of animal victory spreads on the blackened faces of the Canadians around him as they pull souvenirs from bodies and peer into darkened holes. Their artillery has slowed down on either side of them, though, and Elijah knows it will not be long before Fritz pours reinforcements into this place.

He is surprised when the scream of artillery begins to come, shells landing close to this section of trench. Just as a shell lands near enough to send one of the Canadians' legless bodies flying up and over the parapet ten yards away from him, Elijah realizes that Fritz has caught on that this section of trench is no longer his and is directing his own artillery into it, seeking revenge. The raiding officer's whistle shrills and they all scramble over the walls of the trenches, dragging their prisoners and souvenirs with them, scurrying now not like majestic beasts but like rats, shell-hole by shell-hole down the hill, back to their line, not stopping any more when the eerie green or red light of flares pops up over them but running, running, the *rat tat tat* of Hun machine guns behind them knocking some of the Canadians headlong toward their own line, Fritz not caring any more if the bullets find the Canadians or their prisoners. Elijah is over his own parapet and back in the safety of the listening post as others crawl over as well. He can see that most of them have made it back tonight.

When he returns to our dugout to tell me most of this

night's adventure, the possession in his kit bag almost pulsates, he thinks. I watch as he lies down on his blanket and lets the night slow down enough for him to sleep. Just before he drifts off completely, he is startled awake and mutters to me that in the rush and clamour of the raid he forgot to find himself a German sniper rifle.

When we are moved behind Arras for a few days, Elijah finally admits to me that he sees that the medicine has caused him to lose too much weight while at the same time he's not been able to relieve his bowels in any satisfying way for a long, long time. I'm not sure why he tells me all this. Maybe he feels guilty. Maybe it's because he and I are two of the same in a place of strangers. Probably he sees that I am depressed and he gives me little bits of himself as an offering.

When he's gone too long without the medicine, he tells me, he becomes fragile and headaches cause him so much pain that death seems a good alternative. When he does not take the morphine, he is afraid of the world, and that is not a good feeling. I tell him that he must stop using it, that his fear of being without it will leave him soon enough. I tell him that he can request a trip back to Blighty for a few weeks where he can recover.

But when the golden liquid is in his veins! Even at night the world is bathed in a soft light. He hears men talking and he understands what they are truly saying beneath their words. He can make himself float from his body at will and look down at the world below him—the world that man has created—and still see the beauty in it. He becomes the hunter at these times, the invincible hunter who can lie still for hours, for days, only moving to refuel his body with the medicine, using his osprey's vision to spot the enemy.

KIMOTOWIN
Stealing

PAST MIDDAY I AM HUNGRY, and so I paddle Xavier and myself to shore. I make bannock with river water, wrap the dough about a stick and bake it by the fire, turning the stick every little bit when the dough begins to brown. Xavier still won't eat anything. I grow a little frustrated with him, but keep it inside. When I look at him and see the pain cross his face I remind myself that he suffers in a way I can't see. He will have to eat something if he is to live. This evening I will make a broth and force it down him if I must. For now, I will feed him another story.

I move closer to him, even though I can tell from his body that he wants to sit off alone. I take a long stick and poke it into the fire, stare out at the river moving by us, this river that carries us deeper into the bush. Again today I do not recognize much of this land. I try to push the thought away, the fear that we have entered a place we've never been before, but it continues to taunt me like a mean child throwing stones from the bush along the shoreline.

You are too young to know your grandmother, Nephew. She died long before you were born. Her illness came suddenly, and it consumed her. One month we were sitting on the bank of a river fishing together, the next she was a skeleton shivering in a blanket in her lodge. I tried all of the remedies and cures that I could think of, but nothing worked. The cruelty of living and dying can be astounding.

I buried her in the tradition of our family, placing her tightly wrapped body in the highest bough that I could find so that her *ahcahk* was free to travel up without hindrance to find her husband, my father. My mother had come from west of James Bay. She was born an Ojibwe, but had met my father on a trading expedition. The two tribes were not all that different, even shared much of the same language. But the Cree and Ojibwe did not always get along very well. My mother and father, in their own small way, tried to make that better.

It was summer, and I sat under my mother's tree for days watching over her. I was wild as any animal by then, having left men and their churches a handful of summers earlier for the loneliness of the bush. Other women my age had children who would soon be ready to enter into adulthood. I had only myself. At that time, I could not imagine having my own children or going back to the people in that town.

I was left alone, and being alone, I found it easy to pity myself. The seasons came and went, sometimes so quickly that I lost track of my own age, sometimes so slowly that I felt I would go mad. My sister Rabbit, your mother, still lived, but the talk was that she was a drinker of *wemistikoshiw* rum and had abandoned her only son to be raised by the nuns in that residential school. The thought of my blood left in that place to fend for himself gave me no end of misery, but I had little choice in the matter.

The other *awawatuk* continued to ask favours of me sometimes, but besides that, my only conversations were with the sky and the forest animals. I dwelled on the Frenchman more than I wanted to, sometimes late at night believing I'd done wrong, but the loneliness I felt, even years later, of waking by myself every morning, served to remind me of what he'd done to me.

In the autumn after my mother's death my recurring fits and their visions returned. They scared me. I was alone now, with no one to watch me. The fits were violent and painful. I worried about choking on my tongue or hitting my head on a rock as I fell into the unwanted spasms. But they came, and more and more I would awake and find myself staring up at the sky, a cold sweat raising the goosebumps on my skin. From the dryness of my eyes, I guessed that they remained open while I was in that other world, but it was only fleeting images that I could usually bring back with me. The one thing I did know was that their return meant some change was coming. And at this point in my life, I had no reason to believe that the change would be good.

I continued on with my life best I could, following my traplines and hunting, collecting roots and herbs, always storing for the winter months. I moved with the game, my summer a little easier than winter, which was so frozen and still that certain days I was convinced I was the only living thing on this earth.

I would know a fit was coming by the change in light. The world would suddenly take on a sharper hue—the sky would go bluer, the water might turn a deeper black. And then the light would go soft, and my fingers and toes would tingle. The first pain was a lightning bolt through my temple, and it was always the one I dreaded most, the jolt of it dropping me to my knees while I was still conscious, an ice bullet through the head. Not until I entered this painful gate was I allowed to slip into unconsciousness and flashes of vision, faces I knew suddenly many years older, other faces I did not recognize.

Sometimes I found myself in a circle of others around a council fire, other times I was alone. Once I came back from the other place with a vision of a metal wagon, moving of its own accord, black and shiny and noisy on a wide smooth path. Sometimes I saw the place where animals would be, other times I saw a great barren plain, the trees cut down and the water filthy with human waste. The visions were random, confusing, frightening or joyful. And when I returned, I had to scoop the fragments from the waters of my confusion and try to piece them into a story I could understand.

My loneliness combined with my fear in the year after my mother's death so that a plan began to form in my mind. During one of my fits the face of a boy came to me. There was no doubting that he was my relation. His nose was mine, his eyes carried the same sharpness. His ears stuck out from his head. I realized I was seeing you, Nephew, that you needed me as much as I needed you. In the long, quiet hours of the bush, the thought of you kept me company.

From what I knew, you were only four or five winters. The nuns could not have damaged you too much already. You needed to be out of that place as much as I had needed it when my mother took me. It would be a relatively simple thing to sneak you from there. They would not concern themselves too much with one little boy. Children ran away from there all the time. And even if they decided to search, no *wemistikoshiw* lived who could find me.

That winter was especially long and cold, and in the nights that seemed to stretch on forever, I convinced myself of what I needed to do. Many problems presented themselves to solve, the biggest one being that I didn't know what my own nephew looked like or even his name. Surely they would have given him one of their names, and I had to find it out. A greater problem still was whether I'd even be able to force myself to go back to that place again.

I struck out by canoe just after the blackflies died off. Now that mid-summer had arrived the rivers would allow me a silent and untraceable route of escape once I found you. Not only this, but I knew from my brief stay in the residential school that most of the children were allowed to return to their parents for a short while in this season, and I hoped this would make finding you much easier. If what I'd heard was true, my sister was in no condition to keep you, and you'd be lonely and likely willing to leave if I invited. And that is how I finally decided. I would not take you by force. I would ask my nephew if he wanted to come with me. If you said no, I would respect it. If you said yes, I would bring you with me to be raised in the old ways.

I travelled for three days, paddling from first to last light. As I had remembered, the smell of the town came to me long before I could see it. A copse of pine stood near the school, a place in which I could hide and watch. I had to rely on the vision of you I'd brought back from the other place. It felt fresh in my memory. I just needed to look for the boy with eyes like mine and ears that stuck out. How hard could it be?

I entered the town at night, fighting off the fear of coming face to face with the Frenchman again, even though I knew full well he was dead. It wasn't his physical body that frightened me. Just as I remembered, the pines near the school offered protection, facing the blank wall full of windows, the top floor the place where all the children slept. I took steps to make sure I would not be discovered, carefully hiding my canoe and covering my tracks, building a shelter of pine boughs far away from the trail that ran through this place. A cooking fire was out of the question, and so I'd brought enough smoked fish and meat to last me a number of days. I settled in and waited, my body full of jittery anxiety for what I would find.

As I had expected, only a few children remained in the summer. They came outside to play at the same time every morning, as carefully watched over by one of the nuns as goslings by a mother goose. Six boys of similar age played with one another. I watched them from a distance. By the second day I'd made my guess which one was my blood.

In the afternoons, an old nun, the one I was sure went by the name Magdalene and who had taken such a dislike to me, went out in a canoe with the little boy, and while he paddled her up and down a stretch of the river, she fished from the front. He was a small boy, and her weight was great enough that the canoe did not lie level on the water, but he tried hard as he could to take her to the places she pointed at. It didn't take long before he tired against the current and her weight, and when he rested she would turn around and smack him hard on the head with her paddle. She was a horrible fisher, banging about in the canoe and demanding he paddle her to places where no fish would want to feed. But he was patient, and did not give up or complain. I had no doubt it was you.

Two days later I watched while the children played. They kicked a hide ball back and forth to one another, and I moved close to the edge of the trees. You were one of the children and you were closest to me, and I waited patiently until the ball was over-kicked and you were the one to pursue it. When you were within earshot, I made the sound of a grouse, just loud enough that you could hear. Your ears perked as I knew they would. After kicking the ball back to the others, you crept into the trees. I made the sound of the grouse again, and you came closer.

'Nephew,' I whispered. You stopped short, tensed to run. 'Do not be afraid. You are the son of the one they call Anne.' I spoke in Cree, for my English was not good enough. But you understood. You nodded. 'I am Niska. I am your Auntie.' You followed my voice, and I watched as you saw me for the first time. Your eyes widened. I realized then what I must look like, my hair long and black and wild, my body covered in hides.

'What do you want of me, Auntie?' you asked. You spoke Cree with a *wemistikoshiw* accent. You were bold.

'I came to ask if you would prefer leaving here and going into the forest to live with me.'

You did not hesitate. 'Yes, Auntie.'

I smiled, and as I did I realized it was my first smile in many months. My eyes watered.

'Meet me here tomorrow.' You smiled too, then turned back and joined the others, chasing the ball.

When you came the next day, I explained that we'd leave in the afternoon, that I would paddle up to the canoe while you fished with the nun.

'But why can't we leave now, Auntie?' you asked.

'There is something I have waited many summers to do,' I said. 'And I would be honoured that you would be a part of it along with me.'

Later that day I waited in my own canoe underneath a thick overhang of willow. As I knew would happen, you appeared on the river, Nephew, paddling the fat nun Magdalene. When you were across the river from me, I called out the sound of the whiskeyjack. You turned toward it. There was no question whose blood you were.

I listened as the nun shouted out directions. You steered the canoe closer to me. I waited, and, not wanting to miss the moment when she was no more than two arms' length away from me, I let out a great wail, the wail of years of hurting, so that the old nun stood, then stumbled and rolled out of the boat and into the water. I slipped out of the willows in my canoe, and in the English I remembered said to her, '*You* paddle home.' I took my paddle and clipped her sharply on the head for emphasis. She stared up at me from the water, terrified, her black robe billowing around her, her thin grey hair plastered to her forehead. I motioned for you, and you jumped in my canoe. Do you remember, Nephew? We left that place slow and smiling.

The months that followed were the happiest in my life. We spent our days wandering and trapping and hunting in the bush. Amazingly, you had very little knowledge of any of it, and so I taught you everything I could. You learned quickly and naturally, and your ability to walk invisibly and to shoot was obvious.

One afternoon in late autumn, when the frost in the morning was heavy on the ground and the last of the geese were flying south high on the currents of air, the familiar tingling in my toes and fingers came to me. We followed a river that promised moose, and I wanted to warn you of what was to come, but was too late. The piercing pain shot through my temple and I collapsed to the ground. As I drifted off to the other world I could hear you calling out to me and crying.

I do not know how long I was gone, but as I gradually returned from that place, you remained hovering over me with a tear-stained face.

248

'Were you dead, Auntie?' you asked me. I smiled and shook my head. 'Your eyes were open, but they did not see. You said words I did not understand.'

'Don't worry,' I said. 'When you are old enough I will explain.'

That winter and the following summer and the winter and summer after that were plentiful and very happy. You adjusted to the ways of the bush better than I had hoped and became a talented hunter and reader of signs. I taught you all I knew about the bush, the best way to snare rabbits and how to use their fur for protection against the cold brutality of winter, how to weave and walk in snowshoes through the deep snow, how to approach a moose downwind and even how to snare one, how to make your own clothing and moccasins, what plants and herbs were edible and which had healing properties.

But as always happens, the good times bled into harder times and our third winter together proved long and difficult and very cold. Some days were so difficult for us that you cried with hunger and I was reminded of my own childhood, of that winter long ago when my father still lived. Once or twice late at night as you slept fitfully by the fire, I even found myself questioning if I had made the right decision in taking you from that school. At least there you had a full stomach and warm bed. My fits began to come back to me more often, and they were something you could not understand, but at least became used to, for you realized I always came back from that other place. What I didn't tell you, Nephew, was that I brought back with me the knowledge that soon a visitor would come to us, a visitor with a request I could not ignore.

ONATOPANIWIW
Fighter

THE STORY AUNTIE TELLS me brings a smile to my lips. I remember that nun who liked to switch me. I can still see the look on her face when Auntie scared her into the water and struck her with the paddle. I smile at Auntie and this makes her eyes bright. Niska is a good woman. She is a good and crazy woman.

The sun is warm on the river, and I no longer feel guilty that I do not help paddle. She has the current and we are in no rush. I lie back and run my hand over the rough wool of my pants, feel the nub of my leg through it. The skin covering it is still a burnt red and puckered and so ugly that I can't look at it. When I first realized I'd lost my leg, I stared at the wound for days, watched as blood seeped through the white bandage, life leaking out of me in a trickle. Maybe it was then that I decided to die. I know that was when I discovered why Elijah loved the morphine, and the nurses were generous with it.

I struggle to stay awake for a while, the canoe rocking me on a fast part of the river so that I'm reminded of the trains Elijah and I rode to join the army, the trains moving further and further south until we came to that frightening place called Toronto. I remember how we lined up in rows of soldiers in new uniforms, how we ate and marched together. The barracks were just like the ones in the school of my childhood. We children had lined up just like soldiers to be inspected every morning and evening. Elijah and I were always together in my short time at the school. He protected me and I protected him.

We schemed after our switching in front of the other children. We lay in our beds beside one another, whispering late into the night, going silent when we heard the nun making her rounds with her candle.

'We will run away from this place,' I would say to Elijah in our tongue. 'We will take a bit of food from the pantry each day, just enough that it won't be noticed. We will find a place to store it, and when we have enough, we will leave late at night and be so deep in the bush by morning that no one will ever be able to find us.' This was before I knew you existed, Auntie.

'We will need more than just food,' Elijah would whisper back. 'We will need an axe and some matches. We will need extra clothes and shoes for summer and boots for winter.'

I was surprised Elijah needed so much. 'Where will we keep it all?' I asked. 'The nuns can smell too good. They will find it. They find everything.'

'We will hide what we take near the river, and we will steal the canoe that always sits by it,' Elijah answered matter-of-factly.

'But the animals will eat our food,' I said, and this kept Elijah quiet for a long time.

A rumour floated from ear to ear amongst the children that two boys had once run away from here and were never found. The other rumour was that the next year, little bones, too small to be an adult's, were found in the barn by the school.

'We will hide only the things that can't be eaten by the river, and we will hide the food somewhere here in the school,' Elijah said finally.

251

I doubted this plan would work. The nuns found everything we tried to hide. But I said nothing. I wanted the plan to come to life.

'One of the nuns keeps a rifle,' Elijah said as I was falling asleep. 'She keeps a good rifle and lots of bullets. I have seen it in her room.'

This information made me open my eyes. 'Really?' I asked. He nodded. That settled it. I was kept awake wondering if Elijah had really been in her sleeping place. We were all strictly forbidden to go anywhere near it. Elijah was not good enough at sneaking that he wouldn't be caught trying to get in. It wasn't until a long time later that I found out he'd really been in her room. And though Elijah and I were forever planning our running away, it remained just whispers in the dark before sleep.

Niska hums a song to herself as she paddles. The sun on my face makes me sleepy, and the tide of memory pulls at me again, this time taking me to France. I struggle against the pull. I do not want to go there right now. Instead, I try to figure out what day today is in the English way of keeping time. It is high summer, but what day, what month? I slip into a light sleep, remembering that in the way that they keep time, it has been a year now that Elijah and I have been here. I am a different man. I am thinner than when I left Canada, and harder in so many ways.

The late winter and early spring brings cold rain that turns to snow but does not stay. The engineers constantly work, and Elijah has explained to me that I must decide to be either a carrier of bags full of wet mud or a hunter. All winter I have suffered this miserable thing called depression. To make it all worse, I cannot forget that girl, Lisette. For weeks after I left her I was a mud carrier. My mind could not focus in the field, and that is dangerous when what you hunt hunts you as well. But now I am sick of mud. The idea has grown in my head all winter, so that now I cannot shake it. If I can see her again, my depression will go away. I think of ways to accomplish this, to see her again. But she lives far away from Vimy Ridge. Lisette was my first woman. When I see her again, I want to be able to tell her stories of adventure. And that is why I am again Elijah's spotter in the field.

We've found what promises to be a good nest in a pile of brick just behind the front trench. In the event of trouble, a communication trench lies just to our right and leads to the support trenches. When the sun is out, for most of the day we stay still and choose potential targets, the sun in our eyes so that we must be careful not to let it glint on our field glasses. But the sun is rarely a problem. The wind blows from the west constantly, carrying with it heavy, low clouds that spit upon us. Elijah is friends with the officers who have authority to call artillery in to specific areas, and he uses this friendship, asks them to blow holes in the Hun parapets. The odd Fritz wanders by and Elijah has made a game of keeping a running tally of the hits and misses we each make.

'We'll use your Mauser as the prize,' he says. 'After two weeks we tally our scores and the winner takes the prize.'

I just smile at his proposition. This is a fine rifle, one that I will take home and hunt many moose with.

I ask Elijah where I can find rounds for the Fritz rifle. Elijah'd promised me more a while ago, and only a handful is left now. I think he is holding out. Elijah covets this gun, but I am responsible for taking down the Hun sniper who loved the dead. The night of the day I killed my first human was the first time I felt like an ancestor, an *awawatuk* raider and warrior. I prayed to *Gitchi Manitou* for many hours on that day and the following day, thanking him that it was I who still breathed and not my enemy. Since that time I am able to shoot at other men and understand that what I do is for survival, as long as I pray to *Gitchi Manitou*. He understands. My enemy might not understand this when I send him on the three-day road, but maybe he will on the day that I finally meet him again.

From our position we watch the hill that Fritz has dug into and from which Fritz watches the Canadians. Our engineers work at night, digging like moles into the ground, and Elijah and I debate whether they are digging another tunnel under the German line to fill it with explosives or whether the digging is for another reason. I think that what they are doing will surprise everyone, but Elijah says that you can't teach an old dog new tricks. We do agree that something big is coming, though. When the ground thaws, I imagine. More and more troops huddle in the cold behind the lines when Elijah and I are sent back to rest. I see, too, that the supply dumps grow in size and horses pull up the big guns while the earth is still frozen enough to keep them from sinking.

On a night that we have come up from the support trench to take our position at the front again, an idea comes to me that I cannot shake from my head. Through my fine German scope I see that a group of three dead Fritz are not too far away, strung on the wire. A listening post juts out within an easy shot from where they are tangled up and turning black, and I think that they must have bullets for a Mauser with them. I consider mentioning this growing idea to Elijah in the hopes that he will join me in the adventure, but then decide I want to do this alone. It's dangerous, I know, but that's the point, isn't it? I can almost hear Elijah saying this in his funny-sounding *wemistikoshiw* tongue. I fear being caught by my own and the trouble that will come from it as much as being caught by Fritz.

On the night that I choose to do my raid, everything feels wrong. A lot of troop movement bustles through my part of the line. Fritz has picked up his shelling and focused it on the Canadian wire, and I am not left alone long enough to blacken my face with burnt cork and sneak over the top without being noticed. When the middle of the night has come and passed and I still sit in my dugout, frozen by indecision and trying to find a good time to make my move, I finally and bitterly tell myself to call it off. I lie back on my blanket, the dark of the night sinking into me. Elijah would have just gone, I tell myself. Elijah would not have worried about anyone else or anything else but focusing on those dead Fritz and what was in their pockets and he would not have let any excuses, any fear, stop him. He would have just gone. I do not sleep all night, this defeat that I've suffered biting at me like scurrying, passing rats.

Elijah and I are called into McCaan's dugout in early April. We both know, as all of the soldiers around us know, that an offensive comes soon. McCaan talks fast and I can't make out all of what he says. It isn't that I can't understand English. I've become good at that. It's my ears. They ring constantly and sometimes I can't hear anything at all. But I know Elijah listens closely, and I will ask him to repeat it all to me in Cree later. I watch McCaan's lips move, and my ears whine as if plugged with dirt or wax. I try to clear them with my finger, which usually helps a little, but now they only feel plugged more. I am relieved when Elijah and I are dismissed.

'What did he say?' I ask, my voice echoing in my head. Elijah's lips move, but nothing seems to come out. 'Louder,' I say. I tug hard at my earlobes and this seems to work some, but the whining continues somewhere deep.

'We are to begin scouting out positions in no man's land as close to Fritz as we can comfortably get,' he says. 'We are to take as much ammunition with us as we will need, along with rations and drinking water.' Elijah smiles. 'We are to try and spot Fritz's machine-gun nests, and on the morning of the 'operation,' as McCaan calls it, we are to take out as many of them as possible.' Elijah looks at me strangely then. 'You are going deaf,' he says.

For the next few days we scan every inch of ground in front of our section. Our biggest challenge is that Fritz has the high ground and without much difficulty will identify almost all of our hiding places. An area stretches out fifty yards in front of the Hun wire, though, where a pile of old bricks and a mud breastwork was formed by one of the bigger shells. We both agree that this is the best-looking place and that we will check it out this evening.

Elijah reports to Breech and he gives us the go-ahead. I try to sleep a little after stand-to, but as usual I can't. Instead, I lie back in my dugout and count the flares that go up and cast shadows on the wall of mud across from me. I'm worried about my ears. The deafness comes and goes, followed by the ringing, which is enough to drive me mad. When the ringing does die down, I feel as if I am living in a hollowed cave.

We blacken our faces and only the two of us go out, just like old times. We make our way down the now familiar listening-post trench and slip out when enemy flares die down. Fritz is nervous because of all the recent trench raids, and I know to move cautiously and silently toward him. When a flare goes up we lie still and flat, knowing that we won't be seen in the shadows. In this way we make it to the place we'd agreed upon earlier.

This seems a good spot in the darkness, but Elijah is tense here. He motions to me and makes his sign that Fritz is close, two fingers pointing to the ground. We lie unmoving and listen to the darkness, but I cannot hear much of anything. Elijah motions to our left and in front, in sign language lets me know that someone's twenty or so yards away, four or five of them. We scan the horizon and I note that this place will be a good one for our purposes, with lots of spots to crawl into and take refuge in, while offering a wide view of Fritz's line. We make our way back carefully and report to McCaan.

'We've found a suitable place,' Elijah tells McCaan. I stand beside him, listening best I can. 'But Fritz has a listening post twenty yards or so from it. I imagine it will serve as a machine-gun nest once we begin our advance.'

'Well, then,' McCaan answers, 'I suggest that that post is the first thing you take out when the attack begins.'

Elijah nods and smiles, before turning with me and heading back to our dugout. We will be given word on the evening before to head out to our position, and we have been told to be ready to move at a moment's notice.

Neither of us speaks in the dugout that we've claimed for our own. The day was a quiet one and already another evening approaches. The rest of our section has been given sentry detail in shifts tonight, and I can hear Fat snoring in the dugout next to ours, Gilberto muttering angrily for him to shut up. I listen as Elijah shuffles in his kit, hear the now familiar glass clink of a small syringe and the light slapping of his arm, the heavy sigh when he is done. I think he is asleep but then his voice drifts to me. My hearing is all right tonight. I hope it stays that way.

'I have something for you in my kit,' he says. 'A gift. There are two magazines of Mauser rounds that I've been saving for you. Use them wisely.'

I reach over and feel for his knapsack. I pull it to me and dig my hand in. Something soft and furry. I pull my hand back in case it is a sleeping rat that will wake to bite me. Maybe Elijah plays a trick. I feel the outside of the bag but there is no warmth or movement inside. I reach cautiously into it again and pull out the soft thing. I cannot tell what it is in this light, a small hide, maybe, but the fur is too long to be a rat's. When I raise it to my nose to sniff the hardening leather side of it, the familiar reek of rotting human flesh makes me snap my hand away in disgust. I realize just what it is that Elijah keeps.

I place it back in the kit and extract the magazines. Lying there for the second time in as many nights, I watch the shadows on the trench wall and listen to the thunder and rumble of the big guns. I run my finger along the cold flat metal of a bullet casing and wonder what is happening all around me.

Two nights later, McCaan gives us word to take our position in the field. The trenches are alive with movement. Companies of men move in until they are all shoulder to shoulder. The engineers have finished their digging, and men and rifles and Mills bombs and machine guns fill the tunnels that lead up to Fritz's line. To try a frontal attack in the open and up Vimy Ridge would create a slaughter, and so we've done the natural thing, dug tunnels that lead under and out into no man's land where Canadians will pour from the earth close to the German line and take it by surprise. Elijah is shocked and even a little angry that he was wrong and I was right.

We make our way out to our position, lugging knapsacks full of ammunition and our rifles and our rations, our line's shelling masking the movement. I had less than two dozen rounds for my Mauser, and so McCaan put out the word up and down the line. A number of soldiers came forth with more, and now I have many.

We dig ourselves in at the place of brick and mud, and I create a loophole in the brick from which I can fire my rifle. It will be well hidden from Fritz. Elijah works with handfuls of mud and loose brick and does the same. The German line almost hums, I think. The Canadian bombardment lands close to us and the earth shudders below me like a living thing. Fritz must know that something is coming, and now that they have gotten a taste of the Canadians at Saint-Eloi Craters and the Somme and here at Vimy Ridge, they know their opponent is worthy.

Fritz's listening post is still nearby and it's causing us to work very slowly. The Germans close by will not be able to hear Elijah and me over the din of the bombing, but they will spot movement if we are not careful. Elijah motions to me to lean toward him. 'Stay put,' he says. 'Offer me cover if I need it. If I do not make it back, hold this place and kill as many of them as you can in the morning.' He slips out with trench knife and crawls into the darkness.

I am sick with worry. Elijah has let the medicine drive him mad. I don't want to be left in this position alone come daylight, facing the machine guns and their accuracy, the artillery and point-blank whiz-bangs.

Nothing for me to do but lie still and wait. The world explodes around me, shells landing fifty and a hundred yards ahead, wrecking the German line. I order my mind to drift, to shut down, but it will not.

It feels like hours have passed when finally I sense rather than see or hear a form close by. Elijah. I can tell by his scent. He crawls up and his eyes are wide with excitement.

'Three of them!' he whispers. 'I slit the throats of three of them so quickly that I surprised even myself! I am truly a ghost man now!' His hands look black in the dark, and I realize that they are covered with blood.

'Did you cut the hair from them?' I ask.

'How did you know?' he answers, excited like a young boy who's taken his first grouse.

We settle in and wait.

The lightening sky in front of us puts the urge in me to begin crawling back to my own trenches before it's too late and I'm caught here in the open. The temperature is below freezing and I feel cold and stiff in my greatcoat. We scan the still-dark horizon, waiting for that moment when the sun peeks up in front of us and sheds light on their line. Very soon the shelling will begin. Elijah and I were warned by McCaan that it'll be a huge and intense event. The artillery will rip apart the Hun trenches, and there will be an absolute silence for just a moment before we hear the shrill whistle behind us that signals for the Canadians to begin pouring over the top and then the world will explode once again.

Every minute that passes brings the dawn a little closer to the horizon. Without warning, the artillery behind begins with a roar and quickly reaches a crescendo. I watch as shells scream overhead, close to me, sounding like they will land upon me, but beautifully accurate on this morning, flinging mud and shrapnel and sandbags and human remains and showers of sparks into the air. For a second I wonder if this will be the last morning of my life.

Elijah nudges me and passes me a canteen. *Drink,* he mouths, and I take it from him, tipping it to my parched throat. The taste is not water at all and as it burns down my throat I realize that it is rum. 'McCaan gave us double rations. Drink!' Elijah shouts over the din.

I tip the canteen and drink again as deeply as I can. I need this, I think. When I pass the canteen back, I can now make out clearly the details of Elijah's blackened face in the approaching light, the high cheekbones and hollowed cheeks, so gaunt from the medicine. His eyes sparkle like sunlight on water and I stare for a while, taking all of him in. He is beautiful, like a wild animal. Too delicate, it seems, for what he is so good at. Elijah stares back at me quizzically, and then his face breaks into a wide smile, the whiteness of his teeth startling me.

Elijah turns to his rifle, sliding open the bolt and checking the action, pushing a round back into the chamber. He shoulders his rifle and peers into the scope, then looks to me, shouting, 'Do you see that knoll there?'

I look up at Fritz's breastworks and nod. A large mound rises directly ahead of us in the slipping darkness, like a pimple on the earth.

'You are responsible for everything on your side of it. I will be responsible for everything on my side. There will be machine-gun nests for sure in that area over there.' He points to small mounds that rise up from their parapet, sandbagged reinforcements, I assume. 'We'll pour our fire into them,' he says.

261

We can both tell from the light that there will be no sun this morning. The day is birthing a heavy grey and a wind has picked up that blows past us and sweeps up the hill into Fritz's line. It is cold and thick flakes of snow swirl about. All of this is good for the Canadian boys, the wind at their backs and natural cover falling. It will be more difficult for me to find my targets, but that is a small price. With the snow in Fritz's eyes, he will have a far more difficult time spotting the attackers.

Just then the shelling stops.

A hum rises in my ears from a quiet I haven't heard since leaving Mushkegowuk.

A whistle, high and piercing, echoes somewhere in the cottony air behind me. A moment later, the desperate roar of men scrabbling their way over the top and approaching me a hundred yards behind.

Elijah and I peer through the falling snow for signs of movement. I keep one hand by the trigger of my rifle, the other shielding the scope from falling snowflakes. Enough light now that I can make out the details of their line, sandbags and brightly coloured cloth, no discernible patterns in it. The shelling appears to have been accurate. Huge gaps have been blown in Fritz's line and there is still no movement anywhere to be seen. I swing my rifle along the blasted trench, scanning through the snowflakes for any movement. Nothing. Is it possible that we've blown Fritz into the other world? I can hear the approach of men behind me. The terrain's difficult and they are obviously struggling up it with their heavy packs and rifles and muddy boots. But still they continue their shouting, more desperate and breathless now. I move my eye away from my scope and squint at Fritz's line. Unbelievable.

Still no movement. Maybe all the talk of this place being an impregnable fortress was lies.

That's when I spot something.

I peer through my scope and focus in on the clear outline of a rounded Fritz helmet and below it the pale face of a young man struggling, his tongue sticking out, to do something with his hands that is out of my view. I am mesmerized by the young German. He feels so close through the scope that I might reach out and touch him. Just one man. Only one man is left who has survived the shelling!

But then my stomach goes into my throat. Soldiers pop up from nowhere through the settling smoke of the barrage and fall into place along the parapet, rifles trained directly at me. In the seconds that I watch, their line fills up with the outlines of shoulders and heads, all pointing rifles toward the soldiers approaching behind us. It dawns on me that through all of the winter that the Canadians dug tunnels toward the Hun, the Hun have been digging down deep to hide from the shelling.

'Look at them all!' Elijah says.

Without thinking, I place the crosshairs of my scope squarely on the chest of the struggling soldier that I first saw and firmly squeeze the trigger. My rifle bucks and the soldier sails backwards as if pulled from behind with great force, a startled expression flashing on his face before he disappears from view. The concussion echoes dully in my head and I realize that this is the first rifle shot to shatter the morning. Then the world seems to erupt once more.

The Canadian artillery opens up again in a creeping barrage somewhere nearby in the falling snow. I squeeze my eyes shut and pray that it is in front of me and not behind. The

Canadian barrage falls so close to us in its attempt to cover the advancing soldiers that the air is hard to breathe, most of it sucked up by the concussions. I want to run screaming but my body is an impossible weight stuck in the earth. I cannot dig deep enough to escape it, but try anyway, burying my face in the mud. Is it in front? Yes! It is!

Gradually the tremendous pound recedes just enough to let me know it moves away and not toward. McCaan's calculations and Elijah's instincts were right. We are just behind the invisible line where our artillery begins its pounding cover. The whole earth is on fire in front of me, exploding in huge fountains of mud and fire. I can feel the rumble below me, through me, swallowing me. My whole body vibrates with it. We both remove our arms from over our heads and watch the shells steadily creep forward toward the Hun.

But audible just below the shells is the sound that empties the stomach of every infantry soldier as he makes his way across open ground toward the enemy. The rattle of machine guns barks out into the grey morning. Elijah systematically fires, reloads, fires, reloads, picking off soldiers whose heads appear suddenly through the snow and smoke and spraying mud, then just as quickly disappear. My greatest fear is that we will give away our position, but so far the bullets are well over our heads.

I try to locate where the machine-gun nests are, but in the snow, seeing much of anything is difficult. All I do know is that with every minute, their bullets are hitting Canadians. Elijah nudges me and points in the direction of a rise. When I look long enough I see what Elijah has caught, the flash of muzzle fire that gives away a nest's position through the thickening snow. We both train our rifles on the flash and I aim mine just above it, hoping that with luck I might hit the soldier working the gun. We both begin an even, methodical fire, but the flashes continue. Elijah pauses to reload a magazine and I have two bullets left before I must do the same. I aim through my scope again, and in a brief slowing of snowfall think I can make out an outline hunched above the flash. I squeeze off one shot, then another. The flash of the machine gun stops. I wait for it to begin again, but it doesn't.

'I think I got him!' I say to Elijah, excited.

'Impossible to say,' he answers.

We will keep up a covering fire until our troops make it to this position, then we are to stand and join them in the sweep up the hill. From the sounds behind me, they are getting close.

Dirt and pieces of brick kick up in front of my face. Somebody has spotted my muzzle flash. I sweep my scope across the parapet but snow has fallen onto the lens and makes it more difficult to see. More bullets zing by my head. I duck out of the line of fire and look over to Elijah. He continues to focus in on a target, fire and reload. A slight smile has settled on his lips.

'We've been spotted!' I shout to him in Cree.

He apparently doesn't hear what I say. That or he is ignoring me. Bullets cough up dirt all around him. I look back. The Canadian soldiers are only forty or fifty yards from us now, but another machine gun cuts large holes in their line.

I look over to the secondary position that Elijah and I had scouted last night. I can slip down into the shell crater behind me, crawl along it and take position there without being seen by their line. I shout my intention to Elijah and then make my move, not waiting for an answer. He's in his own world. I

265

scramble in case I'm not as invisible to them as I hope I am. Once in place, I pull some dry cotton from inside my coat and pat my scope dry. I nudge my rifle barrel between two piles of brick, make sure I have a clear line of fire and once again begin searching for the machine-gun nest that is inflicting so much damage. A pillbox lies a hundred yards or so in front and to my right. The pillbox is so blasted by shells that it's now more a pile of rubble than a structure. Elijah and I had both known it existed but assumed that it was too damaged to be of use. But something tells me to train my scope on it. I scan the blasted concrete and brick but there doesn't seem to be any place to fit a machine gun in the flattened wreck.

That is when I see the telltale flash of muzzle fire spitting out, not from somewhere on the bottom of the pile, as I'd assumed, but from up on top. They've cleverly concealed themselves with canvas, grey like the colour of the flattened pillbox. It seems obvious to me now. I would have done the same thing. I should have known better.

The machine gun continues its stream of fire. I squint through my scope and in the lightening snowfall can once again make out a soldier's head just above it, peering down his sight. I can also see that the machine-gunner's partner is beside him, feeding the gun its belt of ammunition and spotting for him. It makes sense to me to take out the gunner first, then his partner. Breathing out, then in deeply, then out again, I try to steady my nerves. I let out half my breath as my crosshairs find the place just below the lip of the gunner's helmet, and I gently squeeze the trigger. Once again my rifle bucks, but I keep my eye on the target long enough to see the soldier jerk back. I move the scope to my left and focus in on the other. He hasn't noticed yet, his gaze on his hands doing something below the point where I can see. I watch him look up and see for the first time his dead mate. His mouth makes an O and then he hurries to take over the position behind the gun. Once again I breathe and exhale. Nothing exists except the sound of my own breath in my head. I pull the trigger and the soldier falls back in a spray of red.

The first of the Canadians make their way to us now, their mouths open and chests heaving, no longer screaming so much as whimpering in the clatter of rifle fire aimed at them. Their faces are grimy and drawn and their eyes are wide. Their bayonets are attached to their rifles and look heavy in their hands.

I reach down to my belt and feel for my bayonet, pull it from its sheath and slide it onto the barrel, clicking it into place. I lie on my back for a second, feeling the snow fall on my face, and try to calm myself into standing up in this stream of fire. I sit and breathe deeply, my face toward the sky. The snow feels cold, good on my face. I look over to see if Elijah is still alive and am surprised to see that he is no longer there.

Men begin to pass me more frequently now, and I stare up into their faces as they run as fast as they can, at a slow jog now, staring ahead at the rifles that shoot at them. I see a face that I recognize approaching. Gilberto. Gilberto sees me too, and turns toward me, offering his hand to help me up, an expression on his face as if he's finally found a long-lost friend. I reach up to take it, just as the smile on his face blooms into a red flower. He collapses onto his knees and falls across me. Screaming, I struggle to push my friend's heavy weight from me. When I manage this, I stand up and begin running with the others toward the German line.

The rise gets steeper the further I get. Men all around me

scream and fall to the ground grasping themselves. Others slump like sacks of flour. I think that in a little while no one will be left but me. The world has gone almost silent in my head but for a deep hum and what sounds like the faraway surge of waves crashing on a beach and then pulling away. I try not to think, but a memory of me playing on the muddy shore of the Great Salt Bay comes to me, a presence near me, my watchful aunt protecting me. You, Niska. I don't know why I think of you now as bullets zing by my head so close that they whisper to me. One cuts through my coat and I can feel my side burning. I think I have been shot but the pain is almost absent, just an annoying bite. I begin to mouth your name over and over, like a protection against the bullets. *Niska,* I whisper as I run up the hill and approach a stretch of barbed wire. *Niska. Niska. Niska. Niska. Niska.* I realize as I stumble and fall to my knees that the sound of the waves crashing in my head is my own breathing.

I look up to the wire in front of me and see that it is still a tangled mess despite the shelling that was meant to blow it apart and despite the efforts of the sappers, many of whom lie dead and tangled in grotesque positions on the wire. Others all around me shout and scurry toward it, their mouths moving but no sound coming out. I stand again and push ahead. A break in the wire and men bunch up at its opening, trying to get through. Not knowing what else to do, I head toward them, but see that too many are being shot and too many corpses jam up the hole for anyone to get through now. I look along the stretch of wire and notice that a few others have found another place to get through by throwing themselves on the ground and crabbing under it. Others are climbing over the bodies of the dead or throwing planks of wood carried up from their trench to create bridges over the wire. I find a place that will allow me to scamper under it.

Bullets tear up the ground all around my head, tossing up painful clods of dirt into my eyes. I make it through the wire and see that I am close to their parapet, Germans leaning over it and shooting point-blank. Lying on my belly, I aim my rifle, the scope useless now that I'm so close. I fire at one soldier who seems to be doing a lot of damage. The soldier drops and I reload and fire at another, dropping him too. I want to just lie here and keep shooting until I myself am shot, but the legs and bodies of the other Canadians block me from shooting any more. I stand up then and with a desperate scream join them on the charge at the parapet.

For the first time, the faces of the Hun look nervous. The Canadians are so close now that rifle fire is almost useless, and the ones just ahead of me are on the German sandbags, stabbing with their rifles at the men below them. The Canadians pour over the line and into the enemy trenches. A great panic takes over the men as I stare for just a moment at the chaos below me. Soldiers battle with rifles, frantically using them like pikes to stab and parry. There is none of the smoothness of our training in their movements. Others desperately struggle with their hands, strangling one another or using whatever they can, helmets, rifle butts, pieces of wood, to smash each other's skulls.

Gripping my rifle in both hands, I jump into the trench. A young man with startling green eyes runs at me, his rifle pointed, his small frame almost like a child's in his oversize coat. I sidestep the rifle and let the momentum of the German's charge carry him onto my Mauser's bayonet. The boy's eyes go wide and I feel the knife's length cut into his body. Then the point hits something hard and stops. The young soldier opens his mouth as I try to pull the bayonet from him. But it is stuck and I am forced to raise my boot to the soldier's belly and kick hard to dislodge it. He falls back, clutching his stomach.

I turn from him to stop myself from throwing up, just as another soldier runs at me, this one much larger, a giant of a man it seems to me, his red hair and eyes wild as if on fire. He carries a war club in his hand and swings it clumsily but with great force at the top of my skull. I jump to the side and the force of his attack carries the man forward and onto the ground so that he is on all fours. Before he can get up, I raise my rifle with both hands and drive the bayonet into his back. I can feel it bounce sharply off his spine before it finds a softer spot and sinks in halfway. The big man falls onto his stomach as I struggle to pull the bayonet out.

The German swings his arms wildly behind him, trying to reach that centre place in his back as if he has a great itch. I pull with all my might but the bayonet is stuck. I have no choice but to stand on the man's back, and as he writhes around I pull up hard, the knife suddenly coming loose so that I fly off him and land on my tailbone, the breath knocked from me. All around me are the legs and torsos of men struggling with one another, and as I gulp air I can only watch in horror as the red giant stands up with dazed anger in his eyes and on wobbly legs bears down on me, hands outstretched to squeeze my neck. The man leans down so close that I can smell his sour breath. He mutters something I cannot make out, and it is then that I realize I'm going to die now, my diaphragm relaxing in this knowledge so that I can breathe a little again. The German's hands are calloused and very strong as he begins squeezing, and all I can do is stare up into his angry bloodshot eyes. He is no monster, just a man, I think, as my eyes bulge and I stop breathing once again.

Throat burning, I catch the movement of someone coming up beside the big man, and as I look over I see McCaan with his officer's revolver drawn. He places it to the side of the big man's head and I watch his finger pull the trigger. The man's head pops open in a spray of red and grey that covers my face in its warmth, a startling feeling in the cold air. I suck in a great breath of air and blood, then begin sputtering. McCaan calmly moves on, aiming his revolver and firing as he walks along the trench.

When I have the strength, I stand up, but then fall back down again. From what I can tell, the Hun are retreating. My eyes close, but I am still alive.

ISHINAKWAHITISIW
Turning

WE ARE OUT OF THE LINES for a few days' rest and all of the Canadians around me are loud and happy. We've taken the place where hundreds of thousands of Frenchmen and Englishmen died in their attempt to do the same these last years. We are an army to be reckoned with suddenly, no longer the colonials, as the Englishmen call us, looking down at us.

Fat took a bayonet to his lower leg, enough to send him to Blighty because it swelled and became infected. Word is that he did it to himself halfway across no man's land, which makes sense since there were no Fritz around for a couple of hundred yards at the time he claims he was wounded. The story that came out later was that he stumbled and fell, somehow cutting his leg badly in the process.

We are billeted by the wreck of what was once a town, the only standing building an old half-destroyed hotel that still serves us liquor and food when it's available. Those lucky enough not to be running supplies up during the night to the front line stay out late, drinking and playing Crown and Anchor, and trying to be the ones to bed the couple of local women who accept food just as readily as money for their friendship. I miss the girl called Lisette, the one with hair blonde like I've not seen hair before. I fight the urge to begin walking north the thirty-five miles or so to see her. I've actually worked it out over and over in my head. I can walk the distance overnight, spend the day with her, and walk back the next. I would probably not be missed if I were to do it. There is much madness around here with reinforcements arriving and departing and supply wagons and artillery rumbling through this place night and day. We now have the ridge that looks out and over the long Douai Plain, and we have forced Fritz back to his deep trenches, the place they call the Hindenburg Line. It is the first Allied victory of this war.

I don't remember much after gaining their trench and the hand-to-hand fighting. My mind cracked after Gilberto was killed in front of me, broke further when the big man began strangling me. I am told I stood after McCaan shot the man in the head and that I continued on with the others, helping to secure the first trench, then offering cover fire when we stormed the secondary trench and eventually the reserve trench. Elijah found me slumped over a parapet and was sure I was dead. The way Elijah tells it to me, when he turned me over I opened my eyes to Elijah and told him I'd been talking to my mad aunt, to you, Niska. Elijah picked me up then, strung my rifle over his shoulder along with his own and carried me all the way back to our morning trench, where I slept under Elijah's careful eye for thirty-six hours.

And now it is spring and we are here on top of Vimy Ridge rather than below it. The snow and blowing wind that came to us that morning has left, and I wonder if it wasn't sent by you to help us, Niska. A warm day arrives, the first in a long time, and the sun comes out. We take off our shirts and lie by a small river that runs close by. The braver ones swim in the ice water. I sit with Elijah and Grey Eyes and Graves, and Fat just back from Blighty. We are the only original privates left, and all of us look up at the observation balloons that try to keep track of what Fritz is up to. The others' chests are as white as fish bellies, and even Elijah's and mine seem paler than I ever remember them being. Nobody talks of Gilberto. He is gone now. To invite his memory will only invite sadness, and sadness can collect here as quick as rain in trenches, until it drowns everything. Elijah speaks of writing Gilberto's wife and children a letter describing his bravery and kindness, but I don't know if he ever will.

Someone points up to the sky and in the distance we hear the drone of an aeroplane. We all strain to see which direction it comes from, ready to bound away for cover if he comes in to strafe us. 'There it is!' Graves shouts, and I see the flash of sun on its propeller as it pops out from a cloud and aims itself at one of the balloons. Its machine gun is just a *tick tick tick* in the distance and we watch mesmerized as the observation balloon it heads toward pops into flames, the basket and men in it plummeting to earth. The plane turns and heads for another balloon, and it too erupts into flames, the men in it specks tumbling to the ground. Again the plane turns and this time begins firing at a third balloon. This one, rather than becoming a candle flame in the distance, simply goes limp, the air in it gone so that it spins lazily down. Some of the Canadians cheer as two more planes appear on the horizon, ours by the way they speed toward the other. The three planes swoop and fire, chase one another in circles and dives until an orange flame and thick black smoke erupts from the German plane and it falls to earth, disappearing behind the rise of Vimy Ridge.

'I would give my left arm to fly in one of those aeroplanes,' Elijah says to the others.

I can't imagine anything more frightening. Elijah begins to speak softly, so that the others around him must lean toward him. Everyone, it seems, wants to hear what he says as he begins to recount the events of that morning on the ridge in no man's land, and my English and my ears today are good enough to understand most of it. I must strain to hear Elijah, though, even though I lie close to him. I live in a world now where my head feels permanently stuffed with cotton.

Elijah talks of sneaking out in the pre-dawn darkness, slipping into a Hun listening post and slitting their throats. I notice that he has left out how he cut the hair from their heads. I also notice that he doesn't speak with his Englishman's accent much now that he has discovered the morphine. He tells of how the creeping barrage nearly caused him to soil his pants, how the shells landed so close he could taste the Canadian-made metal in his mouth, how he cursed his own artillery for being so accurate. The men around him laugh. He talks of hearing the chatter of their machine guns before he could see them through the snow and explosions, how he took out at least three nests from a distance and countless soldiers who were foolish enough to have their heads above their parapets. He stood and ran with the others, shooting from the hip, too close to use his scope, and joined the rest of the men around him in bayoneting the frightened Hun until the survivors ran from their trenches and down toward the Douai Plain, Elijah carefully and casually picking them off as they ran. It is as if I was not even there, as if I did not do as much as him in the attack.

One soldier pipes up and claims he witnessed Elijah hit a retreating Hun from at least five hundred yards away, says he's never seen anything like it in his life and probably never will again.

'Until the next time you are with me in a similar situation,' Elijah answers him.

They all laugh.

I look around and realize that I know very few of the men by name any more. So many have come and gone that I've lost track. Amazingly, Elijah seems to know all of them, acts as if he has known them for years. One of the new ones asks if it is true that Elijah was mentioned in dispatches that day. He nods.

'He'll probably get a bar added to the MM they promised him,' another says. 'You're the pride of the company.'

Elijah's eyes glow with the medicine in his veins. He has not mentioned me once.

We watch as a small duck flies along the stream, looking for a place to land. It skitters onto the water and floats with the current, maybe one hundred yards away. The soldier who's been praising Elijah says, 'That would be something nice to eat for supper,' looking to the others for a reaction. I can see that the duck's a fish eater and know its meat will be greasy and stinky. 'I'll bet Whiskeyjack could hit it from here.' The others around us laugh and agree. Elijah picks up his rifle, checks the action and slides a round into the chamber. He sits with his knees up and rests the rifle on one. We all go silent, watch for what will happen.

His shot cracks out and the water a foot ahead of the duck sprays up, sending the animal into a panicked flight. I watch as it lifts up high, then circles, looking for another place on the water to land. The men laugh and say, 'Nice shot,' anyway. The duck comes back in and lands not far from its original place.

I pick up my rifle and slip in a round, then take careful aim through my scope. With half a breath released, I pull the trigger and my rifle barks. The duck's feathers spray up, then slowly float back onto the water, landing on the surface and around the ripped carcass. The men around us stare at me as I stand up and walk away. Me, I won't let them forget who I am.

Two months pass and all I want is home. I'm sick with wanting to be back there now that summer has arrived here and small red flowers bloom in the most unexpected places on the front, around dead soldiers and their rifles, a feeble attempt to cover up the horror before the flowers are pounded into black slime by artillery. If I cannot be back home, I will be with Lisette, even if for just a night. Every day I plan how to do it, and in its small way this takes my mind off the desire to be home.

It seems that none of the generals around here know exactly what to do. No one had expected the Canadians to take Vimy Ridge and there was no follow-up plan. Command has us going up through the caves and tunnels of Vimy to spend our time on the front line, then we are moved to the support line, and then to the reserve line. It seems to me that everything these *wemistikoshiw* do is in threes. They are obsessed by that number. The front line, the support line and the reserve line is just the beginning of it. Their work parties are split into groups of three, and they are ordered to count off accordingly. Soldier one is sentry while soldier two and soldier three work. They've even divided their army into three sections, the infantry, the artillery and the cavalry. And these three sections are put through the same three rituals of training, then combat, then recovery.

This whole love for that number has trickled down from the ones who give the orders to the ones who take them. As soon as we are moved from the lines for rest, we follow the same pattern. Food, then rest, then women. We even die in threes. I have watched countless times how a soldier dies. He is a man before the bullet strikes, but when he is hit and the pain crashes into his body and he realizes that he has only moments left on this earth, he becomes a desperate animal. Finally, inescapably, he becomes a corpse. Sometimes I attend the prayers that the *wemistikoshiw* meet for and in these prayers they invoke their three *manitous,* the Father, the Son and the Holy Spirit. Maybe for this reason the *wemistikoshiw* do so much in threes.

But it does not stop there. I too have begun to see the world in threes. It was Elijah who taught me when sniping at night to look for the flare of the match in the Hun's trench. He showed me how to focus in on the match and to fire after slowly counting to three. The first soldier strikes the match to light his cigarette, and that is what we spot from our position. He then offers the match to his friend's cigarette, and that is when the sniper sights in on the flame with his rifle. When that soldier offers his match to his third friend, the sniper is given enough time to fire before that unlucky third soldier inhales the smoke.

I lie deep in the trench when the day is calm and think about how the world of the soldier consists of staring up at the sky, crawling upon the earth at night and living beneath it during the day. In the dark of night I think that my life has been divided into three for me by these *wemistikoshiw.* There was my life before them and their army, there is my life in their army, and, if I live, there will be my life after I have left it and returned home. They must have some magic in their number of three. I know that you, Niska, taught me that we will all someday walk the three-day road, and now I'm left wondering what connection there might be between their world and mine. I need to find out if we share something, some magic. Maybe it will help me get through all this.

Elijah and I spend most of our time on the front line patrolling the Douai Plain, sniping and scouting. He is able to settle comfortably into his madness when I am around and does not have to put on his Englishman's mask to cover it up. He carries his scalps with him and has dried them out to prevent rot and strung them together. I don't know how many he has. He talks to me late at night in whispers as we keep watch for movement on the plain or patrol the vast cave and tunnel complexes that not so long ago housed the enemy. 'The French will respect me,' he says, eyes glowing. 'I am better than Peggy. He cannot take a scalp. He cannot do what I do.'

I must listen to him carefully to hear what he says. My ears go deaf for a time, but usually it does not last long and then I can hear a little again.

We've found plenty of Fritz's gear in his old trenches. Lots of mess kits and helmets and articles of clothing and photos of smiling women and children, candles and boots and bullets, plenty of Mauser bullets for my rifle. We've found a couple of Mausers too, but none of them seem to suit Elijah, and none of them have the fine German scope that mine has. Elijah still tries to talk me out of it. It is like a game to him, but behind his friendly smile burns an obsession that is frightening. I fear many things in this place. But I do not want to fear my friend.

The craziest thing we have found was in a bunker thirty or forty feet below the earth. Behind a red velvet curtain are comfortable couches and chairs and candles everywhere and even electric lighting. And in the middle of the room is a grand piano. Elijah and I found someone who can play it, and this place soon became the officers' mess and we are not allowed to go there any more.

By mid-summer word trickles out that our section will be moving to another area, which means that we will soon be sent into another offensive. I am sick of this. I don't want to fight any more. Something needles me, is trying to tell me that the worst is still to come. But I can't imagine much worse than what I've been through. It is in mid-July, our last night at the front before we are to be sent back for rest, that I make up my mind. I will walk if I have to and see Lisette one more time. We have at least a few days' rest, and besides, no one ever seems to notice that I'm around.

Luck is with me on the first evening behind the line. We are bivouacked near a road and lorries carry wounded heading north. I listen carefully to the drivers talk, and through the tinny echo in my head realize that they are heading to a place only a few miles from where Lisette lives.

I grab a roll of gauze after evening roll call and make my way toward the convoy. Sitting with my rifle and pack close by me, I cut a small length across my arm with my bayonet, then dip the gauze into it, absorbing the red. The lorries begin to roll away, and I look around but no one seems to be paying attention. I walk to the lorries as they crawl toward the main road, and at the last possible second as they are gaining speed I jump onto the back of the last one and crawl between the canvas covers. I peer out to see if anyone has seen me, but the men in my company lie on their backs or sit and talk casually with one another.

As I begin to close the flaps, I spot Elijah. He stands on the road, staring at me, a quizzical expression on his face. He looks like a boy left out of the game. I wave to him, then settle back into the darkness of the truck, wrapping the gauze about my head so that I will appear wounded in the event that I'm discovered. A strange, good feeling washes over me now that I have broken away from him, now that I am the one doing and not the one left behind. The men all around me are crammed on stretchers or sitting slumped against the truck's wall. They moan and babble and occasionally shout, but worst of all is the stench. Tinny and sharp with a hint of rot. It is the smell of desperation, the stink of the dying.

I stick my head out of the back of the lorry. Even the choking dust kicked up by the tires is better than the reek inside. I breathe through a handkerchief and as night falls I stare out at the glow on the horizon and the flash of the big guns to the south where the war rages in earnest. The lorry's exhaust reminds me of the smell of that city called Toronto. I think back to those last few days of freedom before Elijah and I joined the army.

It seemed that every place we stopped on that train no longer had a recruiting depot. We stayed on the train and eventually it did stop. I panicked among all the people and the noise and so we found somewhere to camp by the great lake, away from it. The sand is warm in the sun and behind us a copse of trees stretches out to a marsh filled with the warbling of blackbirds.

'You'll get used to all this,' Elijah says. He points behind him to the sprawl of the city only a quarter-mile away, amazed at this quiet beach so close to the chaos. 'At least we found this good spot.'

Elijah leaves to explore the city while I walk through the bush that surrounds me. I find the tracks of a small deer, spend the day making snares along its route. Before Elijah makes it back the next morning I have the animal gutted and the hide in a small creek held down by rocks. It is a good thing. When he finally returns we are very hungry. We eat roasted deer and he tells me the story of his adventure.

He had found a cemetery on a hill that looks back down at the whole wide view of the city. At a quiet spot under the shade of a maple, he stretches out and stares up at the sky. White clouds scuttle along. His eyes are heavy.

Some time later he wakes with a start to the sound of voices. Turning his head, he sees a young woman and two children by a grave. The woman's head is bowed and she whispers to herself. The children fidget and kick at the grass with their shiny black shoes.

One of them looks up. Elijah sits and crosses his arms over his knees. The child, a small girl, smiles to him. Elijah smiles back. She looks to her mother and then to Elijah again. She walks toward him without the mother noticing.

'Hello,' she says.

'Hello,' Elijah answers.

'Who are you?' she asks. Her hair is almost white, a colour he has never seen before. It shimmers in the afternoon sun.

'I am Elijah,' he answers. 'Elijah Whiskeyjack.'

'You have a funny name,' she says.

'What's your name?'

'Suzanne,' she says.

'Do you have a last name?'

'Of course!' she giggles. 'Erikson.'

'Hmm …' Elijah says. 'Erik Suzanneson. That truly is a funny name, especially for a girl.'

'No, silly!' she squeals. 'Su*zanne* Erikson.'

'Oh, I apologize.'

'You have dark skin,' she says. 'And long hair like a girl.'

Elijah smiles.

'Where are you from?' she asks.

'A long way away,' he answers. 'A place called Moose Factory.'

'Moose Factory!' she says. 'That is a very silly name!'

'Yes.'

After a time, she points in the direction of her mother and brother. The boy is a little older than her and stares back at them shyly. 'That's my father,' she says, pointing again at the two.

It takes Elijah a few seconds to realize what she means.

'He died in a war,' she says. 'He died in a place called France.' She appears a little puzzled. 'His body isn't even in that grave,' she says. 'They buried him in France.'

Elijah nods.

'The dirty Huns killed him with gas,' she says, then shrugs as if this is something that happens to her every day.

'Suzanne!' her mother calls suddenly. 'Come here right away!'

'Bye, Elijah,' she says brightly, then turns and runs off.

By the time the lorry rolls to a stop it is the dead of night and my kidneys ache from the truck's constant pounding on the pitted road. I get out and am greeted by the hands of orderlies trying to lead me into a building bright with electric lights. I shake them off and they stare as I make my way into the darkness. A couple of them shout at me, but they are too busy to pursue me as they unload the wounded from the truck.

If I remember correctly, the road leads out of here south and west toward Lisette's village. I begin walking it, keeping an eye out for patrols and for sentries. They will throw me in a prison if I'm discovered here, and to be locked up so close to Lisette will surely kill me. When I reach the end of town, I head out into the darkness of the road that stretches across fields and dykes and through what were once orchards. A mist rises all around and in the darkness I'm reminded of my first month in this place, when it seemed I'd been thrown into an underworld full of skulls and quick, brutal death. So much has changed since then. I realize that the place hasn't changed. It's me.

I sense rather than hear soldiers coming toward me in the fog. I dive for cover in a shallow ditch and lie prone, rifle at the ready. Voices come out of the darkness and four bodies appear, ghostly in the fog. They support one another, and I realize it is a song they are shouting out, their voices swallowed by the night. They are drunk, I see, returning from Lisette's village, trying to make it back before dawn and roll call. A knot forms in my stomach when I realize that in a few hours it will be discovered that I'm missing. When the men are past safely, I move on.

I can hear the estaminet from a long way off. Not too long before dawn now, but it still hums with life. Little has changed here, which makes me feel good. Men sit on the ground outside of it, drunk. They pay me no mind as I make my way to Lisette's door beside the drinking place.

I decide to find out if there is a back door, and walk around the small building. I see one. My stomach is in my throat as I softly knock. Lisette lives with her mother, I think I remember her telling me. I do not wish for the old woman or Lisette's father to answer the door. No one comes to the door so I knock a little louder. Maybe she has moved away? My heart speeds.

I knock again, and finally see the flare of a match touching candle in the window upstairs and hear the slap of bare feet on stairs inside.

The door opens a little and there is Lisette, her blonde hair shining in the light of the candle she holds. Her eyes are sleepy like a little girl's, and my whole body fills with warmth. My legs tremble. But her eyes do not change when they focus on me. We stare at each other for a few moments.

'You are hurt,' she finally says. 'Do you need some water?'

'I am not hurt,' I say in my best English. 'I ... I came very long to see you.'

'You cannot see me,' she says, and I realize that I still have the gauze wrapped about my head. I tear at it and pull it away to show her that it's me.

'It is me, Xavier,' I say.

Something in her eyes brightens and I think that now she will know me and let me in.

'I remember you!' she says. 'You are the Indian boy, the boy from Canada!'

'Yes,' I say.

'You can't stay, Indian boy,' she whispers.

My stomach feels as if it has been punched hard so that all the air has left it.

'I am with another. He is upstairs.' She points with her finger.

An anger sweeps over me so suddenly that I feel I might fall down. 'I come very long to see you!' I shout, and it is strange to hear my own voice, the voice that I have used so rarely in this last year.

'You must go now!' she says, and then a voice behind her startles me.

'Who's there!' he demands in a British accent. His face appears in the candlelight behind Lisette. He has a long moustache, the moustache of an officer.

I do not answer, just glare at him with a hatred I have rarely felt.

'Who are you, soldier?' he demands. 'What regiment do you belong to? What is the meaning of all this?'

My eyes might burn a hole into the officer's head.

'You are speaking to an officer!' he shouts, and as he does so I swing at him over Lisette, hitting him squarely in the nose, the force of my arm sending Lisette to the ground too.

Immediately I feel ashamed for hurting her, and try to reach down to help her up. She screams, though, and the officer behind her moans with his hands cupped over his nose.

'Leave!' she cries.

I pick up my pack and rifle and turn from her, running from her courtyard, running down the road and out of the village as fast as I can. I keep running along the road until I can run no further, my pack bouncing on my back, my rifle in hand. The sky glows at the edges and a mist is slowly burning off the ground. Something in me has gone dull and hard, and I force myself to keep running. My ears hear nothing now but the shallow *whoosh* of my own breath in my chest.

I avoid the place with the hospital and begin making my way south along a dirt road, no longer caring that I will be court-martialled when I make it back. I will just keep walking along this road until I'm with my section again, and then if they let me, I will go back to the trenches and commence killing. I pass rows of soldiers marching north for a brief leave, their faces lined and dirty and tired. I blend in with a company making its way south, and we march to a place where more lorries wait to take us back to Vimy.

Not caring if I'm caught, I line up with the others and climb into the open back of a transport, a few of them looking at me but not saying anything. We begin the bumpy ride south along pocked fields of mud and the ruins of little villages. The rain begins, a steady mist that soaks through my clothing and gives me chills. The others in the truck, like me, seem resolved to it and they keep their heads bowed with knees close to their chests.

It is dark once more when I recognize the crossroads near where my company rests. I jump from the truck and land on one knee. Pain shoots up and through my crotch so I feel like I've been kicked there. I let the intensity of it burn away everything else inside of me and limp toward the darkened camp. I slip by the young sentry who is new to us. He is half asleep, and I must stop myself from reaching out and tapping him as I pass in the darkness. This one has much to learn, if he does not die first.

When we are called into formation in the morning for roll, Elijah stands beside me. 'Where did you go?' he asks in Cree.

'I do not want to talk,' I say.

'I see,' he answers. 'You went to find that girl, didn't you. I could have saved you the trouble and told you she was a whore, but you would not have listened.'

I look over at Elijah, remember how he first approached her, talked to her. The truth begins to creep into my head. Something I've never felt before rushes over me. I want to beat Elijah with my fists until he is bloody.

McCaan and Breech appear before the line. Breech walks up and down it, inspecting the troops as McCaan calls out names. Mine is one of the first, and when McCaan calls out, 'Private Bird!' I answer, the men around me turning their heads to look. McCaan pauses briefly, then continues to call out, and I am left to wonder what is happening. When McCaan is done calling names, he takes his place and Breech steps up.

'An important announcement, gentlemen,' he begins, looking up and down the rows, his tall riding boots shiny in the morning light. 'You might have heard the rumours, which are true. We will shortly be sent to a new undisclosed location. It appears that our victory at Vimy has made us the darlings of the British Command and we are to spearhead another offensive.' It does not seem to be the news anyone around me wants to hear. Shoulders visibly slump. 'On a separate note,' he contin-ues, 'I've just received word that medals have been awarded to our company for valour in the field. Sergeant McCaan, Corporal Williams and Private Reardon have all been recommended for bravery in action.' Breech pauses. 'I am especially proud to note that Acting Corporal Whiskeyjack has been recommended for the MM for unmatched bravery in the face of the enemy.'

The men all around me cheer. My ears have begun to ring again.

'A more formal ceremony is promised before we move out,' says Breech. 'Dismissed.'

The men relax and turn to Elijah and in the commotion and the press of bodies I feel crushed. I really must be invisible to them. And then I hear McCaan's voice booming over the others'.

'Private Bird, report to me at once! Private Bird to the lieutenant's quarters!'

My stomach fills with sour juice. The men look at me and

then avert their eyes. A few mumble half-heartedly.

'No worries,' Elijah says to me in Cree. 'I will come with you. Just speak in Cree and I will translate.'

I glance at him, then spit on the ground and look away. I move forward toward McCaan, who waits in the middle of the impromptu parade ground. We then move single file, McCaan first, me second, Elijah third.

The lieutenant's tent is cool and dark. He stands when we enter and asks Elijah his business here.

'Private Bird's English is very poor, sir,' he says. 'You will need me to translate.'

I know that McCaan knows better, and wonder why he does not speak up at this.

'It is a desperate army indeed that allows non-English speakers into it,' Breech mutters. 'Does the private understand that the penalty for desertion is immediate execution by firing squad?' He pauses as if to let this point sink in. 'Ask the private his whereabouts last night and the day before.'

Elijah's eyes capture mine, and in Cree he says, 'I've got an idea. Just speak in our tongue and I will do the translating. Don't fight me on this.'

'I do not give a shit any more,' I say in Cree. 'Let the bastards shoot me. Fritz will anyway, sooner or later.'

Elijah turns to the lieutenant, and in his funny accent begins to speak. 'The private says that he went out in search of fresh game for the men. He became lost in this foreign environment and was only able to make it back late last night. He'd planned on reporting to Sergeant McCaan directly, but had not been afforded the chance to before roll call this morning. By then, it was too late.'

Breech appears a little puzzled. It is not the answer he had expected. 'Surely the private must understand that absence without permission is a dire offence? Ask him this.'

Elijah turns to me. 'Pretty good lie, eh?' he says. 'You went out in order to help the others. I knew it would catch him off guard.'

'Tell the lieutenant that I fucked his mother last night,' I respond. Elijah pretends a cough to cover up the grunt of a laugh. I look into his eyes and ask, 'Why did you fool me about her? And why do they overlook me for all of the honours?'

Elijah turns back to Breech. 'The private has not been himself since our offensive at Vimy. He took a tremendous blow to the head in the midst of some very brutal hand-to-hand fighting in Fritz's trenches. Sergeant McCaan witnessed this.' Elijah's eyes find the sergeant. McCaan nods his head in agreement. 'He has been suffering bouts of forgetfulness and nausea since,' Elijah continues. 'He only meant to add to our fresh meat supply when he disappeared. There isn't a man in our company who would argue that Private Bird is not an excellent soldier and person.'

Breech is silent for a while, contemplating all of the information. 'Has the private been examined by a physician since the battle?' he asks.

'I hope that you made that hussy sore for all of the trouble she has caused you,' Elijah says to me.

'I am sick of this army and want to go back to Mushkegowuk,' I say.

Elijah turns again to Breech. 'Private Bird is somewhat fearful of the English form of medicine. He is used to a much more primitive practice of healing. I've asked him to see our medics, but he is disoriented, afraid.'

Again the lieutenant pauses, curling the tips of his moustache as he thinks. 'I will not even dare ask what sorcery this heathen practises in the wild forests back home.' He shakes his head sadly at McCaan. 'I order Private Bird to three days' confinement under the watch of a medic. After that time it will be decided if he is fit to go back in the field. Tell the private this and ask if he has anything else to say.'

Elijah says to me, 'You are a lucky bastard. You are lucky that I am such a good friend.'

'Tell Breech that his mother is a loose and lousy fuck with moose mittens for tits. Also tell him that I am going to escape tonight and make my way back home.'

'The private asks that I say thank you and says that he looks forward to care and rest.'

Elijah is allowed to walk with me and the military policeman to the place where I am to be held. 'You were miserable back there, Xavier,' Elijah says.

I clench my fists.

'I knew that a woman would be good for you but that you would never visit a whore, and so I did this for you to help you, not to hurt you.'

'Bastard,' I say, and spit again.

'I paid a lot of money for her time with you. If I knew you were going to fall in love like a fool, I wouldn't have done it. Now I wish I hadn't.'

'Shut up now and go away,' I say, not looking at him.

He turns from me then and heads back toward the others.

The cabin in which they've put me is still and dusty and hot. They have taken my rifle and given me fresh clothes that are itchy and too warm. A guard has been posted outside of the door and every few hours the medic comes to peer into my eyes and ask questions slowly. I stare out the glassless window at the patch of sky and high white clouds. The only entertainment is a barn swallow that has made a nest in the corner of the cabin near the window and swoops in and out, busy feeding her noisy young. I watch her work and it is the comfort of the bush that wraps around me. The bird reminds me of home. I watch it all afternoon, fascinated.

In the early evening with the sun beginning to slant lower, I hear the guard outside say something, and then Breech comes in the door, followed by Elijah and the medic.

'How is the private doing?' he asks, surveying the room.

'I think that he suffers exhaustion and that rest will do him a world of good,' the medic says.

'Ask the private how he is doing,' Breech says to Elijah.

'I brought you a piece of goose that I got from a farm last night,' Elijah says in our tongue. 'It is here, under my shirt.'

I don't want to do it, but I nod to him.

'He is feeling much better, sir,' Elijah answers.

The swallow has come back in the room but is angry at the intrusion. It seems to have taken a dislike to Breech and perches on a rafter near its nest, calling out noisily at him. Breech looks up, annoyed.

'Have the private remove that bird and its nest at once,' he says. 'This is no way to keep one's quarters!'

Elijah reaches for a broom in the corner, hands it to me, points to the nest.

I refuse to take the broom, glare back.

'It is just a bird,' Elijah says. 'It is not worth the trouble. Breech is testing you. He needs to feel that he controls you.'

'Fuck the lieutenant,' I say.

'Tell the private to stand up and sweep down that nest!' the lieutenant shouts, suddenly angry.

I don't move.

'Do it,' Elijah says.

I stare up at the ceiling. The swallow chatters louder. Elijah takes the broom and sweeps the nest hard, knocking it to the floor. The baby swallows tumble out. Two are lifeless, killed instantly by the fall. The third raises his featherless head, bewildered, its eyes large and round above its small yellow beak. Its tiny wings beat frantically on the floor, then more slowly. The mother bird cries out. The baby swallow's lids sink and it ceases to move. I turn my head away from all of them.

KA NIPIHAT WINDIGOWA
Windigo Killer

I MADE XAVIER SMILE with my story of smacking the nun with my paddle, and this gives me hope. Steering the canoe slow through the afternoon I watch him drift into sleep. It is a restless time for him, and his face looks like a scared child's when he cries out. To try and ease him a little, I start talking again. The story is not a happy one, but something in me has to tell it. There is truth in this story that Xavier needs to hear, and maybe it is best that he hears it in sleep so that the medicine in the tale can slip into him unnoticed.

I ask Nephew if he remembers the sunny day after a large snowfall when the branches of the trees were covered and glittering. He was still a small boy. It was the day an *awawatuk* from the turtle clan came visiting us. His unexpected arrival reminded me of another visit long ago.

You sat with me, Nephew, in our winter lodge. Do you remember? We brewed tea and I sewed while you played a stick game in the corner. We both went quiet at the sound of snowshoes. Fearful that *wemistikoshiw* approached, I motioned for you to sit and wait while I went to see who it was. Outside I recognized the face of an old hunter.

The old man spoke immediately. 'One of us has gone *windigo* this winter,' he said, and the words brought all of the memories of my father back to me so that I was light-headed and feared I might fall. But I had to appear strong. I stood and waited and listened.

'A young man went out in the bush and did not come back for weeks. We assumed he was dead. But when he came back he carried a pack full of meat that was obviously human. He has gone mad and threatens to destroy all of us.'

'How many are you?' I asked.

'Twelve,' he answered. 'Most of us are relations. The young man is my nephew.'

I had no choice. 'Where is your camp?' I asked.

'Two days' walk from here,' he answered. 'At the place near Thunderhouse Rapids.'

'We will leave at once,' I told him, and turned to go inside and gather my things.

The travelling was difficult in the deep, wet snow. We walked hard for two days, you struggling to keep up. The walk stretched into a third. I would have preferred not to bring you to this place of sickness where we were heading, but it was too risky to leave you alone at my camp. Possibly, I wouldn't return myself. I wasn't sure what awaited me.

I knew that the old man we walked with wondered about the little boy accompanying me. He knew I was not a mother, but the old man kept his stare straight ahead, his wizened eyes not giving a hint as to what he was thinking. We built a shelter at night, kept warm with a fire. We'd stop a few times during the day to eat jerkied moose. The old man kept the pace quick. He was anxious to get back and be rid of the badness that had descended on his people.

I pieced the story together over those days of travelling. The tale was similar to what I had witnessed as a young girl, except this time the wife had died and her husband, the old man's nephew, had eaten her. He'd come back into the small community of *awawatuk* half mad with sadness and anger, not trying to hide the fact that he'd gone *windigo,* attacking his old uncle, who with the help of the other men was barely able to hold him down and bind him tightly. When we were close to his village, the old man rolled up his sleeve and showed me where his nephew had bitten him. A purple welt tattooed his arm, teeth marks clearly visible. It looked infected. I would apply herbs to it when we got to his home.

I expected some kind of noise or movement when on the third morning we finally walked into the clearing with a few *askihkans* that was the old man's winter home. But the place was as still as death. The fear that I'd been holding back surfaced. I questioned if I was ready to take on the role of my father. The immensity of what was expected of me made me doubt my ability. That the *windigo* had escaped his ropes and had killed everyone was a secondary fear, and in realizing this I was able to ground myself a little. I saw smoke coming from the fire holes of the *askihkans* then, and pushed away my doubt as best I could.

As soon as I saw the *askihkan* where the nephew lay, I pointed to it and said, 'He's there.' The old man nodded, his eyes telling me he wondered how I was so sure. But it was as if the *askihkan* glowed from within. An aura as bright to me as the North Lights pulsed from within it with a great sadness. I realized then that sadness was at the heart of the *windigo,* a sadness so pure that it shrivelled the human heart and let something else grow in its place. To know that you have dese-crated the ones you love, that you have done something so damning out of a greed for life that you have been exiled from your people forever is a hard meal to swallow, much harder to swallow than that first bite of human flesh.

The old man tried immediately to take me to the place where his nephew lay bound and guarded, but I told him I needed a place in which I could prepare and pray for a while. He led me to his shelter and I was left there, you quietly waiting nearby. I sat in the darkness a long time, not praying, not thinking even, just rocking on my haunches and waiting for the *ahcahk* of my father to come to me.

My mind was blank as I left the old man's *askihkan,* not full of light or strength or anything else. I told you to stay until I returned. The old man sat outside waiting for me, gazing off into the bush. I saw the faces of a couple of small children peering out at me from the entryways of their *askihkans,* but hands quickly pulled them inside. The sickness of the *windigo* could spread as surely as the invisible sicknesses of the *wemistikoshiw*. I was the surgeon summoned to carve the illness from this small group, the one assumed to have the skill that the others did not.

The old man led me to the lodge where the sick one lay, and in my numbness I couldn't help but feel like a prisoner being led to confinement. The pain emanating from the *askihkan* pulsed stronger as I approached. I felt as if I was walking against a strong current, as if I might be swept away at any minute. The old man pulled aside the hide covering and I stepped into the darkness, my eyes slow to adjust. Two men sat by the doorway, keeping watch over the form covered by a blanket. I asked them to remove the blanket. When they did I was surprised by the smallness of the man left exposed, bound hand and foot, staring back at me with goose-black eyes. They didn't appear human at all, those eyes, looking at me with the inquisitiveness of an animal. And I watched as those eyes changed when they realized who and what I was. They went cold and lightless as a stone, and he turned his head toward the wall.

I had arrived with no plan, hoping that what I needed to do would come to me. I told the two men to untie him and to hold his arms above his head, knowing that this would make it more difficult for him to fight. Their eyes searched my face for just a second, then they did as I asked. I told the old man to sit on the *windigo*'s feet, to have his knife ready in the event it overpowered us. There was no struggle as the men untied his arms from his sides and then lifted them above his head, holding them there so that he was stretched out on the blanket. I pulled a stick from the firepit and my rope from around my waist and knelt beside him. He smelled sour, like he'd pissed himself, but there was a deeper musk too, one that I'd not smelled before and hoped not to again. I straddled his chest so that my slight weight was on him. Finally he turned his head to me and looked deep into my eyes.

I could see that he understood. I reached under his neck and placed the rope around it, wrapping both ends around the stick. All I had to do now was twist the stick around and around until the rope tightened and cut his breath off. I started to whisper a prayer to *Gitchi Manitou* and began twisting the stick with each sentence of my prayer. The rope bit into his neck and he began to struggle. I twisted more and prayed louder. His eyes flooded with an animal's panic, and he bucked me hard, trying to throw me from him. I squeezed my thighs tighter around him and kept twisting so that his eyes began to widen and bulge. The men holding his arms strained against his strength, cursing and breathing hard. From the way the *windigo* writhed and flopped, I knew that the old man too was holding on for his life.

The *windigo* began to pant and speak in a tongue I'd not heard before, the voice scratched. His eyes burned into mine and I realized that he was cursing me. I prayed louder to *Gitchi Manitou*, asking to deflect this curse, to carry it away on the smoke of the fire and out of the lodge into the sky. My hands stung from the work of twisting. The *windigo*'s face had turned purple and I was afraid that his eyes would pop from his head. His words melted into a long groan and his thick tongue stuck out from his mouth.

With one last great shudder, he tried to throw me from him. My body and feet went into the air and, just before the point where I was about to flip off of him, my body's weight came back down hard onto his chest. With a great gush of spittle and blood, the last stinking air in his body left him and splattered onto my rough cotton shirt. His eyes remained open, the whites turned a deep red from the strangulation. The two men who'd held his arms fell back in a heap. I turned around and saw the old man crouched, looking at me.

I stood after a time, my legs shaking. I felt the warm trickle of my blood running down the insides of my thighs. A sound in the corner caught my attention. I turned quickly. You sat in shadow inside the lodge, watching us. You'd sneaked in, and I could tell by your face that you'd seen everything.

The next day I gave the men directions on how to dispose of the body. I told them to construct a large fire of hardwood and build up the hot coals for a day. When the fire was at its height they would place the body upon it and would keep the fire burning until there was nothing left. They would then carefully sweep up the ash and burn it upon another fire. This was to be repeated a third time, and when the ash was carefully collected from the last fire they were to sprinkle it in the river and let the current carry it away.

The old man offered to walk me back the two or three days to my lodge, but I told him that I wanted to go alone with my nephew. We set out early the next morning, my head crowded with too many thoughts, like children vying for attention so that I was unable to deal with any of them. Had I rid these people of the *windigo* in the proper way? Maybe word of my deed would make its way to the *wemistikoshiw,* who would come after me and condemn me as they had my father? Just as I had witnessed it at your age, you had now seen something that you were too young to understand fully. I needed to explain to you that I was a healer, and that sometimes healing entailed cutting out the sickness. Once I had fought the role placed upon me, the struggle as difficult as trying to tame a wolf or fox for a pet. Back then I was young still and wanted to live free of it all. But I was older now and knew that such denying was not possible.

You finally spoke to me, Nephew, on the morning of the third day, when we were close to home.

'Why did you kill that man, Auntie?'

I had expected the question, but not so soon. After a long time, I said, 'Sometimes one must be sacrificed if all are to survive.' You nodded as if you were a grown-up, even though you couldn't fully understand. I had taught you all about the physical life of the bush, and it was time to teach you about the other life.

You and I continued where we had left off, and I was as happy as I'd ever been now that you were near me. You grew strong in the bush, your hair long and black by the time you were in your twelfth summer. You wore it braided and I wove into it a strip of rawhide and a thin red length of yarn so that you wore it the same way my father had. You seemed more than content to forget the *wemistikoshiw* ways, and it was rare that we spoke any English at all, or even talked of that place.

You asked about your mother, Rabbit, but I knew little. After my father died and we were forced to go to the town to survive, her will dried up. It is very easy in those circumstances to find comfort, to soak in *wemistikoshiw* drink, and this is what your mother did. I explained to you that I found my comfort in the sweat lodge, and many of the answers that I needed in the shaking tent. Over the years I taught you how to cleanse yourself, and, much more difficult, how to divine answers yourself. This last cannot be taught so much as nurtured, and many days I saw the spark of true talent in you. But you were much more interested in the hunt, spending longer and longer periods out alone in the bush.

One day you came to me and asked me something that took me by surprise. But it made sense to me. It was quite natural.

'I want a friend, Auntie,' you said that evening when you'd returned from your traplines with three fox and a marten. 'I am lonely.'

I looked up from my sewing and saw that indeed you had grown up over the last winter. 'Do you mean a girl?' I asked.

You turned red and blurted out, 'No! I want a friend who is another boy who I can hunt with and play games with. I will wait for a girl until I am older.'

I laughed, but saw immediately that I had hurt your feelings. 'I do not mean to laugh at you, Nephew,' I said. 'It is just that you are very rational. You aren't afraid to hide your feelings either, and that is a good thing.'

We sat for a long time. I helped you skin the animals. 'Not too many people live around here,' I finally said. 'Where will you find a friend, especially one your age?'

'We can move closer to the town,' you said.

I hadn't been ready for this answer.

'If the *wemistikoshiw* were to find you, they would take you away and put you back in that school.'

'No *wemistikoshiw* can catch me, Auntie,' you said. 'I do not want to live in town, just close enough that I can find my old friend who will come out into the bush with me to hunt.'

'We shall go when the weather allows it,' I said after a while.

You smiled.

Although I didn't like to admit it, living back near other humans again felt good. That I did not see anyone didn't matter. I was comforted a little by the fact that a half-day walk was all that separated me from other Cree. You were much happier too. I worried each time you'd make your way to the town, but you always returned, and within a few months you began to bring back a boy with you who was your age and who enjoyed to hunt as much as you. Your friend spent many days in the summers with us, and I worried that his parents would grow concerned at his long absences. One night, as politely as I could, I asked him about this.

'My mother is dead, so she doesn't worry much about me,' he answered. 'I was told my father traps for the Hudson's Bay Company but I have never seen him. If I didn't come out here to stay with you, those fat nuns would make me paddle them around while they scared away all the fish in the river.'

I laughed at his talk. It brought back memories of years before.

'I think that I would like to stay with you rather than go back to the residential school in autumn,' he added.

'I do not think that is possible,' I said. 'They would surely come and look for you and throw us all in one of their prisons.'

'Well, we should think about it,' he answered.

He knew little of the bush, and I watched proudly as you taught him, Nephew. And how he liked to talk! For hours he could talk about anything, the stars, the rivers, the school, the people that he knew, places he didn't know, far away across the ocean. Late each night I would fall asleep to his chatter. You lay beside him, Nephew, your eyes open wide as you listened to his stories.

Your friend began to return to our camp with a rifle and many bullets. I still had an old musket that had been my father's, and had traded with other *awawatuk* for powder and balls of lead. But his was a fine rifle, a repeating Winchester that was almost as tall as you two boys. I wondered where he would get such a fine rifle, patiently waited for the story to come out. I did not have to wait long.

'I took this from one of the nuns,' he said to you one day while we sat around a fire outside, smoking fish for the approaching winter. 'What does a nun need with a gun, anyway? I've seen her shoot it, too,' he added. 'She is the worst shot I have ever seen.'

'I don't know if it's right to take something that isn't yours,' you said to him.

'I am a warrior,' he answered. 'I will use this gun far more and far better than her. It is small payment for her always wanting to bathe me.'

You both laughed at this, but the words echoed in my head for days afterwards.

All the rest of that summer you had shooting competitions with one another, and I watched how quickly both of you excelled. You shot at rocks you'd placed upon other rocks across the river, you shot leaves from trees, you shot the heads from grouse that roosted on the tops of tall pines. Neither of you missed very often. Your competition was friendly but serious.

'Nephew,' I called out one day after the two of you had repeatedly tried to shoot a small rock a great distance away, 'the two of you are truly talented marksmen.' You smiled at me. Your friend took aim carefully at the rock, fired, but missed.

'Why does she call you Nephew and not your real name?' he asked.

'Nephew is my real name,' you answered. 'I am her nephew.'

'Does she ever call you by your Christian name?' he asked.

You shook your head, looked at me nervously. 'My name is Nephew.'

'Your name is Xavier,' your friend answered.

It was not said meanly. I could tell from his voice that the boy was simply trying to understand.

'Your Christian name is Xavier,' he said. 'And mine is Elijah.'

TAPAKWEWIN
Snaring

AS NISKA MAKES CAMP for another night, I take a needleful of morphine, enough to send away the pain in my body, but not to kill me. I no longer have enough to stop my heart, only enough to get me through, at best, tomorrow. What will happen to me after that? I decide not to dwell on this now but instead to enjoy the warm river of it.

I must figure out what happened to Elijah. If Elijah can come back to me, he will help me. We will fight together again, fight against this medicine that consumes us. We will get better together. He will help me overcome the pain and I will help pull him from the war madness that swallowed him whole. Where is he?

I remember when he began to explore the places that aren't safe to explore. I remember him learning to love killing rather than simply killing to survive. Even when he went so far into that other place that I worried for him constantly, he still loved to tell me stories. He never lost his ability to talk. I think it was this ability that fooled the others around us into believing he hadn't gone mad. But I knew.

Elijah tells me a story. One night in late September he finds himself in a Hun trench. He's not sure how he's gotten here. More and more he finds himself losing pieces of his day. His face is blackened by cork and he's alone. He remembers patrolling one of the small, crushed villages with a number of

305

others close by Hill 70. And now he's here. He must have slipped off on his own and made his way through their wire. He's here for a reason, he's sure. If he could only remember what it is.

He looks in his hand and sees that he's holding a spool of thin wire he'd found by an ammunition dump. Now he knows! Before he's discovered, he forms a slip-knot with the wire and wraps each end to support beams on either side of the trench wall. It is a wonderful place for a rabbit run, the snare placed carefully by steps that lead down a few feet deeper. With luck, a man close to Elijah's height will put his head right through and, as he jumps down, meet his end.

Elijah climbs out of the trench and finds a place to hide and watch. Amazingly, no one comes, and so he pulls a Mills bomb from his pack, is about to pull the pin, but thinks better of it. He places the bomb back and cups his hands by his mouth. Constricting his throat he makes the call of the goose, the honking sound as sweet and gruff as he's ever remembered. A long time since he's made that sound. It feels good. This will surely get men running. Still nothing. Another idea comes to him. He cups his hands around his mouth again and calls out, 'Here Fritzy, Fritzy, Fritzy.'

Within a minute he hears the stamp of boots coming down the run. Four or five soldiers approach, slowing where the trench traverses. One and then another and another passes by the snare and jumps down unharmed. Has he made some miscalculation?

Then another soldier comes running and jumps down the steps, but stops abruptly, his feet kicking wildly a number of inches above the ground. He grasps at his neck, but the wire is buried now so tightly in his skin that all he can do is struggle himself to death. Within seconds he hangs there twitching. A couple of soldiers come up from behind him and, seeing their comrade apparently floating, stop dead and stare, not quite sure what is happening. One approaches and figures it out. He shouts for the others. Men come running, and as they are busy talking frantically and trying to release the body from the snare, Elijah slips back into the night. If he tells, who would believe it?

There are days behind the line when all he wants to do is stare up at the sky and look for aeroplanes. He's asked about how one might get to fly. Nobody seems to know. The light of day hurts his eyes, he tells me. He eats very little. He does not shit. He drinks water and tea with lots of sugar and whiles away his time until we are sent back into the front line. That is his home.

He tells me that when he sleeps he dreams of being sent into a freshly dug mine shaft under the Hun line. He's sent in carrying a great sack of explosives and travels deep into the shaft, the walls around him getting closer and closer. Without warning the tunnel ahead and the tunnel behind seal shut. His torch is extinguished. He's left in a stifling black hole with enough explosives to tear out the bottom of the world.

One morning after stand-to we are given the order to change our socks for dry, clean ones. We've not been wearing our moccasins since Hill 70. Thick-soled boots are more sensible for walking over the shattered brick and sharp stones. Once his boots and old socks are removed, I see that the toes on Elijah's left foot are a bit black. He rubs them and I can tell by his face that the pain shoots through his morning haze. He tries to cover them before someone notices, but McCaan is nearby.

'Look at that foot, Whiskeyjack!' he growls. 'It stinks of rot. Report to the medic immediately.'

He limps down the line and finds Driscoll. The medic pushes his glasses back on his nose and takes Elijah's foot in his lap, staring at it intently. 'You've got the beginnings of a nasty case of trenchfoot, Corporal,' he says.

Driscoll pulls out a tin from his medical kit and opens it, scoops what looks like grease onto his fingers and rubs it onto Elijah's foot. The pain makes Elijah feel faint.

'Whale oil,' Driscoll says. 'I haven't seen a case of trench-foot in months. You mustn't be taking very good care of yourself. Don't let an officer see this or he'll put you up on charges.' Elijah laughs, but he sees Driscoll is serious. 'Change your socks twice a day,' Driscoll continues, 'and use the whale oil liberally each time. If it gets worse, I'll report you myself.'

'No need for that,' Elijah says as cheerily as he can. 'Hardly hurts, hardly hurts.'

Driscoll hands him a small vial of tablets. 'If it gets too much, pop one of these in your mouth and let it dissolve under your tongue. It's morphine.' He winks at Elijah. 'Just don't take any before a patrol.'

Elijah begins to walk away.

'Corporal,' Driscoll calls out before he's made it too far. Elijah turns back. 'You're looking rather anemic. Are you eating properly?'

'Just fine, sir.' Elijah walks away, limping and whistling.

WE ARE ORDERED TO GO over the top near a town called Lens. Our battalion crouches, backs to the mud wall, faces between knees. Shells scream and slam into the enemy trenches nearby and my body vibrates with the earth. I look over to Elijah beside me. He smiles.

Later, he tells me that he hums to himself a song that's become popular with the soldiers. He can't hear what he hums over the noise, just feels the vibration of the song in his chest. Everything shakes so badly he wonders how it is that the world keeps from falling apart. The soldiers around him squat too, wait for the barrage to end before they pour over the top. They keep their eyes squeezed shut, hands by their faces for protection. Elijah looks at those beside him, at me, at Graves, at Fat, at McCaan, at all the newer ones, wonders who he won't see after today. The barrage reaches a crescendo. All that exists in the universe is noise, he thinks. The thought makes him begin to laugh.

And then all goes still. His ears hum an electric buzz and he can hear his own breathing deep inside him. There are places in the world, far off, where men are not about to do what Elijah and the others tense and wait to do. Elijah imagines men at this very moment still sleeping in their beds beside their wives. He imagines Indian hunters rising with the dawn to track through the forest. Although the silence only lasts for a few seconds, Elijah imagines it goes on for hours, his mind ticking like a pocket watch, the medicine in his veins illuminating the true meaning of all of this, moments before it will change so completely for so many.

A shrill whistle breaks the quiet. It sounds like the lone call of some crazed bird, makes Elijah's stomach drop. Breech begins screaming, giving the order. Elijah's waited all night for this, made sure to inject enough medicine into his bruised body to keep him calm without putting him to sleep. We've drunk our rum. Now we climb over the parapet screaming.

Immediately the machine guns start rattling and men on both sides are falling. Fat struggles to climb over, and Elijah and I turn back and pull him up with as much strength as we can muster. Fat's trip to Blighty wasn't long enough. He lies there like an invalid, trying to catch his breath, and so Elijah and I turn to begin the advance. It rains metal, bullets ripping the ground and the sandbags right beside us.

When we begin the short run to the Boche line, Elijah and I find ourselves behind a thin row of soldiers who have taken the lead, but many of them kneel and lie, or are thrown down by the machine guns, and soon it is only Elijah and me, it seems, running headlong to the barbed wire. We hear the *boom* and feel the thunk of mortars crashing all around. Tossing ourselves in front of the German wire we wait for the sappers with their Bangalore torpedoes to come up from behind. Only one arrives and he slips in beside, slides the tube into the wire, lights the fuse, then orders us to roll away and cover our heads. We do as we're told and the tube blows a nice wide swath through the wire. I roll first, Elijah follows, and we crawl fast as we can through the hole, a machine gun now trained on us and the bullets whistling just over our heads and exploding into the earth and creating showers of dirt.

Once through the wire both Elijah and I set our grenades and lob them into the area that holds the machine-gunner. Elijah carries an automatic rifle that McCaan gave him to use today. He carries his sniper rifle strapped snugly on his back, and he trains his machine gun on the smoke and dust in the place where it seems that most of the firing has come from. The gun is heavy and kicks hard in his hands as he sprays the nest. The nest goes quiet. We advance quick, bent over double, and jump into the advance trench, ready to begin shooting at close range.

The place is blasted. Two Boche lie slumped over the gun and others are scattered about in deformed poses, legs and arms bent at strange angles. One is still alive, moaning and cursing. Elijah walks over to him and empties the rest of the magazine into his chest. He reloads and drags what barbed wire he can into the trench, twenty yards on either side of us, while I keep watch. It will slow down any counterattacking Hun if they decide to retake this section.

I wonder where the rest of the enemy are, but then realize that this is just one small advance trench of many that surround the ruins of coal-mining villages that we've been ordered to overrun. We sit tight and wait for any of the others that might make it to us. Soon other soldiers begin trickling in, McCaan, Graves, Grey Eyes. I'm happy to see Corporal Thompson slide into the trench with us. He's back from Blighty and looks thin and paler. Finally, Lieutenant Breech makes it in and immediately begins to bark out directions.

Heavy fighting continues in all the little trenches around us. Chaos. The trenches are like spiderwebs, shooting out in all directions, some leading nowhere, others leading into the heart of the villages thick with Boche infantry and snipers and bombers and machine-gunners. We must find our way in and take over these places. In doing this, we will control the place named Hill 70 and will, for once, be the ones staring down at the Hun, with a bird's-eye view of the city called Lens. But first we must go foot by foot through these trenches that wind through the rubble of this village and kill every enemy we can find.

'Bird, Whiskeyjack, you go forward with Thompson and

get a feel for what's ahead of us,' Breech says. 'I want you back within a half-hour to report directly to me.'

We check our weapons and begin making our way down the trench at a crouch. From what I can see, the trench leads pretty much straight into the smoking rubble of the village. The trench gets deeper as we advance, winding along so that every ten or twenty yards a new stretch of dirt walls opens before us. We can see by the ruined brick on either side that we are at the village's border. A sharp traverse in the trench appears ahead. We pause by it and Thompson takes out a small mirror, carefully holds it so that he can peer around the corner. He hands Elijah the mirror, whispers that there is the ruin of a church that he's sure will contain a sniper or machine gun. If we try to advance further we'll be walking straight into view for more than thirty yards.

Elijah peers at the mirror and sees the layout. With the sun higher now and behind us, we will make perfect silhouettes if we go forward. Elijah notes a dugout in the wall ten yards down the trench, one that he can make safely, he says. We squat on our haunches to work out this problem.

'I can make it to cover ten yards down,' Elijah says to Thompson. 'That will draw the fire of any sniper who might be there. It will be up to you two to see where he's firing from.'

'You're assuming there will only be one,' Thompson answers.

'One, two, three, what's the difference?' Elijah answers. 'Just make sure you get their position. Put X in that spot there where he has a clear view of the church.' Elijah points to a brick pile that juts out from the trench corner, with a hole through it that creates a natural loophole, a place where I can lie down behind and fire from, without exposing any more than my rifle barrel and scope. I like this idea. I get down and carefully settle myself into place, aligning my rifle so that I have a view of the church. I scan along it. I'm ready.

Thompson stands above me, puts his mirror into position.

With his rifle in his right hand, Elijah takes a breath and then walks out and around the corner. He does not run, but goes as slowly as his body will allow him. Thompson whispers loudly through clenched teeth, 'Move!' but Elijah wants to make sure anyone in the church can see him. When he is five yards down the trench a rifle cracks out just as he jumps to the side. A bullet crashes into the mud wall where he'd been standing. He walks forward again and then jumps backwards just before the rifle fires a second time, another bullet whistling by very close. He then walks directly to the dugout and slips behind it as a bullet punches into the wall. Elijah looks back at where he came from and I can tell he sees Thompson reflected in his mirror, shaking his head at Elijah.

'Did you get a look at where the sniper is?' Elijah calls back.

'There are two,' I answer in Cree. 'One is shooting from the ground level, the other from that higher place where the bell is.'

'Well, shoot them,' Elijah says.

Maybe he thinks this is a sure way to get me out of the funk I'd been in since my trip to see Lisette. And it is great fun for Elijah too, I can tell. From where he is he can watch me quite clearly. I lie still, breathe calmly, peer through my scope. I know that Elijah thinks that it makes more sense to shoot the man on the ground first. The one higher up has a much more difficult time of escaping if he feels pinned in his perch.

My Mauser cracks the silence and Thompson whistles out, 'Good shot!' I reload quickly as a bullet tears into the brick close to my head. The other sniper has spotted me. I fire almost simultaneously, my finger jerking the trigger. It is not the shot I'd intended. The bell gongs out hollowly.

Elijah laughs. 'Shoot again, quick!' he calls out.

I reload just as the sniper answers my shot. Dust rises up by my ear. I swear, steady myself. I sense Elijah watching me take a breath in, then letting it half out. I fire.

'Got him!' Thompson calls out, as the sound of a rifle clattering to the bricks below echoes down the trench.

Beyond the church ruins, artillery fire begins, and a lot of rifle fire from the trenches on either side of us. We make our way to the church and see that the wreck of the steeple where the dead sniper lies is high enough to offer a good view of the surrounding area. Elijah tells Thompson and me that he's going up.

'A half-hour has passed,' Thompson says. 'Breech will want us back.'

'Better to secure the high ground,' Elijah says. 'It won't take long.'

He has to make it across a pile of loose brick that is wide open to anyone on either side. I cover the church in the event that there might still be Boche waiting there, and Thompson has the impossible job of covering everything else. Without wasting time, Elijah stumbles his way up the mound. Rifle and machine-gun fire clatters and pings off the bricks. Elijah dives into the broken doorway of the church.

The next part of the story Elijah tells me afterwards. He makes his way into the little church, letting his eyes adjust to

314

the darkness. He knows now that this is a hot area, but he's got that good feeling, the one that is like a shroud around him. Nothing will go wrong right now.

The roof has been blown mostly off. The steeple is close to collapse. Elijah makes his way up the rickety stairs and reaches the top. The dead sniper lies on the floor face down, like he is napping. A penny-sized hole in the back of his head leaks out blood and grey brain. Elijah waves to Thompson and me, then turns him over. His eyes are still open. They are very blue but beginning to cloud up. Like a pickerel's eyes, Elijah thinks. The dead one is young, with not much experience. A hole no bigger than a small shirt button oozes in the centre of his forehead a couple of inches below his thick hair. A wonderful shot. Elijah sometimes forgets how good I really am. How ironic, he thinks, this Hun killed by a weapon from his own country! If Elijah or I ever were to be captured, there would be no pity for us.

A new wave of small arms fire erupts on either side of Elijah. He peers through a hole blown into the side of the wall and indeed this perch offers a good view. He can see much of the way down the trench from where we just came, and in the distance he sees the plain on the outskirts of town and a number of Canadian soldiers moving along it. He makes his way to the other side of the steeple and cautiously raises his head above a small window ledge. Fallen walls and rubble block much of the view, but he can make out trench lines running through the village that are definitely not in Canadian hands, yet appear abandoned. He still must figure out where all of the fire he attracted has come from.

Leaning back in our direction, he calls out to me in Cree. He does not want to risk a Fritz soldier hearing who knows

English. 'Tell Thompson he and I will hold our positions while you go back and bring the company forward to us. But be quick. If Fritz decides he wants this church back, he will take it fast.'

After a minute, Thompson shouts back, 'All right,' and I head back to retrieve our section.

Elijah settles in with his automatic rifle and begins trying to figure out where the enemy is hiding. A lot of rifle fire echoes about, but not as close as what was aimed at him.

'Do you see anything?' Elijah shouts to Thompson. Before he can answer, a spray of machine-gun fire rakes the wall that Elijah crouches against, vibrating it. They know exactly where he is. He considers making his way out of the steeple to better cover below, but if he does that, he'll lose his sight advantage. At least now he knows roughly where the Fritz are. They are to the south and east just a little way. That is the only direction from which the machine-gunner could fire and hit the wall at his back. He wishes he had Thompson's mirror so he could get a good look without exposing his head to them.

'I can guess their location but can't see a damn thing,' Thompson shouts out to Elijah. 'Let's just hold tight and wait for the others.'

A tense half-hour passes and Elijah's very surprised that Fritz does not attempt to take back the church. The fighting has moved further into the village, and he assumes that Fritz is in a controlled retreat. He decides to risk peeking over the ledge. Slowly, he raises his head. The sun is bright and hot now, at its apex. If a sniper's waiting, he has a clean shot at Elijah.

Elijah waits. Nothing happens. He can see an entranceway into a pile of brick that he guesses is where they are sheltered.

It seems to lead into a basement. Much of the other area is crushed stone and broken timber. He can't see a lot of places big enough to hide more than one soldier. They must have retreated from that basement when the going was good. When I arrive with the others, Elijah knows, we will throw some eggs in just to make sure.

Elijah sits back and relaxes. A whine echoes in his head, and his arms and arse ache. A sure sign that he needs a little more medicine. He reaches into his kit and removes a readied syringe. The supply is running low. He'll have to get more soon, maybe question Grey Eyes. Not even bothering to pull his pants down, he jabs the needle through the wool and into his thigh. The prick of it feeds his anticipation. He pushes the plunger down and feels the heat and fullness of the morphine going into his leg. No injecting directly into a vein when he needs his wits about him. The world shrinks back a little and the harsh light diffuses to a pleasant glow. Even the ache of his bowels that have not been emptied for years, it seems, goes away. His hearing sharpens, and as he lets his eyes close he makes out the scuffle of boots coming down the trench. His section, coming this way. Further away he picks out the voices of whispering Boche. Where are they? Not close enough for Elijah to worry about them right now. His listening for them makes Elijah in turn think of me. Poor Xavier, Elijah thinks, he is going deaf but does not want to admit it to anyone.

McCaan's shout forces Elijah to raise his eyelids. 'Corporal Whiskeyjack, have you spotted the enemy?' Elijah crawls to his knees and peers over the ledge toward us. We've clattered to a halt and sneak looks over the trench toward his perch in the steeple, rifles aimed at the stretch of crushed village ahead of us.

'Indeed, Sergeant, I have. But I believe that they have retreated. There is a hole leading into a basement to the south and to the east that looks dangerous, but nothing that a few bombers can't take care of.' He hears Breech bark out some orders. Breech isn't used to all this front-line activity. Graves and a new private who doesn't even shave yet are handed Mills bombs and sent over the top to take care of it. I see Elijah climb slowly onto his knees to get a good view of the proceedings. The fighting clatters on, hundreds of yards away. Graves takes the lead position and walks toward the entrance. The young private walks six or seven yards behind.

'Don't forget to pull the pins,' Elijah shouts. The others in the trench laugh.

'Hop to it, Private!' McCaan barks out to the young one. 'The faster you do this, the quicker we can get to the action!' Everyone laughs again. This is the private's first mission. Graves has done this sort of thing dozens of times.

Looking back to the basement, I make out the figure of a man who has emerged from it while we were all laughing. A rag is tied across his nose and mouth. He carries what looks like a rifle in his hands but it is attached to a tube that runs under his arm and to a large tank on his back. Blue flame falls from the barrel of the strange gun and splashes onto the brick. Everyone else must see this very soon after I do. The laughing stops and Thompson shouts out, 'Move!' Graves stops in his tracks. He seems about to turn, stops himself and then continues forward, raising the bomb in his hand like a club.

'Lie down, Graves!' Elijah shouts, reaching for his rifle, and I realize just as he must that the words are in Cree.

Graves looks up to Elijah, confusion on his face. A stream of bright yellow fire spits from the tip of the strange gun with a great *whoosh* and engulfs Graves's body. He raises his arm to Elijah as if waving, his hair and moustache burning. Within seconds he is a ball of flame writhing silently on the ground. The young private turns and begins to run back to safety but trips on the brick, landing with arms stretched toward the others, the Mills bomb he carried flying toward us. Men rush and tumble over each other around me, trying to get out of its path. Another flame spits from the gun and engulfs the private, who screams shrilly and stands, then runs blazing in a greasy yellow fire until he crumples to the ground. Only then do I realize I must pick up my rifle and end this.

Then the bomb explodes in the trench, sending men flying.

Before I can get off the ground and aim at the fire shooter, a couple of men in the trench do it. One of them hits the tank on the Hun's back. A fiery explosion shoots up into an orange and-black ball of flame. What was a man is now burning pieces of carrion on the ground. Elijah rushes down from the steeple. Graves is a smoking heap. The young private is still alive, the flames out now, but they've burned the clothes from his body and he reminds me of the charred moose that Elijah and I found on the riverbank so long ago. He is unrecognizable lying there, gasping, the pink inside his mouth the only colour that stands out against the oozing and charred black of his body.

A soldier screams in the trench. Another lies dead. Their two bodies muffled the explosion and it is pure luck that the whole section wasn't killed by the blast. I am all right, but shaken. Fat walks in circles, muttering. Graves was the only one who treated him kindly. A couple of the others stare down at the screaming soldier in the trench. Others stare confused at the burnt kid. Nobody knows what to do. We are stunned by this new weapon used against us. McCaan begins shouting for a medic. It breaks the spell.

Elijah and I take covering positions and keep an eye out for any other Boche. That is when we hear another sound coming from the direction of Graves's body. I turn around and watch as Fat sits beside the burnt corpse, slapping his own face hard as he can, crying.

By day's end we've cleaned out the coal-mining village and word trickles down that the First and Second Divisions have taken Hill 70. The Canadians are poised now to go into the big city of Lens. Word also comes of more of the fire attacks against us, and more and more Canadian troops are being stretchered down from the front lines, bodies melted and black. The smell is sweet enough to make the stomach feel bad. Rumours travel that the Germans have introduced another new weapon, a type of gas that is fired long distance by shells and burns the skin. We've entered into a fire war, Elijah says to me.

Elijah tells me he dreams of Graves on fire, waving to him. Elijah sees and smells his blackened body. And this makes Elijah dream of Sean Patrick, a neat hole in his throat, his life blown out the base of his skull. He dreams of Gilberto, of me describing how one moment he was there smiling, the next his big body was lying across me, lifeless. Elijah looks up. They stand around him in his dugout. Smoke wafts up from Graves's head. Sean Patrick is grey. Gilberto's brain leaks out from his mouth. 'Do what you can,' they all tell him. 'There is nothing sacred any more in a place such as this. Don't fight it. Do what you can.' Elijah wakes with a start.

Through the rest of August, we hold the hill and the small

surrounding villages that we've taken. From this vantage we continue to pound Lens, but just as before, our forward movement has crunched to a stop. Elijah's crazy with the boredom of routine. Little action in the way of trench raids, just night patrols in no man's land. He asks Lieutenant Breech permission to resume sniping with me, tries to win his argument by explaining that we have great advantage in being on a rise, looking down at the Hun for once. It is not long before he and I are searching out good spots again, and this helps relieve the growing ache inside of Elijah that he cannot stem. We lie still for days, searching out targets. We're after officers and must be very patient. Thompson had once told us that spotting officers is easy. They are the ones who aren't doing anything when everyone else is working.

In the long hours of hunting Elijah tries to understand what is growing in him. He talks to me about this through the nights we spend out in the damp and mud. Mist rises from craters and swirls in the stink. In the end, the answer that comes is simple. Elijah has learned to take pleasure in killing.

Elijah says that something in me has hardened in the last months. I talk even less than before, do not smile at all any more. He knows that I want to be home, that I am sick of all of this, but he tells me I must realize that the freedom of this place will not present itself again. But this freedom he talks about, this freedom to kill, is a choice I no longer want.

We've found a place that is three hundred yards from the Boche line. Elijah and I have a good view of it, but very little cover is offered here and we will be easily spotted as soon as we fire. One shot, two at best, then we must get back to our line. We wait and watch.

There is an officer who appears in the Hun line, but only

for a moment each morning at stand-to. He was clearly visible this morning, and Elijah had a shot, but was still groggy from a long, restless night. He tells me he will not let that chance go by again tomorrow morning. We spend this day looking up at the sky, waiting for the aeroplanes to swoop across the trenches, strafing and bombing. But none come. 'I want to fly in one of those once before I die,' Elijah says again.

The night is even longer than the day, but Elijah's kept awake by the image of the officer coming into the sight and Elijah pulling the trigger. I pretend to sleep lightly beside him as he reaches into his kit and extracts a syringe. He needs some to steady his nerves, to take away the aches that are now a part of his every waking moment. He nudges me when dawn is approaching and he peers through his glass at their trench. Enough light now to make out forms in the darkness.

When the grey breaks from the black over the horizon, Elijah places his finger on his trigger. Just as yesterday, the same soldiers' heads appear for stand-to, and just behind them a lieutenant appears, hands behind his back, inspecting the line.

'You have your shot,' I say, and Elijah doesn't hesitate.

His crosshairs are on the officer's forehead. The officer stands there frowning. Elijah squeezes the trigger, but the kick of the rifle prevents him from getting a clear view of the outcome.

'He is dead,' I report, and Elijah begins to laugh. He is better off where Elijah's sent him. I turn to gather our little gear and make a quick exit from our cover.

Already Elijah can see through his scope the startled looks of the soldiers, the veterans training their guns on our position. He reloads and finds another target, and although he knows better, he fires again, this time at a soldier whose head is higher than the others'. The soldier drops from the impact, but the muzzle flash of the rifle has given us away. The crack of rifle fire travels up the rise, bullets zinging close by us.

'*Ashtum!*' I call out, already five yards closer to the safety of our line. Elijah collects his gear and crawls out of his hole, stretches lazily up to the sky and smiles to the sun. Bullets rip the air all around him. 'Put yourself in danger if you like, but not me!' I shout in anger as I turn to run.

Elijah turns too, and begins walking casually. 'I'd only meant to add a little excitement to your morning, shake you out of this funk you've sunk into,' he shouts back.

I have rarely raised my voice at him. I can tell he is hurt.

The nights are getting cold again. Goose-hunting season back in Mushkegowuk. Word has trickled down that we are to be moved north, to a place called Passchendaele. The name is a pretty one. It makes me think of women. But then I am told it is near the place where Lisette lives and so my heart hurts all over again. When we are pulled off the line we are sent to a town far behind it. A pub that the company has adopted as its own sits in the middle of the village. I don't like to go to it, but Elijah makes me anyway. 'There are other Lisettes,' Elijah tells me. That makes me mad.

We will drink till we fall down tonight. I am not a good drinker and it won't take me much, I think.

The pub is crowded and noisy and full of smoke. Men bang glasses and bottles on the long, scarred wooden tables. A feeling here Elijah says he doesn't like. We buy drinks from the old woman behind the bar. Her nose is thin and crooked. She has long white hair that unravels from her braid. She reminds me of an old grandmother, a *kokum*. I look across the bar then and I see him. I'm shocked by his face here in this place. A face like mine. I've seen other brown men, a troop of brown men on horses, white cloth twisted high on their heads and long beards tied neatly so that they looked frightening and beautiful with their swords rattling at their sides. McCaan told me they were another type of Indian. 'Indians from India,' he said. 'Some of the King's best.' But the one here in this pub is an Indian like Elijah and I are Indians. He's Anishnabe. He looks Ojibwe.

I nudge Elijah and whisper to him to look to our left. At one of the tables the short brown man with black hair sits laughing with some others. It takes Elijah a moment, I see. He first thinks it might be an Indian from Moose Factory that he's not quite remembering. But then he sees the stripes of a corporal.

'Is he the one they call Peggy?' Elijah asks me.

I shrug, take a long swig from my glass as if I don't care.

He does not look at Elijah and me but we know that he knows we are here. Elijah buys a second bottle of wine from *Kokum* and goes to sit by him.

'Wachay, wachay,' Elijah says, handing him the bottle.

He smiles at Elijah. The smile is wary.

'Three Anishnabe in the same place,' the corporal says, nodding. He speaks in his tongue, but it is close enough to ours that we understand it. 'Some things are beyond chance.'

'And how is your hunting?' Elijah asks. 'I hope it's as good as mine.'

I snort a laugh. It is good to laugh again. The white men around their table look at us oddly. They do not like that the Indians talk in words that they can't understand.

'You must mistake me for someone else,' the corporal says.

'There are more Anishnabe than you might guess who wander these battlefields. We all want to be warriors again.'

Elijah looks at me. I smile and then laugh again. It strikes me that I'm drunk.

'My guess is that you are Whiskeyjack, and this drunk fellow beside you is Bird,' the corporal says.

'I'm not drunk!' I slur the words. It is their turn to laugh.

'Your reputation walks ahead of you,' the corporal says, looking away from Elijah. 'From what I hear, you are one of the good ones.'

Elijah stares straight ahead. His mouth is tight, but he can't help but smile slightly.

'You know that the *wemistikoshiw* do not care to believe us when they hear about our kills in the field,' the corporal says. 'We do the nasty work for them and if we return home we will be treated like pieces of shit once more. But while we are here we might as well do what we are good at.'

'Let's not talk of dying tonight,' Elijah says, knowing right away that to kill him would prove nothing. 'Let's drink instead.'

By midnight they are drunk too. Everyone in this place is drunk. He is infantry like us, and his company, like the others, will be soon leaving to Passchendaele.

'You know,' Elijah says, leaning to him, 'you and I are not so different.'

'From what I have heard, you've killed many. How many? Be honest.'

'One hundred ninety-four, to date,' Elijah answers. The corporal's eyes open wide in astonishment. 'It's true!' Elijah shouts. 'X, how many have I killed?' he asks in Cree.

'What?' I shout back.

Elijah shouts louder. 'How many Fritz do you think I have killed?'

'Too many,' I answer. 'More than one hundred sniper kills that I have observed. You are always sneaking off too. I do not know how many you have dispatched in the darkness of night. And don't forget the hair you keep in your kit bag.'

'We shall not talk of that right now,' Elijah says, shaking his finger at me.

'There is another one, a Métis,' the corporal says. 'His name is Norwest. He's from Alberta and the rumour is he has killed more than you, even.'

'I'm sick of hearing about the feats of others,' Elijah says. 'What do you really want from me?'

The corporal smiles. 'Think of me as your conscience,' he says. 'And you can be mine.'

Outside the air holds the cold of autumn. The smell of fire is on the breeze and Elijah and I are reminded of home. This corporal is too, I imagine. We walk down the main street of the village, back toward our respective camps. None of the three of us says anything. It gives me an odd feeling to be walking like we walk at home. An aeroplane drones in the distance. It is coming this way. Elijah says he hopes to catch a glimpse of its wings flash in the moonlight as it passes us.

The drone comes closer. The hair on the back of my neck rises. 'This way,' I say, pulling Elijah's sleeve and motioning with my other hand to the corporal. We slip into an alley as the plane passes over, low and fast. A bomb falling from under the plane screams in the cold air, then we hear the *whomp* of splintering roof as it pierces wood and the tiny breath of silence before the explosion. Flames shoot high. Men shout and scramble. Over the sound of burning wood Elijah says he can make out the drone of the plane coming back. It runs the length of the main road, its machine gun strafing the people who have come out to the road to investigate.

When the plane has left, we walk back onto the street. The pub where we'd been moments before is a smouldering bonfire. So are the buildings on either side. Bodies lie on the street, men attending to them.

Later, Elijah tells me that in this chaos the corporal leaned to him and whispered that he had twice Elijah's kills in the field. Elijah says it would have been simple to slip his skinning knife into the corporal then, into the soft muscle between his ribs. He tells me he is happy he did not take advantage of the opportunity. He's not sure why.

MASINAHIKEWIN
Writing

XAVIER TELLS ME HIS MEDICINE will soon be gone and when this happens he will become very difficult, like the worst child I have ever seen. He says his heart will probably stop. He says he will struggle first, and the pain of his leg and his arm and the pain in his heart will kill him and he doesn't want me to be sad when that time comes. He tells me all of this when the medicine he takes has him in its grip. He's smiling as he talks, and I think that this medicine is far stronger even than the root I've heard that the Anishnabe far to the south take for visions.

I look down at him as he lies beside the small fire I've built on the beach. In the light his cheeks are hollow like an old man's, but the smile is young. I've made a broth of moosemeat and roots. I move closer to him as the sun continues its descent, the sky still bright enough near midnight that I can clearly see the tree line across the river.

When he goes quiet I begin to hum an old song I'd hummed to him when he was small, and the smile remains on his lips. He keeps his eyes open, though. They are disquieting, glistening in the firelight. I wonder what they see. It is not this world here in front of me.

I begin to lift his head onto my lap and he lets me. I continue to hum the song, running my hand through his hair. He's taken off his jacket and I look at his brown, scarred arms, at the hollow chest where his shirt is unbuttoned. I cry when I look at the empty pant leg. Even if he were to survive this paddle home, how will he survive in the bush? He is clumsy on his crutches. In a few winters I will be too old to continue hunting for him. What then?

I look at his arms again. They fascinate me. Scars all over them, white against his brown skin. I wonder where they came from. The *wemistikoshiw* at the trading post explained to me how the enemy used sharp wire to prevent men from crawling up and surprising them. They told me stories of how bombs blew apart into little needles that penetrated everything around. Xavier's scars must be from this. As I look at these scars that crisscross his body I am angry at the ones who did this to him. My tears stop and I clench my teeth to stop myself from screaming out. I will not let him go easily.

The broth has cooled. I take a little in my mouth and bend to Nephew. His eyes are still open, but they do not see me. I place my mouth against his and in this way feed him so that he swallows in little gulps. At first he fights it, but I do not give in to his weak protest. I don't feed him too much, afraid he will throw up what I've given him. He doesn't.

After a time he begins to talk again. 'Elijah,' he says. 'Do you know how many he has killed?'

I look down at him. He's still far away.

'I've killed many too. But Elijah, he is truly talented.'

'What has happened to Elijah?' I ask. The words come out of my mouth before I can stop them. Nephew continues staring, but his fingers fumble and wrestle with one another. He rolls away from me and moans long and low so that his voice travels across the river.

He tries to stand up, but without his crutches he falls back down hard. I offer him help but know he will not accept it. 'Nephew,' I say. 'Let me tell you a story. It will help pass this night.' He turns his back to me, but doesn't try to stand again.

When the time at the end of summer came for your friend Elijah to go back to the residential school, he did not want to leave. I wasn't surprised. You boys had grown close, more brothers than friends, and for a long time after Elijah was gone, you stayed quiet, knowing that it would be the rare times that you'd be able to see him during the school year. Elijah left the rifle. Do you remember, Nephew? After all, he could not bring it back to the school with him, and so you carried it everywhere. I did not like the way the gun had been obtained, but you were old enough to make decisions of your own, and to live with the consequences. You continued to shoot the rifle often, as if you hoped to impress Elijah with your ability when he returned. Elijah was one of those rare people who everyone always seemed to want to impress. I found it humorous that even I had found myself wondering what he thought of the food I cooked or the moccasins I sewed for him.

You were at the age that I needed to begin the next step of your learning. Late that autumn when the snow was in the air and we'd smoked enough geese to last us well into the winter, I built a hot fire and placed the shoulder blade of a moose upon it. I asked you to think about the animal, its habits, its scent, what it most enjoyed to eat. I told you to speak out loud about the animal, to talk about your last successful hunt. You watched carefully as you talked and I prayed. When I felt the good feeling of an old friend come to join us in the tent, I began to drip water onto the bone. It sizzled and popped, and finally a pattern that I could recognize began to emerge on the face of the bone.

I let the fire die down, then removed the still-hot shoulder blade. I studied the lines for a long time, talking as I did so that you might begin to understand the thinking. This animal had lived all its life in this country, and just like all of us it carried an internal map of its life, where it liked to eat, to rest, to mate. And where this moose had been, others surely would congregate. The job of the diviner was to coax this information from the animal.

'This crack,' I asked, running my finger along it, 'does the way it forks into three remind you of any creek you might have been on?'

Immediately you answered, 'There is the creek a half-day's paddle down the river that looks much like that.'

'But there are many creeks that split into three,' I said.

You stared at the bone for a long time. 'But the creek I think of runs from another creek that looks just like this one.' You pointed to another crack that ran into the one split into three.

I smiled. 'Do you get a good feeling from it?' I asked. You looked at me quizzically. 'When you picture walking up this creek, do you get the feeling that you will find a moose here, or do you feel nothing?'

You thought about this, your eyes closed, then finally answered, 'I get a good feeling.'

'You will leave tomorrow before first light,' I said.

You were very happy early the next summer when Elijah returned. Both of you had grown and were young men now. Elijah made his announcement that evening as we ate.

'I am old enough now that I no longer have to return to the residential school. I am free to live with you.'

'You will go mad within a month,' I teased, 'with no one

331

but an old lady and a friend who would rather hunt than speak.'

'The town is not that far away,' Elijah answered. 'Xavier and I can go there when we grow bored. No one will recognize Xavier any more. He looks like just another wild bush Indian with his long hair and his clothing.'

I looked at you, Nephew. Elijah was right. The only hint of your childhood was your ears that still stuck out a little from your head.

'You must grow your hair out now too,' you said, Nephew, looking at Elijah's short residential cut.

'I like it this way,' he said. 'It is easy to take care of.'

But over the months of summer I watched it grow longer as he became a wild thing of the forest once again.

The years passed quickly for me then, Xavier. My fits grew less frequent with age so that I began to believe they were gone forever. You and Elijah reached the age where you began to spend some of your time in town where there were young women. The two of you were happy, and I was glad for this. But then without warning the light began to change and the tingling returned. As surely as if the earth opened up beneath me and I was swallowed by it, I was taken to that other place, shown tormented visions of black horizons and constant thunder and more dead men than a woman can count or cry over. Soon I understood.

'A war has started in that place called Europe,' Elijah announced when you'd returned one day from a trip to town. 'The Canadians have entered it.'

To me, Europe was that place to which the Hudson's Bay Company sent furs from the bush. I knew little of that place except for its hunger for pelts.

Just like little boys again, you and Elijah stayed up late into the evenings, talking. The focus of the conversation was obvious. I prayed to *Gitchi Manitou* that you not be taken away from me, but other plans were in the making that I could not yet see or understand.

Do you recall the morning you came to me, eyes cast down? I knew what was coming.

'Auntie,' you said, 'Elijah and I have made a decision, but I want your approval.'

I continued to sew the shirt I'd been making for you and kept my eyes down too.

'We have decided to paddle to a town where we can join their army,' you said.

I was silent for a while. Finally I said, 'Is there anything I might say that would change your mind?'

You shook your head.

'It will not be as you picture it,' I said. 'Know that you go to a place that will change you forever.'

You nodded.

My next words were difficult to speak. 'You must do what you must do.'

I watched over the weeks that you and Elijah prepared for the long paddle. Elijah seemed eager to get started.

'This war will not last long. We are going to miss it,' he began saying every day that he did not leave.

But you, Nephew, you seemed less anxious to go. Maybe you wanted to enjoy the quiet days of summer before being swallowed up by the *wemistikoshiw* and their ways. So much was still left for me to teach, but time had suddenly grown too short.

A little while before you set out, I once again heated the

stones and built the *matatosowin*. I took you and Elijah into it and prayed round after round until all of us were so drained that we could not enter again. I prayed to the four directions, I prayed to the spirit animals, I prayed to *Gitchi Manitou*.

On the morning you were to travel, I tied a small medicine bundle around each of your necks. I see that you still have it. I'd chosen the ingredients carefully, pinches of all of the protective herbs I had, along with the tooth of the lynx that would offer you speed and invisibility and vision. I did not watch you leave, you know. Instead I took a long walk in the forest and cried. When I returned, I entered the shaking tent and summoned the lynx, begging it to follow and watch over you. The lynx did not answer.

I went back to living as I had as a young woman, alone and quiet. Another winter came and went, and I survived to see summer again. I prayed for you boys every day, sent up offerings with sweetgrass that you be protected. I heard little bits of news from Cree who tended to their traplines. None of it was good. Thousands were dying, and a war that was supposed to have ended in a short time suddenly had no end in sight. I hungered for more news.

When an old one named Hookimaw visited one day, bringing with him a fat goose for me to roast, I was troubled by what he told me. The *wemistikoshiw* had gone mad with war and had invented tools to kill one another that were beyond belief. I plucked the goose and prepared it for the fire while Hookimaw talked, claiming that the enemy had created an invisible weapon. When you breathed the air that it rode on, you choked to death. Was this true? Another invention was a great metal machine that rolled on tracks and fired exploding bullets.

'The *wemistikoshiw* at the trading post follow the war carefully,' Hookimaw said as we ate. 'They sit and talk of it all day long.' As if knowing what I was thinking, he added, 'They might even have news of your nephew.'

Before the week was over I'd packed what I needed into my canoe and paddled to within a short distance of the town. I made a summer camp and then, when I was able to summon the nerve, paddled in.

For the first time since I was a young woman, I walked openly on the streets of that place. Just as years before, the people stared at me. Cree and *wemistikoshiw* alike talked about me as soon as my back was to them. I became self-conscious, as I never had to be when alone in the bush. I was an old woman now, my hair long, black still but streaked with grey. I was thin and wiry, the veins in my arms protruding like a man's. My clothes were in the style that had not been worn for years, my cotton shirt so threadbare it could almost be seen through. I ignored them best I could and walked toward the Company store, all the time worried that their police would arrive to lock me up.

Without warning, a great noisy rumble approached me from behind. I spun toward it, ready to protect myself, and watched as a black metal wagon bumped along the flat road, moving of its own accord. The one they called Old Man Ferguson sat in it, wearing goggles and steering it with a wheel. I stood dumbfounded as he passed, the dust from the wagon drifting up, then settling down on everything around me. The smell of it was horrible, a burning smell that was sweet and sickening at the same time, the smell of this new era that I'd managed to live into. He halted it by the Company store and the noise rattled and choked to a stop. The air was suddenly quiet again and the birds continued chirping. They'd grown accustomed to this strange thing. I was amazed.

The store was cool and dark inside. Just as old Hookimaw had said, men sat around a table with papers opened before them. They stopped talking when I came in. I sat in a corner and waited for whatever was to happen. They began to talk about me, pointing at me with their thumbs. After a while, Old Man Ferguson came up to me and began speaking in his tongue. I did not understand it. He looked angry. He made the movement to grab me, but I was up and out of his reach before he could react. He looked startled, then began to roar.

An older Indian that I recognized stood up from where he was sitting in a dark corner and began to speak in English to Ferguson. Ferguson spoke back quickly to him. The Indian looked at me.

'They think you are a witch and a heathen and say you must leave here now or you will meet a violent end.'

'Tell them that I simply come to find out about my nephew who fights with the Canadians in their war.'

The Indian turned to Ferguson and spoke. Ferguson shook his head and replied angrily.

The Indian turned to me. 'He says that you are a dirty bush Indian and a sorceress to boot and he will not have you in his store even if you have a hundred relatives in their army.'

I smiled. 'Tell him that I may be a bush Indian and a sorceress, but I also know where to find the thickest, shiniest furs that any of these fat bastards have ever seen. If he allows me to find out about my nephew, I will consider repaying him the favour.'

The Indian looked nervous to say this, but did so haltingly.

Ferguson bellowed, made a move toward me again, but was grabbed by one of the men at the table. They exchanged words.

'Did your nephew go to war with the one called Elijah Whiskeyjack?' the Indian finally asked me.

I nodded.

He told the men at the table this and they talked excitedly. 'And you will begin trading furs with the Hudson's Bay Company only and not have any dealings with the Revillon Brothers?' the Indian continued.

I nodded again, smiling.

The Indian spoke with them in their tongue once more. They spoke back. He turned to me. 'You can find out what you may, but they do not want you here permanently.'

He looked sorry that he had to be the one to report this. I liked the laugh lines by his eyes.

'You must sit away from them and you must not touch anything in the store. They say you must leave by week's end and return at winter's end with as many furs as you can.'

Again I nodded.

The men sat back down uncomfortably at their table and opened the papers before them. Gradually they began to talk again, but self-consciously. After a while, they forgot about me and began talking more openly. I couldn't hear them, so I moved closer. They stopped talking and looked at me. Two of them blessed themselves. I was close enough to them that I could smell the stink of their sweat.

I did not move, but sat, my hands folded in my lap. After a time, they began to talk again. They chattered like old women. But I could not understand, and asked the Indian, who I recognized from my childhood, to translate. I remembered his name. Joseph Netmaker. He was about the same age as me.

'Old Joseph,' I said. 'Tell me what they say.'

At first the others at the table seemed irritated by his talking to me after anything was said, but after a while they seemed to forget about us. They talked of many things that I could not fully understand, talked of many place names—Festubert, Saint-Eloi, Mount Sorrel, the Somme—all these places the sites of great battles. The battles were no longer fought in the traditional way of the *wemistikoshiw* where men rode horses and walked on foot headlong into one another. They dug themselves into the ground and lived like night animals, all while the sky was raining down iron that exploded and killed many men. I learned much on that first day, Nephew, sat there with them until it began to grow dark and they stood to leave.

I came back the next day, and the next, and always Joseph Netmaker was there to translate, but I learned little about you, Nephew, where you were, if you still lived. The feeling inside me told me that you did, and so I kept going back to that Company store. It seemed impossible to me to track you and Elijah. So many men were over there. How would I ever begin to figure out how to find you?

As I listened I began to learn things about their army. Joseph, who had spent childhood summers near our family by the Great Salt Bay, explained that men who joined the army from the same place were often kept together. This meant that you and Elijah at least had each other for protection. I asked if the men from our North Country would be sent to a particular place over there. An idea was coming to me.

Joseph spoke my question to one of the old men who

constantly read and reread the papers that trickled into the Company store. The man talked for a long time, and Joseph's face turned worried. I waited impatiently for him to translate to me.

'It is not as simple as I thought, Niska,' Joseph said when they were done talking. 'So many men are killed and wounded that their groups are absorbed by bigger groups and these bigger groups constantly move to different places. The *wemistikoshiw* did tell me that the Company store would receive word of soldiers from our country who are killed or wounded. They've received nothing regarding your nephew.' He paused, and then said, 'That is a good thing, is it not?'

I nodded.

I blended into the store well enough that they forgot about me, and so I stayed longer than I was supposed to, listening to what Joseph told me of the war. The summer was growing late, though, and I was ill prepared for a winter out in the bush. The time had come to head back out and do what I needed to do. One day I told Joseph this, and he looked like a hurt little boy.

'Why stay far away in the bush, Niska?' he said. 'You can stay with me for the winter and find out more about your nephew. I have a comfortable cabin that I made myself, and it is far enough out of town that you will hardly know you are near it.'

I laughed. 'You are very kind, Old Netmaker. But I have always only known living by myself. I would drive you mad with my habits and my stubbornness.'

I turned then and left, did not plan to come back to that town until the snow lay deep and I could walk in by snowshoe.

Being back by myself again was at first a difficult thing to adjust to, but after the passing of two full moons, I wondered how I'd ever been able to stay in that town for so long. I did miss Joseph's easy company, though. I missed his round face, and once in a while he made the trip out to see me, bringing any news that might be of importance.

He appeared one bright winter morning by snowshoe, and I knew by his expression that he had something urgent to tell me. I invited him into my *askihkan* and brewed tamarack tea.

'Old Man Ferguson claims that word continues to come of your nephew's friend, Elijah.'

I braced myself for Joseph to tell me that he had been killed.

'Ferguson says that reports come back of his bravery and his exploits in the military papers.'

I breathed out with relief. 'This must also mean that they have some idea where Nephew and Elijah are,' I said.

'Yes, if they are indeed still together,' Joseph said.

'Well, I shall go back to that town and find out from Ferguson where they might be.'

Joseph smiled. 'I've already found out this information. I thought ahead and asked Ferguson to write all of it down for me.' He pulled out a piece of paper and on it were written English words that I could not read.

We sat in silence for a time, and I stared at the fire, wondering who I might trust enough to do what I needed to do. Joseph looked away, then his eyes came back to me again.

'Obviously you want to say something,' I said. 'So speak.'

'I do not understand why it is you need to know where they might be, Niska,' he said.

He chose his words carefully, spoke, I knew, so as not to offend.

'Will knowing where they are somehow ease your mind?'

'I wish to do what the *wemistikoshiw* do. I wish to write him a letter. I need to tell him that he will return home safely.' I shook my head. 'But there is no *wemistikoshiw* I can trust enough to do this.'

Joseph smiled again, this time broader. 'I can write it for you!' he said happily.

'You can write in their language?' I asked, unbelieving.

'Of course. I was forced, just like all the others, to go to their school. You are one of the few who did not, you know.'

'I don't believe you,' I said.

'I will prove it.' Joseph picked up the piece of paper and ran his finger along it, his lips moving silently. He looked up to me. 'Ferguson has written that they are in the Second Division of the Canadian army. They have wintered in a place called France. Ferguson says that the army won't say more about where, for they worry about spies. But he did say that Elijah, and your nephew, I suppose, are in something called a battalion, and its name is the Southern Ontario Rifles.'

Not much of this made sense to me, but at least it seemed that now I could send a letter which might very well get to you, Nephew. 'If we are to write a letter, what then?'

'It is very simple. I take it to Ferguson, and he sends it with the other mail. It will take some time, but the letter will travel out by canoe, and then by train, and then by ship, and then by train again to your nephew.'

I travelled this route in my mind, saw you at the end of it being handed the letter, a look of wonder on your face. 'Then we shall sit down right now and do it,' I said.

Although I didn't need to say much, the going was slow. Joseph used a small nub of a pencil and wrote painstakingly on a yellowed piece of paper. He listened carefully to what I said, then put the words into English and onto the page. I told you what I had wanted to tell you but had not been able to the summer you paddled away. I said you must return home, for you were the last in our family line. One day you would raise your own child and teach him what had been taught to me. I told you that in war you must do what was necessary to survive, and that in this circumstance *Gitchi Manitou* understood if you had to kill. Elijah must know this too. I told you to make offerings with Elijah to *Gitchi Manitou,* to pray for guidance and to do everything you had to do so that you could return home.

When we were done, I asked Joseph if he had translated my words carefully. 'Yes, Niska, yes,' he said.

I could see in his eyes, though, that he was not so sure.

The next day Joseph left, the letter in his pocket. I headed out to my traplines to see what furs I might find to bring to the *wemistikoshiw* store come spring. Something did not feel right, and I could not figure out what it was.

I stop talking now, and see that the sun is not far away. I have kept us up all night. Nephew's eyes are closed but his breathing suggests that he is conscious. He seems to rest a little better than he has the last two days. I am happy to see this, lie back onto my blanket and let myself drift off into memory again.

MICISOW
Feeding

AUNTIE'S TALKING SUDDENLY SOLVES A MYSTERY. I would laugh at it all if the letter had not done such damage to me. It soured me and I lost my desire for survival. Should I tell her the mistakes Old Joseph Netmaker made with his words? That would bring nothing but more sadness. Instead, I slip back a year to when I received the news.

We herd into flatbed trucks that drive all night along bumpy roads that make me feel like I will be shaken apart. When we finally climb from them with bruised tailbones, we relieve ourselves by the side of the road. I look down at Elijah.

'Look at your piss,' I say. 'It is red with blood.'

'Yours is too,' Elijah says.

And it is. My kidneys ache from the lorry's pounding.

We move toward that place called Passchendaele, and get a view of our new home in the first light of morning. I have never seen a place so depressing. Rain without stop for weeks and now in front of us lies a stretch of mud and shell-holes filled with water and bodies of the dead. This place is one vast field. Not a tree or a bush left standing. The trenches are not so much trenches as shallow water-filled craters joined to one another by slimy, caving-in walls. The Hun, as usual, have the higher ground and are smart enough to have built pillboxes instead of trenches, machine guns poking out of slits in the concrete. The Canadian artillery is useless here. The mud is so deep, I have heard, that every time a big gun fires, it sinks. The crew then has to pull it out and re-sight it before trying to fire again. They are not hitting much, but it is not their fault.

What are they thinking in putting us here? I wonder, walking through the deep mud with the others. I have reached the point where nothing makes sense to me any more, especially the actions of the ones who move the soldiers about and order them to their deaths. I hate them for what they make me do, but I do not speak of it, just let it fester like trenchfoot. Elijah tells me that it's my attitude that keeps me a private when I should at least be a corporal by now with my skill.

The other divisions have the unfortunate job of being the first waves sent against the pillboxes. They are to overrun the crumbled ruins of Passchendaele, are to clamber somehow through the sea of mud before them and through the machine-gun fire and take over Fritz's positions. I am sorry for those sent in, but I'm grateful that for once it is not me. The rest of us live in holes thigh deep with cold and stinking November water. In desperation, men climb out of the holes to try and find a drier patch of earth to sleep on, only to be picked off easily by the German snipers.

Incredibly, impossibly, the Canadians do what is asked of them, but at a heavy loss. I watch from the rear position as men crawl back through the mud with stretchers perched on their shoulders. Rumours are everywhere that men who are wounded but who are not picked up by the stretcher-bearers quickly enough are drowning in the mud. It must be true. I tried walking to the side of the boards that lie like little roads everywhere. I sank to my waist and was sinking further when Elijah pulled me out.

And still the rain falls and the shells pound and churn the

mud. That is my nightmare, to be wounded and in my agony, sinking into the mud to be swallowed forever. Gone. Missing in action, and you, Niska, waiting for me for years to return.

And then it is my turn to pick up the fight. Elijah and I are sent as advance scouts into the crumbled city. I'm happy to be out of the mud. We pick our way through the rubble, wary of Hun snipers. By halfway through the village we've had no resistance but are suddenly pinned down by rifle fire coming from the window of a low, smashed building. It appears the only structure left standing in the whole town. Elijah and I drop down behind a shattered wagon. The shots were very close to my head.

Both of us are useless pinned down here. One will have to make a break for a broken wall twenty-five yards to the right while the other offers covering fire. Then we will be in a much better position to take out the sniper in the building.

'I'll go,' Elijah says, but I tell him that I want to do it. Elijah nods. 'If you've got the shot, don't hesitate. Take it.'

I take some deep breaths that echo in my clogged ears, hunch there, then at the agreed time stand and run hard. Elijah immediately swings his rifle over the side of the wagon and I hear the *crack crack* as he fires into the window. I am almost there when a bullet whizzes close enough to me that I don't know how it missed. I dive behind the shattered wall, skinning my hands so they bleed. Rolling onto my back, I check my rifle, then roll to a small break in the wall from which I can sight in on the building with my scope. I search the windows through my scope and catch a glimpse of movement in the bottom left one. I can't make much out except the shadow of a crouching body. Breathing out half a breath, I squeeze the trigger. The rifle's explosion in my ear is a hollow echo. The shadow slumps and I know I've hit it. I signal to Elijah. Elijah signals back for me to cover him while he comes over.

We decide to go into the building to investigate. If it was used as a command post, we might find valuable papers. I have to read Elijah's lips to understand. The hearing will come back. It always does. We make our way along the wall and to the side entrance of the building, leapfrogging, one covering the other as we go. We know of no more than one shooter so far, but we must be wary of others. The one that I killed was a straggler. I do not know why he stayed behind.

We let our eyes adjust to the darkness, then make our way in. Not much interior of this building is left. The walls are mostly gone. I point to where I hit the figure.

He lies face down. Elijah rolls him over with his boot. I had hit him high in the chest and there is a large pool of bright red blood on the floor beneath him. Lung blood. Elijah goes through his pockets and finds a little German money and his papers. Nothing else worthwhile. He was just a private. His Mauser is an old one, not worth keeping. A deserter, from what I can guess.

'Search the rest of the building, would you?' Elijah says in English.

'There is no one else here,' I say.

'Be a good chap and do it anyway. I know that you don't like what I am about to do.'

The look in Elijah's eyes is frightening. I can only believe that this war has made my friend this way. Elijah, he will get better when we are gone from it, I think.

I nod and then turn away, wandering far enough that I don't have to think of the tearing of scalp from skull.

I walk into what remains of another room. A table rests in

the middle with a little food on it. My stomach rumbles. As I head toward it, I catch a movement to my left coming toward me. I turn and fire my rifle just as I see that it is a young woman. She flies backwards, her face startled. She slumps against the wall. I peer quickly around me to see who else might be in here. A small child huddles in the corner, staring at me with wide eyes. She begins to cry when I approach the mother.

'I am sorry, I am sorry,' I repeat over and over, to the child, to the mother. 'I am sorry.' I turn toward the child to try and calm her, come close enough that she begins to swing her fists with terror at my legs. I hear Elijah's boots as he runs into the room.

A rifle shot explodes and the child goes still, a red hole punched in her chest by the bullet.

'Mo-na!' I scream. I spin around to Elijah and he stands there with a blank look on his face, absorbing the scene.

'I didn't know it was a child,' he says, staring at her. 'All I saw in the darkness was her fighting with you.'

'You couldn't tell that she was a child?' I yell at him.

'I am trained not to hesitate in situations of danger,' he answers coldly. He glances to the woman as if to make his point.

She is breathing shallowly, each breath gurgling red spittle. What was she doing in such a place? I lean toward her to see if I might do anything to help. I already know. A large red bubble forms at her mouth. She stares into my eyes. Hers are dull. She's thin and brown-haired. Plain, Sergeant McCaan would comment of her. My hands tremble. I reach out to her, but stop myself.

*

347

WE ARE KEPT IN PASSCHENDAELE only until the end of November, but in that short time we have done what was needed. It is our third big victory in a year. The Canadians are proving to be the only ones who win their battles. It makes the men around me happy, but I realize that this only means we will continue to be sent in as the spearhead to the rest of the hellish places that have been created here. Nobody is sad to leave this place as winter sets in and the mud fields begin freezing in the night. Passchendaele is by far the worst place we've been.

The faces of the woman and child haunt me. Elijah did not report their killing to battalion headquarters. There would be too many questions. It would not look good. But he did report the killing of an enemy sniper, giving me credit for it. I am too numb to care.

We're sent back south to the old familiar country of Lens. My hearing continues to leave me, but for longer stretches now. It is punishment for my crimes, I think. Many times I look over to Fat or McCaan or Grey Eyes only to find them staring back at me with a strange expression on their faces, waiting for me to answer a question that they have asked. I play it off as my not understanding their English too well, and they leave it at that. They all know my silence so well now that they do not question it.

Their big holiday approaches once more, in a week or so, the one called Christmas that celebrates the birth of their *Gitchi Manitou*. Already, I have spent two with them. This Christmas will be my third. The time is one of celebration and of drinking, but me, I don't see much of their god in it. Their god is a fighter *manitou,* I assume, although this is not how their holy men talk of him. When they talk of him, they use words like *forgiveness, virgins, children*. But I believe their god must be a warrior, for he is the one they all pray to before they go over the top. I will never understand this god, these people.

Fat and Grey Eyes and McCaan are the only originals left. All the others are dead. I don't bother getting to know the new ones who come in any more. No secret now that the one who comes in to take Sean Patrick's place is always very young and always dies within a month of arriving. Nobody bothers getting to know the new one. The rest all look, thinking that the new boy is cursed but not daring to say so.

This Christmas celebration of theirs bleeds through a week to another celebration of the beginning of the new year. I realize that all of this drinking and false celebrating just masks the sadness. They all talk about what has happened in the last year and speak of how they hope that the next year will be the last year of war. This new year that begins they call 1918. I know that this is how many years have passed since they say their god was born as a man.

This sadness and reflection rubs off on me. I do not like their way of keeping time. Their way is based loosely on the moons but is as orderly as the officers try to keep the trenches, full of meaningless numbers and different names for days that are all the same anyways. I worked it out and I have been with the *wemistikoshiw* twenty-seven full moons. I've been in the battlefields for nineteen full moons. It is a long time, and there is no end in sight for this war they have created.

On the night of the eve of the new year we are in a reserve trench and are given double rations of rum. Elijah's gone missing. I am the only one to notice. He slipped away to try and find the Frenchmen he met a year ago when I was with him in that town. They are the ones who told him about keeping trophies of the enemy, but his madness is all his own. He goes to meet them and show his skill as a hunter. All he carries now in his pack are the trophies of the dead. He collects them like pelts. His pack is full.

Elijah seems to have no more need for food. He is thin and hard like a rope. He is a shadow that slips in and out of the darkness. He is someone I no longer know.

I drink the rum and more is passed around. I take it greedily. Anything is better than another night of waiting for the shell to land close enough to kill us. I drink with the others and the shells continue to land in the trenches up front and punctuate the songs that they sing all around me. I stand up and walk away from them. I want to be alone tonight. Without thinking, I walk up a support trench that leads to the front line. Soldiers scurry and duck when shells scream in, but I ignore them. Another battalion is up here on the front line, one I do not recognize. Most of them do not pay any attention to me.

The world feels unreal, like it is not me but someone pretending to be me walking along the front-line trench and not caring. I've drunk a lot of their rum. At a dugout where a small group of men huddle, I stop.

'Do you have rum for me?' I ask.

They look up at me. 'Who the hell are you?' one of them asks.

'I am Xavier Bird. I am a sniper with the Southern Ontario Rifles.'

'You're a drunk Injun, is what you are,' one of them says. The others look at my Mauser slung over my shoulder, at the scope.

'I've heard of this one,' another says. I have to read his lips to understand. 'Works with a fella called Whiskeyjack. Quite the reputation! You can have a drink on me any day!'

He hands me his tin cup and I drink from it deeply. My legs start to feel unsteady, like I have not used them for long.

I wave and walk away. Down the line a starburst erupts, illuminating the sky and no man's land. I get onto the fire-step to get a better look. The ground is lit by a red glow, like a fire is burning just below the surface of the earth. I can see Fritz's line of barbed wire, the hump of his parapet.

I pull myself up as the light dies down, go over the top. I stand straight and begin to walk along no man's land, along the length of the trench. I stop and stare at Fritz's line. I walk toward it, then back toward my own. I feel free for the first time in a very long while. Walking further, I follow the sand-bags of my trench. No sound. Even the shells have momentarily stopped falling. Silence but for the constant buzz in my ears.

I notice movement from my trench. A man waves frantic-ally for me to come to him. His mouth is forming words, but I can't hear them. Another starburst lights up the sky. Everything is suddenly bright like daytime. I walk toward him and jump into the trench beside him. He is saying something to me but I can't hear it. Something in my head pops and the hearing in one ear returns. Rifle fire on either side of me, the heavy breath of shells down the line, the *whomp* of their impact.

'Are you all right, mate?' the soldier shouts at me over the din.

He has red hair and a red moustache like McCaan. I shake my head. 'There is a dead woman and child in Passchendaele,' I say, walking away.

When Elijah comes back a couple of days later, he tells me of finding some of the Frenchmen who'd taught him to scalp his enemies last year. He has brought some meat with him, a gift from the Frenchmen, he says. We sit a long way behind the line and Elijah cuts the meat into thin strips, fries it up in his tin cup and passes me pieces on the tip of his trench knife as soon as they are cooked. I try not to think of what that knife has done. This is the first hot meal I've had in weeks. Elijah explains how he found the Frenchmen, that they let him know where to look for them, but I do not inquire further.

'If they did not know last Christmas that I am a hunter to contend with, they do now,' Elijah says. 'All they did was stare when I showed them my trophies.' He smiles at the memory. 'They acted nervously around me after that. My reputation is sealed, I think.' He gloats on this.

I wonder how it is that I go missing for a day or two and am put under guard, but Elijah does so without punishment.

The meat is gamy and a little tough. 'Is it horse?' I ask, pulling gristle from my mouth.

Elijah smiles his wicked little-boy smile. 'No. It is human. German, to be exact.'

I jump to my feet before I know that I do it and approach Elijah with balled fists. Then I find myself reaching for my knife. But what he has said makes me gag and I kneel down and stick my finger down my throat. The contents of my stomach come out in a slimy glob.

'X! Calm down!' Elijah says. 'I am only joking. What? Do you think I'm crazy? I was kidding. It's just horsemeat.'

His forehead creases innocently and the gleam of the trickster is in his eyes. He pops some meat in his mouth, chews it and swallows.

MASINAHIKAN
The Letter

THE WINTER IN LENS is a quiet one. Both sides, it seems, are licking wounds, preparing for the warmer weather of spring before they resume killing. The Germans, everyone agrees, will go on the offensive, and try to gain back the ground that they lost over this last year.

Americans are in the struggle now, and their addition has been a welcome thing. I haven't seen many of them. They are to the north and massing in the south. They have a lot to learn, a lot to catch up on that the others have mastered over the last three years.

Elijah and I are kept sharp by being sent out on patrols. The Germans are well dug in to the Hindenburg Line, and trench raids are out of the question in this sector, but there is plenty of action in no man's land to keep my mind occupied. I find myself taking chances more and more, not being as careful as I once was, not caring to.

One night Elijah and I crawl through an area where reports of a Fritz work party came in the night before. We crawl and listen, crawl and listen, freeze flat on the ground when flares go up. But we find nothing. Usually, I am the one to tell Elijah it is time to head back, but tonight I don't bother.

We are out so long that dawn is approaching when Elijah says we should head back in. My ears have been buzzing and I've had to rely on Elijah's movements to let me know when danger might be near. I've learned to read Elijah well. He's wound tight like a hare when we are on the move, but when he smells the enemy close by his body goes loose and fluid, just the opposite of anyone else that I have ever been in this position with. As we turn away from Fritz's lines, maybe two-thirds across no man's land at this point, Elijah stops and points back in the enemy's direction. We stare into the dark that is beginning to lighten and both of us see two forms that slither quickly into a shell-hole. Getting this glimpse of others doing what we do out in this dangerous place gives me a jolt. Sometimes when we are out here I feel like Elijah and I are the only ones in the world. In not very long, the sun will be close enough to the horizon behind the German line that Elijah and I will be shadows for Fritz to shoot.

We make our way to a shell crater twenty yards closer to our line. Elijah peers over the top and begins to shout in English.

'Fritzy!' he yells. 'I saw you, Fritzy! Tomorrow night we will be back in this same place and I dare you to come out to play with us.'

Despite my better judgment, I laugh. Elijah has shouted loud enough that even I can hear him through the ringing.

As we crawl out of the crater to make it back along the route to our line, I am surprised to hear a voice shout back to us. I can't make out what he says, only the word *Tommy*. Elijah laughs, and we scurry on.

'What did he say?' I ask Elijah once we are back safe and have drunk our morning rum.

'He was a funny one,' Elijah says. 'He called us Tommy and said he'd be there waiting for us tomorrow.'

'Are we going to go back?' I ask.

'No point,' Elijah says. 'They will not be there.'

When we are given a few days' rest, we wait for the rain to stop. When it does, we all congregate by the cook wagon where it is warmest. Men sit and talk or stare out at nothing. I stay by myself, watch the others and what they do.

I see Elijah talking in a low voice with Grey Eyes. Their relationship is now one of convenience. One will rely on the other when he is short of medicine. They talk in code. One day Elijah might ask for a cup of tea, the next day Grey Eyes might ask Elijah for a bandage, the next a cigarette. I used to worry about Grey Eyes, that he would make a mistake that would cause some of us to die, as he did with Sean Patrick. But since that time Grey Eyes has become a shadow. Nobody really notices him any more, which is best. McCaan and Breech know better than to send him on anything more than work detail. McCaan must have some idea that he takes the medicine. For reasons I do not understand, McCaan does nothing. But if Grey Eyes is caught sleeping on sentry duty, or lets happen what happened with Sean Patrick and is blamed for it, there's no question he will be sent behind the line to face a firing squad. Grey Eyes knows this too, and this fear keeps him functioning.

Fat sits by a small fire and eats a large piece of chocolate that he received in the mail. Fat has lost weight. He is still fat, and he will never have any grace or think of anything but his comfort, but he somehow has managed to survive in a place where so many others have not. Some people carry luck like others carry weight. He carries both.

McCaan discusses with Breech the winter's action, and what they expect in the approaching spring. He continues to watch over us like a father. Lines have grown across his forehead and beside his mouth from the strain of all this. His red hair is going grey. He is a strong man, a good man. I know that he carries the burden of each death in his section, and sometimes I worry for him.

Lately, I have seen a change in McCaan's eyes. I don't want to admit it, but I know as surely as I know anything. McCaan knows too. I want to approach McCaan, tell him to leave this place, go to England, go back to Canada, anywhere but here. But you can't run from it. It finds you when the time has come. We both know McCaan doesn't have long, but neither of us says anything. There is no point.

But I do not worry for Bastard Breech, the man who is so concerned with appearance, waxing his moustache to points every morning, slapping his riding crop against his leg as he talks to us like we are children. He would make a good teacher at the residential school.

I wish as much as Elijah that it was Sergeant McCaan and Corporal Thompson in charge of us and that Breech would go away. Although Thompson is not one of our originals, he is the one who taught Elijah and me about scouting and patrolling and raiding. He is quiet like an Indian and stays to himself. Rumour is that he was a lawyer back in Toronto. Nobody knows much about him and he likes it that way. Thompson notices Elijah more than he does me, and I've become used to it. Elijah. He fools everyone but me. I am the only one who can see through his mask.

I stay awake the whole night before we are to go back up the line. In the middle of the night I'm forced to face something I have been fighting. Elijah is mad. The acts he does will bring bad luck onto all of us. Something is coming, but I cannot quite see what it is.

Our battalion is moved back to the caves and tunnels of Vimy late in the winter. Talk is that this is where the Boche will focus their spring offensive. The Boche like the high ground, and the Canadians have the ridge now.

One night word goes out of a trench raid, the first in a while. The plan is simple. Go in under cover of a box barrage, and once we are in, inflict as much damage to the trenches as we can. This will be one of many small raids. The call goes out for five volunteers. Elijah and me, Thompson, a new soldier, and McCaan. I'm surprised that McCaan is going with us. He's better at staying back and helping with the barrage.

We are over the top and crawling across no man's land late in the night. Artillery laid down an unnecessarily large barrage earlier in the evening that went on too long in the hopes of picking apart the section of Hun line that we head for. We make it through the wire with little problem and I am spooked to find that when we slip into the enemy trench, no enemy is there to engage. It seems as if they've abandoned this line. Then the realization hits me.

They have abandoned this section for a reason. I'm beginning to think that the barrage has given us away, and whisper this to Elijah as the first shell screams in and the young soldier ten yards away disappears in a flash of white and red. The rest of us are thrown to our backs. It was a German shell. It came from that direction, not the Canadians'. Fritz has been waiting.

Another shell screams in, then another. They are landing so close that the air is sucked out of my lungs and I cannot breathe. I roll onto my stomach and begin crawling. I have no idea what has happened to the others. Shards of frozen earth rain down on me as I find a dugout and roll in. Impossible to see anything in the smoke and darkness. The earth smells burnt.

The shelling stops as quickly as it started and I know that Hun will swarm into this section any moment to finish us off, but I'm too stunned by the explosion to move. My ears hear only silence.

Where are the others?

I force myself to crawl from the caved-in dugout. In the darkness I grab onto a leg. I pull myself along it but find it is not attached to a body. The leg belongs to one of us, and a sick wave washes over me. Nothing for me to do but crawl back over the side and make my way back to our line. Up on the parapet I look down once more. Some of the smoke has cleared and I can see McCaan on the ground.

'Sergeant,' I call to him. He's looking up at me but his eyes don't seem to take me in. I see that his arm is gone. Blood spurts out of him in pulses. He struggles to sit up. I'm frozen up on the parapet, my legs and arms not responding to what I ask them to do. 'Sergeant McCaan!' I shout, and my voice is muffled in my head. His eyes focus on me then. A smile comes to his face and his red moustache curls with his lips. He stretches his remaining arm to me.

I see the movement to my left. A couple of soldiers run up with rifles pointed and stare down at McCaan. One of the soldiers shouts at him and the other lifts his rifle and aims at McCaan's head. I see the spit of fire come out of the barrel and then McCaan lies still. I squeeze myself flat, trying to disappear into the earth, frightened like I have never felt before. If I make a sound they will kill me too. I watch them move on a short way, and when their backs are turned, I force myself to roll away from the parapet's edge. Now I can move to save myself, but I could do nothing for him. I am a coward, and the thought of living through this moment takes over my limbs. Tears and smoke burn my eyes as I turn away and crawl back across no man's land alone.

Morning is close and I am the only one who has made it back. I report to Breech the confirmation of McCaan's death. Word travels out to the company quickly. We begin to fire our artillery all afternoon, a great barrage in anger and sadness and revenge. Nothing has changed by early evening. The three most popular men in the battalion, all lost in one night.

Late that night I am awakened by Elijah's ghost. He is so thin that I think I can almost see through him. Elijah laughs and talks but I can't make out what he's saying. I turn away from him to go back to sleep and Elijah pushes at me. I turn back and see that it really is him.

'I had to hide out in a shell crater not ten yards away from their line all day!' he says, excited.

'What of the others?' I ask. 'Speak louder!'

'I dragged Thompson out just before Fritz arrived,' Elijah says.

I think of my inability to do the same for McCaan. The thought crushes something inside me.

'That new private was killed instantly,' Elijah continues. 'I couldn't find you or McCaan and I had to get out of the trench when I heard Fritz coming.'

'McCaan is dead,' I say. 'I watched it happen.'

'I'm glad you're alive,' Elijah says. 'Thompson was hit bad. I'm lucky I was carrying morphine or his cries would have given us away. I helped him to sleep out there through the day. He was gut shot so bad I can't imagine he'll make it. But I got him back to our side in the dark.'

I look at Elijah, follow his lips moving. He's found a way to remove himself from the pain of all this. None of this seems to affect him.

Everyone is stunned by the death of McCaan, but Elijah's and Thompson's miraculous survival takes a bit of the sting away. The men have something positive to focus on. I too feel some relief that Thompson has made it. McCaan is gone forever, though, and this continues to eat away the small part left in me that keeps me walking forward. Thompson won't make it. I know this as surely as I knew McCaan's fate before he did. I grieve in my own way for my two friends, burn sprigs of dried grass that I find along the roads that lead in and out of this place. The prayers sent up on the smoke seem so small. McCaan and Thompson were the ones who anchored the company, made Lieutenant Breech bearable. I realize I'd come to think of them as my relations.

Not long after this, my name is shouted at mail call. I'm as surprised as anybody. Elijah and I used to joke that we were the only ones in the Canadian army to never receive mail. 'If only your heathen aunt could write English,' Elijah took to saying. When it's passed to me, all I can do is stare at the letter in my hand. I open it carefully and look at the piece of paper for a long time. I will need to find someone who will read it to me. Elijah can read, but I do not want him to be the one. He might lie about what it says or play a joke. I go to Fat, take a long time to build up the nerve to ask him.

Fat humphs and then begins to read it in his nasally voice. 'It says here that you must return home.' He stops reading, looks up at me. 'This is very difficult to read, X. There is no punctuation and the handwriting is childlike. From the best that I can tell, it says you are the last in the family. You must raise a child so you can teach him what you were taught.'

The wind is knocked out of me as surely as if a shell has exploded at my feet. Does this mean Auntie is dead?

Fat continues. 'It says that God understands if you must kill Elijah.' Fat stops and glances up at me. 'This is nonsensical, X. Kill Elijah! My word!'

'What else does it say?' I ask him, barely breathing.

'Not a lot. It says to pray and do what you must to make it home.'

He hands me back the letter and I sit on my haunches. 'Is there a name upon it?' I ask, desperate.

Fat takes the letter and looks again. 'It's child's scrawl, but it appears to say 'Joseph Netmaker.' What kind of name is that? My word!'

I think hard, remember Joseph. He wasn't a homeguard Indian, but one of the good ones who still lived the old way. He wouldn't lie or play a joke like this. I approach Fat again, take him aside and ask him to read the letter once more, slowly and loudly. 'There is no mention of my aunt?' I ask.

'No, it clearly says that you are the last of your family.'

My heart falls to my stomach.

'And it is followed by the sentence that God understands if you must kill Elijah. I have a mind to turn this in to Lieutenant Breech, X.'

He gives me the letter once again. I fold it carefully and put it in my pocket, get up and walk far away so that I might figure this out.

I sit alone and let the words echo in my head. Auntie does not know how to write their language, never mind speak it. This letter says she is dead. It even talks of the madness that has taken Elijah. Why would old Joseph send this? The world is suddenly less real than it was yesterday.

We are in the caves of Vimy, waiting to be moved up to the front once more, when Elijah comes to me, carrying a sack. Elijah's eyes look wild and shiny again. He has been taking too much of the medicine, has explained to me that he has built up such a tolerance that one of his doses would kill a normal man instantly. I want to tell him of the news of Auntie, but can no longer rely on him.

'Come with me, X,' he says. 'I need a big favour of you.'

He leads me through the winding tunnels back to the surface at the bottom of the ridge. We are outside in the evening of an early spring. The sky is still light in the west. A fresh breeze blows from the south. A nightingale calls out. We walk to the edge of a small copse of trees that survived last year's shelling. Elijah looks excited.

'Let's build a fire,' he says.

We do this together, choosing nice dry hardwood that has been lying here since last year. We sit by the fire and gaze into the flames.

Elijah continues to put wood on the fire even though there is no need for it. The night is balmy still. 'Go easy with the wood,' I say. 'You'll have Fritz spotting it and shelling us.'

'I need to get it very hot,' he says. 'I want you to do something for me.'

I wonder what craziness he wants me to do with fire. He reaches for the sack and pulls out a whitened bone. It is slightly concave and smooth and looks like a bone I recognize. Elijah hands it to me. I turn it over, rub my fingers along it and realize what I have. 'Where did you find the shoulder blade of a bear?' I ask him.

Elijah smiles. 'It is not from a bear. It is German.'

I drop it immediately, look at him to see if he jokes once again. He doesn't.

'I need you to read the bone,' Elijah says, staring at me. 'I want you to divine for me.'

I am confused. 'Why? What do you think I can decipher from it?'

'It is just the same as conjuring a moose, is it not?' he says. 'You have read moose bones in the past. I have watched you. And often it has worked. You have led us straight to them before.'

'But this is different,' I say.

'What is the difference?' Elijah asks. 'To hunt is to hunt.'

'I hunt for sustenance,' I say.

'And so do I,' Elijah answers.

I'm not sure I understand what Elijah's saying. 'Are you telling me that you eat Germans now?'

'Don't be so literal, X,' he says. 'I have found the one thing I am truly talented at, and that is killing men. I do not need food when I have this.'

We stop talking for a while and stare into the fire.

'Although,' Elijah continues, 'there are those who will eat the eyes of their enemy to see what he sees. Thompson told me of them before. Those Frenchmen verified it. And besides, the Iroquois eat their enemy's heart to take his power. We grew up with those stories.' He stops as if to consider this.

I shake my head. 'You are not yourself, Elijah.'

Elijah goes quiet. Small tremors begin to shake him. His fists are clenched and his face contorts in a sneer. My fear of him returns stronger than before. I do not want any part of this. As if he realizes this, he unclenches his fists and a mask of calm falls over his face. He smiles, but it isn't genuine. I must get away.

'If you want me to divine for you where you can find Hun,' I say, standing to walk away, 'I will. They are over there.' I point over Vimy Ridge and to the Hindenburg Line.

When we are again sent back to rest, an idea comes to me. I search for good rocks and borrow old canvas from the quartermaster. I search the sparse woods behind where we stay and find an appropriate place, then construct a *matatosowin* and build a hot fire nearby, heating the rocks all day. I do all the work myself, and when the rocks are ready, I carry them in one by one with my trench shovel, followed by a pail of water. I strip down so that all I wear is my medicine bundle around my neck.

I crawl into the lodge and circle it in a clockwise direction, then take my place. A cupful of water poured on the stones makes them hiss red and release a billow of steam. I breathe the steam in so that my lungs burn. I want the steam to release the prayers from inside my head so that I may send them up into the sky.

Nothing.

I pour more water on the stones and the wet heat sears my skin. My body feels on fire.

Once again I pour water on the rocks and this time the steam is so painful that I bend down at the waist and suck in the cooler air from the ground. I stare at the stones glowing red in the blackness. Light white fissures of heat pulse from under the red. I gaze into them and they begin to dull. Another cupful of water onto the stones makes them hiss back to life. I begin to panic. The air is too hot to breathe. To exit the *matatosowin* now would be failure. I calm myself best I can and bend down so that my face is buried in the ground. The pain of the heat on my back makes me moan.

It is too hot to concentrate, so I wait and try to master the pain. No prayers will come. I think of the four directions, I think of you, Niska. I think of home. I try to see if you truly are dead. Nothing. I ask out loud what I should do, what I can do. Nothing. That you are gone and the letter is true, Niska, seems all too clear now.

Finally, it comes to me. I begin to think a simple prayer over and over. *I want to hear. I want to see. I want to hear. I want to see. I want to hear again. I want to see what I should do. I want to hear again. I want to see what I should do.* I pour more water and the billow of pain that washes over me turns ecstatic. I pray until I have left my body and float out over this place, rising so high that I'm looking down at the lines of the trenches scratched into the earth. I try to read their pattern, to understand it. Lines cut into the earth's skin. Scars. I can't read their language, but I know I must go.

I am light-headed leaving the *matatosowin*, stumble when I bend to pick up my clothes. Still no answers. The heat has sucked everything out of me. My skin is red and tender. The air outside is deliciously cool. My will does not guide me at this point. Something carries me. I've been in the lodge for hours. The world now is a colour I've never seen, a blue-black so sharp that the sky feels close enough for me to touch it. A half-moon floats above me. I let whatever this is pull me along, take me where it will.

As I slip into one of the tents, in the darkness I hear the slow regular breathing of Elijah. I walk to it. Elijah sleeps the sleep of the medicine. I crouch by him, look at his peaceful face outlined in the little light. His kit is beside him. My hand goes to it, feels inside for a syringe of his medicine. I take it out, stare at it.

I sit with my back against Elijah's bed and lightly touch the sharp end of the needle. I roll up my sleeve. I want to feel what Elijah feels. Maybe I will understand better then. With the sharp needle to my skin, I begin to push, but as the first layers of skin break, something stops me. Another idea. I know what to do.

I turn and kneel, face Elijah again. I feel for his arm and take it gently in my hands. I feel with one finger for the bump of vein, the one that runs inside of Elijah's elbow. I take the needle's point and place it gently along the bump, like I've watched Elijah do. Elijah never takes more than a little bit this way. The syringe now is full of the golden liquid.

I push the needle tip into Elijah's vein. It slips in, first with resistance, then smoothly. I place my thumb on the plunger and, before I flush the medicine into my friend's vein, search his face one more time.

His eyes are open. He has a slight smile on his lips.

'What are you doing?' he asks in Cree.

'I am giving you medicine,' I say.

'I do not need more right now,' he says.

We stare at one another for a long time. We are caught in this moment.

Slowly, I pull the needle from Elijah's arm, place it back in his kit. I stand up, weak-kneed, and leave the tent.

PIMINAAWIN
Flying

TODAY IS OUR THIRD FULL DAY on the river. I will soon begin to recognize the country where I grew up. The weather continues to hold, but ahead of us, to the north, grey clouds rise up from the Great Salt Bay. I don't care if rain falls. I became so used to living in cold rain, to life spent shivering in wet wool, that living felt incomplete when the sun shone.

I hold the last needle of morphine in my fingers, and twirl it so that the sunlight captures the golden liquid and makes it glow. My stomach is cramped badly and my arm screams where a Mauser bullet entered.

'Auntie,' I say, twisting around to her. She looks down at me as she paddles. 'This is the last one. After this there is no more.' I turn back and pick a small scab from a vein on my arm, then slip the needle point in. I push down the plunger and feel the slight burn as the liquid enters me. Nice not to have to hide my habit any more, but I laugh to think that just as I come to this point, the medicine is all gone.

My breath catches and the sun shines bright behind my eyelids and the canoe rocks gently and the water drips from Auntie's paddle and I float up from the wreck of my body. The warm wind tickles my skin. For the last time I feel the full embrace of it. In a few hours I will fall and shatter on the rocks of this hard place, but for now I will float free of myself and won't feel any pain.

From up above I see Elijah and me standing at attention in an open field with the others, rifles smartly resting in our right hands. We've been issued fresh uniforms and the new company sergeant has ordered haircuts for all of us. Elijah says his scalp burns from the rip of dull shears on his skull. Despite what I tried to do to him with his needle, despite my claiming I don't want him to talk to me any more, he still does. Incessantly, like a child. Maybe he thinks if he stops talking to me, he will pop like a sturgeon bladder puffed with too much air. He talks to me as if his life depends on it, his eyes wet with the morphine. To make up for long stretches out alone hunting in no man's land he spends the nights whispering his thoughts to me while I try to sleep.

He is front and centre today, has taken more medicine this morning than he'd meant to. The sun is painful in his eyes. His pupils do not retract as much as they should in the light any more. Elijah looks around at the others. Very few of the old faces. Me. Fat. The bastard Breech. Grey Eyes went missing a week ago. Nobody knows if he's dead or alive.

I can see that Elijah sweats. His legs feel wobbly. We all sweat in our itchy wool uniforms. The sweat runs down Elijah's back and sends shivers through his body. We've been standing here an hour, waiting.

Finally, the one we've been waiting for arrives on horseback with his attendant. He is a general, speaks at length with the new sergeant named Colquhoun and Lieutenant Breech. Elijah can see Colquhoun point to him, the eyes of the rest of us following. Elijah swallows the urge to wave to the officers looking at him. The man on the horse speaks at length, uses words like *bravery, the good fight, honour, victory*. He dismounts from his horse, is handed a small velvet box by his attendant and walks directly to Elijah. The man opens the box, utters the name Whiskeyjack in the same sentence as he does the King of England, takes out a medal and pins it on Elijah's chest, fumbling with it just a little. Elijah salutes, standing in this heat and sun, his eyes swimming. He sees a bird floating on a current of air on the horizon and focuses on it. Elijah is flying.

ELIJAH DOES NOT KNOW what to make of me. Elijah can't forget that a few months ago he awoke from sweet dreams to find me sticking a syringe in his arm. He accused me of taking the medicine too, but Elijah knows that I don't. I fight my own struggles just as Elijah does, and every other man, Canadian, English, German, French, Australian, American, Burmese, Austrian, fights his. We all fight on two fronts, the one facing the enemy, the one facing what we do to the enemy.

I see a hunger in Elijah that he can't satisfy. He goes out on his own to snipe now that I don't want to go into the field any more. He tells me a story about crawling in the mud and finding the place where he will not be seen. He burrows into the mud like a mole so that just the tip of the barrel of his rifle pokes out, burlap over his scope to deflect glare. He wishes that I would let him use my fine German Mauser. He lies still for hours, for days sometimes, only moving for his medicine, waiting for the shot that will count. He lets many targets pass, waits for just the right one. Men are beasts of habit, and he lets this be the thing that keeps him patient. He looks for corporals, sergeants, lieutenants, all of them spotted by the way they move. More confident. More sure. Officers always seem to have the skinny legs. Elijah runs his tally higher in the ripe fields around Vimy, comes back with just

369

his word that he has killed, but his word is enough now.

One day he's reached the point with his sniping that the Boche have begun to shell our sector heavily and our own soldiers nod to him and say, 'Push off now, do your business elsewhere,' when he passes. He decides to move on to a part of the line that the troops assume is dead. He has a feeling about it.

He crawls through no man's land at night, listening, stopping often, looking for a good place come morning. Finally he finds one. The lip of a crater offers a fine vantage point. He makes a nest, spends all night doing it so that in the morning it feels right. All that day he peers through his scope, resting his eyes every little while, then peering again. By all accounts this does look like a dead stretch of line, but then, at the end of the second day, he glimpses movement.

A cat, fat and happy, sits on a wrecked parapet and licks its paws. Elijah stares at it for a long time. What is a cat doing here? The cat is well fed and groomed, not wild. By all accounts the trench rats would have eaten it. Somebody is keeping it, and the only ones with such luxuries are officers.

He lies and watches all day, and deep in the night leaves his nest and crawls silent to where he'd seen the cat. Whispers come up from the trench. He listens to the words. There are three or four of them. What are they doing in a deserted section of trench? A quickly called meeting, maybe? No mind. They will soon be dead.

With revolver in one hand and war club in the other, he slips into the trench, looks about so as not to be surprised himself. He watches them in the darkness. They sit in two groups of two. He walks up behind the first group, swings his club at the one closest to him before they even know he's there. The officer screams out and falls, holding his head. Elijah must work fast now. He swings and hits the one beside the fallen man across the temple, and this one also stumbles and collapses. Now the other two are up. One runs in the opposite direction, the other runs at Elijah, a pistol in his hand, aimed. He fires frantically, misses. Elijah raises his revolver and fires, striking the Hun square in the forehead. The man is dead before he hits the ground. Elijah pursues the other who has run away. This one is not hard to catch. Only fifteen yards down the trench he lies on his side, grasping his chest. He is having a heart attack. Elijah helps end it by bringing the war club down on his skull. He holsters his revolver, takes out his knife and begins cutting.

Elijah turns back to the others. The first two are still alive, moaning. One has crawled a considerable distance. Elijah walks up behind him, sits on his back, pulls his head by the hair so that his neck is exposed, and cuts across it deeply. He turns back to the other whose eyes are open but not seeing. Elijah closes them gently with his hand, then places the revolver to the officer's forehead. The gun cracks and the officer's body bucks, then goes still.

Elijah exits the trench after taking their hair and searching their pockets. All of them officers. As he makes his way back to his nest, he changes his mind and turns back. Crawling into the trench once again, he removes the insignia from their uniforms, goes into their dugout and finds a satchel full of papers and maps. He wants no one to question this evening's claim.

Back in his nest he medicates himself and lies on his back, his body shivering. As he drifts into the sky, a familiar woman's voice comes to him, asking if he does not feel anything after such killing. Something walks across his leg and he jolts awake. He does not want a rat bite. He reaches down to throttle it and his hand grasps the warm fur. The animal purrs. The cat has followed him back. He lies back and closes his eyes again. The cat walks up him and snuggles in the crook of his arm. They fall asleep together.

In mid-summer we are sent back for rest to a quiet place alongside a river. I find it hard to grasp that a couple of days ago we were in trenches surrounded by strands of rusted barbed wire and rats eating bodies and today we are camped in tents in a farmer's field staring out at the wind running its hand over fields of wheat. As if in passing, Lieutenant Breech puts out word that Corporal Thompson has died from his wounds.

'He was a good man,' Elijah says to me as we gaze out at the field. 'I hope that he died peacefully.'

'I imagine they filled him with the medicine,' I answer. I'd believed from the moment I saw him that Thompson, more than anyone, would be the one to survive this war. With him gone now, I have only Elijah and myself to rely on.

Nearby sits an airfield, and every morning Elijah's up before dawn, watching the pilots and the mechanics preparing their planes for flight. The mechanics rush around, tinkering with engines and running hands over wings and loading ammunition into machine-gun belts. He watches as the pilots dress for flight, pretty white silk pants and shirts first, then wool trousers and tunics, and then warm coats, silk scarves, hats and gloves. When they are done, they look ready for winter in the heat of July, and they climb awkwardly into the cockpits of their planes.

But then they become a part of the machine. He watches

from the edge of the airfield as the engines cough to life, smoke puffing out from the exhaust pipes, the planes bumping over the rough ground to the airfield and then whining louder and louder, picking up speed, racing across the ground until the moment the wheels leave the ground and the planes swing steep into the air, jostling on the currents of wind, climbing higher and farther away until they are droning specks on the horizon. Later in the day he listens for their return, wonders which ones will make it back and which ones won't.

On our last day of rest Elijah is asked if he wants to go up in an aeroplane. The pilots have heard that Whiskeyjack the Indian sniper is billeted nearby.

'I would be delighted,' he says, and it's as simple as that, the dream that he has carried is to be realized.

Elijah tells me everything, even though I say I do not want to hear. But his tone is different with this story. He doesn't sound like a madman whispering of killing. He sounds a little like himself again.

First the pilots give him soft silk leggings, and then woollen trousers to pull over those. He's given the flyer's coat with its sheepskin collar. A silk scarf is wrapped about his neck and a leather helmet and goggles are placed on his head. He climbs up onto the wing and into the forward cockpit, his head buzzing with the excitement. The pilot sits behind him. The man is thin and handsome, his sharp profile like the profiles of the men on recruiting posters, staring bravely toward the horizon.

'We'll keep you well behind the lines, but keep your eyes peeled still,' he shouts over the noise of the engine as it coughs, then roars to life. 'Fritz likes to sneak up on us from above with the sun behind him.'

The pilot steers toward the runway and then they are bumping along it, the plane accelerating to speeds Elijah's never known before, the trees flashing by. And then, the moment. The wheels leave the ground and Elijah knows this because the plane quits shaking along the ground and vibrates smoothly instead, the ground below him suddenly further away. The pilot steers sharply into the sky and Elijah's insides drop near out of him. The engine and wind in his ears combine to a roar and he looks down at the earth below, petrified. He can't move.

The pilot veers to the left and Elijah's given a view of the battlefield in the distance, the trenches cut into the earth, just like he's seen in his dreams. The pilot flies the plane sideways so that the left wing points directly to the earth. Elijah has the sudden panic that he might fall out of the plane at this sharp angle and begins grasping in the cockpit for something to hold onto. The ground looms far below. His body tightens so that his stomach aches. He can see the puffs of shellfire on the German side. The sky is blue when he turns his head away, gives him a sickening feeling like he struggles on an ocean with no land in sight.

The wind is a sharp knife, even through the layers of his clothing. The pilot climbs higher. The earth shrinks away. Elijah feels weightless strapped in his seat, a part of the sky, but not in the way he'd ever imagined.

Nothing holds him from plummeting. He pictures himself falling, arms in a frantic wave, the world coming upon him fast until he is smashed upon it. He's held locked into the seat of this vibrating thing that coughs and sputters. He has no control.

The pilot veers to the right and signals for him to look

down. A river snakes along the earth, glittering in the sunshine. Elijah's head is so light it feels like an empty bubble. He wants to be back on the ground. The exhaust from the plane's engine nauseates him.

The pilot must sense this and begins to descend to earth, and that is when a great pressure builds in Elijah's ears and a pain shoots through his head. He does what he was instructed to do and begins swallowing, but the pain does not go away. Elijah grabs his head with both hands and squeezes. The pain is so intense that he begins to think it is going to kill him, so bad that he begins to throw up, his stomach straining and heaving as he keeps his head between his knees. When he's about to scream, there is a pop in his head and the pain drains away immediately. The earth is right below them and suddenly they are jostling on the ground once more, the plane shuddering as it strains to slow down. He's back on the ground now, and the weight of the earth is back upon him as he climbs out shakily and walks to the mess to have a drink with the others.

Is he meant to walk on the ground and not fly? he asks me. He's not thought about his own death before this, except in the abstract, even during the most intense bombings. He was always different from the others. As the pilots toast with their shot glasses and light cigarettes and trade their stories, Elijah realizes that now, something has changed.

NIPAHIWEWIN
Murder

WHEN ELIJAH WAS A CHILD, his mother died of a coughing sickness. He was young and would not accept that she was dead. He continued to talk to her, picturing her in front of him. The nuns who watched over him at the residential school grew angry at his behaviour, and began to punish him whenever he and his mother talked. So he did it more and more until often his body ached badly from their paddlings and whippings.

Not long after this he met me, and I in turn introduced him to you, Niska. The moment Elijah first spoke to you was the moment that he stopped talking to his dead mother.

The days out in the bush with you and me are memories that glow inside him still. Elijah's sad to see me this way, he says, this unhappiness that burns inside my stomach. I am not meant for war like Elijah is. I am meant to be alone in the bush, hunting moose and snaring rabbits with you, not crawling through mud in search of men.

Elijah's not one to waste his time reflecting on the past, but in these warm days of summer he grows a little sad. He, like me, misses home. But Elijah's able to banish this sadness by talking about his triumphant return there. 'I will go back and become chief,' he says to me. 'I will become a great chief of the people and I will grow into old age pining for these days.'

I look at him and see that he isn't joking. This is what he's decided he wants.

By August, the rumour of another great Allied offensive comes true. Fritz tried with everything he had to end this war in the spring, but he is weakening. Elijah and I see when the Canadians take over a section of the Boche trench that the Boche are not eating much or well, that the battle for food is as constant as the battle against the enemy. Elijah says he's concerned that they will stop fighting sooner than he wants them to, and he's anxious to see more action.

Early in the month we are sent under cover of darkness to a place east of the city called Amiens. On the way we pass by a battalion of Australians and exchange cigarettes and gossip. Elijah finds out that the French will be on our right flank and wonders if he might find the friends he'd made. Only half of them were left living when he snuck off to visit last Christmas. They are a secret society and do not admit new members easily, even when their own ranks are so thin now. Elijah was amused to realize that as mad as they are, they looked at him as somebody far more so. Is he mad? Elijah wonders. Who isn't in such a place?

We walk across the darkness of no man's land. Elijah's laughing, rifle in hand and bayonet fixed. He walks beside me, standing upright, not crouching like he has all of the other times we've been in this place between. The smell of exhaust fumes from the tank ahead makes us light-headed. It lumbers and squeals, moans and creaks, Fritz's machine-gun bullets bouncing off of it uselessly.

The shrill whistle to go over the top had come in the dark and fog of night. The sun won't even begin to climb up for another hour. The plan is wise. To attack at dawn is the standard for both sides. The popular theory is that large groups of soldiers can't operate as one body in the darkness. Imagine the mass confusion. But the Canadians challenge that theory on this morning in early August. We take Fritz by surprise.

The tank that we walk behind drops big hooks behind it, pulling the barbed wire out of the way, creating a wide path for us. The tank rolls right into and then out of the German trench. Elijah and I can see the silhouettes of soldiers in the fog desperately climbing out and running. We jump into the trench, walk up and down it, shooting and bayoneting the brave ones who stay behind to fight. Elijah finds a box of potato mashers, picks it up and calmly walks to each dugout, pulls the fuse of a potato masher, lobs it in, then walks on, the grenade exploding behind him with a muffled boom, destroying the contents of each place.

When the fog lifts at mid-morning, we give pursuit to the retreating Germans, following them into the sun. For the first time it feels like Fritz has finally had enough. Fritz is running. By noon, the Canadians have advanced three miles into German territory, by afternoon, ten.

I lose sight of Elijah in the confusion. I do not see him the rest of that day, and begin to wonder if he has gone too far this time and will never return. The day after taking Amiens, our battalion moves further into what was German territory a short time ago. Fritz continues to fall back. Still no Elijah.

On a road flooded with sunshine, our platoon marches in a haze of dust. We are tired, but happy. Up ahead on the road, Elijah walks toward us. I feel both relief and something else. A number of soldiers shout out to Elijah when they see him.

'We were beginning to assume you were dead, Whiskeyjack,' one calls out.

'Me dead? Never!' Elijah shouts back.

He's been away from us two days, and walks tired but alert. I've seen him like this many times, and know that he has the medicine in him. Elijah claims he walks with one foot in this world, one firmly planted in the other world. He says it's as if he's watching himself from ten feet above and can see a little way into the future.

Lieutenant Breech nods to Colquhoun, the one who has come to replace McCaan. I watch him march up to Elijah. Elijah does not like Colquhoun. He is out to prove himself.

'You were absent without leave for two days, soldier,' he shouts at Elijah, and all of us go silent, watching. Elijah's a bit taken aback, is used to McCaan's calm and patient ways. 'I will have you put up on charges unless you have a very good explanation for your disappearance.' He stares at Elijah, challenging him. Breech watches amused from behind.

'I was out killing Fritz,' Elijah answers.

Some of the others choke back laughs. Colquhoun grows angrier.

'You obviously do not understand the seriousness of this, Corporal. I have a mind to court-martial you. Just because you have been awarded citations does not mean you have immunity under my command!'

Ah! So this is what it is about! Colquhoun and Breech are jealous. Rather than say anything more, Elijah remains silent, must bite his tongue so that it does not say what he will later regret. The silence that ensues is awkward. Elijah can see me behind Colquhoun, but I try not to look at Elijah.

When we've stopped marching for the evening and

completed duties, Elijah searches me out to tell me where he has been and what he has done. He doesn't sound proud or sad. He speaks in a low voice. On the day we took the trenches of Amiens, Elijah continued advancing fast as he could. He moved all afternoon, staying close to a company of retreating Fritz, stalking them.

With the sun behind him now, Elijah finds a place on a ridge and sights in his Ross, follows the retreating soldiers as they run desperately across a long, open plain. He places his crosshairs square on the back of each retreating soldier, one by one, and squeezes the trigger, watches him tumble forward and lie still. Elijah feels badly after his tenth kill. The shooting is too easy. He's almost out of bullets now, and continues knocking the Hun down until he has no more.

When the sun of this glorious day is setting, he stands upon the ridge and looks about him. He's completely alone and realizes that he's gotten far ahead of our section and has lost us. No one to witness this killing spree. He calculates in his head and his conservative estimate is twenty dead, all within a half-hour. His rifle barrel is too hot to touch, and the bolt is sticking from the expansion of British-made shells. He turns back west and follows the dirt road he's come up from.

Elijah passes companies of French and smiles at them, looking for familiar faces. They smile back, handing him cigarettes and bottles of wine to take pulls from. By the time the sun is down, he decides that it will be impossible to find his own, and walks up to a quickly constructed camp of Canadians.

Taking water and a little food, he only then realizes that he sits among the 48th Highlanders, the old rivals from our days of training back in Ontario. He recognizes none of the faces, asks about the little marksman who was such a challenge to him and me so long ago and finds out that he is dead, killed by another sniper while out hunting. The battalion took the little sniper's death hard. He'd surpassed a hundred kills and was a legend. Elijah has reached 356 kills as of today, and these are only the ones of which he's quite positive. Today is a new personal record for one day and he says as much to the others that sit around a fire and talk with him. They offer congratulations and look at him when they think he does not notice, stare at the thin Indian with the sharp nose and blackened face, cheekbones glinting in firelight, rifle with its scope mounted on the left lying next to him, wrapped in burlap. So many knife cuts in the stock it looks hand carved.

His head pounds through the haze of wine and rum, and he reaches for his kit to find another syringe, only to find none. He asks where he might find the medic, and is pointed toward him. The medic is in a large open tent, working by lantern light. Soldiers lie in rows, moaning or unconscious, and he rushes with his batman from one to another. Elijah watches all this from the darkness and knows that to try and approach him with no obvious malady would be a great mistake. The medic has time only for the wounded. Spotting the wooden box, he's sure it contains what he's after. It lies beside a man who drifts in and out of consciousness, and Elijah should have easy access without being seen. When the medic and assistant are at the opposite end of the tent, he walks up and sits on the side of the bed of the soldier. Elijah looks down at him and the soldier opens his eyes, grasps his stomach. Elijah looks at it. The man's middle is bandaged tight but has bled through. Elijah can smell the stink of the man's bowels. The man's mouth moves but Elijah can't hear the whisper. The pallor of death is on his clammy skin. Elijah leans closer to his mouth.

'Morphine,' he whispers.

Elijah smiles.

'Morphine,' he says again.

Looking up, Elijah sees that the medic will not notice. He walks to the box, squats, opens it and grasps at the row of shining glass. He grabs handfuls and places them in his kit. There will be time to wrap each one in cloth later. He goes back to the soldier and sits on the side of his bed once more.

'Who are you?' the soldier whispers, then falls into mumbles.

Elijah takes out a syringe, takes the soldier's arm in his hand and searches out the vein that he desires. Elijah peers over his shoulder and sees that the medic remains busy. Elijah's own body screams out for the needle. He doesn't listen to it as he slips the needle into the soldier's arm and flushes the medicine into his veins. Elijah watches and imagines the dull warmth spreading through the soldier. The man's body relaxes, his face goes slack and his eyes close.

Elijah takes another needle and slips it into the same tiny hole in the soldier's arm, flushes more into his veins. He watches as the slow shadow of death creeps across him, watches as what was once alive goes cold and tightens.

I listen to Elijah tell this story, watch his mouth moving, watch his eyes. His eyes absorb the light, don't want to reflect back what he has done. I can't listen any more and so get up and walk away with ringing ears.

After our victory at Amiens, we are moved north once more to the familiar country near Arras. We are not given much rest before the orders arrive to march the

Arras–Cambrai Road and into the bitter fighting near the Canal du Nord.

Even though I walk away from Elijah when he tells me these stories, he doesn't seem bothered. He simply searches me out like a pesky child. Not long after the story of killing the Highlander, Elijah tells me of a dream that begins to come to him every time he closes his eyes and drifts into sleep. A family sits in the snow, cold and starving. They are too tired to move. Elijah can feel their cold, the gnaw in their bellies. Death is everywhere around them in the forest, staring at them from behind trees. But something far worse than death crouches close by. It is felt rather than seen. It waits for the moment when they close their eyes to approach.

Is this an old story of yours, Niska, that's come back to haunt him? Elijah tells me he has no room for such things in his head. He pushes the dream away.

Near the front lines, Elijah and I are told to report to Lieutenant Breech's dugout early one evening. The sky is grey and it feels like it does before bad weather strikes. The Germans have begun another bombardment, but the shells are farther down the line, and when they explode I feel a dull shuddering up my legs. In the dugout, Elijah and I are surprised to see Grey Eyes sitting in a chair beside Breech. He's been gone a few weeks, and we all figured he'd either deserted for good or been killed, but here he is beside the lieutenant. He is as thin as ever, and his uniform is dirty and torn. His eyes have the look of a wild animal caught in a snare.

'This private brings some serious charges against you and Private Bird, Corporal,' the lieutenant says. He talks to Elijah, still assuming I cannot speak English. 'Among other things, he

383

claims you are an addict of the morphine and that you have been committing atrocities on the battlefield.' The look on Breech's face is smug in the knowledge that he has finally gotten Elijah.

Elijah looks at Grey Eyes, who stares at the ground near his feet. The shells continue to erupt. I wish for them to come closer so that we can get out of this mess.

'Now why would you want to do this to me?' Elijah asks. 'What happened? You deserted and were captured and to save your own stinking life you are turning me in?' An anger blossoms in Elijah that grows uncontrollably.

'What is this you're saying?' the lieutenant says. 'And what of this claim that you scalp your enemies like your heathen ancestors?'

Shells begin to scream closer. All of us but Elijah look up at the rafters as they shiver down bits of dirt and dust.

'I am saying that he acts out of jealousy and out of fear.' Elijah reaches for his revolver and snaps open the holster. 'And jealousy is what prompts you to threaten to court-martial me for doing my job too well.' The blackness of his anger boils just below his skin. His voice shakes with it.

Breech sees what Elijah's doing, does not seem to want to believe it. 'We'll have none of this, now stand down, Corporal, and do not make matters worse.' His eyes are suddenly frightened.

A whistling starts in my head. Later, Elijah tells me that the same pain that he'd experienced on the aeroplane came back to him in Breech's dugout and he had trouble seeing. The rage inside him grew. Does he not go out at night into great danger for men like these two in front of him? His revolver is out and is pointed at Grey Eyes. Grey Eyes stumbles from his chair and pulls it in front of him. Elijah's head is going to explode, and it is all Grey Eyes' fault. The whistling becomes a scream and a bright light flashes and a concussion sends all of us flying into the air. The air is sucked out of the dugout as earth rains down and the world goes black.

I'm on my stomach and force myself up onto all fours. How long have I lain here? It couldn't have been too long. The dugout is still mostly intact, but the smoke is thick and I find it difficult to breathe. I crawl over to where Elijah had been standing and find him. He is bleeding from the head.

'Quick, help me,' Elijah says, tugging at me.

I shake myself out of my daze and we crawl to the lieutenant and Grey Eyes. Elijah checks and finds that both are breathing. He lost his revolver in the shelling, but he mutters that that was the wrong weapon anyways.

Searching the ground, he finds a solid piece of wood. I watch stunned as he grabs it in both hands and sits on Grey Eyes' slight chest.

'Grey Eyes,' Elijah calls out. 'Wake up.'

He opens his eyes and looks up at Elijah. Elijah raises the wood in both hands and swings it down hard as he can onto Grey Eyes' forehead.

'*Mo-na!*' I shout out.

'We have no other choice,' Elijah answers. 'I do not want to spend the rest of my life in one of their prisons.' He swings the wood again and again, battering the little man's head until the life has left him.

'We've got to get the lieutenant to a medic,' I say.

'Are you kidding?' Elijah answers. 'The little prick knows everything.' He crawls over and finds Breech, turns his head to just the right angle and begins smashing it with the wood.

385

Elijah feels wonderful solving the last problem to confront him. I can see it.

Slowly, the anger in him begins to subside. He throws dirt across the two men and then lifts loose boards onto them. 'Providence,' he says. 'And the pain in my head. All gone.'

Elijah turns to me. I sit with my head in my hands.

'Let's go,' Elijah says.

I don't move.

'We had to do it,' he tells me. 'Would you rather have faced the consequences, X? Don't you see that we are free of it all now? We have no more worries.'

I hear voices shouting outside, and Elijah calling back for help.

Over the next few days Elijah continues to talk to me when night is blackest. He is fighting what's become of him, he tells me. One memory has come back to him lately. We are going out to hunt for a few days. Mid-autumn and the air is cold. He and I say goodbye to Niska early in the morning before the sun has come up. We travel along the river in our canoe for a day. We are fifteen winters and think we know the world well.

The bawl of a cow moose travels to us when the sun is setting. We head toward it but it grows too dark to go any further. After making a camp and building a fire, we sit by it and talk of girls.

Without planning it or wanting to, Elijah tells me the story of the nun, Magdalene, who liked to bathe him each week when he was a boy. He tells me of how she would rub her soapy hands over him, how Elijah would get an erection, how she would scold him and then take his erection in her hands and rub him until his taut penis thumped against his lower belly in a spasm.

Elijah tells me of the first time that he actually ejaculated in her hand, a little white current shooting out of him. He was horrified. He thought he was broken. She looked at it on her hand. She began screaming at Elijah until he was afraid she'd gone mad and might try to drown him. He ran from her then. Many months later he had the chance to steal her rifle, the very one we had with us hunting the moose.

Elijah tells me I just stared into the fire after he told this story. I didn't say anything. I was always like this with Elijah, he says. Quiet and calm and listening, but never saying what Elijah needed to hear.

The next morning we got up before the sun again and found the moose tracks. We followed them and flushed the animal out of the thicket where it was hiding. Elijah shot her through the lungs and she did not run far before collapsing. Between the hide and meat, there was almost too much for us to paddle back with. But we did. You were happy, Niska, to see our prize. You smiled proudly at us from the shore, your long hair loose in the wind. You were always worried about having enough for us to eat through the winter. Elijah never quite knew why you worried.

And he never spoke of that experience again.

Elijah and I are tired and we're actually relieved to find that the Second Division is to stand back while the Fourth and First Divisions spearhead an attack on a canal. We sit behind the line a little ways one night and watch the flash of the big guns like lightning across the horizon. Another new lieutenant has been sent to us now, and he is young and proper and understands that Elijah and I are *corps élite*. Elijah does not think he will bother us much.

We sit with a group of others by a fire tonight, and I notice

387

that Elijah smiles a lot, the warm flow of the medicine carrying him along. The smell of roasting meat is in the air and we know that in the next couple of days our brothers will do something brave and great once again and push through Fritz's desperate lines. They must ford a canal, though, and it will be dangerous, miserable work. In this early autumn evening, Elijah tells everyone he's happy for once to sit back and let it happen without him.

I remain my silent self. Elijah jokes a little with me, knows I do not like what he did, but he feels he had to if he and I are to survive. We talk in Cree. Elijah does not want the others to know what we say.

'Fritz has nearly had enough,' Elijah tells me. 'It will not be too long now before this is all over and we return to Mushkegowuk.'

I nod, but do not answer. I am very sad, Elijah sees.

'I know I've done horrible things here,' Elijah says. 'I know that you think I have gone mad.' He pauses. 'Sometimes I feel like I was mad too. But I feel like I must leave this place, that I am ready. We will go back home and you and I will return as heroes.' He points to the moccasins that he wears, the ones I made him so long ago back in Ontario. I have re-stitched them many times, but they are clearly near their end.

'There's no fixing those,' I say.

'Despite what I've done here, what you've done here,' Elijah says, pulling my eyes from the campfire, 'we can still go home together like we always planned.'

Still, I do not answer. Elijah needs me to. I can see that this emptiness inside him cannot be filled up.

'We can go back into the bush and live with Niska,' he says.

I turn to him when I hear this. His words release the agony that I have not been able to face till now, that I have not been able to speak aloud until now. I have lost everything. 'No, we can't,' I say. 'Niska is dead.'

WEESAGEECHAK
Hero

WE ARE IN THE LONG PART of the afternoon. Only
wispy remnants of the medicine remain in me. My body cries
out for more, not wanting to believe there isn't any. 'Paddle
me to shore, Auntie,' I call out.

When the canoe's nose settles into the mud of the bank,
I pull myself out and crawl into the bush, nothing more than
a wounded animal. I get my pants down just as the badness
of my body leaves me in a stinking rush. The cramping eases
a little, and I clean myself best I can with leaves. I pull
myself back out to the shore and see that Auntie is making
camp. It is a good place with a flat grassy plain and dried
hard driftwood lying about.

'We will camp here,' she says when she sees me. 'And I will
help you through this.' She builds a fire and leaves me by it to
go into the bush.

I am sweating. My shirt is soaked through. Waves of
cramps hit my belly, bend me over and make me grit my
teeth. It feels like the stab of a bayonet. My body has been
wrung out and yet great invisible hands twist it more until I
want to scream. I place a small piece of wood between my
teeth to ease the pain in my jaw. Just one more needle. I
wish I had one more needle. I begin to think of all those
times I took the medicine in the last months when it wasn't
needed. I might better have saved it up, stored it away for

the hard months. What was I thinking? Didn't I realize this day would come crashing into me? Elijah would call it my lack of foresight.

Elijah. He should be here. We could help each other through this. A pain squeezes my guts so bad that I cry out in a long growl. I need to sleep. Sleep will help me.

I look over to the woods where Auntie went, a little like the woods in our last days over there, a thick stand. Nicest woods I have seen, the trees big, the ground soft and dark. The section advances quietly, makes our way through a mist that hovers about our knees so that we can't tell what we are about to step on. Me, my ears are no good today. A dull buzz, people's voices echoing in my head. I must rely on my eyes and keep a watch on Elijah. Elijah will be the first to notice anything.

Fat keeps tripping and falling, and Elijah turns to him. *You will kill us all if you keep this up,* his dull eyes say. The rest of the original section is dead. I find it hard to believe that Fat is the only one to have survived this long. None of our dead friends would have believed Fat would outlive them.

The *crack* of rifle fire echoes back, bouncing through the trees. We crouch and continue. We are close. Elijah stops and motions for us to split into two groups. I watch Elijah telling me to take one and go fifty yards up the right flank. A pocket of Hun wait ahead, his lips say, holed up in a deadfall. I will know it when I see it. Both groups are to lob Mills bombs into it, and then Elijah's side will advance to mop up while my soldiers offer covering fire.

Just as Elijah called it, I find the deadfall ahead. It is as if Elijah's been here before, has seen the lay of the land.

I let Elijah's side throw the first bombs, and I follow suit.

Screams and shouts and the muffled racket of Elijah's group charging in travels my way. The sharp smell of cordite tingles my nose. I see movement through the mist, bodies advancing toward me from the deadfall. They are running from Elijah. I point for the others to see and they shoulder their rifles, kill the first few who approach us. Their startled eyes. The stragglers that follow throw up their arms and we quickly take them prisoner and collect their weapons.

'There is no time for prisoners,' Elijah scolds when he comes up to me and sees the men I've captured.

A dull anger thumps in my rib cage. 'Would you rather I kill them, Corporal?' I ask.

Elijah looks at me, something like sadness in his eyes. 'X, you'll have to take them back. Fat, you go with him.'

I am satisfied to do this. I no longer have the stomach for what I do. Fat and I begin the journey with our prisoners back behind the line. Five of them walk along, three very young-looking, one my age, the fifth old enough to be the father to all of them. Blood runs from the old one's ears. Our Mills bombs must have popped them. Rumour on both sides is that we do not take prisoners, that they are killed on the spot or taken back and tortured. I offer these five cigarettes, place the cigarettes in their mouths and light them, smile so that they know I mean no harm. Their eyes have the look of long and terrible fighting, of seeing things that men should not be witness to, the same look that is in my eyes, I should think. For them, at least, the war is over. I wish I could say the same for myself.

An idea comes to me late at night when I'm most vulnerable. If I'm wounded badly enough, they will send me to Blighty, maybe even home. But how to accomplish this? I could ask Elijah to do it. No, not a good idea. In his blood-lust Elijah would probably kill me. I laugh to myself. Am I a coward for thinking such thoughts?

The air in the mornings is sharp, the smell of hardwood fires travelling for miles across the open country. We've broken through the Marcoing Line and stand before Cambrai. The city is important, Fritz's major rail centre. To take Cambrai is to be a short way to victory. At least this is what the officers tell us.

We make our final preparations on an October evening. I watch as men write last letters to wives and children, clean rifles and check gear, pray silently with moving lips or just stare up at the sky.

Elijah and I are sent in before dawn. We are to be advance scouts, report back on what we find, on troop movement, on how well fortified the city is.

We sneak into the first crushed outer buildings of the city just as the sun is threatening to rise. We crawl over rubble, keep one eye out for the enemy, one out for a good place of cover, and steadily move into the town. It is deserted. Elijah stands up from his crouch and boldly begins to walk along the street that we'd been leapfrogging along. I tense, ready for the shot of a sniper to ring out, but nothing happens. Elijah walks further down the street and I follow. The sun is up now. No one's here. They have abandoned the city.

Elijah is ahead of me and his shoulders are shaking. I think he must be upset. Me, I'm happy that we've not had to fight any more today. Elijah turns around, but anger is not on his face. A smile broadens it. He looks young again, like himself.

'What is wrong with them?' he laughs. 'They are not ready to give up already, are they? They are going to do this to me?'

He begins to laugh louder and I want to believe it's a crazy laugh. Elijah walks away from me, back toward our line. I follow at a distance.

After Cambrai we are relieved, given time to recuperate and prepare for our pursuit of the Germans. The others talk of how Fritz retreats further back toward his homeland, refusing to surrender. The Germans still have the capability to keep this war going for months, even years. The thought depresses, then infuriates me.

Telling a superior about the murder of Grey Eyes and the lieutenant begins to appeal to me. Telling might purify, something that the *matatosowin,* the sweat lodge, can no longer do. Elijah crossed the line, crossed it long ago. He won't stop. Is it up to me to stop him? I wish that I had you here to ask, Niska. You are the only one who might help me figure this out, but you are gone. I'm alone. It's as if I've lost my way in the bush, and the panic is starting to flash its ugly face from behind the trees.

We've been surrounding, then attacking villages for the last couple of days, clearing them of our enemies and liberating the towns. The villagers are ecstatic at our arrival, dance in the streets and give us flowers and wine. Elijah fights hard, takes many chances. Sometimes I find myself hoping that Elijah will go too far, will be killed in action. I will be able to rest easier then, my conscience clean enough at least to turn myself in for what has been done, to the woman and child, to Grey Eyes and the lieutenant, to the countless others Elijah has surprised and massacred in the night. The others watch Elijah in action, say that he is brave, a warrior of the highest order. To me he is mad. I am the only one now to know Elijah's secrets, and Elijah has turned himself into something invincible, something inhuman. Sometimes, though, I feel as if I'm going mad too.

On a beautiful morning we've advanced as far east into France as any of us has been. I am once again alone with Elijah, advance scouting and looking for enemy movement. We come out of a stretch of trees and to the beginning of a pretty meadow. I find it hard to believe that a war ravages it. The meadow rises slowly and becomes a slope, the top of which is covered in trees. Perfect place for an ambush. I can see that Elijah senses this too.

'I'll go up twenty yards and stop. You cover,' Elijah says. His hair has grown longer. It is dirty and matted. 'The grass is tall enough to disappear into if I come under fire. Just try to mark where you see it coming from.'

'Why don't we just wait until the others get here?' I say.

'No time. No time.' It seems as if Elijah knows that something approaches. An end to this, maybe.

Elijah slips into the grass, and I can follow his movement a little way before he disappears completely. I wait tensely for a minute, then for another. A rifle shot cracks out and I hear a shout, and finally silence. Quickly as is safe, I move along the small indent of a path that Elijah's left.

Elijah kneels in the tall grass, a young German pinned below him. The German is bleeding but still alive, looks up in shock and fear at Elijah. Just as I approach from behind, Elijah cuts hard into the soldier's solar plexus with a knife, muttering. I can't make out what he says. The man below him writhes and screams. I watch as Elijah plunges his knife once again into the man. I can see the horror in the eyes turn to the dullness of death as Elijah's hand moves to his own face.

'Elijah,' I mutter.

Elijah turns to me. Blood is smeared across his cheeks. His eyes are wet with tears.

'Why did you kill him?' I ask. And why is his blood on your face? I want to ask him.

'What do you mean why did I kill him?' Elijah asks calmly. 'Moments ago he was trying to kill me.' He tries to wipe the blood from his mouth, but smears it more.

Our company has been moving so fast that we must wait for our own artillery to arrive. A cavalry company is camped by us. This is one of the only times in four years of fighting when they have been able to advance and be used as intended. I can smell the horses. I'm reminded of the Exhibition Grounds in Toronto, of the ship over.

I sit by myself and look at the horses in the dusk. They are tall, healthy animals pawing at the earth, some with noses to the wind, a few with heads bent to eat. Elijah suddenly stands beside me. I did not hear him approach.

'I was talking to you,' he says. I am used to reading lips now to compensate for my ears. 'I stood behind you and spoke to you but thought you were ignoring me. Your hearing has worsened, X.'

I nod to him. I don't want to be around him right now.

'If you desired, we could go see the medic together. We could explain to him that you cannot hear properly any more. They can do tests. The medic will see that it's the truth and they will send you home as a hero.'

He talks as if he is the Elijah I once knew. I feel drawn

toward his concern, comforted in this place of loneliness. I struggle not to fall for it.

'I'm not crazy,' Elijah says. I continue to stare at the horses. 'You must listen to me, X. This is war. This is not home. What's mad is them putting us in trenches to begin with. The madness is to tell us to kill and to award those of us who do it well. I only wish to survive.'

'You've gone beyond that,' I say.

Elijah kicks at the ground. 'Listen to me, X,' he says. 'I should never have gotten in that aeroplane. Before that I believed nothing could hurt me over here. But I lost something up there is what it feels like. I need to get it back.' Elijah reaches his hand out to a horse. It shies away. 'I can see that I went too far into a dangerous place for a while. But I see that.' He stops talking, then starts again. 'Does that mean something?'

I'm not sure if he wants me to answer. I'm not sure of anything any more.

The sun is behind Elijah now, and his face is in shadow, light shining brightly about his head. 'Do you know what I think?' I say softly. 'I think that you did more than just kill that young soldier yesterday.' I look at Elijah as I say this to see his eyes, but he remains a shadow.

'Why do you say that?' he says. He speaks loudly so that I can hear him.

When I do not answer, he seems about to walk away, but then looks in my eyes, makes sure that I can see his lips, see what he is saying. 'I came to talk to you to offer you help. We have a great future after this war. We will return home as heroes. I will become a great chief. I won't let you or anyone else take that away.' He turns and walks away before I can answer, hands in his pockets.

My stomach cramps again and makes me cry out. I lie on my side in the sand, staring out at the river and the late afternoon sun sparkling on it. Niska, what am I to do?

ONIIMOWI PINESHISH
Little Bird Dancer

I DRAG WHAT I NEED out of the bush. Willow branches the width of my fingers, hardwood for a hot fire, roots of secret plants, bark from a tamarack. I don't see Nephew immediately, and so I go to collecting the stones that speak to me. None of them are very large, but all of them have a character of their own, call out to me as I pass them. *Niska, choose me. I will give off heat without cracking. I will spark in the darkness and tell you of your grandfathers. I am older than the others.* I make a pile of them and build a fire nearby, use the hardwood I have gathered so that it burns hot and bright.

Only then do I begin to wonder about Nephew. I look around, see his odd tracks in the sand and mud, the solid, single boot print, heavy on the heel, the two deep holes off on either side of it made by his crutches. His step is unsteady, and I can see clearly that he has fallen while trying to walk and dragged himself toward the river. I panic for a second, imagining him pulling himself into the river and drowning in the current, but then see that he has crawled into the canoe. I walk to him.

He lies in it, sweats and shakes without control. He crawled into the canoe for protection. I bend to him but he looks at me with eyes that don't seem to recognize me. He is close to leaving me for good and all I want to do is hold him, but he weakly pushes me away. I let him lie in the canoe and I sit on a rock beside it, my fingers worrying themselves. He looks like he is caught in a bad dream. He calls out English words I do not know, covers his face as if shielding it from danger. He dreams of his war, and this causes the fever inside him to burn.

I leave him and build up the fire again. Carefully, I place the rocks into the centre where they will heat. The coals glow white and red. Heating the rocks properly will still take hours. It is only late afternoon, and the sky will stay bright long into the evening.

I construct a willow frame carefully, weaving the thin branches into a suitable length, then digging the butts into the earth so that in the end I have built what looks like the skeleton of a small wigwam. In the centre I dig out a pit for the rocks, fill my bucket with river water and put it beside the pit. I take the canvas from the canoe and place it over the frame, pile more rocks around the edges so that no heat will escape and no light will come in. In the end the lodge is just big enough for Nephew and me to crawl into and sit comfortably.

I check the rocks heating in the coals of the fire, then I leave to search out some spruce boughs and to fill my medicine bag with twists of sweetgrass.

When Nephew is more conscious and is calm enough, I pick him up out of the canoe and lay him down on a blanket by the fire. His weight is that of a child. He can't eat, and the tremors continue to shake his body.

The dusk of high summer approaches. I have thought hard for the last hours. I have tried to figure out what Nephew needs, what will help to staunch his wounds before it is too late. I know of roots and stalks for headache, for stomach sickness, for infection. I know to use the skunk's glands to cure snowblindness. But what Nephew suffers from has been inflicted in a place I do not understand. What he has gone through I will never fully understand. For much of my life, during many of my fits, I have seen flashes of the killing and of the earth exploding in fountains of mud, but that is a small taste of the reality, even though the images haunted me for days. A fever is eating him alive.

I remember when I was a child and came to my father scared or hurt. I remember what he would do to help me. He made stories for me. About me. About how he imagined me before I was ever even born. I have no medicine that will help Nephew, but in these memories I find something.

Nephew continues to shiver in his blanket by the fire. Sometimes he calls out names and words. His dreams are bad. Maybe he won't last through the night. I cannot let him go without telling him his story. I lie down with him and gently place my arm over his thin frame. Our relationship has never been one of physical closeness, and it feels strange to mother him in this way. I put my mouth close to his ear so that he can hear me whisper. His skin burns. He doesn't respond, but I don't let that worry me. If I choose my words right, and speak from that place inside that tells no lies, he will hear.

Nephew, before I ever knew you, I had dreams of you. I dreamed that I used to take you out hunting before you could walk. I would bundle you tight in your *tikonoggan* and carry you on my back through the bush. You were very good. You watched everything. And when we came close to game, you knew to stay quiet. Even then in my dreams I knew you would one day become a great *hookimaw*.

He stirs a little, tries to push me away, but I hold onto him and keep whispering in his ear. His sweat begins to soak through my shirt too.

I dreamed that when you were old enough to walk, we would go out into the bush for days. We'd take only what we could carry in our *mewutikans*. In winter we would strap snowshoes to our mukluks and your body grew strong from this weight on your shoulders and legs. When I dreamed, I saw from the first time you pulled a bow or fired a rifle that you had something more than others, a calmness of breath, an eye that saw for great distances, steadiness.

He moans out loud and begins to shake. I cling tighter to him and hold back my tears. I am afraid of losing him. I don't want to lose him.

Listen to me, Nephew, when you were no more than five winters I came and took you away from their school, from them. I didn't have to live in visions any more. And this story that I tell you is the story of you.

I stop for a moment and listen to his breathing. It is panicked and shallow.

Your first winter with me we followed bull moose tracks through deep snow. We followed them for miles. You held me up with your short steps, even though I cut a good path through the powder in front of you. Slowly, I got further and further ahead until I disappeared from your sight. You were left alone for the first time in your life. Your sobs echoed in the frozen air. But you kept walking.

I cry as I tell him this, but I keep my voice firm and slow.

You crossed a long, open plain and my tracks led you to a place of thick undergrowth, so thick that you must have wondered how even my small body could make it through the tangled branches that reached down and grabbed at you like bony fingers. You kept walking through trees that grew so close they sucked the sun's light into their black bodies. You had to strain to see my tracks below you. You crouched and listened for the sound of me ahead. But you only heard your own breathing. You had no choice but to push on.

I can feel his heartbeat through our thin frames.

The bush began to open up and you saw in the better light that you were not following my tracks at all. You were following the long ragged drag of the bull moose as he fought his way through the snow. A fear you had not known before must have bloomed low in your stomach then. It must have rushed up until it flooded your mouth like the taste of bad meat.

You squatted and held onto your knees so as not to fall down. When the dizziness left you, you stood up again. I'd warned you before of panic's danger. It comes quick like an accident does, out of nowhere. Even then you knew not to let it take you. You stood there for a while and you must have thought of the stories I had told you around the fire, of men deep in winter being eaten alive by their own fear, men who tried to run away from it and grew hot from their running so that they tore their clothing off to cool down and help them run faster, men who were found half naked in the dead of winter by hunters, their faces stiff in a grimace at the sight of their fear catching them.

You stood then and picked up the bow I'd made you. You thought then that I would find you. And if I did not, you would track this moose alone and shoot it full of arrows and clean it and bury it in the snow. Then you'd find your way home. You would go then and find me, Nephew, and you would lead me to sustenance.

He cries out a name I don't recognize. McCaan. It sounds like the names of Hudson's Bay Company men. I think of all the other young men who fought in that war alongside Nephew. There must be so many that have come home damaged like this. He continues to moan and shiver, calls out other names in his sleep, names I don't know. *Gilberto. Sean Patrick. Grey Eyes. Graves. Breech*. So many names, but not that of his childhood friend.

After a time his eyes open. He stares vacantly at the fire, his body still quaking. I once again heat moosemeat over the flame. If he doesn't eat soon, he will die. I chew a choice bit in my mouth to soften it, and when his eyes are closed, I slip the meat from my mouth into his. He tries to spit it out, but I hold his mouth closed until he swallows. I repeat this again, and then again. He keeps most of it down.

The sun is low now, and still warm. I fall into a light sleep but am awakened by his voice.

'Look at my leg, Auntie,' he whispers. There is anger in his tone. 'Look at what is left of it.' He has pulled up the material of his pants and a red nub pokes out above where his knee should be. The stub is inflamed and makes my stomach turn a little. His eyes are wild with the fever. He mustn't waste his little energy.

'Hush,' I say. 'You must rest.'

'What am I to do with this?' He pounds on the stump weakly.

'You will learn to walk on crutches almost as well as you walked on two legs,' I say to him. 'When you put your mind to it.'

He swears and tries to spit into the fire but it dribbles down his chin. He is not fully in this world right now. A part of him has died already and tugs at what is left to follow.

Not knowing what else I can do, I pick up the story again.

When you found that you were following the tracks of a bull moose and not the snowshoes of your Auntie, you made up your mind not to be afraid. This was a brave thing for a boy who'd only seen six winters. But as you followed the tracks you saw that they cut back into the deep bush, and when the branches scraped at your face once more, you could feel the bravery slowly draining from you.

But you kept going because there was no other choice. A half day of following the tracks brought you to the edge of a lake. The snow was deep. You followed the moose's belly drag onto the lake. Halfway across, you stopped to catch your breath, and there the moose was, by the other shore. The sun shone on its massive antlers. You knew from what I had told you that we were now in the month of the coldest moon and this meant that soon the moose would drop the antlers from his head to travel through the dense bush and deep snow easier. New antlers would sprout and begin growing, so fast that by summer they would be massive again, to be used against other bull moose when it was time to mate.

Remember how the wind was in your favour and the moose did not know of your presence? I'd also told you that the animal's only real defence was his sense of smell. *Mooso* is as nearsighted as an old grandfather. Your fear all but disappeared as you stood as still as you could and thought of ways to sneak up closer.

When you looked down at your arrows, they seemed tiny against the bull's mass. You figured, though, that if you walked very quietly, the moose wouldn't notice you. He was too busy eating. Do you remember slowly pulling the mitten off your hand with your teeth? How you reached to your quiver of arrows at your side and pulled out your straightest and sharpest? It must have felt like forever and already your hand was aching from the cold, but you managed to nock the arrow without being heard.

Nephew cries out, but calms down once more. I continue whispering in his ear.

Your first steps in your awkward snowshoes were deliberate and quiet. It was then that you thought to yourself, He cannot escape me. And suddenly, as if you had shouted this thought out loud, the moose jerked his head and looked right at you. He blew a white fog of breath from his nostrils as if a fire burned inside him. He shook his antlered head in disgust, then turned and walked into the underbrush, snapping branches as he went.

You stood for a long time and listened as the moose crashed away through the forest, your bare hand throbbing in the cold, the branches cracking like gunshots in your ears. The cold must have come while you stood still so long, and the fear, hidden in it, came back too. To fight it, you put your mitten back on and began to walk again, following the tracks. If only you had a rifle, you thought to yourself. 'If I had a rifle today, I would be feeding us through the hard months,' you said out loud.

You began to create your story, how you craftily followed the tracks, some of the time through a blizzard, even! How you could smell the great beast before it smelled you, how your arrows bounced harmlessly off his thick hide, and did this not prove you were beyond childish toys and needed a man's weapon? How the beast turned and when he saw you his antlers fell off in sheer terror. Your Auntie would have to give you a rifle then and there. But then the thought of me and your worry that you might never see me again came back fast, forcing tears from your eyes that froze before they could reach your chin.

Bit by bit, as you followed the moose's trail, you took a bite of the fear and swallowed it, let your hungry belly dissolve it. Auntie would pick up your tracks and find you. You would come to a place you recognized. You would double back and find your way home. But the dark bush you'd already come through stopped you from turning around.

Was it then that all the stories of the *windigos* came back? Tall as trees with mouths full of sharpened teeth. You imagined them as you struggled through the snow that glittered painfully in the afternoon sun. You'd heard the stories that Auntie was a *windigo* killer. You came from a family of *windigo* killers. You knew *windigos* were real.

Nephew struggles when he hears the words. He calls out once again and I wait for him to calm.

When the sun had passed its low winter zenith and there was still no sign of Auntie, you heard a great racket arise in the dense forest ahead, a noise you'd never heard before. You were sure you'd stumbled across a *windigo*. It sounded like feet stamping in snow, like many people whistling to one another and rustling dead tree branches. When you realized there was nothing else you could do, you re-drew your bow and crawled up to the clearing where the noise came from.

In the midst of it, on a bare pine, the needles long fallen off, stood the biggest grouse you'd ever seen, wings spread, its voice calling out. Below it there was a circle of other grouse, thirty or forty of them at least, moving in unison around the tree. Do you remember how they danced side by side, around and around, the big grouse calling out, leading them, how you watched transfixed so that you lost track of time? And then something amazing happened. The big grouse stopped beating his wings, called out, and the other grouse immediately stopped, ruffled their feathers so that they appeared to grow twice their size, then started dancing again, but in the other direction. You'd never seen anything like it in your life. Nobody would believe such a thing, a bird dance in the forest!

As you watched, their pattern reminded you of something else you'd seen before, out of the eyesight of the watchful nuns. Your own people gathering in summer to celebrate an easy season, a tradition they carried on despite the stern words of the *wemistikoshiw* church. You stared at these birds dancing in the snow, the sunlight reflecting in it in thousands of tiny ice crystals. You saw in their movement the movement of your own people as they travelled from winter to summer to winter again, dancing through the years.

You saw for the first time the circle. Even though you could not yet express it in words, you understood the seasons, the teepee, the shaking tent, the wigwam, the fire circle, the *matatosowin*. You saw all of life is in the circle, and realized that you always come back, in one way or another, to where you have been before.

Nephew is quieter now, breathing easier, staring into the fire and the rocks that heat at its centre.

And here you are back on the river where you started your journey, but this time with me.

I fall silent for a while, empty for the moment of words. I force a little more food into him, feed him by mouth. Not much of the food or the story remains. I don't know how many of my words he has heard. I think that some of them have slipped into his head. I start my story the third time, the last time.

And so, Nephew, you watched these birds dance in their circle and you realized how much we are alike. You'd forgotten about your fear as you watched them, and just as quickly as it had started, the dance ended. The big grouse and a few stragglers remained, but soon the big grouse flapped his wings and flew off. You must have been lonely then, and hungry. You'd not eaten since the morning.

A straggler, a female by her colouring, sat alone in a pine by the clearing. You picked up your bow with an arrow meant for a *windigo* still nocked in it, and you estimated the distance. Your muscles were cold and aching from being still so long. You aimed a little above her. You let go of the arrow, keeping your right arm straight and your left fingers by your ear as I had taught you. The arrow whispered off, moving quickly across the distance, then through the bird's chest. She dropped from her perch, dead before she hit the ground. You stood and walked to her.

You made a cook fire with some dried branches and built it big to warm yourself. Placing the grouse on her back, you spread the wings out and placed a foot on each of them, close to where they met the body. You grasped her feet and pulled up so that her naked breast popped out of her feathers. You wasted no time in skewering it on a stick and placing it in the fire. As it cooked you plucked her little wings and placed them over the fire too. You were hungry. As you waited, you sifted through her innards and pierced her gullet to see what she'd eaten. Just some pine needles.

And that is when I walked up to you. 'It smells good,' I said, scaring you so that you almost fell into the fire. 'Will you share with me?'

We ate the bird without speaking. You were very happy to see me. I told you that you had done well on your own today, even if you had scared off the moose. I told you that not many people get to witness the mating dance of the grouse. You realized then that I had been close to you all along. Instead of being upset, you seemed very proud. I knew then that you would be a great bush man, Nephew.

I stop speaking for a while, listen to his breathing. The little tremors return every few minutes.

We continued to follow the moose the next morning, caught up to him two days later. Do you remember that? I gave you my old rifle that was taller than you were, told you to aim below and just behind his shoulder. You aimed and fired perfectly, and as we followed his blood trail I saw that the bullet had pierced his lung. When we found him we butchered him and ate until we could eat no more, then we packed what we could carry and buried the rest.

When we returned home with our prize, we invited all the other *awawatuk* who could come to a feast. It was a special time for you. Do you remember all of the bush Indians coming to us, Nephew? How they brought you little gifts, eagle feathers and necklaces, charms and bullets? Do you remember how well we all ate, bannock dipped in fat, dried berries, meat?

After the eating we sat laughing and talking, more than ten of us, the men praising your hunting skills as the fire cast shadows in our bark house. We all sat on fresh-cut spruce boughs. Do you remember the smell of it?

My voice is desperate now. He burns so hot that the

sweat dries on his body as quickly as it is made. Now is when he will decide. I can feel him struggle.

I asked you to tell a story of your first hunt. Your face blushed, but it was from pride. You told the tale of your day, how you lost me but continued on, how it seemed that the moose snorted laughter at you on the frozen lake, how you worried about *windigos* getting you, and how you came upon the grouse and watched their dance. Your hands danced with the story, Nephew, and the children who were there listened with open mouths.

'Show us how the grouse danced,' Old Francis said, and drunk from the attention, you stood, and made everyone else stand around the fire too. You imitated the big grouse, and everyone lifted their arms and moved around the circle. Do you remember? You called out and we moved around the circle, and then you raised your arms and called out again and we all touched our fingertips above our heads and moved the other way, you rustling your arms like feathered wings and everyone laughing. And that is when I said, 'From now on we call you Little Bird Dancer,' and everyone laughed and agreed it was a good name for you.

Nephew goes still. I hold my breath to see if his is still there. I begin to cry. His heart still beats through his thin frame.

I drift off to join him in sleep and try to dream what he dreams, images of nights bathed in greens and reds, faces of soldiers he has known. The air turning poison. Men wearing monstrous masks. Nephew running from something. All of them running from something. Great fear. Turning to look. It is Elijah.

NIPIWIN
Dying

I AM BESIDE A FIRE with Auntie when I awake. I know my pain was so great that I crawled into the canoe to escape it. Now I am here and she has been telling me the story of my childhood. Days before Elijah.

I can no longer escape him. I do not have the energy. I remember our last day together.

Orders are given to advance across a length of open field between two hedgerows. There is a problem with this, though. The enemy has a machine gun and plenty of whiz-bangs somewhere near the border of the village that our company is to secure, and every time a soldier tries to cross, he is shot down or blown up before he gets halfway. The field that separates the Canadians from Fritz erupts as shells land in it.

The C.O. back in the safety of his bunker decides that if we can't get across singly, we will go as a group. When I hear this latest order, I want to scream. I want to find the C.O. and force him at gunpoint to go across first. I begin swearing in whispers and the whispers grow louder. The others look at me. They are not used to hearing me speak, never mind in anger. I spit out all the evil words I know in Cree and English.

Fat laughs. 'I say! That was a good one!'

I reach for the twine with its IDs about my neck and rip it off. 'I am not a part of such a stupid army,' I shout, throwing it into the field. I leave my medicine bundle about my neck. That alone is who I am.

'What's the disturbance here?' the lieutenant says, coming up behind us.

We huddle and stare across the field. I want to protest but the English words in my head become garbled before they can leave my mouth.

'Let's go, gentlemen, shall we?' the lieutenant says, standing, then jumping out and starting at a trot across the field.

As soon as the rest stand and follow I hear the *thunk* of a rifle grenade and then watch as the lieutenant shoots up into the air, arms waving, as if he has suddenly discovered the secret of flight. I realize before he lands that his legs have been left lying on the ground in front of me as neatly as if he'd taken them off and placed them there. I trip over them, which is a good thing because the machine gun opens up with its *rat-a-tat* and the bullets sing just above my head.

I stay on the ground and crawl as fast as I have ever crawled before, others falling on me dead or dying as they hit the ground. Elijah bounds past, firing his revolver toward the machine gun and diving behind the hedgerow to safety. I stand then and run too, full out, bullets kicking up earth at my feet, making me run harder. I make it to the other hedgerow and turn back, see others running or falling.

A whiz-bang catches one of the soldiers square in the middle of the torso and he disintegrates into a red spray of chunks. Fat is behind him a little way and shields his eyes, screaming.

'Run, Fat, run!' the ones behind the hedgerow begin to shout to him, and he seems oriented by the voices. He lumbers toward us, machine-gun fire all around him like

413

angry bees. Impossibly, he reaches the hedgerow, falls in a sweating heap at our feet. Three of us drag him to more cover.

Elijah is left in command now. He peers through the hedgerow as bullets above us rip it to pieces. 'We can't stay here forever, boys.' And as he says this the artillery shells scream in again, first from the German side and then from ours. The German shells pound closer to where we hide.

Elijah points out in the field to a large crater with a nice lip to it, but it is twenty murderous yards away. 'X, you come with me,' he shouts, smiles. 'All of the rest of you begin firing and don't stop. Somebody needs to take that machine gun out. When X and I get to the crater, head back and let the C.O. know to send up reinforcements.'

Immediately, I realize the error in Elijah's judgment. The worst thing possible is to leave the two of us alone in the crater without any covering fire. Why does Elijah want to be alone with me out there?

He stands and waits for me.

My body reacts against my will and I stand too. Elijah's pull is so strong. These last years since we left Mushkegowuk we've been on a river, and now the river has led to rapids. It's too late for me to bail and get to shore. I stand and join him.

'Ashtum,' Elijah says. 'Come.'

We break out of the hedge and run fast as we can, bent at the waist, toward the crater. The machine gun erupts again. Bullets whine by my head, one of them tearing a gash through my shirt sleeve. My arm begins to burn. Elijah is ahead of me and zigzags as if he knows exactly which path to take. I try to keep up, waiting for the bullet that will throw me down. It doesn't come. We launch ourselves into the crater and crawl to the bottom.

My arm has gone numb, and does not respond well when I try to move it to look at the wound. I can see that a bullet has caught me through the meaty part of my biceps. Blood pumps out with each heartbeat.

I pull a tourniquet from my pack and, holding one end in my teeth, wrap the other above the hole in my arm and pull tightly. I feel no pain. The blood pumps out a little less quickly. My ears ring. I look at Elijah. He lies on his back, laughing at the sky. Blood runs down his cheek in a constant stream, maybe from a piece of shrapnel. He doesn't seem to notice.

'Is this not beautiful?' he shouts. 'Come on.'

He rolls over and crawls to the lip of the crater to peer over. Machine-gun bullets burrow into the dirt all around his head. His dirty hair is longer now than I've seen it in years. It sticks out from his head in clumps. The blood from his cheek runs down his neck into his tunic.

He ducks back down. 'Give me your Mauser,' he says. 'I can take him.'

'*Mo-na,*' I say, pulling my rifle from over my head. 'We both can.' I do not want to be without a weapon right now.

'All right, then,' he says, removing his from over his head. 'Let's each take a position on either end of the crater. When I say go, start shooting.' He grins at me.

I make my way to the far edge and carefully crawl up the side. I remove the rag from my scope, check the action and push a round into the chamber. I look over at Elijah.

'He is twelve o'clock,' Elijah shouts. 'You can't miss him.'

We slip our rifles over the lip of the crater at the same

415

time, and I search frantically through my scope for the machine-gunner. We have confused him. He shoots first at me, missing by some feet, and then swings toward Elijah. I catch the flash of his muzzle in a dirt bunker ahead of me and focus in on it. The machine gun continues to fire at Elijah.

I have a straightforward shot, but wait.

Elijah fires and misses, reloads and fires again. He is shouting, laughing. 'Shoot!' I think he says.

I place my crosshairs just above the muzzle flash of the machine gun. 'Niska,' I whisper, 'Auntie,' and pull the trigger.

Immediately the world is a dull buzz again.

I crawl toward Elijah. Once I'm beside him, I lie back and stare at the sky. Elijah lies on his stomach still, peers through his scope. Without looking up, he reaches inside his coat. I tense. He pulls out a packet of cigarettes and hands me two, still staring through the scope. The numbness has left my arm now. It feels on fire.

Light them and give me one, he says. *You always were the better shot.*

I look over to him to make sure he said what I think I heard.

The metal case of my lighter clinks open, and just as it does, the earth ahead of us lights up in a great flash. I hear the shrill whistle of a shell streak overhead and explode nearby. The world erupts around us once more. Elijah continues to stare through his scope.

'We have to get out of here,' I shout. 'This bombardment's too heavy.'

Elijah finally takes his eye away from his scope, looks at me, a sad smile on his bloody face. He says something to me, something I can't make out in the noise.

We both can't ... he mouths, and then a shell lands close enough to blow and suck a hot wind across us.

'What?' I shout, my eyes fixed on his lips.

Leave, he mouths, still smiling, his teeth glinting.

Elijah sits up and reaches as if to hug me. When his hands touch me, a cold shock runs the length of my body. I push him back, my wounded arm heavy. Elijah struggles up and reaches to wrap his arms around me again. He's no longer smiling. His mouth is twisted in an angry grimace.

No thinking any more. I fight against Elijah until I am on top of him. His face is calm, his mouth now set in a thin line. Elijah tries to reach with one hand into his own coat, his other hand pushing up against the weight of my chest. My hands wrap around Elijah's throat. I don't know what else to do. I straddle Elijah's waist and squeeze with all my might. My hands are slippery with his blood. Elijah's eyes go wide for a moment, then narrow to slits. He begins swinging at me with his arms, hitting my head, my nose, my sides, my wounded arm. I scream and squeeze harder. Elijah's tongue sticks out. His face turns dark.

'*Mo-na,*' Elijah gasps. '*Mo-na.*'

A whistling begins, faint and far away at first. Another shell lands close to our crater and flings me from Elijah. I am on my back, gasping for air, my mouth and eyes filled with dirt. I rub my eyes. When I can see again, Elijah is on his knees beside me, looking down at me.

Why? his lips ask.

My head feels split open from the explosion. I can't move, can only stare up at him, his mouth.

'Are we not best friends, Xavier?' he asks. 'Are we not best friends and great hunters?'

He is my old friend again. I see the hurt child in him now. I nod.

'You were always the better hunter,' he says.

He reaches for me.

'It has gone too far, hasn't it,' he says. 'I have gone too far, haven't I.'

His words wake my body. Elijah's hands reach for my throat. He squeezes it hard, and the words from that letter come back to me then, Niska. *Do what you have to*. I can't breathe. He is killing me. My good arm grasps at the ground beside me. My fingers grab a rifle. I swing the butt of it awkwardly at Elijah. The hard wood of it cracks the side of his head. He falls over.

With all the strength left in me, I roll up and onto my knees, the rifle in both hands. It is my fine German Mauser. Elijah is on his back, dazed and staring at the sky, a slight smile on his face. I straddle him once more and place the rifle across his throat. I look into Elijah's eyes. Water splashes on his cheeks. I think it is rain, but then realize that it is my tears. I push down on the rifle. He struggles, legs kicking.

'Elijah,' I whisper, eyes blurring from the tears. 'Elijah.'

Elijah doesn't struggle any more, just stares up at me.

'You have gone mad. There is no coming back from where you've travelled.' I press down harder. Elijah's eyes shine with tears. His face grows a dark red. He tries to whisper words to me but I know that I cannot allow Elijah to speak them. I must finish this. I have become what you are, Niska.

I lean all of my weight down across the rifle. Elijah begs with his eyes. I desperately want to stop what I've started but something else controls me now. My tears fall heavier on his face. His mouth opens and closes, gasping for air. Veins bulge from his forehead.

Just when I think that he is made of something unbreakable, the rifle in my hands sinks down and I feel through the stock the collapse of his windpipe under the rifle's pressure. He goes still. His eyes are open, still watching me.

How long have I stayed here, straddling my friend, staring down as my tears leave streaks in the dirt and blood of his dead face? Finally, I sit back and grasp my knees, rock slowly as the shells scream in and explode all around me. My friend lies still, arms stretched out from his body as if he welcomes the sky. Finally, I turn to him, lean over him once more.

I reach around his neck and grab hold of his medicine bundle. I tug at it. It does not want to break. I tug hard and the hide rope gives. I pull it from the neck, his ID wrapped about it. I place them in the inside pocket of my coat. I reach into his other pockets and take out his few possessions. His comb, a few bullets, his medal in its nice case, a picture of the two of us taken long ago in Toronto. He smiles at the camera while I look away, nervous. Boys. Our haircuts new. Our arms awkwardly around each other. Like brothers. I stick that in my pocket too.

As I close his lids, the bombardment picks up again. I begin to throw handfuls of dirt across him. I cannot give him a proper resting place in the trees. But his *ahcahk* is strong. It will find its way. When I've covered him as best I can, I lay my rifle across him, the same rifle he has wanted for so long.

I stand up in the crater and feel, more than hear, the shells continuing to explode around me. I walk up the crater's side, head toward where I came from. I stumble across the churned field, my one arm dead beside me. Nothing matters any more, and just as I think this I feel a thud and I'm enveloped by a bright flash and I'm in the air as high as I have ever been, looking down at the ground far below, where I swear Elijah stares up, smiling once more, arms outstretched to me.

DIFFERENT FACES STARING DOWN. I float along, through darkness and then back into light. *No, won't make it,* one with a long moustache says, staring into my eyes, tracing something onto my forehead with his finger. I float away. Shells scream across me. I can see them as they streak through the sky above. I'm not floating any more. I'm on the ground in the mud, men lying dead or dying beside me. They stand and pick me up and I'm floating again.

This must be the three-day road, I think.

I'm travelling still. Another man stares down at me. *This one's a mess,* he whispers, turns away. There is no pain. I float on a warm river in sunlight. *Still alive?* another says. *This one's famous, a hero.*

Elijah! I call out, but my voice does not work. I'm stuck inside myself. He can help me figure this out. But then I remember and I begin thrashing until a man comes up to me and pricks my arm. I drift on a sunlit river again.

Violent rocking. A dark place. Souls all around me, moaning. Screams and shouts. This is the place the Christians talk about. I am a bad man. Something pounds the wall beside me, over and over, rhythmic. Elijah pounding to be let in? I want my friend beside me. I need to say I'm sorry. The big room I'm in turns sideways and I'm rolled out of my bed. Pain shoots dully along my arm, along my legs. Is it pain? It is! It is all over me suddenly like I've stepped on a nest of wasps. I want to stand and run, but can't. Somebody is picking me up. A big man. *Hell of a storm. That last wave almost capsized us. Don't usually get them this big in the channel.* Then I'm back in softness again.

I'm in a room, on a bed, staring out a long window. A tree limb outside is black and bare, silhouetted against the grey sky. I'm able to turn my head slowly with much effort. Just one in a long row of beds. They are all full. I glance down at myself covered in a white sheet. Something is wrong. What's missing?

The echo of singing down the hall. It comes closer. Like a door opening, the song is all around me. Women in white all around me, smiling and singing. I can hear their voices, tinny and far away, like the phonograph I once heard, the volume turned very low. One comes up to me, bends over me and smiles sweetly.

The war is over, she mouths. *The war is over.*

I grasp at her. 'Elijah.'

Yes, Elijah, she mouths back. *The war is over, and you are a hero.*

When I awake from the blackness now, a great pain shoots through my left leg. It runs up and sets my arm on fire. I was shot in the arm, I remember that now. But what came after? Reaching for my arm, I run my hand over the bandage. The pain in my leg grows, throbs so badly that I try to scream, but all that comes out is a sad croaking. And then I remember. It was not a dream. I did what I did. I try to sit up, try to stand, to run, to get away. My body won't respond. I cry out.

A woman in white walks up to me. A nurse. She gently pushes me back on the bed, hushes me with her pretty mouth. *Lie back,* she says. *Tell me what is wrong.*

I search for the words in English. So much is wrong. 'My leg,' I finally whisper. 'This leg.' I reach and feel for it with my hand. 'It hurts me badly.'

Her eyes are sad. *It is called phantom pain,* she tells me.

I follow the movement of her mouth. I don't know these words.

It was too badly damaged, she says. *The doctors had to amputate it.*

I feel my eyes go wide. I don't understand, don't want to believe. Moving my hand along the bed I find no leg there. I feel the stump that sticks out from my hip, and blackness rushes across my eyelids.

It will be all right, Corporal Whiskeyjack, she mouths.

I stare at her.

You are going to live. You are a great hero.

'Mo-na,' I whisper to her. 'Xavier Bird.'

Your friend Xavier did not make it. She looks with sympathy into my eyes.

I begin to struggle against her. I must get up and fix all of this. I'm not Elijah. I'm Xavier Bird. I see her call out. Another nurse rushes up with a syringe, puts it into my arm before I can stop her. I hear the warm river approaching, and softly, softly, I float onto it.

I come out of the blackness and the warmth more often, into the hurting grey. When I feel my body, I want to go back where I've emerged from. When my friend comes to me, I want to say I'm sorry. But instead I try desperately to crawl back into the darkness. The only thing that allows me this solace is the needle, their medicine. I find myself begging for it when I'm conscious enough to do so. Usually the nurses take pity on me, caress my forehead and mouth to me that

I'm a hero, that I've served king and country beyond the call, as they slip the point of the needle into my arm.

Why do they call me Elijah? Is this some joke Elijah plays on me from the other world? I am Xavier. Am I not? But there is something calming in the idea that I am Elijah. There is something appealing in being the hero, the one who always does the right thing, says the funny thing. Now I understand his love for the medicine. It takes all of the badness away. The world is warm and close with the medicine surrounding me.

The grey light that comes into the room does not change for a long time. I watch the rain pelt the windows. The war is over. I don't feel anything. The others in the beds around me, they either begin to get up and walk slowly with the help of the nurses or they are simply gone one morning. I know where. Me, I don't try. I'm stuck between these two places. All I have to look forward to is the comfort of the river. Sometimes I can hear people speaking when they are close by, as if they are talking through a long tube. But mostly there is silence, and this silence helps a little.

The doctor sits on my bed one morning, talks to me in a loud enough voice that I can hear him. *I have crutches for you, Corporal Whiskeyjack. It is time for you to try to begin walking again.*

I see him as if from a long way away, watch his lips moving, then turn my head.

The nurse with the pretty mouth makes an effort to befriend me. She wants me to try to get up. She talks to me as she sits at my bedside. She realizes my ears trouble me. One morning I awake and she holds a board to my face, English words written on it. I shake my head and look instead at her eyes. They are grey, but the grey of the sky after a rainstorm before it becomes blue again, not the grey of the sky outside this place.

'Can't,' I whisper.

You must get better, Corporal Whiskeyjack, she says to me, her lips moving slowly so that I can understand. *You are a good man. You are so brave that they want to give you another medal.* Her expression is sad then. *Your friend, Xavier. He is dead.*

I stare at her mouth.

But you tried to save him. Soldiers saw you walk from safety and into a bombardment trying to rescue him. They say you were looking for him. That is the most any man could do for his friend.

I'm awake one night, sweating. I've not called out for the medicine for a whole day. My body radiates pain. I need my head to be straight, to be clear. I need to figure out this horrible joke being played on me. I try to sit up. The pain shoots through me. I try again, and then again. I feel for my leg and find a stump. That is all. My arm does not respond when I tell it to move. I roll over to my side, see the bedstand. It is empty. I reach with my good arm and feel for a drawer. I pull it open and feel inside. A soft pouch. My medicine bag. I pull it out and an ID dangles from it. I pull it close to my eyes in the low moonlight from the window. The English words for my name are not on it. I recognize the shape of these ones, though, the order of them. Elijah's name. That is when it comes back, roaring through my head like a bush fire. I see Elijah dead in the crater, see my own hands taking Elijah's medicine bundle, his ID from around his neck, sticking them in my pocket. I threw my own away. A moan begins deep in my chest, finds something inside that helps it to grow until it is a cry, and then finally a howl.

A long time has passed. Many days. I don't know how

many. I've made the decision to live, and each morning crawl out of my bed and pick up the crutches beside it. I am able to hobble down the hall now. The others pay me little attention.

I do not know how to make them understand who I am. To them I am Elijah Whiskeyjack, sniper and scout. Hero. When I want medicine, I tell the pretty-mouthed nurse that the pain is too bad, that I need a little of it. She leaves for a short time, comes back carrying a needle. I spend hours staring out the window, rubbing at the stub of leg through the pinned-up material of the pajamas, feeling the warm river rushing below me. It is easier not to tell them anything, easier not to explain at all. I allow myself to believe that I am Elijah. In this way he is still alive.

One morning I walk along the same hall that I walk every morning, crutches swinging forward, followed by leg. I see the door that leads out to a street, a place filled with people. I'm tempted to go outside and lose myself in the rush of bodies, but know that I'd be sorry I did. For the first time in a long time I think of home. No one is there for me. I cannot live in the bush like this by myself. The thought of living in the town is punishment. Maybe they will let me stay here. The nurse with the pretty mouth, the grey eyes, maybe she will look after me.

On an afternoon not long after, two officers come to my bedside and salute. I look away. The past has caught up with me. One opens an envelope and reads it. I watch his lips carefully. The officer is telling me that I am to return home at my earliest convenience, that I am a decorated soldier of the war and will be afforded comfortable passage on a steamer.

It still rains in this place on the morning that I am dressed in a new itchy uniform. The nurse with the pretty mouth helps me into a chair with big wheels, helps pack my duffle and places it on my lap. Tears well in her eyes.

She bends to me. *How is the pain?* she mouths.

I stare back at her, my eyes filling too. I need to tell her that I want to stay with her.

She slips an envelope into my lap, takes my face in her hands. *Use these carefully. Only take a little when you need it, when the pain is too much.*

I need to tell her that I wish to stay with her, but can't find the English words. I think I can hear the clink of needles in the envelope as I am pushed away from her.

The ship is as big as the one I sailed on years ago. But instead of being led down below the deck with the horses, I am kept up high above the water, put in a room of my own with a window from which I can stare out at the water. Officers come to visit me, lieutenants and colonels and even a general. They want to meet me, this Indian sniper of supreme talent whose reputation matches that of the one they call Peggy. They have learned that my hearing is mostly gone, speak to me in great loud baritones, bring bottles of rum and cigars. The winter ocean is rough, and they try to keep steady as they stand and talk down to me. I stare at them, try to smile, wait for the one who will discover my secret, this lie.

On the nights, the nights that stretch on forever before dawn comes, on those nights when the rain pounds at my little window and the waves rock and beat the ship like Elijah coming to haunt me, I reach shakily into my duffle and feel for the envelope, feel the warmth of the sunlit river coming to lift me up.

NTASHIIHKEWIN
Home

THE NIGHT IS UPON US NOW and the stones have heated. I pick them up from the fire with two sticks and carry them into the *matatosowin* one by one. They pulse in the darkness. I wake up Nephew then and let him gain his senses a little. He holds his stomach and leans on me as we go to the river. I help him remove the *wemistikoshiw* clothes that he has worn so long, and wash his body in the cool water. I remove my clothing too, and then take him inside.

In the *matatosowin* the heat is good. When we are ready I close the flap tightly. The darkness is complete.

'I am glad you are here with me,' I say loudly enough that he might hear, as I pour water on the stones. They hiss alive and glow and a wave of steam washes over us. 'Tell me if it is too hot or if you do not feel well.'

I acknowledge the four directions and then the earth, the sun, the sky and the moon, sprinkling a little sage onto the rocks as I do. I thank *Gitchi Manitou* for Nephew's return. I sit and breathe the steam, open myself to the *manitous*.

I know that Nephew will have trouble hearing me and so I feel no need to talk out loud. The heat is pleasant, relaxing, a good first round. The rocks dull a little and so I sprinkle more water on them. As I stare at them the image comes to me of Nephew leaving that morning with Elijah so long ago. I tie a medicine bundle around each of their necks, kiss each of them

427

on the forehead. I stand on the riverbank and hold my hand up to them. Xavier and Elijah turn and smile at me as they paddle away. I smile now in the darkness, remembering.

When the time comes, I crawl to the flap and open it, and we lie outside on the cool ground and breathe the air deeply. After a time, I open the flap and crawl back in. He follows me.

Once more I welcome the *manitous* and then pour a little more water on the rocks, make it hotter inside. I sprinkle more sage onto the stones and it sparks and dances. I know that Nephew stares at the glow as well. I chant my prayers, and as I do I see flashes in the darkness, the shouts of fury and of killing. I see the confusion, feel the anger, but mostly the fear. My body shakes with the vibration of their bombs exploding. I watch as men fall dead with bullet holes in their foreheads or are blown to pieces by great blasts. I watch as green gas crawls across the ground, seeking out all the breathing things so that it might choke them to death. Pain. So much pain. But it is their fear that leaves me weak. The fear of crawling over the sandbags and running headlong into the enemy. I talk out loud then, ask that men be forgiven for their mistakes. I sprinkle more water onto the stones so that the steam may carry it away. When it is time, we leave once more and drink in the cooler air outside.

The third round I am consumed by Nephew's pain. I can feel it settle on my chest as surely as if someone is sitting on me. I pour water on the rocks and the steam rushes into my lungs like poison. It is difficult to breathe. I begin to feel panic, something I've not felt in this place since childhood. I want to rush out of the *matatosowin* and breathe fresh air. The heat sears my lungs, and so I bend to the ground and try to breathe the cooler air there, whispering words over and over to *Gitchi Manitou*. Nephew is chased by something horrible, even in here. And it threatens to take me too. I am a child again and this is my first time in the *matatosowin,* the darkness and heat and hot moisture making me desperate to get out.

My father's words come back to me. I concentrate on my racing heart and ask it to slow down. I breathe shallowly from the ground and let the heat burn my back. I whisper over and over. The pain that Nephew has carried inside of himself for so long is leaving his body and swirling around in this place. It swooshes and screams and scratches at me until I think I am bleeding. It tries to enter me, first through my mouth, but I purse my lips and spit out a prayer at it. It slips down my breasts, my stomach, my thighs, a tongue of fire, searching. It tries to slip up inside me between my legs but I cover myself with my hands. It bites my fingers with sharp teeth. I want it to be burned up by the heat.

I pour more water on the rocks, and then more. Nephew bends to the ground too, moaning and crying and whispering. I am worried for him, that his body is not strong enough, but if the illness stays inside him it will kill him.

With the squeal of stone splitting in half from the heat, the presence is gone. A rush of cool air comes as if the flap has opened and closed quickly, and I suddenly feel something else inside, sitting down beside us.

Nephew begins talking into the ground and it is hard to hear what he says. The other presence in the *matatosowin* isn't threatening. It neither challenges nor calms. The other is pure, and it fills this space. It is a young man I once knew who loved to talk. Nephew speaks, then stops as if listening. *'Ponenimin,'* Nephew says. 'Forgive me. I had no choice.' He speaks more, says *ponenimin* again for killing his friend over there in that place.

I am sad to hear this, but it is no surprise. Nephew was never one to keep secrets. A long silence, and then I listen in the wet heat as Nephew accepts forgiveness too.

'But I cannot forgive everything you did there,' he says. 'It is not my place to do so.'

He speaks again softly. I can't make out the words, nor do I want to. He cries, and in it I hear the fear of his loneliness. I lean down into the ground and hug this presence that has joined us, hug Elijah like a baby in my arms, holding on as long as I can before I must let go. The *matatosowin* goes still. Over the murmur of hot stones Nephew whispers goodbye to his friend, and then it is just the two of us here once again.

I crawl to the flap, open it and carry Nephew out. We collapse on the ground. Above us, the sky has settled into the long black of night. It will be a clear morning. My body tingles. My skin is reddened from the steam. I look over to Nephew and see that his is too. He is so thin now. I can see his ribs. I see where his leg was severed. The cut is clean, but the skin all around it is purple and angry. The scars are thick and ropy and run up his thigh like lightning bolts.

I lean close to him and whisper directly in his ear. 'Just one more round, Nephew. It will not feel as painful or as hot.'

I crawl back in first, then help him inside. I pour more water onto the rocks and once again I'm embraced by the heat. The feeling is good after the coolness of the evening air. Almost immediately the heat brings visions. Children. I see children. They are happy and play games by the bank. The bank of the Great Salt Bay. They are two boys, naked, their brown backs to me as they throw little stones into the water.

Their hair is long in the old way and is braided with strips of red cloth. But this isn't the past. It is what's still to come. They look to be brothers. Someone else besides me watches them. I sense that he watches to keep them from danger. I am no longer on the ground with them at all but above, looking down at this whole scene. I am not able to see the one who keeps his eye on them, and do not want to see. I know who he is, and who these boys are too.

The *matatosowin* is filled with this good vision and I let myself drift in it, in the smell of sweetgrass and the sigh of the old stones. Soon a lightness I've not felt since I was young tells me that we're finished. We crawl out.

It is the dark before dawn. I am surprised at how time passed so quickly. We lie beside one another, our skin as tender as newborns', steam rising from us like we are on fire inside.

On the edge of the evening sky I watch a white mist of washed-out *Wawahtew* begin to pulse. It is too early in the year for their colours to shimmer. For the first time in a long time I think of my father. Something of him is in those lights, the way they pulse slow and even, like a strong heartbeat. He has been all around me all my life, never really left me. It has taken most of my years to realize this. He is in the sky at night. He walks silently beside me when I stalk moose. He follows me even when I go into that *wemistikoshiw* town that he hated so much, the same place that he was taken to and where he died.

After a time, I get up and dress. I help Nephew into his clothes and start a fire. We sit by it and gaze up at the stars that dot the sky. The *Wawahtew* pulse a little more brightly tonight than last. The eastern sky is lightening. It's been a long night.

Tonight I do not worry about making camp. I just pull our blankets from the canoe and we curl up in them and watch the fire. In a little while I will have to add more wood to keep the chill away. Nephew breathes calmly. I listen to the sounds of the night animals not so far away. I hear the fox and the marten chasing mice. I hear the whoosh of great wings as an Arctic owl sweeps close by, and after that the almost silent step of a bigger animal, a lynx perhaps, keeping watch with her yellow eyes. I lie here and look at the sky, then at the river, the black line of it heading north. By tomorrow we'll be home.

Acknowledgments

I WISH TO HONOUR the Native soldiers who fought in the Great War, and in all wars in which they so overwhelmingly volunteered. Your bravery and skill do not go unnoticed. I especially want to honour Francis Pegahmagabow, sniper, scout, and later chief of Wasauksing First Nation (Parry Island). He is one of Canada's most important heroes.

ALTHOUGH HE'S FAR TOO HUMBLE to admit it, R. James Steel ranks among our country's best World War I historians and authors. His patience, wisdom, and especially his astounding knowledge of the war made this a journey I will never forget. Any inaccuracies that might exist in this book can only be blamed on me. Thank you for reading so many drafts of this novel, Jim.

Thanks must also go to the Canada Council for the Arts for their support; it is a vital Canadian institution.

I also wish to thank Greg Spence of Moose Factory, Ontario, for his guidance in translation to the Cree language. *Mikwec ntontem.*

A debt of gratitude to my dear friends for reading early drafts: Jarret Lofstead, Joc Longo, James Grainger, Michael Winter, Carmen and Chris Tozer, Matt Suazo, and David Gifford.

I especially want to thank my brother, Bruce Boyden, for

his wisdom and close military eye to detail. I also wish to thank Marc Cote for his willingness to share his editor's knowledge. Janie Yoon, your attention to the page is something I will not forget.

I experienced the rare and wonderful opportunity to work with a number of great editors in shaping this novel: Barbara Berson at Penguin Canada, your skill, faith, and confidence is deeply appreciated. David Davidar, what can I say? You're the man. Tracy Bordian, you are the finest managing editor a writer could wish to have.

Many thanks also to Paul Slovak at Penguin U.S.A., and Helen Garnons-Williams at Weidenfeld and Nicolson U.K. for your guidance and belief in me.

Francis Geffard at Albin-Michel: You were the first one to take a chance and the first to let me know when it worked and when it didn't. *Meegwetch, mon ami.*

Nicole Winstanley: You are more than just a brilliant agent. You are a dear friend.

On my northern travels I've never experienced anything other than warmth, laughs, and incredible stories. William and Pam Tozer of Moose Cree First Nation, *mikwec* for always making your home my home. *Mikwec* as well to the Metatawabins of Fort Albany First Nation. To Bertha Sandy and her family of Beausoleil First Nation: You've been good to my relatives and me.

Finally, I want to thank my own very large family: David, Raymond, Francis, Suzanne, Julia, Veronica, Mary, Bruce, Claire, Theresa, Angela, and, of course, you, Mom. You are everything. Lieutenant Colonel Raymond Wilfrid Boyden, D.S.O., C.D., M.D., our deceased father and World War II hero, you continue to live in all of us.

As always, Amanda, you've been the best reader a person could ask for. Your support and encouragement made a writer out of me.